The Bottom Of The Spiral

Pablo Castelo

Every book is more than one book; this book is in all the books. It is in debt to Carl Jung, Joseph Campbell, Martin Gardner, Umberto Ecco, Hilaire Belloc, Cervantes, Escher, Borges, Virgil, Ovid, Homer and many others, and each of them.

Contents

Preface

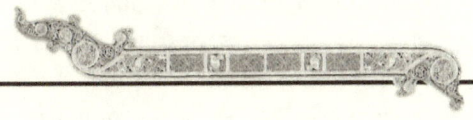

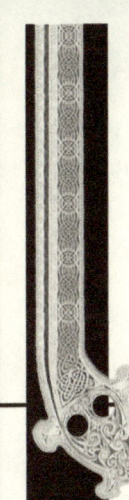ow, that the night of my existence is gaining shadows for my eyes and spends time marking its silver trace on my hair; now, detained by the rigidity, my whole adventure is limited to longingly giving my farewell to those who are departing and watching them get lost among the curves of the path coiled on the mountain; now, and before the decrepitude corrupts events and ruins my memories; before it's too late, I'm going to reveal the extraordinary events of my early life, facts that my perplexed youth promised to record in the peak of enthusiasm. I will not do it, though, because I feel indebted to a drive of my cheerful youth. I'm going to do it because the boy I was found himself caught in the threads of the designs that weave the common destiny that binds us together. These, after having reached me with matters of common interest, ultimately made the anecdote of adventures part of the public knowledge, turning what was a mere testifying impulse into an unavoidable duty. Part of this demand moves me to talk about Reverend Ogli-s-Oöp, my generous master.

Our relationship flourished since the first time we met. He greeted me without etiquette, or should I say, with the unembarrassed rituals with which the boys celebrate their encounters. His large and bright black eyes regarded me as a discovery. I had heard of him, but I never imagined him to be so much like my father. He, too, had a face wrinkled with creases that seemed to have been piled with the same patience as the annual rings of old trees. His eyebrows suffered a resigned fatigue but his eyes shone with a cheerful vivacity. He had an energetic but unhurried spirit. The heavy body of my master was supported on massive legs and what they couldn't hold was leaning on his walking stick, so typical of the highlands, where the tortuous paths are perched on the rocks. His figure was clumsy, leaning forward, almost horizontal, as if he was in perpetual cosmic reverence. When Reverend Ogli-s-Oöp was moving, he gave the impression that he was swinging in collaboration with the same universal rhythm that also waved the leaves and palpitated on the stones, which I never felt again in the transit of any other person. Ogli-s-Oöp was different, he was something more.

Normally, he was the owner of a disarming simplicity, an exasperating modesty. I never saw him slighting anyone by disregarding a concern or finding inconveniences on food, generously given, no matter how strange it was. His depth was born of a playful intellectuality, free of presumptions, with no powers to be proved. His talent was neither more nor less than the practical result of his wonderful sense of beauty. Thanks to his curious knowledge, he knew how to exalt the more insignificant pebble, highlighting his unexpected attributes. He handled a wisdom able to ornate mysteries, which used other mysteries itself, equal or more surprising. My master was wise and humble. He could, however, get angry with ignorance when it was arrogant. I would not say that Reverend Ogli estimated everyone with the same affection -with some, he made a real effort- but he was able to give his life if it was worth the universal brotherhood.

Ogli-s-Oöp cultivated his celebrated authenticity, adjusting himself to it as if the honor of a life would lie on it. Apart from the habitual wisdom of a Szabeo monk, he possessed a great universality. He read Artesio and Grezco almost with as much fluency as his own language, which allowed him access to restricted sources for the common of the scholars. Unlike them, he conceded little importance to such merits. When nothing was urging him a discernment or an action, he was spontaneous and joyful. But he used to mentally isolate himself for hours to concentrate on the interpretation of dreams and to meditate on the multidimensional geometry. He believed he could find glimpses of divinity in the hyperspace.

As a thinker, Ogli-s-Oöp can hardly be considered simple and, even less, popular. This is due to both the complexity reached by the resolution of his thesis and the counted followers of his ideas, especially of his methods. The problem lies in the effort required to rationalize the mysteries. It is also unlikely that the sympathy of Reverend Ogli is due to the diffusion of his theories; on the contrary, they are only to the reach of specialists, for now. Even today, his books spread lazily. For this reason, I have tried where possible to domesticate his reflections -in an audacious way, sometimes- trying to convey his ideas in the same way they were shared with me when I was young. The idea of popularizing his ideas, making them accessible, was originally of Reverend Ogli himself but his pacifist activities never gave him enough time and his purpose became impracticable.

He already had noticed the inaccurate transmission of his concepts and the theoretical complications that make the theme impermeable; he regretted that. As if this were not enough, the rejection that Ogli-s-Oöp felt against dogmatic conclusions inhibited any enunciation of a body of doctrine, which has contributed to the disorientation of those who need a marked trail. Ogli-s-Oöp knew well the intransigence of the arid minds and took care of becoming infected himself. So, he kept an open attitude and refrained from making laws and struggled to fight his own prejudices. This permanent doubt was not due to a pusillanimous will, but due to a creative determination based on honesty.

Some, accustomed to the certainty with which intransigent people ignore the possibility of other truths -and the truths themselves-, saw the personality of a wimp in the Szabeo monk. Probably, Ogli-s-Oöp would have thought that this possibility could not be discarded. That was my master!

I believe it necessary to write down some final comments. Although many will have overturned his curiosity about the total existence of Ogli-s-Oöp, I must clarify that this story will give account for only a part of it; in particular the part he employed to unveil the most extraordinary mystery that led him to his global relevance. There must be other readers who have focused their curiosity precisely in the latter. What happened after our return to the secular and daily life belongs to the public sphere. It is for me to reveal what I, and nobody else can testify.

The facts narrated here are accurate in all its integrity, however, I recognize that my scientific or historical explanations might be amenable to repair. The same issues, seen by more suitable eyes, would claim the ground for a more appropriate version.

In an unconnected way, something was known about our trip through Ogli-s-Oöp himself on those rare occasions when he alluded to it, in an anecdotal manner. These references were quite specific and, inadvertently, left in the general consciousness a fragmentary chronicle of what happened. Unfortunately, it has sought to supplement the shortfall based on assumptions of apocryphal origin, which, though all fantasy was used, has only achieved remote adaptations. I hope this story completely clarifies everything.

I have written these pages as I lived them, in the same order in which facts and wonders were presented to me. With this, I intend to enable an approach to the process that I experienced in my unrecoverable adolescence, without exposing the reader to the dangers faced by a master and his trainee in the most revealing and magnificent of all the adventures that have been forged on or below the surface of Ghesta.

Rev. Ad-d-Tuar
Monastery of Kien
Year III of the Guilar

Chapter I

The Mirror of Ink

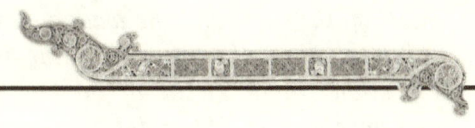

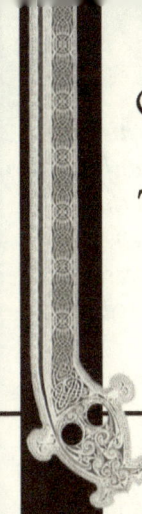he small beetle fled from me over the rough and blackened edge of the well. In its flight, he went over a mark, chiseled in the rocky mass, that must have seemed like the canyon of a dry river to him. Maybe my titanic shadow, or the sensorial cataclysm produced by my approach, took him by surprise and the poor little insect got scared. His hesitated escape on the exposed stone made him easy prey for an infamous finger. Probably, in the absence of a raised point of view over the surface, the beetle could not favor any particular direction and his indecisive route was the result of the immediate solution of obstacles. The roughness of the terrain became a labyrinth, open to dangers.

His fragile and competent structure made me think of a beautiful and elaborate clockwork, an experimental biological prototype. When he reached the edge, where the skin of the rock curved down in a free fall until sinking into the liquid of the well, the beetle indifferently followed the precipitation of the ground as if gravity were only one direction among many others. He began to descend into the pit whose contents began only a hand span from the edge. The frontal encounter with his self-image, over the perfect reflection of the black fluid, did not seem to raise his interest, as he neither faced his image nor stepped back. As he found the thick fluid that filled the hollow of the well, the insect simply chose to continue the flight to his left.

He ran over the wall that surrounded the liquid matter. In his terrified race, the little animal brushed the wet obstacle that confined him to his right-hand side. His infallible antennae measured the escape possibilities. The fearful insect got away, circled the well, and when he was about to find me again, somehow noticed my presence and turned to flee in the way he had come. Soon, he repeated the meeting, the turn, and the walk around.

At this time, the behavior of the beetle did not invite me to any reflection. The anxieties of the bug were an entertainment to me and nothing else. What did arouse my attention was the fact that the insect was not interested in his image. I thought it was, indeed, something to consider. He did not care about his image in the same way wise men and artists do not.

There are, however, other animals that show signs of perceiving their images, but no indication of discovering its illusory nature. The eastern phaisamisjal, bird-chameleon, small and domestic, reacts furiously in front of a mirror, challenging its image to take the most varied forms. Togos and groanes, apparently, are more intelligent because they withdraw their attention after the first skirmish; although some groanes, as one which was with me until not so long ago, are able to bark at the mirror for an entire day. The cessation of hostilities suggests that, eventually, they become aware of the unreality of the image. They suspend the alarm and dismiss the threat. Now, ignoring the image does not mean, even remotely, having come to understand it. Cipamios, however, largely surpass the other animals. A cipamio not only realizes that the other cipamio is harmless but is able to recognize himself in it. His avid curiosity keeps him playing for hours with the mirror. He laughs at himself, which is a remarkable sign of evolution and makes faces to himself. He reflects the light on the walls and irritates his fellows cipamios by blinding them with the splendor. He even uses the mirror to watch parts of his body that he had never seen before. It does not stop there! The cipamio takes advantage of his discovery by using it to scratch his back with better application. The latter made me think of some people who overestimate the value of the thinking beings above the other animals due to the possession of a soul, whose proof of existence lies in the capacity of reasoning. If that were true, then cipamios have enough soul to give it away and the groanes should despise the phaisamisjals. As a Szabeo novice that I was, I knew that I should respect any form of life because God nests in all beings, thus the soul is not a discriminatory essence but rather a unifying connection.

What I did not know at the time was that we, Thinking Beings, resemble togos and groanes more than cipamios regarding our reaction to the mirror. We ignore the specular images believing that we have understood and even worn out the lessons of the mirror.

I did not see the beetle anymore. I was lying face down on the wide edge of the well. It was not an ordinary well. This one kept the shiny darkness that every novice wants to penetrate. My attention was focused on my image, my weight on my elbows, my elbows on the petroglyphs that measured the passage of time and were carved around the well. A slight evaporation of mineral smell separated from the bituminous fluid and reached my nose. Sometimes it was combined with more friendly emanations, wandering aromas, and the last remnants of incense. The well was sunk in the middle of the domed chapel at the south of the convent. Neither was the container made of rock nor were the contents made of water; they were, respectively, magnetite and ink thickened with iron oxides. When some condensed steam dripped on the ink, nothing could be heard immediately, no dripping or splashing. From the impact point, a deft circular wave opened its way through the surface in a cushioning way. Only when the concentric waves had reached the walls of the well did they transmit their disturbance to every atom of the rocky edge. Only then was it possible to hear, like a discharge, the noise of a normal drip which then echoed in the hollowness of the chamber. When nothing altered the splendid reflection of the ink, it seemed to palpitate with light pulses according to the rekindling of the crackling torches from around.

When would it be possible for me to immerse my gaze into the darkness of the well and contemplate all the facets of the world, as the Illuminated Masters, the masters of my masters, do? -I asked myself. How much do I still need to understand before the secrets held at the other side of this mirror trust me and show themselves without the suspicion that drives them away for now?

I put my eyes on the reflections and faced my visage for a long time. I sensed changes on my face. Then, I took off my ring and confronted it with its image. I was trying to find a crack on the conventional to slip through and penetrate the mysteries of the ink.

- I did not know you could already see under the ink! -A hollow voice that came from all and no place said.

I was so startled that I dropped the ring that had accompanied me throughout my childhood into the well. Only then, did I notice Master Garg behind me.

- Ah!... No... Of course not, Master Garg! I was just looking at my appearance.

Of course, no splash was heard yet.

- And... What is it that you observe?

The question gave me a break. I looked inside the well. I considered my ring inevitably lost.

- Well, if I close my right eye, my image closes its left eye. My mole is on the opposite side. If I would comb my hair toward one side, my image would exhibit it toward the other. Everything is inverted!

- Are you sure, Ad-d-Tuar?

- Yes, I think so!

- All areas of any kind of mirror are homogeneous and they should not exhibit different properties, in other words, a mirror surface is isotropic. True?

- Yes, Master Garg! -I said without a complete understanding.

I was more concerned with the idea that at any moment the sound of my ring falling into the sacred liquid would be released. I feared not being able to justify my irreverence.

- Then -he continued- its left and right parts should not behave differently from its top and bottom. True?

- Yes, Master Garg -I said without paying attention to his speech. I was suffering every second, wondering how I would explain about the ring.

- If a mirror is able to exchange the left arm for the right one and turn a left-handed observer into a right-handed again, why it does not invert what is above for what is below, exchanging your head for your feet?

- Well...

- If you thought that the sides of the mirror are bewitched, you could give it a quarter of a turn, setting aside what previously was located above. What happens then? The parts of the mirror that are now felt and right will become the prey of the same spell. Why nature persists in showing itself differently when it comes to right and left if both concepts are just a guidance for orientation invented by the intellect? Huh... Ad?

I had lost the thread a long time ago. I was missing the previous questions. What happened to the sound? My ignorance about mirrors and my unfortunate situation never put me, before or after, closer to the condition of groanes. I was only able to guess that I was completely disarmed in front of an important mystery as high as the height of my severe teacher who was expecting a reply. When I was about to say something...

- Good morning, Master Garg! -a powerful voice intervened- This young man should be...

- Ad-d-Tuar -said Master Garg- Good morning!

- Reverend Ogli! -I exclaimed.

- Do you know me, Ad-d-Tuar?

- Of course! I mean... Not directly. You conceived the method of the Compressed Space. I'm not sure what it is but I know it's important.

- I'm sure you'll know, my dear boy -said Master Garg- That and much more! Even the sacred mystery about the stubbornness of the mirror. You are our most promising novice and for that reason, I have requested for you the best guide a novice could have during their initiation journey: Reverend Ogli-s-Oöp.

With a broad smile on his round face, Reverend Ogli moved toward me holding out his open hand. I never could hear the damn sound.

Following this brief presentation, Master Garg asked me to meet my classmates in the normal activities of the convent. I had, in particular, the task of rejuvenating the decorations adorning the capital letters of ancient manuscripts. But only those that swarmed around the letters but were not part of them

Among these ornaments, there were golden and colorful decorations. These demanded the mastering of a delicate technique achieved only with time. I reapplied only the cobalt blue. The novices had to devote two hours to manual labor, one hour of housework which included taking care of the gardens or cheese-making, and the rest to the following of the Szabeo education on the knowledge of science and the arts.

We had three ceremonies a day. We celebrated the first and last appearance of colors in the sky. At night, the third ceremony greeted the ancient brightness of the stars. For these occasions, we met on the arms of the terraces of the convent and performed the dance of the wind. This caused me quite a fear because, from those terraces without fences, totally exposed to the vacuum, in the same way one could extend the view, it was also possible to fall into the abyss. But instead, I liked to see how the skirts of our habits were lifted when the twists reached some regularly, while the wide sleeves fluttered in the wind. My taste also favored the sessions devoted to the cultivation of Inner Strength and Mental Power where, through meditation and deep breathing, we were initiated on the telepathic, hypnotic, and contemplative arts.

As I rejoined my work, my table-mates began to question me about my Shematt. That was the name given to the meeting where the novice is presented to his guide. The Shematt always happens on the eve of the initiation journey for all Szabeos novices. I could not contain myself and confessed the name of my guide. My companions, who were already in the second level, told me they had heard from Reverend Ub-er, the baker of the convent, that Reverend Ogli had grown from a child among Szabeo monks, participating in their liturgies and chores.

In the mountainous region of Orme, forests of curly mocas filled the rocky armpits where the wind no longer breaks the leaves. Not all of these cavities have forests, but the ones that have always cradle a stream where animals drink and the mochas agglomerate. As they run, these infant rivers unite in every confluence until they finally end up spilling their icy beauty in rapids and waterfalls, forming steps of blue-green crystal that descend over pastoral areas of lower elevation.

Despite its kindness, Orme was once home of death and terror. The modest villages scattered among its greenery were subdued by a heartless little tyrant who exploited the shepherds with taxes. When the shepherds stated that they had no more to give, the tyrant began to torment them because he thought they were lying. Later, he thought they were plotting a revolt and he unleashed such a massacre that it is still lamented today. It is believed that Ogli's parents, in a desperate effort to save him from the sword, left him to his fate in a straw basket on the waters where the Umbre river just begins to be the rugged river that it is. From the region of Orme to the plains of Acqueor, the Umbre river goes jumping. It is not known how the boy survived the descent. He traveled inside of the basket over the Umbre's rough crests. The child went aground in a backwater where

the cook of the Convent of Strioja, who had gone there to fish for arrovos, picked him up and took him to his convent. Arrovos go uphill
over the mountain rivers, overcoming the waterfalls. Some people
see their intervention in this story. The arrovos, they say, cushioned
the fall of the basket with their backs, driving the child to where the
monk used to fish, so the child could be rescued. The truth is that this
monk never fished arrovos again. The other monks missed them until
the advent of the new cook.

Anyway... The child was raised there among novices and monks.
They say that the kid was more reserved than the other children, always away from loudness and objects. I have been told that when the
kid was around seven, he became even more mysterious. He seemed
even more reserved. Watching him closely, the monks found that the
boy, by stealth, took a glass and a jug with water to the warehouse
full of trinkets and remained there for a while. The monks let the boy
go back to bed, then went into the cellar and examined the jug. Then,
they deliberated. A monk kept one eye on him for the rest of the night.
Early the next day, they went to his bed. They asked the boy about the
purpose of his actions, and he replied that, during the day, God takes
care of his things which were many, such as keeping the stars moving
and seeding the plants that are seeded by nobody. At night, God is exhausted and seeks rest in that precise room. His intention had always
been to bring God something to drink because that is what he does
when he gets tired from working in the garden with Master Ert. The
most curious thing was that when the monks went to the warehouse to
take the jug back, it had already been consumed by an invisible thirst.

My table-mates also commented on the trip that I was about to
undertake, getting me excited in many ways. They trusted me how
they had cherished the novelty of being part of a tour through un-
believable scenarios and how the experience had far exceeded their
expectations. They announced splendid buildings that would fill
my sight, exotic landscapes, different people, bleak mountains, and
peaceful valleys with running water. They anticipated that I would
return with a memory loaded with indelible images. My table-mates
also warned me of something that I could hardly understand at that
time: "Whoever undertakes the Path of Gnedh never returns."

Later, in the evening, we had a dinner in honor of Reverend Ogli-s-
Oöp. Nothing ostentatious. The only special thing was that they served
punch to everybody. This is only done on someone's birthday, and it is
only offered to the celebrated one. The Szabeo Order is actually quite
poor as their vows demand. Another modest but very significant detail

was that Master Garg, two days before, asked us to make colorful lanterns. They were made of translucent colored paper and a candle. First, a paper cylinder was formed. It was glued to a cardboard base. Finally, a candle was placed inside of the cylinder. Just before the dinner was over, Master Garg sent some chosen boys to place the lanterns along the edges of the windows, the extension of the ceilings, railings, and friezes, on any length that could produce a necklace of light. So that, when we left the dining room for the halls surrounding the courtyard that was located two floors below, we all got a very memorable surprise. The night was cloudy and darkness surrounded the building, but the glacial whiteness of the walls of the Convent of Kien was shown dotted with bright colors. It was a real show! My heart, still childlike, was full of emotions. I felt a vibration poking my insides as if something significant was happening to my life. That sensation did not leave me that night until, in my monastic cell, I fell asleep only with some effort. What adventures will be waiting for me out there? What things will I see? What emotions will I feel? What did my table-mates mean?

The next day, very early, Reverend Ogli and I left the convent. Master Garg, Reverend Tres, Reverend Zköy, Reverend Ibo and Brother Bóghaz, who, besides being the porter also worked as the organist of the convent, were there to say goodbye. A representative of the seminarians put me on, according to the tradition of Otân-guié, the scapular of the Szabeo order, and gave me two pieces of chewing gjenci obtained from the first spring sprout. Its freshness stayed in my mouth and brought to my mind those airy evenings when I romped over the flowery fields of Sheik, my hometown, where, not long ago, I also heard goodbyes.

The monastery of Kien, perched on the steep heights of the Bujier peaks, dominates the Athamutt mountains. It always seems like either straightening itself up or precipitating into the abyss. Sometimes, I imagined that the convent had emerged from the depth, painfully scraping the mountain gums. As the first teeth, it seemed that at any time the building would get detached, taking us all in its fall. That day, this solitary fang of the mountain bite looked more enormous than ever, but not with the enormity of the bulk that stands out on the plain; it seemed huge because it looked like one among many other giants of a horde where the exotic was rather small. Other times, my imagination made the convent something minimum and drowned. Looking at it from a moderate distance, it seemed to me like a modest ship dragged by the giant waves of an ocean made of granite.

There is a winding path that follows the crests of those waves of rocks and gives hikers a refuge. There, we found provisions for us. We loaded them on a friendly knork that, according to Brother Zek, responded to the name of Oj. He also told us that, although the knork was the slowest of the pack, it definitely was the strongest among those that grazed nearby. His face, covered with fur, had a sleepy expression, like all the knorks. It looked like, in his life, he had slept only a few times. He was very gentle and loving. Reverend Ogli preferred to relieve him from carrying his backpack.

That was a bright day. The horizon, sawed by so many peaks, kept breaking the glow of the dawn. Looking beyond the distance, Reverend Ogli-s-Oöp took a deep breath of mountain air and said forcefully:

- Let's go, little Add!

I felt, then, as if everything had just begun.

lenelom vn
es in dc dach
en dc dey lic
tac licht vn
dcr duuster
nis en noem
tc dar licht
den dach en

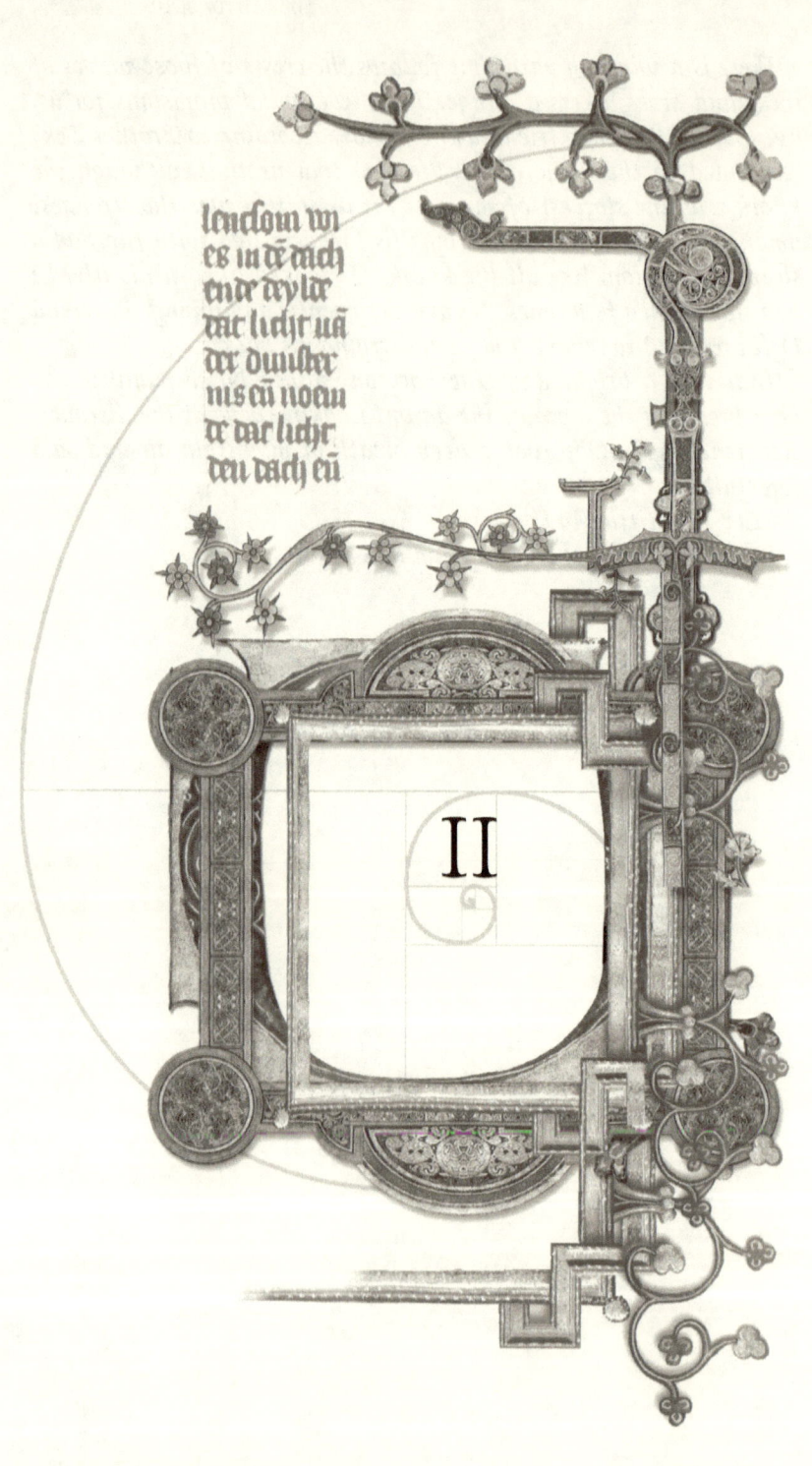

II

Chapter II

The Path of Gnedh

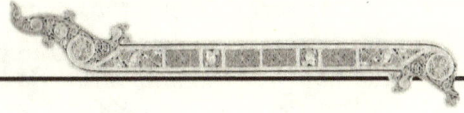

e descended the steep corridor that goes away from the Convent of Kien. The cool wind brought the smell of young grass.

- Aren't you happy for the trip? -Reverend Ogli asked me.

- I have been happy since the day the trip was announced to me.

- What, then, is the cause of that circumspect air?

- It is not that I am discontented. I'm so glad that I was trying to understand what happens to the mirror.

- Ah... The question of Master Garg! Why does a mirror make left what comes right, but it does not put the things upside down? Is that it?

- Yes, Reverend. Ogli.

- You were in trouble yesterday, right?

- Ah... yes!

- The explanation, Ad, is very simple. If you wish, I can explain it to you.

- I would love it. Please!

- Once you understand it, the question seems to be less intricate. Although, as you might recall, you have to get used to not taking your truth as totally genuine and never believe that it's the only explanation. Anyway... As I said, the question is simple and precisely therein lies the problem. Any quest for simplicity implies a purification that leads the individual to break down anything that is not essential until finally, the truth is clean of any mixture.

Reverend Ogli stopped. From his backpack, he pulled out a note-book. He got a sheet of paper and started drawing.

- Imagine a hand in front of a mirror. Your left hand, for example, Ad. Now, think about it, Ad! Does the mirror invert its image or not?

- My left hand appears as a right hand. If I stare at my face, my right eye would appear to the left, my mole on the other side. Of course, the mirror inverts the images, that is clear! My image raises his left hand when I raise my right hand, it closes his left eye when I close my right eye. Sure, it inverts the images!

Reverend Ogli said nothing. He only went back to drawing.

- This new mirror, does it invert the images or not?

-Well... -I gave it a thought and then I was not that sure.

-What the second mirror shows, that would be an undeniable inversion. Do you agree, Ad?

- Yeah, it's true!

- Do you understand, now? In this last case, the fingers of the picture are inverted from left to right. What happens is that, without desire of malice, the mirror shows us forms that have the potential to confuse us. Our brain tries to understand them as best as it can. There is nothing more natural than trying to understand something strange in comparison with something we are already familiar with and understand very well. When we look at the mirror image of our left hand, we believe we are seeing the opposite side of our right hand. This first impression, without further reconsideration, is promoted to the quality of a general rule and thereafter we say that the mirror changes right to left. We hold the mirror responsible for something we do. In the same way, we state many other things, and this happens to us in many different fields of life. The greatest danger, my dear Ad, is that we can become unfair to others.

- I see!

- The mirror, then, does not invert anything. Each of the points of an object corresponds perpendicularly to the points of its image. That is all that a mirror does. If we put a ruler in front of its mirror image, we would make what I have just said more obvious:

- The mirror -he continued- does not change the ruler marks from left to right, but it opposes a proportional distance between each number and its corresponding image.

- I think I understand.

- In the illusory phenomena, the mind always plays a major role. Try to catch it! You will see then how the truth comes out. It seems to us, that the mirror inverts left to right. We do not realize it was us, with the portentous instrument of our imagination, who made the switch. We turned it around from left to right with our mind. This is like the error into which we fall when we accuse the rest of committing what we are not able to see in our own behavior.

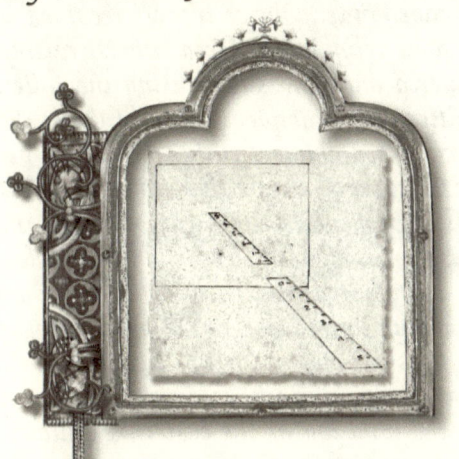

Being consistent is a matter of symmetry. Perhaps for this reason, it is said that only the one who has a conscience at peace can look calmly to the mirror.

- Thank you for your explanation, Reverend Ogli.

- You are welcome! Despite the mistake, there is something wonderful in all of this. We have been able to infer a physical property of an imaginary universe: in the world behind the mirror, everything is the opposite.

As far as I'm concerned, I was very satisfied with the explanation. Now, I have something to tell Master Garg -I said to myself. I was also very pleased to have Reverend Ogli-s-Oöp as the guide for my Ashimathá, this is, my initiation journey. It was then too early to know how privileged I was.

The tour we were about to start was known to those close to the Szabeo order, and only to them, as The Path of Gnedh. Without becoming identical, this itinerary shares some stages, routes, and stations with another pilgrimage pathway of tourist fame: the Aciago Path. Although the idea behind both of them is similar, the difference is substantial: the Aciago Path ignores any church and any religion that is not Cruciglobist; the Path of Gnedh is not discriminatory, their visits look for wider contacts and, therefore, its jurisdiction is greater. The Path of Gnedh is certainly not restricted but, on the other hand, is secretive.

As it may already be assumed, this path is tied with the legacies of religions in conflict with the Cruciglobism which were abolished by it, up to be suppressed from the common memory; memory which is preserved by the Szabeo order. Our scriveners recorded it all while, in the exteriors, some religions replaced others, raising their temples over the conquered ones and substituting the fallen gods with the victorious deities. For example, Aciago of Orqe, the goal of the Cruciglobist journey, today has a cathedral, which before was a temple erected to Eliseo and, before that, to the goddess Sidra. Originally, it was a field of menhirs. The Aciago Path is the youngest of the roads because roads, indeed, were many. Agrodes, king of Lepuria, confirmed -or invented- the discovery of the tomb belonging to a Cruciglobist martyr and rushed to recognize a route of pilgrimage which already existed, and named it "Aciago." Some argue that this was a clever political move because the nascent Lepuria was about to face the invasion of the eastern Lunilaics. Accounting this pilgrimage as part of Cruciglobist assets, Agrodes secured his kingdom with an unbreakable link to the chain of Cruciglobist kingdoms that dominated the Western Continent. So, he got the unconditional support of all the monarchs of his neighborhood, excessively devotees.

In the Middle Era, the Western Continent was shaken by the Lunilaic raids that were pushing to enter the Batzar Strait, either through Arteria or Ariana. Aciago of Orqe was the nucleus on which the religiosity of that part of the world crystallized. On the other hand, the Lunilaics did the same over the surroundings of this area during the Lunilaic occupation. It was at this neuralgic stage when Lepuria became established as part of the Cruciglobist defensive circle, centered on Marteria, the capital of the diocese. When the Lunilaic territories were regained, The Aciago Path became important to the secular and ecclesiastical practice.

From the Piroterio gorges to the Orqelian valley, this religious itinerary has led for centuries countless pilgrims from all over the Western

World along a spiritualizing topography, ideal for solitude and introspection. For this effect, the path accounts, even nowadays, with numerous stations always assisted by hostels, places of worship and piety where it is possible for the pilgrim to rest and collect himself in meditation.

Paradoxically, the deep tranquility and mercy infused by the path get upset by some anti-eastern effervescence that merges into the memories as they come. They are offered to the memory as lashings of rancor, inherited from long ago. They involve the pilgrim in episodes of war and tendentious remembrances, from whose evocations, he emerges unconcerned only with effort. The cathedral of Aciago of Orqe itself has a virulent past and generates conflicting moods in the pilgrim. The original church, constructed by Agrodes, was devastated by the Lunilaics during an invasion commanded by Bn-jal-Umer. The invasion did not leave Cruciglobist monks alive and no statue standing. Of course, we must listen to what the Lunilaics have to say! They also suffered which could outrage to whom is listening without partiality.

Elefo, the Cruciglobist martyr who originated the journey, also embodies a bellicose side. King Nanerdo, on the night his army was about to be defeated, claimed that Elefo had appeared to him, riding a jralen, wearing a wire mesh and wielding a sword from Tiledonia. This caused that, during the reconquest, his image appeared on the banners of the cerontes knights who were fighting the "infidels." Elefo was nicknamed Ejos Killer. "Ejos" was an offensive name used by the Cruciglobists against the Lunilaics. The name of the martyr was transformed into a cry of war. A saint-killer is a figure that the Szabeo doctrine does not understand, and although it does not excommunicate it, it keeps it in quarantine to study it from a distance. It may now be understood that for the pilgrim -more in the Middle Era than nowadays- the journey to Aciago of Orqe symbolized the reconquest of Lepuria, which is the same as the expulsion of the Lunilaicism. This traveling enterprise is considered something close to a crusade. Therefore, the Aciago Path is inevitably soaked in hateful associations. Apart from these antipathies, a deep introspection joins the gentle and the rough, contrite cerontes, shepherds, monks and even criminals in an expiatory mood; all in sincere partnership. Often, there were terminally ill walkers who were convinced of the restoration of their health after the journey because they had heard it from others or they had taken their faith at their own risk. As the influx of pilgrims kept growing, the journey was improved. Hostels and lodgings appeared here and there. The monks of the Convent of Igur wrote a schematic travel guide. The Pensionarian Order arranged a guard of ceronte knights along the way. Apart from hermitages, bridges, and roads, they constructed many shelters for welcoming the newcomers.

Most of the time, the devotee walks without looking around. The happiest landscapes do not relieve him from chewing over his guilt. At some point, though, he faces the captivating views coasting the profile of Lepuria over the Enormous Sea. There, the forest scatters over the coastal slopes, turning them all green. It runs downhill until it is able to see the reflection of its last bush on the bluish waters of the coves. This shore is also famous for being a shepherding sidewalk for transhumant livestock. Then, the penitent will inevitably dissipate his mind following the careless flight of a gliding bird. He may wait for the exhalation of relief with which the waves unload themselves just before they died. He may notice the shape of a delicate herb, a puzzling line discovered on the ground, the frenetic work of the ants, a parade of sea creatures, or the rhythmic navigation of a jellyfish. A handful of wild berries will deliver him some juice and the wind will pick up brief aromas from the sea. Once he finally becomes familiarized with this atmosphere, the devotee suddenly finds himself in front of hermitages and monasteries hooked on the rock as they were gargoyles censuring his weakness and neglect of his penance. The pilgrim, then, will get bitter again.

When he finally reaches the destination, he sees a frontispiece decorated with monsters able to eat impure souls. The frontispiece summarizes and anticipates the apprehensions of death. At the entrance, like a squashed stack of celestial circles, a ring made of multiple concentric arcs closes on itself. This is how the temples mark the separation between the exterior and profane realm and what is sacred. Temple meant in Artesio the site of the augurs intended for cosmic queries.

The Cruciglobist temple -said Reverend Ogli-, like any other, tries to be the reflection and the resonance of the cosmos which is the image of God. It is designed to capture the celestial order and evoke it in contemplation. In order to make that possible, somehow, the temple first has to contain it in its architectural body. Given the vast amount of all agreements and particularities, a summary of the universe would be as impracticable as its enumeration. A breviary of the cosmological fact would be impossible to summarize because its details could not be exhausted. So, in order to confine the uncontainable, it is projected through a converging lens that is capable of concentrating the cosmos on a single point. This mighty lens is the symbolism. The cosmic order is then represented, not summarized. The symbol, although it may succumb to time, has no space; as the point, it lacks a measurable dimension. Therefore, at least temporarily, the symbol contains the universe. The entire cosmos collapses into a point with the gravity of a black hole. Similarly, the finite cavity of a temple metaphorizes and means God. It is because of this allegorical solution that temples explode in meanings at the least survey of the initiated sight. Perhaps now, you can see more easily why the Szabeos are interested in any temple. Thus, from an imprecise time, our monks have journeyed along the path of Gnedh which goes over part of Frigenia, Galactia and Lepuria. They do this when they are about to enter the depth study, as an initiatory approach to the Rarefaction. This is the name given by the Szabeo guidelines to the historical-religious flow. Another pilgrimage is traditional in the middle of the priesthood and at the approach of the end. This is the way the Szabeos remember their reason for being or have been. They devote months of arduous journey on foot to this enterprise, stopping without discrimination in shrines and temples of antagonistic creeds or in ordinary-looking sites interesting only to Szabeos. Part of the Path of Gnedh passes through the border zone between two adversarial faiths, and as it goes over it, it stops equally in the patrimonial heritage of both. This is not because the monks are attracted to the religious or legendary significance of a place less than its architectural wonder. This is because the Szabeos are interested in all religions and none in particular.

Reverend Ogli and I continued going down along the path encouraged by enthusiasm. Three days later, the path engulfs the traveler in a rocky alley of giant walls that stifle the light that falls off the cliffs of its throat. As a result of infinite reflections, what is left of the clarity reaches the bottom pretty exhausted for not using the intuition to know where to step. About halfway down, it is still possible to distinguish the flanks of a mountain canyon populated with thousands of goaty rocks swinging to avoid falling over the precipice. Only the whistling wind travels at ease in this huge crack, aerating the sulfurous sweats of the rocks. No vegetation is there, except for those beings half plant, half animal that infect the stones and devour them. Their name in Artesio means "rock beard." If the traveler finds a place like this, he has reached what is known as "The Piroterium" or Pirufetiemm in Artesio. The name, which comes from very old times, reminds us both of an endemic phenomenon and a legend. It is said that the temperature changes that subjugate the region produce tremendous tensions absorbed by the huge rock masses. These forces are released violently producing bursts of thunder in which the mountain material explodes, raising clouds of dust. Eliseo, the god of gods who ruled over the Marterian mythology, used lightning as arrows. He carried them on his back in a special case as a normal quiver. This quiver, made of stone to keep the rays in an incandescent state, was called "Pirufetiemm." The locals attribute the canyon explosions to the impacts caused by lightning that, not having been used, Eliseo returns to the quiver.

Bridge at the end of the Piroterio

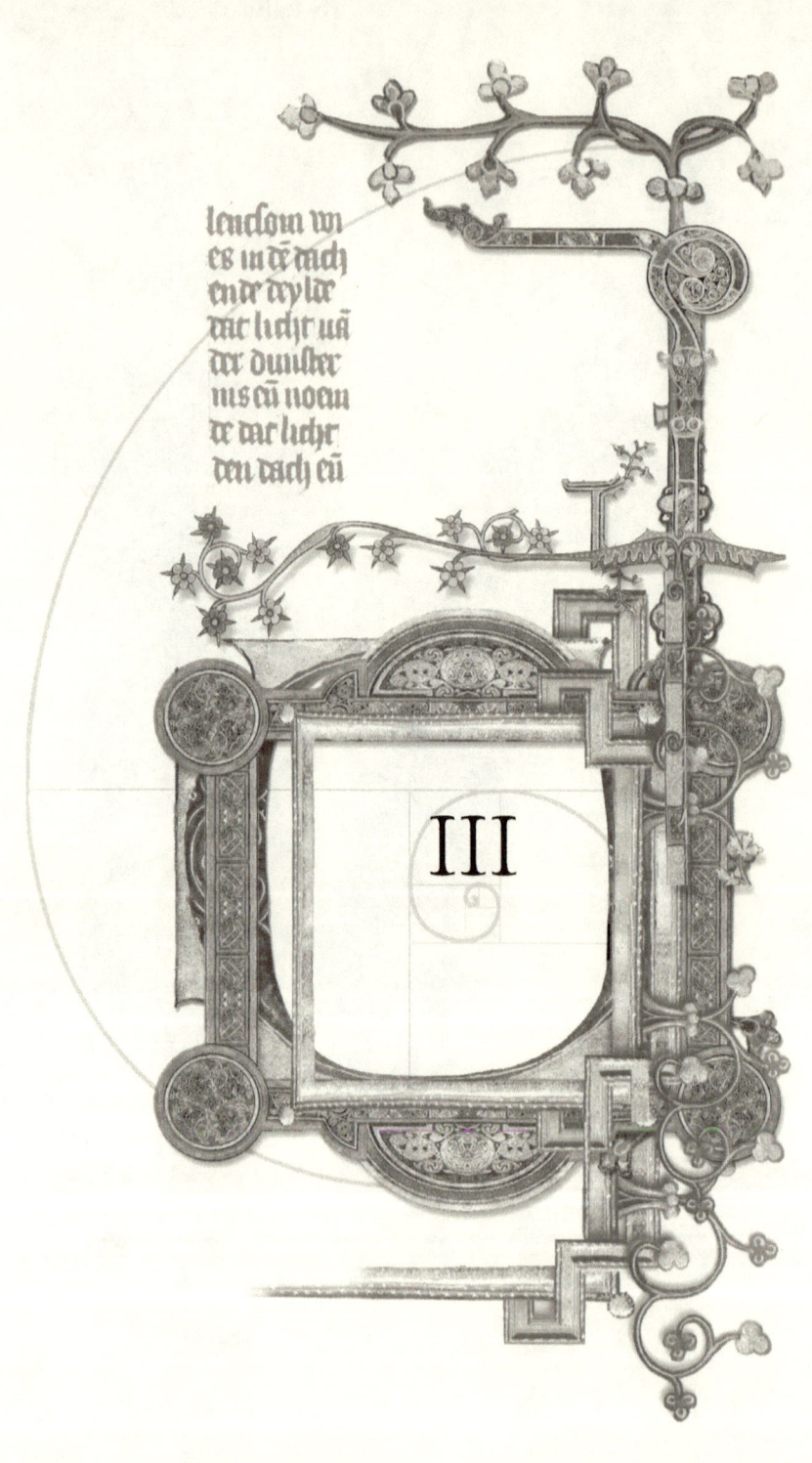

lencforn wi
es in dē dach
en de dey lic
dat licht uā
der duuster
nis cū noctu
te dat licht
den dach cū

III

Chapter III

The Enigmatic Hand of the Past

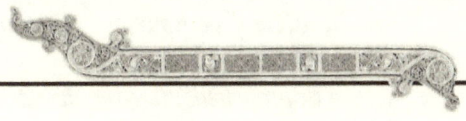

wo days beyond the Piroterium, we entered more kind and green environments with large grazing areas, forests, and crops. We sought accommodation in a little town called Añola and spent the night there.

Embedded in the mountains, Añola is famous among climbers for a couple of Dolomite peaks. These peaks, inserted from behind, hurt the mountain back. There, I tried for the first time Pomera, which is a sweet cream served at breakfast and produced by the people of Añola from cafre musk. This is an odoriferous, lumpy, crumbly, buttery to the touch and bitter-tasting substance. It is obtained from the bag that the cafre carries in its belly. It is also used in medicine and perfumery. In times of war, countless cafres were sacrificed because the musk they produce contains a precursor of the explosive powder used in projectiles.

Early in the morning, we briefly visited Brother Tyl-kro, a secular of the order. Brother Tyl-kro, a good friend of Reverend Ogli, was an old cataloger of infinite progressions. He proposed a universal taxonomy based on the matrix systematization of the genetic code.

Then, without compromising the available time, we headed toward the Alvat, the mountain that lies behind Añola. On the north side, the Alvat makes some room for a little plateau, called La Miranda. That was precisely our immediate destination.

All the region dominated by the Alvat, professes now, almost exclusively, the Cruciglobist creed. However, following the discovery of the J-tamir caves, with the arrival of scholars and tourists, the regional idiosyncrasies suffered a mythological wave from which it did not emerge completely dry. In Añola, you may hear of other gods between doubt and respect; and that is a lot to say. It must be remembered that here, one of the most violent anti-heretical factions of the Cruciglobist Church terrorized the locals. This was the so-called Holy Inquiry. They killed many people after accusing them of witchcraft.

Finally, after five hours of climbing between Añola and La Miranda, we reached our goal.

As we approached the cave, a monument appeared in our way. It was a statue without presumptuousness representing a girl who was inclined on a mirror that was lying at her feet. This was the monument to Nodka, the girl who discovered the images of our prehistoric past.

- Tell me, Ad, did you ever play "how to get the bug out of the mirror"?

- No, Reverend Ogli. What is that?

- It's a game precisely from this region. It consists of writing words in such a way that when you put them in front of a mirror, the mirror completes the body of an insect. The small Nodka loved this game.

Reverend Ogli pulled out his notebook from his bag and began to draw.

- For example -he said- the word "image" produces a bug when you match the edge of a mirror with the dotted line. You must observe the word and image at a time.

After saying this, he reached into his bag and offered me a rectangular mirror, medium-sized, with the edges free of any frame. I put it on the dotted line and looked between the drawing and the mirror.

- Oh, it's true! An insect shows up.

Then, Reverend Ogli wrote the name of Nodka, and I found in it another kind of insect. Then, he drew my own name, and I looked with admiration that my two names, on either side of the mirror, completed the image of a beetle.

- You must observe -he said- that all insects thus formed are symmetrical; that is, the images on either side of the mirror are identical except that one is developed to the left. It is said that one half is "inverted" relative to each other. The line between the two images, in this case, the edge of the mirror, is called "axis of symmetry."

- It's very entertaining -he continued- but it is said that this game is very close to the dark art mastered by the Lepurians witches. According to people with knowledge in the field, they can catch the soul of an individual in a specular insect created from his name. If the witch is in a bad mood, she can send the bug to fly... And the soul of that poor individual will be lost forever! This ruse consists of a sensitive and involuntary handling of an ancient and mysterious calligraphy which draws and decorates itself and by itself, loads and means upon itself the personal world of each individual. The latter is not so strange since any signature carries the microcosm of whom it represents. According to the Book of Illegitimate Occupation by Ülfrido-d-Nera, this skill dates back to when the Word of God had not yet completely abandoned us, when naming a thing was the same as possessing that thing. The wise warned children playing with this, that if the practitioner does not carry the soul free from blame, they run the risk of being bitten by one of these metaphysical insects and suffer unexpected effects.

- Metaphysical?

- Metaphysical! Except for the stroke of graphite that semi-sketches them, most of the insect is just a pure idea; an idea halfway out of this world.

- But is that warning true?

- I do not think so. However, it is significant that as children become adults, they antagonize more and more with this game and ignore the mirror except to accommodate their decorative accessories.

- But then, what happened to Nodka?

- Something rather lucky happened to Nodka. A soil movement unveiled the entrance to a cave. Spurred by tales of witches, Nodka found there a more propitious, mysterious, and clandestine environment to play "how to get the bug out of the mirror," using other people's names. She carried an oil lamp, paper, pencil, and, of course, a mirror. And, although she did not believe in grisly reprisals, some caution did not cost a thing to her. So, she also carried a piece of baptismal candle with a pungent smell of tallow and some holy water as a supernatural insecticide. On one occasion, Nodka went into the cave even deeper than normally. She put down her witchcraft equipment. She brought her lamp closer and outlined with art the letters of a name on a piece of paper. When she was about to exempt a nasty boy from the heavy burden of his soul, she turned over the mirror that had been upside down. What she saw made her shake completely...

- What was it?

- Behind her, a huge monstrous ugante of menacing horns had appeared and was just about to pounce on her. She got terrified. She yelled. He turned around abruptly. She got stunned, though, with the holy water bottle half open. She raised the lamp over her head. The entire ceiling was covered by similar drawings: solitary ugantes, in packs, stacked, lying, or running; all of them outlined as suggested by the rocky relief that had served as a canvas. They were outlined in black. Their bodies had been stained with a blood sepia on the yellowish back ground of the cave which had whitish efflorescences here and there. This warm combination endowed the paintings with a colossal strength that went very well with its large size. Equally astonishing were the graceful bodies of asnifos and gassilopes, elegantly portrayed. Around the paintings, as the stamps used by the Oriental artists to authenticate their works, one could see the shadowed silhouettes of several left hands.

We spent two full days at La Miranda. On the rituals and protocols of the Szabeo liturgy, practices, and sayings, do not ask me to tell because I have taken a vow of silence. I am free to declare, however, what is the relevance of this delay at the gates of a cave....

J-tamir is closely related to the oldest myths. Some more, some less, they fit like a glove. Some, like disloyal boudoir stories, link the most unexpected cultures with fine ties of consanguineous beliefs. A prehistoric bestiary, like J-tamir, inside of a cave, its surrounding characteristics and, most of all, the intriguing hands -so far, with no satisfying secular explanation as opposed to the many dogmatic ones- found no sharper echo than the Grezco and Marterian mythology. Although less coincidental, we do not lack some other legends from which to choose.

Before everything took its final form, there was -in a germinal state- a chaotic and piled up mixture of loosely bound things. There was nothing to shine; neither day. The weight still had not met in the center. All forms were unstable because, at the same time, cold and heat existed, humidity and the dryness worked together, the heavy and the lightweight fought for a place. God or Nature -for the Szabeo monks, it is the same- ended the disorder. He made the opposites settle in agreement: the heavy, down; the lightweight, above. The waters separated from the soil and both distanced themselves from the sky.

The light collected itself in a single star that would mark the day. The air, denser than the sky, stood underneath. Gravity pulled the heavier elements down and thus the ground tightened. So Ghesta was formed. Then God -or whatever was imposing- distributed water and soil around the huge globe at his discretion. He disposed seas and winds, rivers, and lakes. He made the fields spread, the valleys sink, and mountains rise high. He located cold and heat in one and other places. Clouds, thunder, and lightning found their place, partnering with the heights. The sky held the constellations as water admitted the fish and air the birds; as the soil housed the worms, and over it, the beasts. The soil retained some of the divine seed given by his brother, the sky. From the soil, the Thinking Being was born who would dominate everything else; a being somewhat more sacred and more intelligent than the rest. If other animals brought their gaze focused on the step, he held his head up and glanced to the stars. Thus, Ghesta was populated with Thinking Beings who carried the stellar glare in the bottom of their eyes. They admired his Maker in the contemplation of his work, from the immeasurably big to the unimaginably small. That was the beginning.

Thinking Beings did not know about authority because they did not need it; the good and understanding reigned across the globe. Evil, guilt, and fear were absent. At this time, called the Golden Age, Thinking Beings also ignored the sword, ignored violence. Military practices were strange to them. Neither had the soil been torn by tillage tools; it offered its products without hesitation or extortion. Thinking Beings were satisfied by consuming those fleshy roots that sneak under the ground, vegetables or fruits hanging from the branches. Honey was in abundance and it was consumed without the resentment of the bees. Flowers and spikes, born without seed, proliferated to their pleasure, changing the fur of the fields. The wheat glittered in the hills and the homes smelled like bread.

But the bowels of the soil kept the generative momentum. The creative essences were still intermarrying with themselves in the heat of the soil guts. Lower and subsequent life forms saw the light and took their chance in life. However, not all combinations were fortunate; one of the most morbid ones generated a detestable race of giants: The Terrible Lizards. They carried the arrogance in their blood, an unbridled appetite for being preferred, a twisted quest for sumptuousness and, most of all, contempt for others. Soon, they ignored the divine harmony and subjected their smaller siblings. This age, called Carbonic, was characterized by violence and aggression.

That is how the Thinking Beings knew about the desire to possess and dominate; a criminal desire. Truth and loyalty gave place to deception and envy. Ghesta, which was for all before, was parceled into properties. As the lands were coveted, the first wars originated. Then, the Thinking Being discovered the sword and the spear and the death machines. To make them, they lacerated the entrails of the ground looking for iron, as well as gold and silver, because despotism is assisted by the ornaments. The soil felt attacked  and dishonored, and since then, the Thinking Being has to force it to yield its fruits. For the first time, they embedded seeds into the soil and the ground shook. For the first time, the ugante gasped for the weight of the yoke. Since then, the floods lick the soil wounds and the landslides try to heal them.

Finally, the giants turned against God. They coveted his power and challenged him. The giants built huge towers, and on their terraces, they installed catapults of the same disproportion, pointing to the sky. The most daring ones, like the giant Gõtiag and his Anapsid congeners, rose towers as tall that they reached the sky. At some point, Gõtiag was perching on the constellation of Scorpio; others giants were climbing the Centipede and began to ride it to attack the divine abode. It was then when they felt the wrath of God that was unleashed on someone for the first time.

A storm of supernatural rays started far beyond where ordinary clouds are allowed to ascend. A discharge knocked Gōtiag down, who, as he violently crashed against the ground, broke the mountain range that separated the Enormous Sea from what was then the Great Central Valley. The sea waters penetrated the vast opening that is now the Strait of Jvastar, in an unspeakably violent jump as if the faucets of Heaven had been opened. The raging waves swept everything that had breath and had disappointed its Maker. Other giants who accompanied Gōtiag, terrified, turned back and tried to re-enter the atmosphere. At that very moment, they were atomized by a blinding glare coming from the abodes of heaven. One can still see, in the Aurora Borealis, as the tormented ghosts of these giants unsuccessfully try to penetrate the atmosphere.

Among the giants, there was one with a snake body, called Mãleg. During the battle against God, Mãleg was going up through a tornado. God spotted him. He extended his immeasurable foot and crushed the monster against the ground. The monster painfully curled over the untouchable foot of God, becoming a massive stone. God felt repulsion for him, or what was left of him, and grabbing some marine mud with his unimaginable hand, covered it completely, creating a mountain that was later called Mãlegum. The waters transferred from the Enormous Sea and rose for a long time until they almost covered the entire Great Central Valley. Since then, the valley was no longer a valley but became what we know today as the Central Sea.

Most of the giants who did not die in battle ended up drowning. But some survived by seeking refuge in the highlands that, since then, contained the Central Sea. These cold-blooded beings needed external heat in order to survive. God created a cold wave that spread from the latitudes that have always had ice, to freeze the continents and rid the world of them.

But, in the same way, the soil had produced malignant variations, a fortunate variation arose from it: The Artigonians. These were a particularly sensitive kind of Thinking Beings. They had never been seduced by the ambition of the giants. On the contrary, they had distanced themselves from them, inhabiting the hidden caves of the

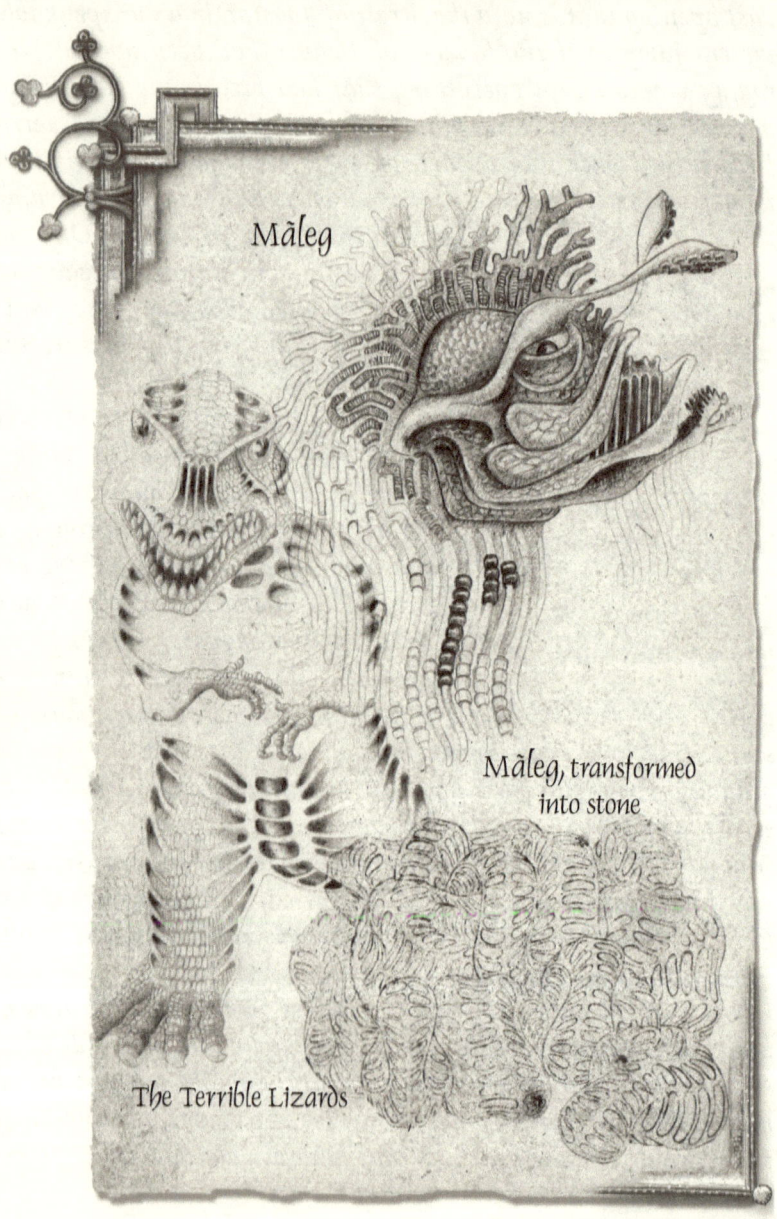

Mâleg

Mâleg, transformed into stone

The Terrible Lizards

highlands. They were skilled and curious which had led them to discover those caves. The Artigonians used their imagination and found pleasure in games, music, drawing, and numbers. They expressed a special affection toward other living beings and considered them their brothers. When the Great Central Valley began to flood,

Ghesta

Asnifo

Ugante

the Artigonians protected their animals to save them from death because they loved them dearly. But despite their best effort, the animals died due to lack of food and the intense cold that came when everything froze in the so-called Ice Age. Then, the Artigonians decided to paint images of some disappeared animals on the walls of the caves as evidence of their existence. They depicted ugantes, gassilopes and asnifos on the rock.

And God saw that it was good and removed the ice. He was proud of the Artigonians, so he decided to trust them and promised to never intervene again. But God did something else before disappearing behind the myths: he gave them the Tablet of the Arcanum, the monolith of carved stone that represented the alliance between the Maker and the Thinking Beings. Thus, the Artigonians became the first custodians of the Tablet of the Arcanum. The Tablet gave them their knowledge as they understood it. The monolith channeled the development of the Artigonians.

Only now, may the importance of the J-tamir caves in the Path of Gnedh and its disturbing concordance with the remotest cosmogonical beliefs be understood, especially those surrounding the origin of the Thinking Being. Despite many similarities, there is only one detail that does not fit: the hands that appear on the cave paintings which were superimposed on the faunal representations.

The hand has always been an important and recurring symbol in archaic religiosity. Therefore, it comes from before the Cruciglobist or Lunilaic iconography. It seems that it represented the link between God and the Thinking Being and this is precisely its meaning nowadays. Even the cryptological numerology gives the quintuple dismemberment of the hand qualities of divine privilege. It is far from clear when the legend of the Artigonians requests the participation of any hand. When the sciences that come to the aid of the excavations stopped around the role of the hand in the cave paintings, they did not dissipate the questions in an unobjectionable way. Generally, the role of the hand has been associated with hunting rituals before an individual begins to hunt. This contradicts the legend because the love for animals is remarkable in it. Whatever the case, on the boundaries of the myth, another one has risen; one that runs outside the Grezco-Marterian mythological body. It is believed that Thinking Beings used their hands on their artistic representations as a signature, as a manifestation of their possession of the Tablet of the Arcanum. This idea, apparently without basis in the mythological records, has always been deeply rooted in the subconsciousness of the population, in such a way that their association with little Nodka's discovery was immediate from the beginning.

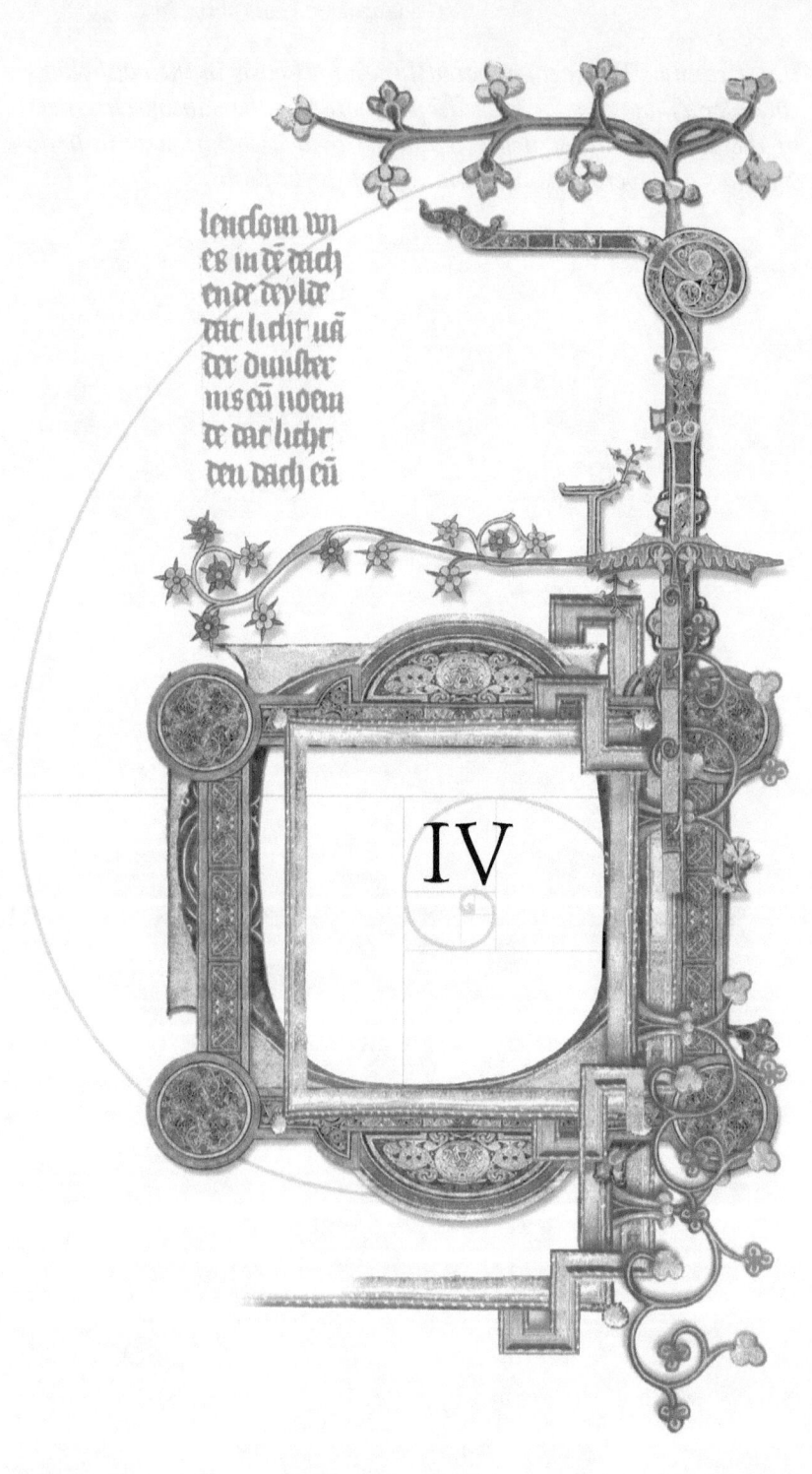

lenderin wi
es in de dach
ende dey lde
dar licht uā
der dunster
nis cū noeu
de dar licht
den dach cū

IV

Chapter IV

The Enveloping Signs of God

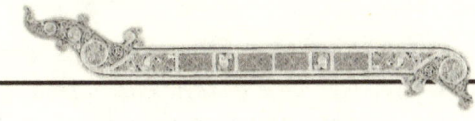

With the Alvat behind us, we turned away from Añola and headed toward the north.

After having ulcerated the gorges of the Piroterium, the ground calls a truce and becomes settled over a shallow depression to create a cradle for a serene valley. If the descent happens early, one can discover it under an oblique angle as the morning light begins to fit in the valley from the side. It gives the impression that the dawn never has surprised the valley resting because from one side and the other, the grazing dings come to the ears, a grazing that must have begun before the light showed up. The first time one sees it, some more than the following times, the eye wants to overflow itself with every detail of this industrious place called D'Iriává Valley. But, despite his best wishes, the traveler must focus on the step because the slope has not stopped being rocky. There is much loose rock, both on the track and cross country. It is possible to find everything from sandstone up to massive rocks strewn over the green mantle that covers the plain. It is as if the rocky mass that one leaves behind has crumbled over the plateau where herds feed.

Halfway on the descent, we entered into a short detour that led us to a small hill surrounded by an arm of rock, from which one can see the entire valley. Almost attached to the rock, a moderate sized Cruciglobist temple suddenly appeared. It was very attractive. It evoked both balance and madness, whether it was contemplated as a whole work or considered in its painstaking detail.

Its prolixity made of it a good example, the biggest or the best, of the Marterian style, which is not exactly the Marteric, and comes from the Low Middle Era.

- This is our second station. What do you think, Ad? -Reverend Ogli asked me, visibly pleased.

- It is very beautiful!

- Yes, very!

We stood there a few moments admiring the building. Reverend Ogli looked at it as if he had missed it for a long time.

- How would not it seem beautiful? -he said- It has every reason for us to like it. Its nice shapes are not random: they are the result of careful harmonization.

- So... Was it built for us to like it?

- Well, yes... to delight us, among other reasons.

- A Lunilaic temple is beautiful too.

- Yes, it is!

- How can two such different things can be equally beautiful?

- First, because they are different beauties. Second, you're looking at the aesthetic fact, without bias that dims your appreciation. Third, because there is no single path to beauty as there is no single way to reach God. The aesthetic planning of a temple, while exploiting the most reputable embellishing resources, focuses on highlighting the forms that every religion considers more significant.

- What are the forms preferred by Cruciglobists?

- Mmm... Actually, there are many. But within this vastness, few are selected as representatives of a specific class of a form. This is, a Cruciglobist temple can have all shapes: triangles, volutes, sinuosities, or cubes, but only one privileged example of each class.

- ...And that choice has to do with the Cruciglobist beliefs?

- Exactly!

Sometimes, his temperate speech had some trim of exaltation.

- In a temple everything has a meaning -he said- Altón, in his "Colloquies," expressed the following conception, probably inherited from the ancient philosophy of the Gregarious school: "... (God) rounded out the world as a sphere because it is the most perfect form. He wanted the world to revolve on itself, around the same point, in a uniform circular motion... He made a circular sky moving circularly... He made seven celestial circles... He wanted three of them moving with equal speed and the other four with different paces." The Cruciglobist church adopted the Altón's philosophy as a subsidiary of its religious doctrine to respond to the intellectual and social development of the secular world. Accordingly, circular and spherical shapes were tacitly privileged as it is evident in the Altonic speech just quoted. For this reason, very often, especially in the Marterian temples, the building is projected around a sphere which crowns its center. The temple we have before us is a good example. It is known as Saint Orafio of The Good Hope. However, the hegemonic role of the sphere and the circle in the Cruciglobist iconography comes from the very sign of this religion: a circle with rays around forming a cross. Its origin is somewhat obscure and Altón was needed to confirm the early Cruciglobist preference for spherical shapes.

- But, if you allow me Reverend Ogli, one can distinguish a sphere in Lunilaic temples as well.

- It is true! However, the incorporation of the sphere within the Lunilaicism is given for different reasons.

R everend Ogli sought the shadow of the building and sat on the stone steps, facing the valley full of paddocks. t

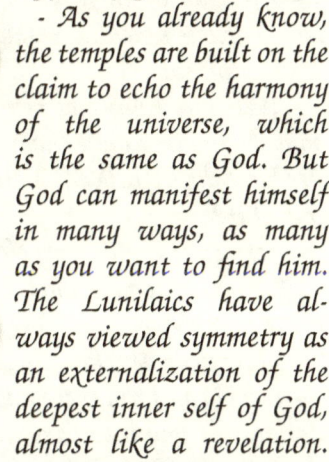

- As you already know, the temples are built on the claim to echo the harmony of the universe, which is the same as God. But God can manifest himself in many ways, as many as you want to find him. The Lunilaics have always viewed symmetry as an externalization of the deepest inner self of God, almost like a revelation.

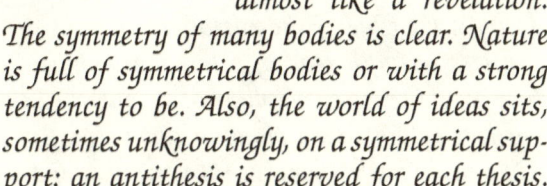

The symmetry of many bodies is clear. Nature is full of symmetrical bodies or with a strong tendency to be. Also, the world of ideas sits, sometimes unknowingly, on a symmetrical support: an antithesis is reserved for each thesis.

Mathematics leads us to infinite through a couple of routes numbered in two opposite directions. In algebra, symmetry distributes the load between both sides of an equation, showing its unique sense of elegance and harmony. In physics, symmetry requires two stirrups on a scale and compares the results of a crash. It enables rocket propulsion and organizes the invisible threads of magnetism. In art, symmetry is a scale for measuring color balance, the weight of the shadows, and the volumes of contours. Symmetry has always been an unavoidable argument in the unraveling of the most intertwined issues. Symmetry is an example of justice. It is a powerful tool for the study of crystals. It is a simplifying key for the different and endless arrangements of the atoms forming the bodies. In botany, symmetry is a census register of inflorescences, making the deployment of petals understandable and systematizing the many forms of all possible flowers. Our knowledge of elementary particles lives in debt to it. As if this were not enough, there is a fundamental law called the Law of Conservation which forces the preservation of symmetry.

- Really? -I exclaimed.

- After all of this, wouldn't you, too, perceive a divine halo, at least curious when no magical, about symmetry?

- I think so!

- Well, the Lunilaics believed it too and deified some figures and some bodies and gave them relevance over the others Do you remember how the little Nodka played with the mirror for getting the bug out of it?

- Yes! That is still very clear.

- Do you remember that the edge of the mirror produces two identical images?

- I do remember that, as well.

- If you can form these images, it means that the edge of the mirror divides the bug into two identical parts. And just for being able to do that, the edge of the mirror can be considered an axis of symmetry. If a body, instead of a flat drawing, is divided, the mirror surface would represent a plane of symmetry. Even a table, although it has legs below, has a plane of symmetry. For you to see, imagine a table cut in half. Then, we take one part and we move it to the front of a mirror until it makes contact with it.

Then, we would see how the mirror restores the missing part and the table appears complete again. The mirror, therefore, plays the role of a symmetry plane, but only represents a plane, because a plane is an abstract concept that, among other things, does not have thickness; the mirror does.

Then Reverend Ogli proceeded to illustrate what he had said with some images and went on to explain the magic backbone of symmetry.

- In the following symmetrical figures, the fine lines are axes of symmetry.

- In some figures there are more than one axis of symmetry -I noticed.

- Yes, of course! Each thin line represents a different way to divide the figure into two. You should notice also that the circle is the only flat figure that supports an infinite number of axes

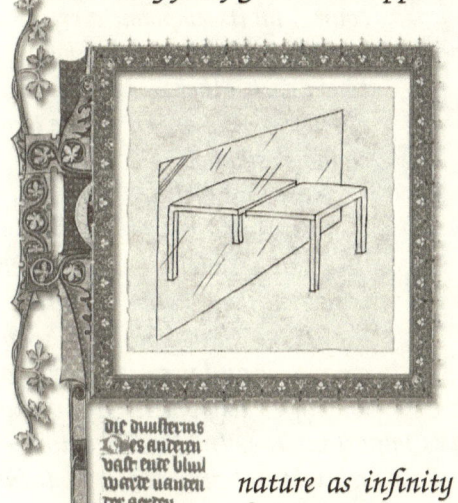

of symmetry. Consequently, the body created by the rotation of the circle, the sphere, has an infinite number of planes of symmetry. And it is for that reason Lunilaics found sacred merits in the sphere. The spherical symmetry, this divine and particularized manifestation, can become absolute up to acquiring an inconceivable nature as infinity itself. This symmetry "infinitization" is interpreted as a return to the insides of God, of which it is a manifestation.

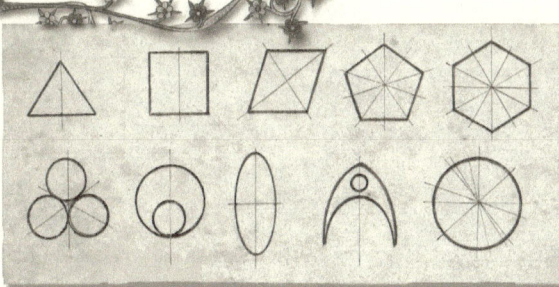

Therefore, one should not be surprised to hear that the spirit of a Lunilaic believer, within the spherical domes of their temples, is reflected an innumerable multitude of times and thus, he undergoes an "infinitization," he somehow becomes absolute. In other words, the believer's spirit meets with God.

- So, the spirit of the believer follows the same path of the symmetry to return to God.

- Exactly! Therefore, the Lunilaic temples also exhibit spheres.

- I see!

- Just to clarify... The sphere is, so to speak, the second in the Lunilaic iconographic hierarchy. The first seat is occupied, of course, by its emblem: a crescent moon whose horns are about to touch each other. Its origin is as obscure as the origin of the Cruciglobist symbol.

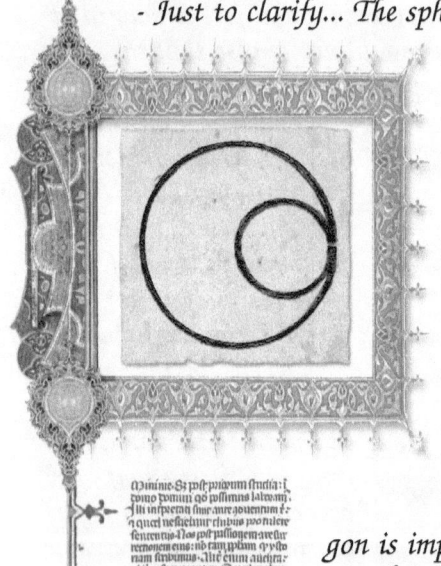

- Reverend Ogli...

- Yes, Ad?

- If, in both religions the sphere is sacred, then maybe it is true.

- From that point of view, among Lunilaics as well as among Cruciglobists, the pentagon is important too. In the conception of Lunilaic architectural structures, if drawing a pentagon was necessary, the architects preferred to delineate it through a method that gets it from their most sacred sign. The Lunilaic half-moon and the Pentagon are twinned dearly.

- Interesting!

- Bravo! That is how a Szabeo monk should think!

- But why is the Pentagon also respected by the Cruciglobists?

- You must remember that another of the cruciglobas precepts is that the circle is the sacred face of the sphere. Traditionally, in the West, the representation of the Thinking Being with his limbs totally open, forming a five-pointed star inside of a circle, was broadly accepted. This representation is a legacy of the Druids from ancient times but was restrained by the Cruciglobism at its beginnings. The "cosmic" Thinking Being of the Druids, in Erdo, their language, was written as follows... - My master drew four signs- Translated into Artesio, it turns out to be Avêmm -he continued- Avem is the name of the first Thinking Being according to the Cruciglobist genesis. So, a five-pointed star within a circle was easily understood as the symbol of the Thinking Being's divine origin. Once this symbol is sketched on a surface, the image of pentagon comes to mind inevitably and automatically, which is not without some magic. Ergo, for the Cruciglobists, the Pentagon is naturally associated with the Thinking Being.

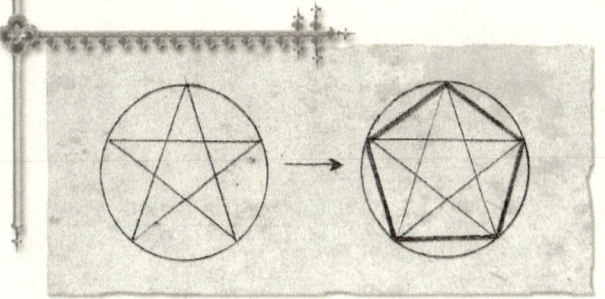

- So far, there are now two sacred symbols common to both religions. Is there anything more? -I asked.

- Well, some people think that the Lunilaic symbol is not a half-moon, but a circle containing a smaller one. In the case of spheres, the biggest would encompass the little one.

Cruciglobist Cathedrals

- That's what I mean! The coincidence of the signs -I said very sure- means that it's not a coincidence.

To my embarrassment, for a moment, the glance of Reverend Ogli hooked to mine in a disconcerting way. I never knew if he was altered so sensitively because I said nonsense or something smart.

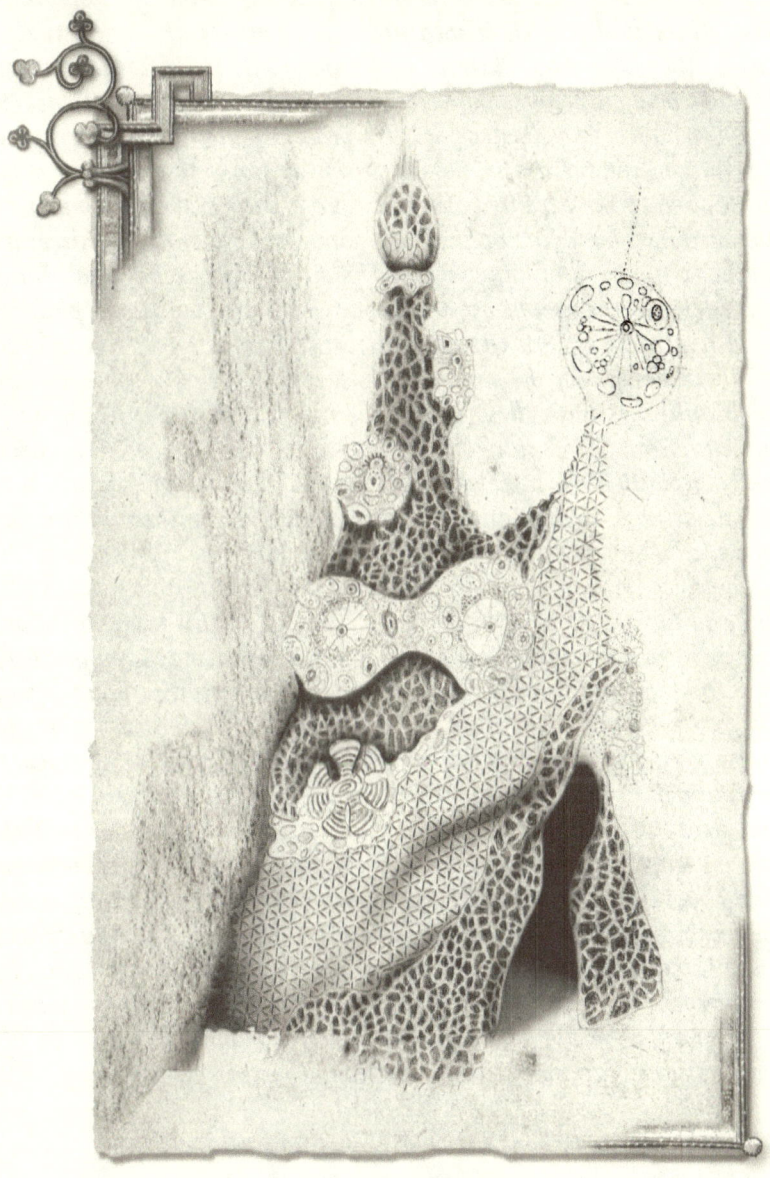

Lunilaic Temple

On Architecture and the Initiate

Architecture is the heritage of God and must be transmitted to the initiate. Architecture is an integrative discipline of many other disciplines with which it measures the goodness of works created with other arts that relate to and support it. Architecture, which because being a privilege of celestial attributes is a secret science, is learned by ear and discreet art. Its practice must be uninterrupted and of continuous use in the execution of works. Its wisdom must be applied to the executed works, to judge their perfection based on the criteria of proportionality and balance. Therefore, architecture without theory is blind; when is orphan of practice, is dead. Those who devoted themselves to it without the assistance of any philosophy, never knew how to materialize the beauty on their works or on their names. On the contrary, those who have only come to raise their buildings with the bricks of the intellect only, did not materialize anything. This happens because in architecture, as in all arts, but especially in it, there are two stirrups on which one must firmly tread: the significance and the significant. The significance is what one wants to represent; the significant is how one represents it. In accordance with this, it is undeniable that the initiate must be skillful and handle both terms with proficiency. In this representation, the initiate has to utilize all the knowledge that has been given to him, because the prestige comes only from the erudite handling of the precepts, and something else. To achieve this, it is necessary to have judgment and good taste, but these are the rarest attributes, even among the desirous ones. But, talent is not everything. The one who has been blessed with these extraordinary gifts, if he feels the presence of God in the forms and wants to praise him with his daily work that is a priesthood of contours, he must study drawing, know geometry, know optics, be vast in arithmetic, be prepared in physics, have facility in grammar, be illustrated in literature, be cultured in history, not ignore the philosophers; embrace the music; answer about medicine; be taught in astronomy; initiated in astrology; versed in alchemy and the melting of metals.

Taken from: The Ten Books Of The Wind. Albana Library. Convent of Kien.

Chapter V

The Algebra of Cathedrals

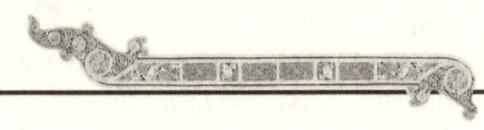

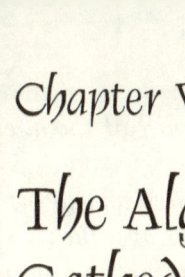 e did not see at what point the door opened. It was the seventh hour when Reverend Ogli and I walked into Saint Orafio. The Marterian temple swallowed us in one bite. Its stony esophagus, carved with aesthetic intricacies like knotted ropes, showed its ribs along the hall. It seemed that we were creeping inside the varicose entrails of a sleeping monster.

The shadows created sequences of chiaroscuro over the endless arcade and made me have sinister premonitions about the fate of my spirit. I felt as if by breaking the thin rays of clarity with our bodies, we were activating an unexpected warning mechanism. I did not want to disrespect or offend anyone, so I tried to silence my steps by containing my gravity. I feared that the shadows under my feet would break as dry leaves, waking up the Lord of this forest of columns and pilasters. Then I discovered that we were watched by the bulging eyes of little creatures sculpted at floor level and tamped down by the weight of the arches. Other creatures followed us from above as nosing our sins.

Perhaps for having previously been saturated by aromas of flowers, mud, and cattle before getting in, their abrupt absence inside the temple was manifested as another odor that my mind could not define. We smelled the difference, the whiff of the alien, the unusual.

We distrusted an old censer that could be seen among the pews. I could not resist the urge to slide my fingertips over the waxy skin of a silent and dark wooden furniture. At that precise moment, the voice of my teacher surprised me as if I had been doing something wrong.

- There are other hidden signs that you must learn to notice in a temple -Reverend Ogli said and immediately was ratified by the emptiness of the nave- Speaking of circles and spheres, the kind of circle or sphere does not matter because there is only one of each. But what about the triangle: regarding the shape, there are scalene, isosceles, and equilateral. Regarding the angles, there are rectangles, obtuse, acute-angled, and equiangular. If we decide to use the isosceles in the construction of temples, for example on the frontis of the facade, the question is: which one? The isosceles triangle is one in which two sides are equal. Now the twin sides may have any proportion to the third. What should be the precise relation between the two for the construction of a temple to rise and trim according to the universal harmony?

- I do not know!... Which one?

- It is a response with some biography. For that, we must go back to remote times... Since long ago, the triangle has been regarded as the triplicity of the unit, the three points on which the self manifests. It was already a revered figure. So, it was taken for granted that the architect, dignity only played by insiders, would take the triangle into consideration when designing a temple. What changed in every town and civilization was the fingerprint of that symbol; in other words, its proportions. The Ajeplos, inhabitants of Faronia, chose the scalene triangle in the 3/4/5 ratio. This same triangle was also distinguished in Frigenia, where it was known as the Druids Triad.

- But Faronia and Frigenia are far from each other, right?

- Indeed. However, it is true. In the Great Pyramid, the floor area of the King's chamber is a rectangle whose sides are set in a 2/4 ratio. The height of the chamber corresponds to the square root of 5. These dimensional relations were not accidental; they were absolutely necessary to draw invisible 3/4/5 triangles inside of the mortuary environment.

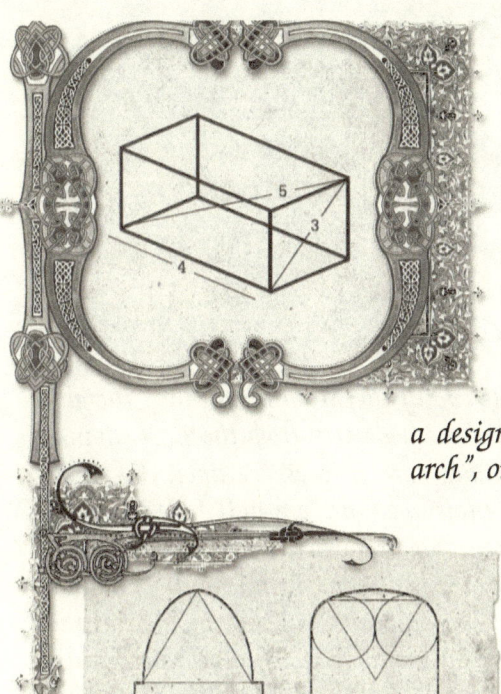

1/1/1 Arch   1/1/1 Half-Arch

- At the dawn of the Cruciglobism -Reverend Ogli continued- vaulted naves were built using the equilateral triangle with a ratio of 1/1/1 for its sides. This was a fairly obvious choice given the Cruciglobist precepts. Then, the same triangle was used in the arcades, but with an inverted position, creating a design known as "three centered arch", or just "half-arch" because its eccentricity is different and seems less high than the first. With this, the sacredness of the content in the equidistant intangibility of the vaults was assured. Another issue subjected to clarification was how to distribute the temple along its length, in the tightest way to the taste of God. How far the central nave should reach? Where do the lateral naves meet the main one? Where the apse should be connected? The older Cruciglobists sought the answer in the same sky, which sounds pretty reasonable if it is all about to emulate God. But the sky, as they understood according to the Altonic theories, was organized in spherical belts at precise intervals. The first five harbored a planet each; the sixth, a paradise; and the seventh, a divine abode. All these skies comprised the sky that revolved around Ghesta. The intervals separating sky and sky were determined with precise quantities and they were worth one, half or one and a half the distance between Ghesta and the moon. The designers directly applied these relations to the plans for the temple. For example, if the length of the smaller naves was set to 1/2, the central nave was worth 1 and 1/2; and the apse, 1/2. Thus, the total length was worth two and formed a cross with a 2:1 ratio between its axes.

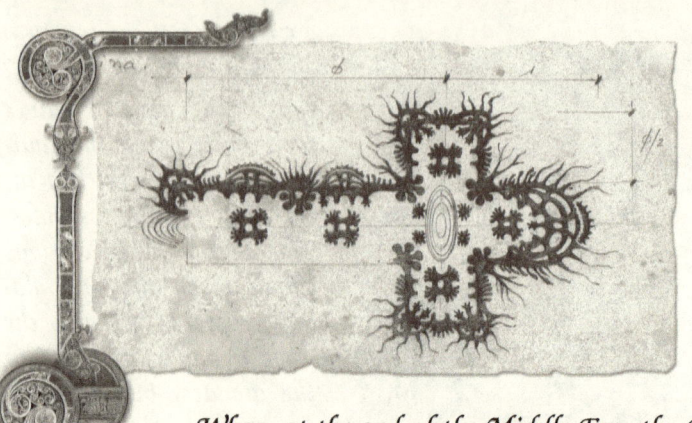

When, at the end of the Middle Era, the Cruciglobists imported the geometry from the East, thanks
to the Lunilaics care to preserve ancient knowledge, they envisioned an eternal and universal
beauty backed by mathematics, which was attributed unanimously to God. To find out what proportion two construction elements should keep in
order to look harmonious, with algebraic beauty,
which is celestial grammar, they inquired mathematics in its own terms:

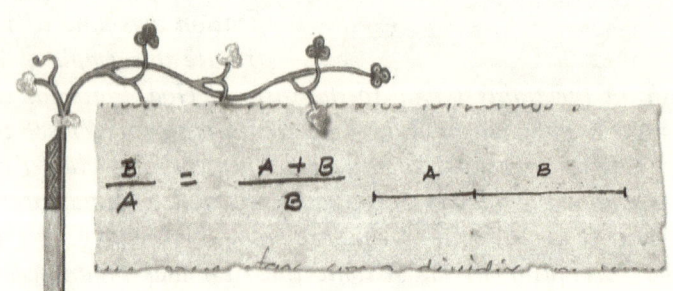

$$\frac{B}{A} = \frac{A+B}{B}$$

- This is the same as asking how to divide a segment,
so the biggest and the smaller piece have the same relation the whole, the entire segment, has with the biggest
piece.
- But... Master -I said, hurried by the short range
of my impulsive reflection- I do not understand what
makes this an aesthetic condition.
- Let me explain. What happens is that this is just a way adapted
to the algebraic semantics, for asking something simple. Actually,

what we want to know is how to divide a segment, so a harmonic progression between all pieces is achieved; this is, the smaller part, the greater and the whole must grow in harmony. Therein lies the aesthetic condition, hidden among the meanings, covertly tele-graphed between the lines:

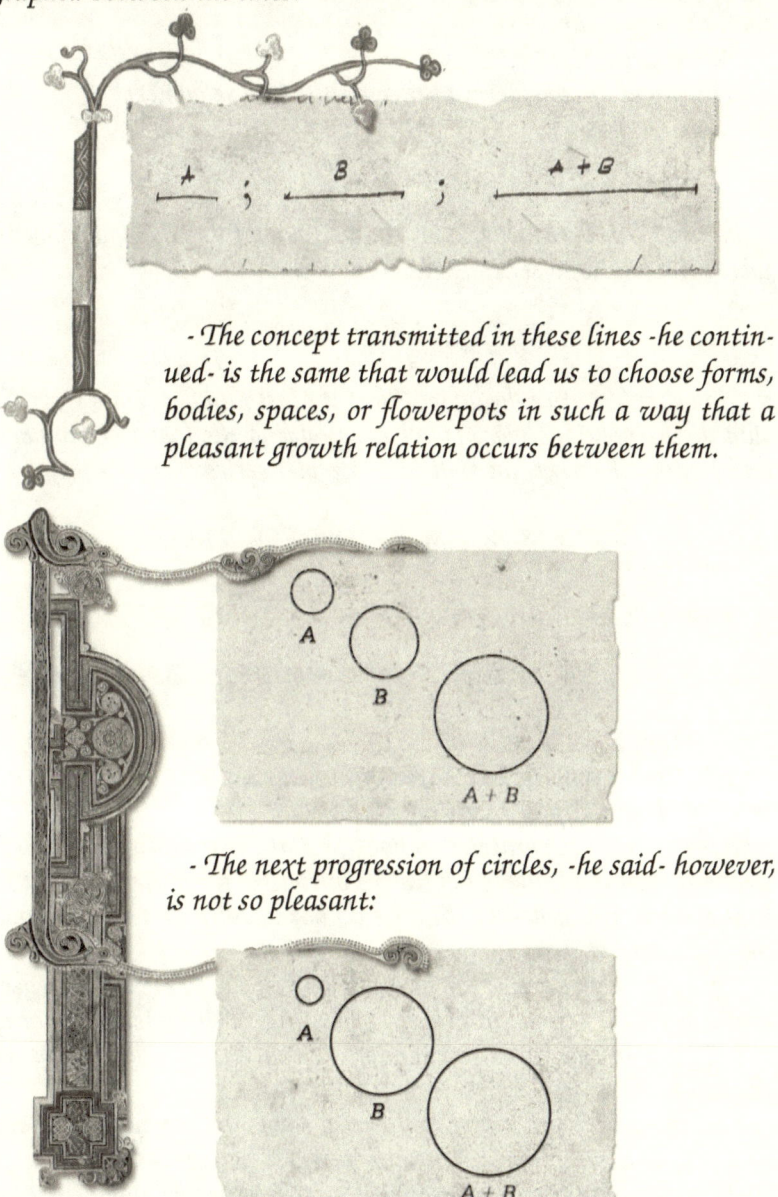

A ; B ; $A + B$

- The concept transmitted in these lines -he contin-ued- is the same that would lead us to choose forms, bodies, spaces, or flowerpots in such a way that a pleasant growth relation occurs between them.

A
B
$A + B$

- The next progression of circles, -he said- however, is not so pleasant:

A
B
$A + B$

- The algebraic expression $B / A = (A + B) / B$ -he added- leads to a quadratic equation that makes B equal to 1.618, which is symbolized as ø (Phi). It is known as the "divine number," "divine proportion," "golden ratio," or "golden proportion." The resolution assumes that the value of A is 1. From this, something else, even more curious than the above, appears.

- What is it, Master?

- If instead of considering the segments in a sequence:

$$A; \quad B; \quad A+B$$

we write, in a sequence, the values found from the equation we were referring to, a series of numbers occurs:

$$1; \quad 1.618; \quad 2.618$$

- You should notice -he added- that the last number comes from the sum of the previous two. If we keep adding the last two numbers and finding the next, we will form a wider series:

$$1; \quad 1.618; \quad 2.618; \quad 4.236; \quad 6.854; \quad 11.09; \ldots$$

- This is the same as writing:

$$1; \quad ø; \quad 1+ø; \quad 1+2ø; \quad 2+3ø; \quad 3+5ø; \ldots$$

... because ø has a value of 1,618.

- Ah! This would be like having a measuring tape to estimate the beauty! -I said happy about my idea.

Reverend Ogli celebrated as a boy at what I just said. Sometimes it was not easy to reconcile his festive outbursts with the fact that he was already 132 years old. Adults do not usually find much happiness in simple things.

- The divine proportion -Reverend Ogli continued explaining- generated a whole new architectural style: The Boric style, in honor of the Bôros, former barbarian inhabitants of Arania who, however, did not discover it.

- I always thought it had to do with some kind of mysterious art and that was why they called that way.

- You mean the term "borïtic" which is Artesio for "magic"?

- Of course! Boric... Borïtic.

- Some say that "Boric Art" is a deformation of "artoric" that, in good Artesio means "sectarian language" or "secret jargon." These same thinkers claim that "artoric" comes from "Ars Ktor" which means "Art or God" or "Art of Light." "

At that precise moment, a beetle landed on my hand. We both looked at it in silence, without wanting to interrupt the evolution of its tasks. When it took flight...

- With the divine proportion in their hands, -Reverend Ogli said - the architects found the divine triangle, the divine pentagon, and the divine circle. The latter accommodates the first ones on the divine square, in one figure of unassailable iconographic value because the ancestral beliefs perfectly found a house in it.

Then, Reverend Ogli sketched a diagram somewhat more accurate than the previous.

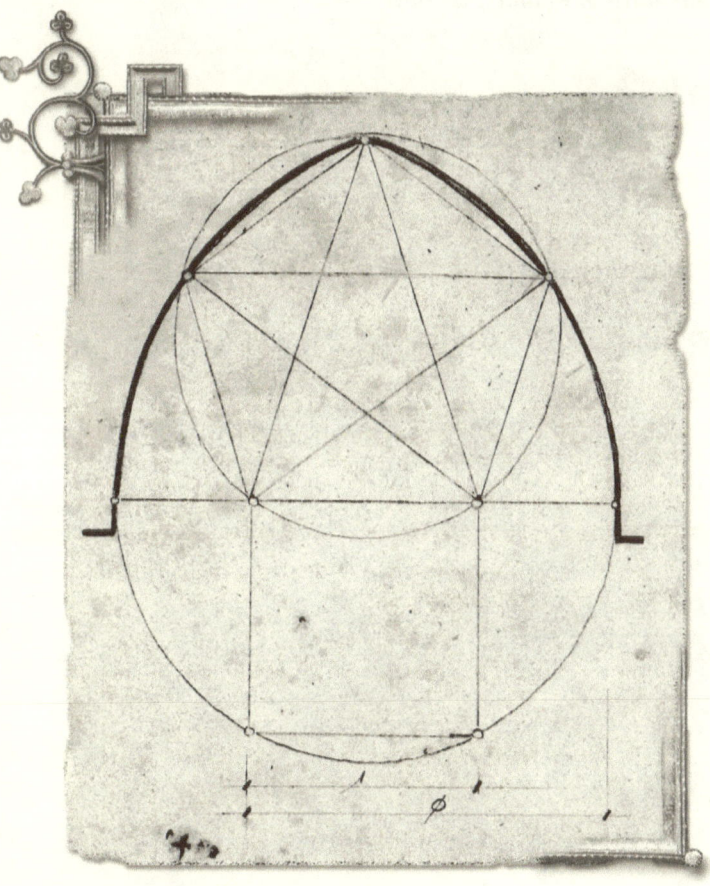

- Ah! -I said- Now, I can see the triangle, the square, the pentagon and the circle!

- It was not a coincidence, then, that upon this invisible network of lines and meanings the Boric ogives were constructed.

- Is this also the shape of the Boric vaults?

- Well... The Boric vaults were built by concatenating ogives arranged in different and creative ways.

- From this point, another branch of our knowledge begins -Reverend Ogli added- All these mysterious ramifications, like the Boric ogives, arise trying to touch, even from a distance, at least the feet of God. For Szabeos, all these intellectual arborescences are considered theological routes. The birth of this other route is as follows. Have you already identified the divine triangle?

- Yes, Master. It is the one formed by the points of the star. It is the one with ø, ø, and 1 as sides.

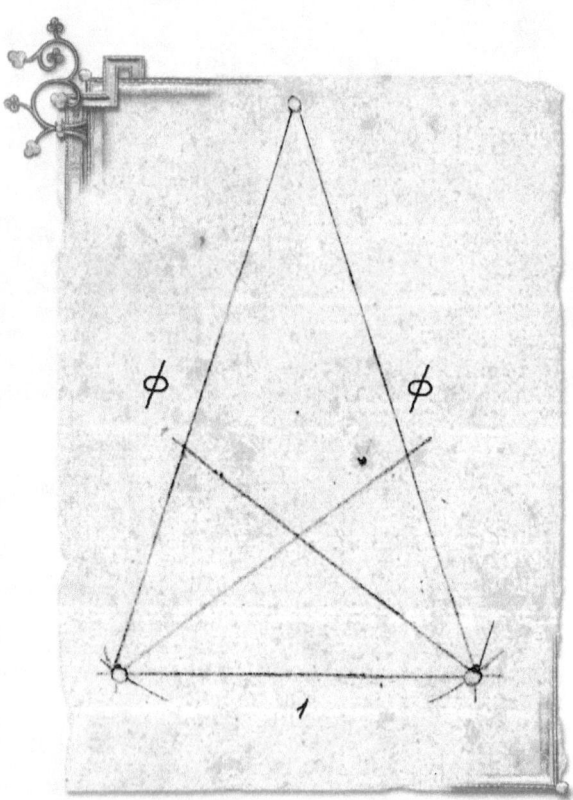

- *Well, that is precisely the issue! If the value of the sides were...*

$$\frac{1}{\emptyset} + 1; \quad \frac{1}{\emptyset} + 1; \quad y \quad 1$$

...We would not be talking about a different triangle -he continued-. This one would be exactly the same triangle.

- *But, that is impossible! -I replied- Anyone can see that ∅ is different than 1 / ∅ +1.*

- *Therein lies the wonder of this matter. Only when we are dealing with the divine number, the value of 1 / ∅ +1 is neither greater nor less than ∅; they are equal.*

- *What! How can it be?*

- *You should notice that ∅ is worth 1,618. So...*

$$\frac{1}{1.618} + 1 = 1.618$$

...If you calculate that, you will notice that this expression is equal to 1,618, or ∅. Try it for yourself and you'll see. With any other number, this equality is invalid. Let's try with the number ten!

- *That's weird! -I exclaimed after trying with other candidates- -*

$$\frac{1}{10} + 1 \neq 10$$

That's weird! -I exclaimed after trying with other candidates- The equation is true only with the divine number!

- *Exactly! -Reverend Ogli claimed. With the excitement looking out his eyes, he wrote with a feverish stroke:*

$$\emptyset : \quad \frac{1}{\emptyset} + 1$$

- *This equation -he continued cheerily- this amazing and unexpected equivalence, true for the divine number only, led to an algebra of esoteric management. With it, all the structures that supported* the Boric cathedrals were calculated. Based on the above equation, called *Penetrating* by the *Hermetics*, the Boric algebra infiltrates into a portentous superior world. This makes it possible to write a series of equations, valid only in that supernatural universe:

$$\phi^2 = 1 + \phi$$

$$\phi^3 = 1 + 2\phi$$

$$\phi^4 = 2 + 3\phi$$

$$\phi^5 = 3 + 5\phi$$

etc...

- And also:

$$\phi^3 = \phi^2 + \phi$$

$$\phi^4 = \phi^3 + \phi^2$$

$$\phi^5 = \phi^4 + \phi^3$$

$$\phi^6 = \phi^5 + \phi^4$$

etc...

- It is curious to realize -Rev. Ogli said again- that the terms $1 + \phi$; $1 + 2\phi$; $2 + 3\phi$; $3 + 5\phi$;... generate the divine series we already know, where a term is the result of the sum of the previous two:

$$1; \quad \phi; \quad 1+\phi; \quad 1+2\phi; \quad 2+3\phi; \quad 3+5\phi;...$$

- Right! -I yelled as I recognized it- That's my measuring tape to estimate the beauty!
- Precisely! If we replace each of its terms by its corresponding power of ϕ, this is: ϕ^2, ϕ^3, ϕ^4,... We have an equivalent way to write the divine series:

$$1; \quad \phi; \quad \phi^2; \quad \phi^3; \quad \phi^4; \quad \phi^5; \quad \phi^6;...$$

- But -he objected- the first one is a series that grows arithmetically, since each term is the sum of the previous two. Instead, the second series grows exponentially, since each term is raised to a power higher than the previous. How can they be equal?

- Yes! How?

- However, as you can verify, these two series produce the same result we already know:

$$1; \ 1.618; \ 2.618; \ 4.236; \ 6.854; \ 11.09;\ldots$$

- With a number other than the divine, different results are produced. For example, replacing ϕ by one million in the series $1; \phi; 1+\phi; 1+2\phi;\ldots$ the infinity would be reached (if possible) at a rate much lower than if we replace it in the series: $1; \phi; \phi^2; \phi^3;\ldots$ But, with the value of the divine number, no matter if we are dealing with the arithmetic or exponential series, the infinite is reached at the same speed since they both produce the same effect: $1; 1.618; 2.618; 4.236;\ldots$

- In other words, with this number, it is the same if we are adding, multiplying raising to a power...

- Exactly! Don't you think, my dear Ad, you're facing a prodigious and privileged way to reach infinity, like the Lunilaic spirit reflecting himself on the dome where the symmetry becomes again one with God? Perhaps, the Penetrating equation truly opens the way to the vicinity of the Maker, where the differences do not count, where everything perpetuates and gets homogenized, where no one is better than the other. No matter if you know too little or too much, if you are rich or indigent, if you are a Thinking Being or an animal in the forest, if you are Cruciglobist or Lunilaic, there is only one equal way to reach God, the Eternal, the Infinite. Don't you feel like being in front of the equation of a religion?

The Secret Revealed

There is a point on the circle
that in the square and triangle is placed.
Do you know that point? Everything will be fine!
Don't you know it? Everything will be in vain!

This is a quartet that appears on the north wall of the Cathedral of Nôtrame d'Teq; it is attributed to the stone-carver monks of the Boric school. It refers to the point that divides a line in the divine proportion. Because all the architectural knowledge of the Boric Era was based on the proportions born from the divine ratio, determining it on a line was crucial. It is understandable then, that this knowledge was kept secret and was revealed only to the disciples in the process of initiation. If you know how to do it, all other geometric constructions based on divine proportion will be accessible and the mysteries of his magical significance will be unveiled.

At one point along the way, Reverend Ogli offered me this precious knowledge and so I was initiated into the Mystical Geometry. The method explained below involves the use of a ruler to measure half of the line in question and a set-square to draw the perpendicular involved in the procedure. To split a line in half and raise a perpendicular at the end of a line with strictly geometric means, see any text on geometry.

Division of a line in the Divine Proportion

Let AB be the line to be divided. Take half the length of AB and with it construct a perpendicular at the end B. This perpendicular, whose value is AB/2, will be called DB. Now, join the D end with the A end. With a compass, take the length of DB and making center in the D end, draw the BE arc. With the compass take the length of AE, making center in A, draw the EC arc. Then, C is the point that divides the line AB in the divine proportion; this is, AC and CB. Let God be magnified!

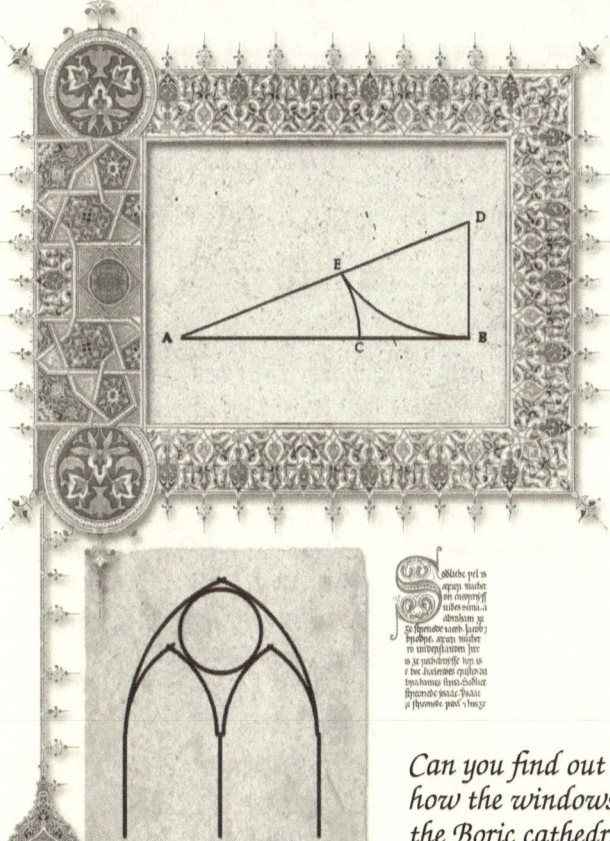

Can you find out how the windows of the Boric cathedrals were designed?

59

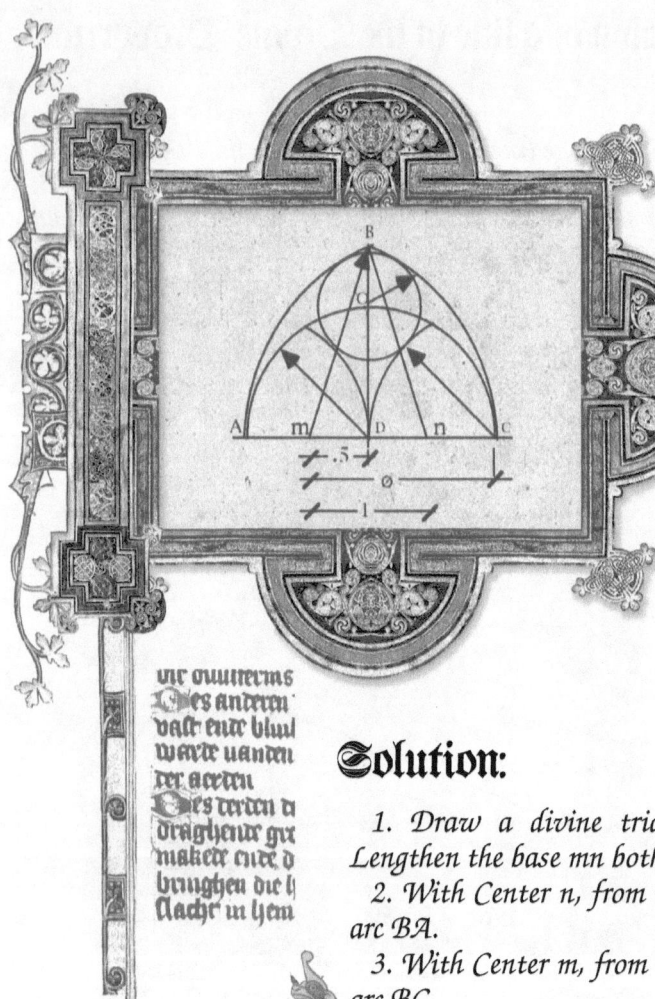

uir oulilterms
es anderen
vast enur bluul
warte uanden
ter acerten
es terten ti
draghenur git
makenr enre d
bninghen die h
Clachr m hem

Solution:

1. Draw a divine triangle mBn. Lengthen the base mn both sides.

2. With Center n, from B, draw an arc BA.

3. With Center m, from B, draw an arc BC.

4. Find the midpoint of mn, D, draw DB.

5. With center D draw the semicircle AC. Determine O.

6. With center A, from D, draw an arc Dp

7. With center C, from D, draw an arc Dq.

8. Finally, from O, draw a tangent circle to the inner arcs.

Chapter VI

The External Manifestation

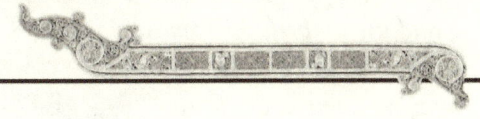

e had planned to continue our march early in the morning and at nightfall, camping halfway between St. Orafio and Qu-et.

Qu-et is the Lunilaic temple which stands at the other side of the River Toss. The majority of Lunilaic buildings that were constructed there touch the ground now, collapsed by wars and time. The Toss River, with an intimidating flow, divides the arid valley of Isor into unequal parts. The waters washed the ground until finding a basin able to contain them. In this way, a big canyon was formed. Its crumbling walls suggest caution to anyone who wants to climb them. It seems rather an open trap over the desert. It is no coincidence, therefore, that the Toss River has always been postulated as a natural boundary for whomever or whatever is imposing hegemony on either side of its channel. And this was precisely the case. In this region of Lepuria, the Lunilaic invasion in the Middle Era desisted from going beyond the river.

Qu-et was not far from where we were and the Path of Gnedh, in good use of that neighborhood, reserved for the Szabeo disciple a first contact with the Lunilaic religiosity. However, despite Reverend Ogli's plans, we were forced to spend a full day under the shade of an orgol, a giant tree that can feed fifteen people through the year with its starchy root. The delay was a courtesy of Oj, our friendly knork. While we were in St. Orafio, Oj got indigestion thanks to some wild berries that made him look green.

Once we accepted the circumstances, we expanded in Szabeo liturgies more than usual. Then we enjoyed the scenery that lay before us. The orgol became a huge beach umbrella when the sky was clear, and the umbrella became a giant rattle when the wind was blowing.

I remember myself enjoying some acid cheese that we carried in the saddlebags when we saw a defeated figure coming up the road at a breathless pace. We recognized him right away. We got up and went to meet him.

- Brother Tyl-kro! -Reverend Ogli yelled while he rushed over the old monk to hold him.

- Reverend Ogli... we need to talk -Tyl-kro said, half asphyxiated.

- Of course! But tell me respectable Tyl-kro, what could be so important to have brought you this far without any guarantee to meet us? I say this because this meeting has been totally accidental.

- I bring a message from Master Garg -he said, still agitated.

- Well, I am listening, Tyl-kro, my friend -said Reverend Ogli.

- Uh... well... -Tyl-kro hesitated, glancing at me.

- Feel free to speak -said my master- Ad must attend all outward manifestation that occurs in his pilgrimage. Remember the Otânguié's Law of Anticipation, brother Tyl-kro, according to which every event that takes place in the Path of Gnedh must be received by the disciple as an awareness that the Rarefaction projected onto him. For each individual, there is a particular pathway, although all pilgrims step on the same footprint. And it is written that there

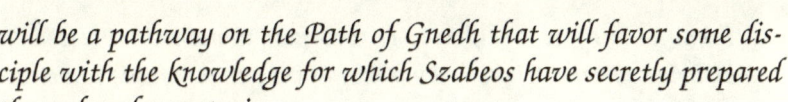

will be a pathway on the Path of Gnedh that will favor some disciple with the knowledge for which Szabeos have secretly prepared themselves for centuries.

- I apologize to your disciple Ad and to you too, Reverend Ogli. -Tyl-kro said- I did not mean to offend you. However, you must admit that it has been the discretion with which our affairs have always been treated that has granted us such a long existence.

- Do not get uncomfortable, my friend. I didn't want to offend you, either. I only tried to encourage my disciple and invite him to pay attention.

- Well, as you know, before you left the Monastery of Kien, the global situation was delicate. Today, we talk of direct intervention by the forces of the Unified Countries against the League of Falanjatos. As you also know, the two sides have weapons that, in the case of war, would put an end not only to themselves but to all life on the planet and to the planet itself. The Secretary of the Sister Nations had been the last to leave the negotiating table and could not achieve anything. The spokesman of the Sammkara government admitted that they have biomolecular missiles pointing to the Western capitals. General D-hu, as a response, publicly declared that he will attack with fusion power. But, you know, although they don't want to admit it, both sides are in possession of antimatter bombs. The Unified Countries have withdrawn their diplomatic staff from the opposing capitals. In Galactia, Primaria and Arania, the television advises the provision of supplies. People are going to atomic shelters and, just to do something, toward the mountains in countries that do not have shelters.

- But this has happened before... four times in three years.

- How do we know that this is not a false alarm? -Brother Tyl-kro asked- At this very moment, a fleet of electronic support is heading toward the Strait of Ammen from a secret base in the Sea of Euda. That means a further step toward the inevitable; now, the danger is greater.

- And each time, it will be higher until finally -Reverend Ogli said, with palpable hopelessness- Are you sure about the fleet of support?

- What I just told you is not a rumor; we have been told by our contacts which, needless to say, are reliable.

- I know, my friend Tyl-kro. It was just nonsense promoted by my discouragement. There is something in me that refuses to believe that Thinking Beings, in many centuries of civilization since the time of the caves, have not won in wisdom; they have only made the methods of murder more sophisticated: from the stick to the transcontinental missile.

- Yes, it is not easy to accept -Tyl-kro said.

Then, he added:

- In any case, Master Garg has asked me to reach you and ask you to seek refuge in the Monastery of Istric, which is the closest to St. Orafio, since Kien can no longer cope. All Szabeo monks once gathered in the various convents will enter into prayer, joining the synchronic singing of the marine mammals to contribute to the ease of tension. We cannot do more.

- It is true! Unfortunately, we cannot do more -my teacher said.

There was a sorrowful silence, as grave as reading an obituary. After a moment, Reverend Ogli restored the conversation...

- Well then, if Master Garg thinks so, we will seek refuge as quickly as possible.

- There's something else you should know, my friend. When there is a threat of total war, as on previous occasions, the people of this region lose interest in work, there are no services, and everything is in chaos. So, to reach the Monastery of Istric, you have no other choice than walking to the Port of Oods and find the way to travel to Frigenia in a boat.

- I was afraid of that -my master responded.

We thanked brother Tyl-kro for his exemplary effort spent to find us. We shared with him our limited provisions. We continued commenting on the global problem for a while. Then, the conversation sought some appeasement in better times. Both of them remembered afternoons they had shared on the river; the innocent theft of fruits on the property of an old miser from which they got a full adventure and a dirty little secret; ball games; the spinning top and milky sweets. Apparently, the friendship between Ogli-s-Oöp and Tyl-kro had united them since childhood. Then we said goodbye as if we meant forever. A deep nostalgia moistened the warm glaze of my teacher as he saw his friend going away and getting lost among the

curves of the road. Now, I think that at that moment, he felt that he would no longer see his friend again. When the atmosphere completely belonged to us, I asked my teacher:

- Reverend Ogli, do you think this time the problem will end in war?

- Things are getting worse over the months. You cannot know with absolute certainty which of the many conflicts will unleash the war. What is undeniable is that any of them may be the last.

- But how did it all start?

- That is a big question!

This was how my teacher began what I summarize below.

The last remains of the creative ferment that was in the soil interstices began their effervescence. Before the astonished eyes of the Artigonians, the random combinations of ferments reproduced animals that Artigonians believed lost. The same happened with plants that had disappeared. The sporadic coincidence produced new species and extinguished others equally unfortunate and accidental. So, the life on Ghesta was restored. The cave where the Artigonians found refuge was at the top of Mount Mãlegum. When the Artigonians descended to inhabit the lowlands, the cave became a temple. There, priests guarded, revered, and studied the Tablet of the Arcanum. The rest of them formed two villages on either side of the mountain Mãlegum; one was called Tre and the other Ert. The land they inhabited was magnificent: forests, orchards, and fields surrounding a large lake of blue and calm waters.

Those who did not grow herded cattle, caught fish, or gathered fruit. But some of the bad examples of the ambitious giants came back to memory. As these fraternal towns grew, the feelings of ownership over the surrounding land also grew. Suddenly, a hill or the water sources were in dispute. Again, the soil of Ghesta was being offended by hurting it with stakes and fences. The rivalry between Tre and Ert increased with each problem. In a short time, they wondered which of the two towns was preferred by God. Then, they developed different ceremonies for the same God who soon began to become different.

This is the origin of the two religions that dominate the world today. Each convinced of being preferred, these two peoples started underestimating each other until contempt. Both found in the differences that distinguished them motives of disgust. Members of both peoples always had bathed in the lake that the mountain Mãlegum dominated. The waters that washed their bodies began to pick up the bad moods produced in the times of hatred. The collected hatred dissolved into the lake, loading it with evil. Hate carries fire because it occurs in inflamed tempers and is able to inflame what it touches. So, once the hatred touched the bottom of the lake, it reactivated the creator ferment, producing the necessary heat to start the creative effervescence again. From hatred and water, the soil made a liquid, viscous and black. This amorphous being thickened with new hatred that was dissolved in the waters of the lake. The more it grew, the greater its desire to become huge. But, for growing, this being needed more food; more and worse evil feelings. So, through the contact with the skin of the bathers, it spurred the Thinking Beings to turn against each other. As a result, both peoples demanded the right to own the Tablet of the Arcanum and both thought that God was interested in their success. They kept an eye on each other and got suspicious of who approached the mountain Mãlegum. Patrols were organized to prevent others from reaching the temple. But this strategy put several of each group in the vicinity of the temple, which they wanted to avoid. Suddenly, the Mount was invaded from two opposite directions. Easily, they went through the temple gates. The custodian priests offered no resistance. The two peoples met each other face to face. The only separation between them was the altar, holding the Tablet of the Arcanum. Around the altar, some monks were protecting the monolith with their bodies. They tried to talk with both sides to prevent them from hurting themselves. But mistrust dominated their actions. Someone misread a sharply raised gesture and threw the first punch, and this triggered an uncontrolled violence. The strength of the meeting brought down the sacred stone. The stampeding crowd moved away to make room for the fall of the monolith. After hitting the ground, the Tablet of the Arcanum broke into three. The lifeless body of a monk could be seen where it fell, having been trampled to death during the commotion. The crowd gathered around him and the violence ended immediately. Everyone froze. The Tablet of the Arcanum had been destroyed and the first murder was committed.

This was all the evil lake needed to rise over the face of the planet and impose his nefarious kingdom. Thus, the lake which was already quite dark and thick, began to coagulate. It became a huge black and viscous mass of suffocating odor. The mass was about to take shape for the monster to arise. From one day to the next, each and every one of the members of the two criminal sides felt tormented by remorse. The first drops, soaked in the guilt of the murder, spread in the waters of the lake. But guilt outweighs hatred; this, the lake did not know. It was loaded with so much guilt that its mass became extreme. When it tried to get up, the floor gave way. As through a huge drain, the monster slipped to the deepest basements of the ground, giving an inconceivable cry. As it passed, the rocks dried out as if they were burned. The rocks cracked. They divided into fragments. They shattered. The fragments were broken down into pieces. The pieces were broken into crumbs that continued fractionating, weakened by the drying of the most microscopic moisture. This is how the desert sand was formed. Where there were waves now there are dunes; the desert keeps the memory of its origin. Does it not seem a sea of sand? This was the origin of the Desert of Azar. Every drop of water that falls on it is absorbed by the black and slimy beast that lies beneath the desert since it wants to be diluted and regain its lightness. Then it could raise itself and conquer the planet. The waters, aware about the evil, avoid it; that is why it does not rain in the desert. But the beast does not know whether to diluted or concentrated because it also needs hate to be what it wants to be. For this reason, it continues goading everyone who lives near the desert by offering water poisoned with rancor in those traps called oases. The water that emerges there comes from the oily supernatants on its liquid body, loaded with malice. This is why the desert is a dangerous land, flogged by wars caused by the beast. When, with sucking machines, the Thinking Beings extract part of the vast liquid mass of the beast, what they get can be used as fuel. When it burns, the fuel merely unleashes the hatred accumulated for millennia. The beast consents to these mutilations because he knows that the fuel is a source of money and power, and those are always big reasons that lie behind the hatred capable of producing wars.

The two people that grew up at the foot of Mount Mãlegum, which were brothers, left like enemies what once was a paradise. Tre's descendants have spread to the neighborhoods bordering the desert to escape its bleak dryness. Ert's descendants went further; hope promised them generous lands. The two groups scattered themselves over everywhere and populated the world: around the Central Sea, south of Azar, on the southern steppes until reaching the northern territories and from there to the Lateral Continent. But since then, Tre's and Ert's descendants, have rejected each other up to the most irrational and violent hatred. No wonder, then, that the boundaries between their descendants have been the scene of wars, massacres, and genocides.

In the new lands, Tre's and Ert's descendants found things they had never seen before and for which they had no name. The more abundant in novelties the area was, the higher the number of words needed to be created. Some Azáritas -inhabitants of the Desert of Azar- never came to see the snow, but the ones who populated the cold lands, such as Frigenia, developed up to twenty names for "snow" in its different conditions. And, as the case of the snow, there were thousands more examples. The different names sounded distinct and produced different verbalizations. Thus, the environmental differences created another distinction: the language. Even among the descendants of the same Azárita people, different languages were spoken. For example, among the descendants of Ert who settled west of the Central Sea, there were those who called themselves Rúsidos and spoke Rusio; the Anátidas and Láridas who spoke Esco; Équidos, Ceúticos, Gypsios, Lepóridos and Axeos -which were the ancestors of the Grezcos- all spoke their own language. From combinations between these ancient peoples, descendants of the Azáritas, the great civilizations were formed; and from them, the modern people arose. We all come from the Azáritas. Hence, racial pretensions, even the most innocent ones, they become absurd, if not ridiculous, to the light of knowledge.

- We must always keep this in mind if we do not want to fall into prejudices and cruel disappointments. -my master concluded- Remember, Ad, ignorance is not a crime, but the one that is based on stubbornness is indecent.

The Unified Countries and the League of Falanjatos are nothing more than modern organizations of Tre's and Ert's descendants, respectively. The first ones are known as Western countries; the last ones, as Lunilaic countries. The first ones follow the Cruciglobist religion; the other ones, the Lunilaicism.

This is the origin of the hatred between them as my dear and wise master, Reverend Ogli-s-Oöp, told me.

lencloun vn
es in de dach
en de deylde
dat licht vā
der duuster
nis en noem
de dat licht
den dach en

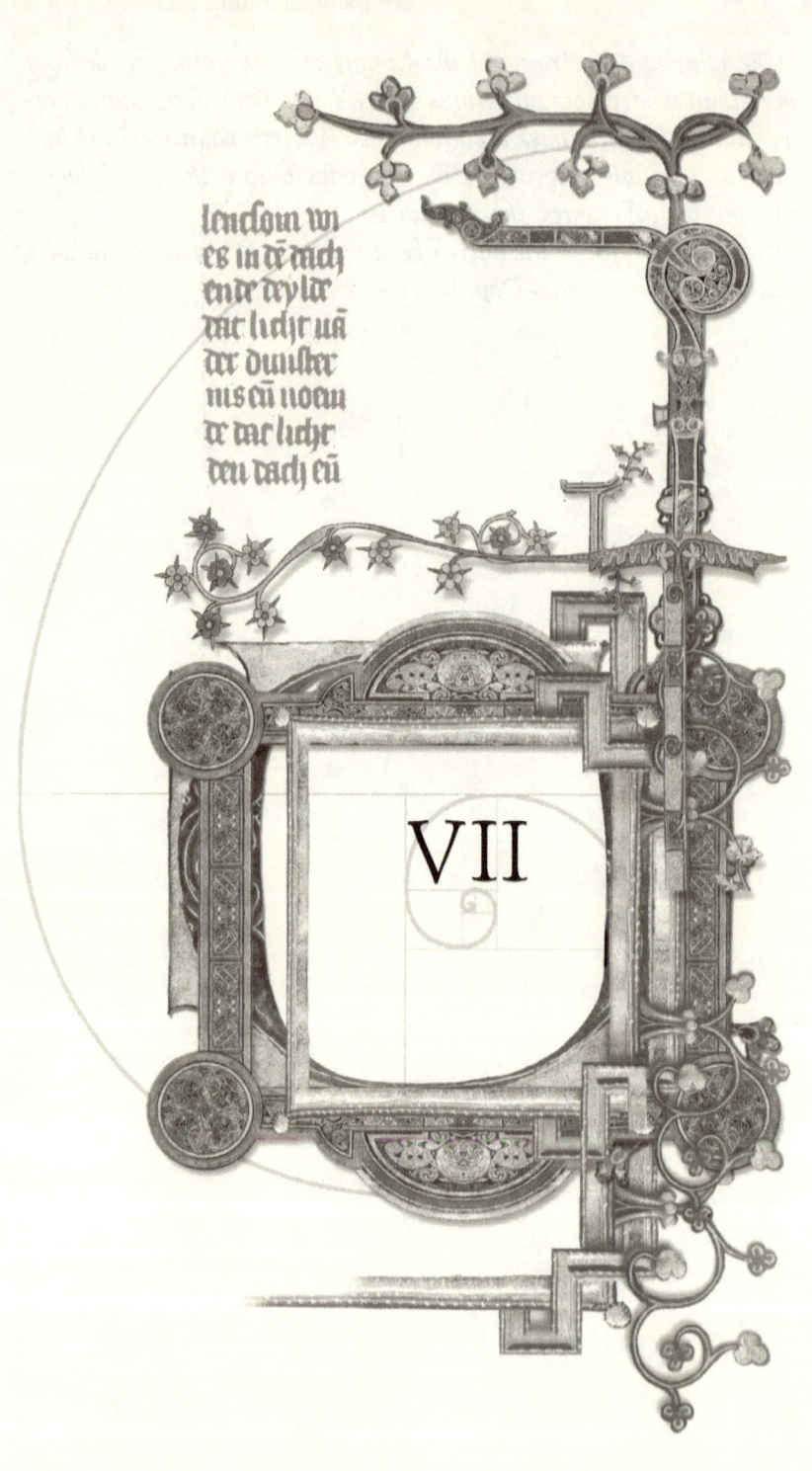

VII

Chapter VII

Chronicle of an Apotheosis

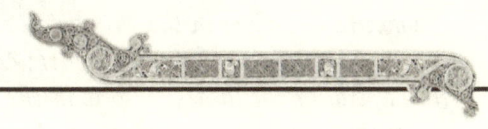

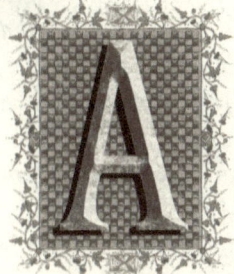t last, we moved.

- Sorry, dear Ad -my master, said- You were so excited about your initiation trip that I hesitated to accept the wisdom of Master Garg. But your journey does not make sense if there is no future for anyone.

- I know, Reverend. Ogli.

- For your consolation, if there can be any, once we disembark in Frigenia, we are obliged to go through Wrestongres, which is one of the highlights of the Path of Gnedh.

- Remember Master, it was you who said that for each individual there is a particular way though all of us step on the same footprint.

- Yes, I remember.

- Then this misfortune can be part of the way the Rarefaction manifests to me. Isn't it true?

- It's true, my dear pupil! Unfortunately, as you've said, it's an unfortunate way to manifest.

- By the way, Reverend Ogli, you have told me what the origin of the global conflict is, according to the mythical and religious beliefs, but... what is currently happening?

- Since, for a better understanding, the explanation imposes some background, I think I will begin by telling you first how Cruciglobism arose.

- As you think necessary -I answered.

- To find the roots of the problem, from the point of view of history, we must go back in time to the origins of the Marterian Empire. Well, the region of Primaria in the center of the Western Hemisphere was comprised of dense mountain forests and was sparsely inhabited in its coastal margins. The Ursids, descendants of an Axeo people fleeing from a war that almost extinguished them, reached the mouth of a river in the Primarian coast and settled there, changing its name. From this settlement, Marteria city arose and became the capital of the largest empire in the history of Ghesta. According to Censato, an Artesian poet, at first, Marteria was just a small market town, but it was led by rulers who valued engineering. They drained the marshes surrounding Marteria, raised fortifications and a temple for Eliseo, their supreme god. For the first time, houses and government buildings took the aspect of a public square. The Republic was proclaimed, which was the first in Ghesta, and a system of law and government was created, which, in its basic form, has survived to our times. Marteria was composed of three neighboring villages: Artesios, Cánidos and Astácidos. Soon, they began to incorporate -by force or choice- all the other people who were in the region of Primaria. And it went further. Starting with the Grezco people, Marteria conquered almost the entire Western Hemisphere: Lepuria, Galactia, Frigenia, Roniav, and Grezca.

- ...And Arania -I completed.

- Arania was conquered only partially and the territories not subjugated became, for Marteria, its limit and threat. Roniav, since then and until recently was called Incidia. It was a hazy border between the cultures of East and West. At one side of the Strait of Arteria, the city of the same name was located. Originally, Arteria was totally Marterian. Later, its name changed to be known as Catatonia. From there, the empire extended its dominions up to the region of Rjostos and over the Illusory Kingdom of Spahá. It reached Sammkara and Asasa. Although with effort, it conquered Ajeplo, that is Faronia. At the end, it could also control Jaraba and Lotaria. In this way, the Marterian Empire came to dominate the entire Central Sea basin.

- When Marterians -he continued after drinking some ki-o he carried in his canteen made of gassílope leather- were limited to the region of Primaria, their civilization was no more advanced than others. Its army, extremely organized, knew how to conquer their neighbors. Smart managers were in charge of governing the provinces respecting their traditions. The Marterians received education from Grezco teachers whose culture they assimilated. They adapted the philosophy, art, science, and religion from Grezca in their own way. At the peak of the empire, all provinces benefited from the contributions of the Grezco-Marterian culture. The communication between people became important and Marterians built a network of paved roads. There was an imperial mail that was responsible for the shipments. Merchant ships roamed the coasts and the maritime transit in the Central Sea was dense. The language also traveled by road, generalizing the Artesio language among the conquered people. The Artesio became the language of diplomacy and science and, of course, also the language of religion and war.

- I thought that the Marterians had no religion.

- The Marterians were deeply religious. They worshiped many gods: one god protected war, another love, yet another the forest, etc. Inside their homes, a minor God guarded the door and another the window. The worship of each god consisted of prayers, offerings and sacrifices. The soothsayers were in abundance: seers predicted the future by analyzing the flight of birds while augurers, examined their livers. The Marterian religion can seem nonexistent because it had no structure, that is, doctrine, and it was the government who was in charge of organizing the ceremonies in honor of the gods. Their deities were imposed throughout the empire. The people of the Marterian villages obeyed the rites as a civic act, as an activity connected to the political world.

- But, I understood that it was the Marterians who spread the Cruciglobism, which is not exactly the Marterian religion.

- It's true. What happened is the result of a process. Marteria, the city, came to have a million inhabitants. But among the luxury in which the aristocratic families, senators, businessmen and military leaders were living, the poorer classes settled. Its members had come to the city looking for work because the empire had outweighed trade and neglected the fields of Primaria which had become poor and disregarded. There was still a more miserable class: the slaves. They could sometimes achieve freedom. In most cases, once freed, they joined the ranks of the poor. The poor lived in overcrowding; the agglomeration caused nauseating odors, accumulation of excrements, and waste. Consequently, the poorer classes were stricken by diseases. Poverty was palpable, and crime reigned. The imperial police showed no mercy to all those who were not influential, and it easily reached extreme cruelty. The same happened to members of the conquered people who did not subdue themselves. Under the empire, the underprivileged souls felt full of anguish and disappointment. The wealthy had surrendered to laziness and had become insensitive. The empire had grown and degenerated to the point where each Marterian was no longer a citizen responsible for the social fate as it had been at first. To forget their poor condition, the upper class occasionally distributed wheat and organized bloody festivals. In a number of cities, public life revolved around these shows. When there were not enough people to be killed, volunteers were

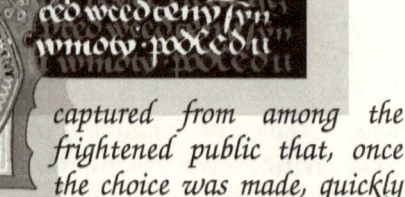

captured from among the frightened public that, once the choice was made, quickly celebrated it. This increased the anxiety for the poor. Losing life was easy. Death waited impatiently for each and every one and appeared at the time when it was least expected. This spiritual anxiety manifested itself in a deep religious concern.

Reverend Ogli drank some ki-o again and continued:

- The gods of the conquered people by Marteria were, if possible, fused with the Marterian gods. In this way, the conquered people could be assimilated more easily because their customs were not disrespected, just readjusted to the new situation. For example, the supreme god of the Marterians, Eliseo, was the same as his corresponding Grezco called Accio; the same as the Faronian god Orupis; equivalent to the Lotarian god Zoor; same as the Frigenian Hirish. Innumerable secondary gods also mingled with each other. Thus, through religious fidelity, Marteria could rule in foreign lands.

- But then,... What happened?

- *Neither Eliseo or the minor gods who accompanied him offered to stop or to compensate for the sufferings of the miserable classes. Sponsored by the reigning discontent, at least two cults arose that differed in some important aspect from the authorized cult. The first arose in the city of Vogadro, in Faronia; the other did not material-ize in a particular place but spread throughout the empire as the excavations have shown. In Vogadro, a large temple called Preuss was constructed for the worship of a trinity of gods who were ven-erated as only one. These were Orupis, Rabis, and Tsis. Its symbol was a winged beetle that dies when it buries its eggs. The other cult took place under the ground, in carved caves that offered a gloomy atmosphere to the worshipers of Sidra. The poor of the empire, who were torn between slavery, cruelty, and fear, disbelieved the priest, the law and custom. They came to Preuss or went into the darkness and blood in the caves of Sidra. Perhaps because some gods were absorbed by others in a process that inadvertently weakened them as they mingled; perhaps because the proximity of death was insuffer-able if it was not conceived as a way of liberation, when the belief in one immaterial god, compensator of miseries, was spread from Jbur, the Thinking Beings were ready to accept this idea.*

That is where the Cruciglobist religion appears... -I said.

- Precisely, dear Ad -my master answered- In a city of Rjostos called Jbur, a tribe of shepherds composed of a dozen families was faithful to the tradition they called Cruciglobist. Their doctrine was collected in a book called The Book of Broc, or just Broc, where the will of their god and the history of that tribe were one. Its name, Cruciglobism, came from the symbol of their god, that is, a cross made with arrows on a circle. The Cruciglobism was the first monotheistic religion on Ghesta. It held the belief that a recognition was waiting for the suffering believer in the next life, where he would be as happy as he had been miserable on Ghesta. This spiritual state, this sacred category, was earned by observing the Cruciglobist standards for a lifetime, including meekness and resignation. No other religion had promoted before eternal life at the expense of the sufferings. Gwell, the prophet who spread the Cruciglobism over Rjostos, Sammkara and the Kingdom of Ghor, attacked patriotism and family ties in the name of God and the brotherhood of Thinking Beings. He also con-demned social classes, personal wealth, and the privileges. Instead, Gwell pondered love to others.

He drank some more ki-o before continuing:

- The Cruciglobist religion spread throughout the Marterian Empire, bringing together an increasing number of converts in communities around the Cruciglobist faith. The attitude of the emperors against the new religion varied as it benefited its policy of respect for traditions or as required by the security of the empire. Thus, its strategy ranged between tolerance and persecution. Sometimes, the intolerant campaigns suffered the most resounding failure because there were those villages where even the imperial authorities were already Cruciglobist. Finally, Marteria came to have a Cruciglobist emperor: Catatonio. He boosted Cruciglobism as the legal religion throughout the empire. He embroidered its symbol on the banners of the army. He overthrew the images of the previous gods, including a colossal monument dedicated to Eliseo that had been built in Erto. He raised temples throughout the empire and, thereafter, they were the only ones allowed.

- So that's how the Marterians spread a religion that was not theirs -I said.

- AHA!

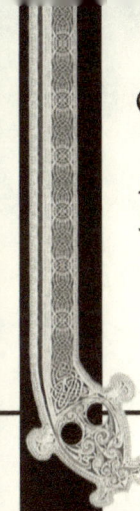

Chapter VIII

Epistolary Revelations

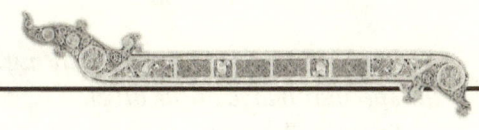

The day was fading, taking the colorful life elsewhere. The green languished on each leaf, in each branch, in the whole body of the forest. The afternoon shadows dimmed the foliage with blurred brush strokes. After being grayed, the forest was retiring to sleep. We also sought rest on a cozy bend. And, as some presences decayed, others were incorporated, celebrating life with nocturnal hymns, sharp sounds of feathery flutes, scratching of serrated legs, vibratos from ample bellies fattened with manure, the darkness sprinkled with fleeting blue-green flashes. Oj, our friendly knork, intoxicated by the insectile spree, began bellowing rhythmically. The resinous scents of the wet wood, which I was setting on fire, reminded me of the lemon fragrances used by the brides of my town. As the wood caught flame, I cooked some soup, and the salty smell of some mushrooms, that we collected while passing through a covered bridge, supplanted all traces of perfume and opened our appetite.

The dinner was very pleasant and left us satisfied. As for me, though, a meal is not complete without taking some ajenta. I prepared a highly energizing, very aromatic, and very black ajenta. As I took the cup to my mouth, I saw the foam breaking away around the larger bubbles. When the foam finally broke up, I could see my face in the blackness of the ajenta. I examined my eyes in the reflection and I felt lucky to be there, on the Path of Gnedh.

- Master!

- Tell me, dear Ad.

- Nobody has the face completely equal from left to right... well, it is equal but... what I mean is...

- What you mean is that one half is not the exact image of the other, as it would be if reflected in a mirror.

- Yes!

- In other words, you mean that not always one half of the face is the specular image of the other.

- Specular Image?

- It is said that the image of an object projected on a mirror is its specular image.

- Specular Image!

- Yes, with that name. It is interesting to notice that specular images of symmetrical forms are exactly like them. For example, place the mirror next to a circle. In the mirror, a circle exactly like the original appears. Do the same with the triangle. You can place the edge of the mirror at any distance from the triangle, but it has to be parallel to the axis, or any of the axes, of symmetry. Remember that it is the existence of these axes which defines a symmetrical image. If you do not try to get this correspondence, we would be in the case of an asymmetric specular image of a triangle. If you do what I said, you would see twin triangles.

Reverend Ogli proceeded to draw them.

- For a moment -he continued- let's imagine that the triangles we have before us are movable. If we could move the first triangle to the right to superpose it on the second, overlaying each other, then we would find that the two images coincide at all points. The second triangle would be perfectly hidden, perfectly overlapped below the first one. This intellectual exercise of moving images, imaginatively, and setting them on top of each other until they completely overlay themselves, is called superposing. Do you understand, dear Ad?

- Yes, Master.

- Very good. Now you may understand the following: the symmetrical images are "superposable" to their specular images; asymmetric images, are not. Let's try, for example, the letter L, which is asymmetric. Could you superpose the letter L to its mirror image? -he asked.

- *No -I answered- The letter L has its leg pointing to the right while on its specular image it is pointing to the left.*

- *This kind of images in which the left and right versions of the same image cannot be superposed, are called enantiomorphic images.* Obviously, only asymmetric shapes have enantiomorphic images.

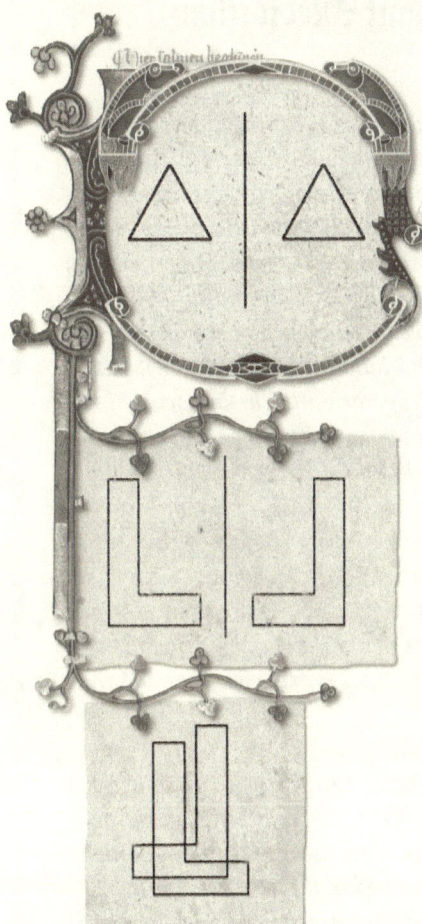

- *Enantiomorphic Images!*

- *Good, dear Ad. Now answer me. Can you superpose the letter E on its specular image?*

After some thought without drawing, I said the following:

- *When the letter E appears "standing", that is, as you type, then it is not possible to superpose it on its specular image. But if it comes lying down, horizontally arranged, then yes, you can.*

After this explanation, we proceeded with our Szabeo liturgy about which I will not speak. All ceremonial activity must be accompanied by a moment of relevant meditation, although no previous ceremony is required if one wants to practice this technique at any time. To ensure proper concentration and achieve the state of balanced stillness, it is mandatory to practice deep breathing. The session ended with a prayer for world peace.

About Deep Breathing, Balanced Stillness and Relevant Meditation:

In order to prevent the nerves of the spine to be pressured, the practicant must perform the breathing exercises with head and neck straight, sitting on crossed legs and looking toward the north, according to the magnetic field of the planet at the specific place where this practice is held. A preliminary approach to the final exercise is to inhale air and slowly exhale it, naturally. The practicant can control the pace of the exercise, counting to ten when you inhale and exhale. He needs to get this pace to set a rate of operation in the integrity of the body. Thus, from the molecular activity up to the waves of thought, they will all be synchronized in their evolution. Only in this way, the practicant can drive all the energy toward the object of meditation, as if there is a single large source of energy. This kind of nervous energy will modulate our body system and nourish our spirit. Practice this breathing for five minutes; that is, count to ten while slowly absorbing air and count to ten again to exhale it. Rest for two minutes and then start again.

It is advisable to practice this breathing exercise three times a day. Wait for about eight hours between each session. So it is said in the Book of Hours of the Szabeo order. If the practicant is out of the convent, he has to discern the most appropriate time. Once he has been initiated in this exercise, the disciple should perform it daily at least for a period of thirty days. It is necessary to warn about the danger of breaking the cycle if good results are expected! The practicant, already accustomed to the rhythm, may disregard the counting and concentrate on the passage of air through the pharynx where an accumulation of nerve endings reside. The practicant must not allow other thoughts to break into consciousness and disturb the concentration. These programmed steps set in the body a natural and instantaneous rhythm which can be evoked at the will of the performer. Achieving this is very important and the reason will be understood later.

The practicant must exercise this breathing without counting, focusing his attention on the pharynx for another thirty days. At the end of this period, your body system and consciousness have created the necessary connection to undertake the next level which is a prelude to the Relevant Meditation. The practicant has to create a phrase of his own that seeks tranquility but has the property of suggesting the same thing with each of its parts. Ideally, each performer finds the phrase that is most immanent to him. If this is not easy, the performer is free to use the phrase given by our venerable master Otânguié, that is: "Let the peace and quiet wrap me with their serene and calm presence." Once you have chosen the phrase, instead of attending the passage of air through the pharynx, the practicant must repeat it mentally in each inhalation and exhalation. As the phrase is repeated, the practicant should focus on what is suggested by the parts and the totality of the sentence. In this way, the practicant will free the miraculous power contained in the words. This breathing exercise should be practiced for two months without any interruption. Thus, an inseparable association between the so-called modulatory phrase and the pacifying modulation of the spirit will be created by the Deep Breathing. The trained performer will discover that he is able to achieve, at his will, a state of calmness putting his whole body into modulation, that is, in Balanced Stillness. It will be noticed how even the muscles of the body get relaxed once it returns to a lower energy state. To do this, it will be enough to mentally invoke the Modulatory Phrase. Thus, if the practicant found himself in a situation of great stress, he could immediately control their anxiety just by using his thought. Basically, this is the fundamental process that a disciple must follow if he wants to educate himself on mental control. If the disciple is attacked by a disease, he could fight it by choosing the appropriate phase; if he pursues some goal, the exercise of this practice will help him to persevere and direct his efforts. The practicant can cause the realization of what he seeks. So, just pick your phrase! The Relevant Meditation is the relaxed reflection on a particular subject. It is needed before reaching the state of Balanced Stillness. Only then, the matter of interest may be convened. In this peaceful circumstance, the consciousness lowers the guard and unveil the wisdom of its hidden side that is part of the Inner Vision. Then, it plays with the possibilities in a carefree way, revealing points of view hidden to the external eye.

With the same skill that the performer has developed to keep other strange thoughts away from the practice of Deep Breathing, he has to maintain in consciousness only the matter in question. Do not pressure the consciousness; it should be abandoned at ease, but always around the object of reflection. The meditation should be free, docile, and offhand. The Relevant Meditation is the most fruitful mechanism to tackle problems by exacerbating the portentous creativity of the mind. When it is oriented toward the spiritual awareness of the surrounding presence of God, the Relevant Meditation is, indeed, a lifting mechanism leading to the so-called Sublimation of the Spirit about which we will discuss in the next mystery.

From: The Substance and the Intangible, Initiatory Library, Monastery of D'orh.

Chapter IX

The Blackmoon Crystal

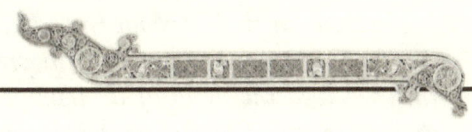

We found the Port of Oods silenced; absurdly quiet for being a market at the edge of the Enormous Sea. We were puzzled and went up where the trucks leave the port once loaded but could not see anything that moved. We walked along several streets sighting in vain. We called for help in vain. We split. I ran for several minutes until I was exhausted from running and watching. There was nobody! The Port of Oods, the vociferous Port of Oods was desolate. Nobody who would like to sail! The twisted and narrow streets, before noisy and gossiping, darned of confabulations and sailor's delusions, had been abandoned. The city seemed hollowed out, as if its soul had escaped. Only the wind lashed doors and windows in the ghostly streets.

I found only an unfriendly old person who had lost hope and desire to speak. Then I went down to the docks. The bare crossarms of the abandoned sailboats made me think of a field of floating swords. Nobody on the docks! A flock of hungry birds was looking for fishermen to steal a portion. This and the breaking of the waves was the only remnant of the usual bustle. The Port of Oods was completely abandoned. Our situation was complicated... Finally, I saw my master approaching me.

- I think we have to move along the coast to get to a small fishing village to the north. Perhaps we can get a boat over there. It is our last hope.

- But do you know what happened here? -I asked.

- People have already left their homes, their belongings, and town in search for refuge. The situation is that serious.

- So, you did find someone in town?

- Yes, I found a small group that preferred to stay here. I was told they received the news of an imminent nuclear war two days ago and all have fled to the coal mines not far from here.

- Why did they stay?

- They said they had lived here all their lives and they would rather die here. However, I think the real reason for staying here is that they were Lunilaics.

- But, getting refuge in the mines could mean saving their lives.

- But in the mines, they must be praying. It would be easy to give yourself away, if the ritual is unknown to you.

- What if the Cruciglobists discover them?

- At this time, the hatred against them should be exacerbated. If they discover them now, their lives would end anyway.

- Why do they hate each other so much, Master?

- It is quite complex for an immediate response...

This occurred in the middle of the morning. Again, we were on our way. The length of the beach gave us the chance to expand on the subject.

- Well, I've already told you the story of the Marterian Empire. Now let's go farther -my master said- In times of Catatonio, Marteria was rejecting the attacks of the nomads from Arania and Emuria. The capital of the empire was moving as the army required. Marteria city, in the region of Primaria, was too far from the conflict zone to serve as a capital. The emperor then, chose the city of Arteria in Gerundia, as the new capital. From there, he thought to rule over the eastern and western part of the empire and also fight the nomadic hordes. Arteria was renamed in honor of the emperor and since then it was known as Catatonia. But history followed an unexpected direction. From Arania, one way or another, the empire was invaded by several clans: Erodos, Anterodos, and Parierodos broke in half the continuity of the Marterian domain around the Central Sea. Nomads conquered the western part of the empire and divided it among them. The Marterian Empire, with its capital in Catatonia, became part of the East. However, the Aranian clans were assimilated almost immediately by the Marterian-Western culture and they turned into its protectors. They awarded titles to themselves, such as kings, dukes, and counts, which are descendants names from Marterian distinctions. They adopted the Cruciglobist religion and accepted the Bishop of Marteria, the Øppos, as the head of the Cruciglobist Church.

R everend Ogli returned to his ki-o. He drank some and continued:
- It was not in the interest of the Øppos to have the empire divided in two, and he tried to unite one and the other. He pursued the imperial unity, but under his paternity, of course. He was motivated by rather mundane than religious reasons. The moment was imperative because there were threats of separation by the Cruciglobist Church of Catatonia. But the Øppos succeeded thanks to a political-religious formula which was accepted with equitable resignation. The Aranian kingdoms of the West had to recognize the Marterian emperor who ruled in Catatonia, although in an indefinite way without vassalage. In turn, the Marterians of Catatonia submitted their church to the authority of Øppos. This stratagem could not avoid the existence of a marked difference between the two cults, both Cruciglobist.

More ki-o...
- In the western part, there were hundreds of bandits who arose as sovereigns. Life remained uncertain and properties were kept by force. To defend the people, the castles multiplied, but the roads were erased. The cities that flourished under the First Empire were impoverished and abandoned. The population stood around the fortresses for protection. The Artesio was transfigured when mixed with the languages of the former Nomads. Only the clergy and some educated Thinking Beings preserved it. The centuries that followed were times of intellectual darkness, ignorance, and superstition. The cultural neglect was such that even the memory of the people was lost.

- I heard -I interrupted- that the inhabitants of the Central Continent at that time, unable to explain the origin of the Marterian aqueducts, said that the devil build them. Is it true?

- It is true! It was about some huge arches that, at that time, no longer worked. How could they know what they were? Marterian science also got lost over time. They did not know who had placed them there or how long they had been there. They did not have better nor a more comfortable explanation than saying that a demoniacal caprice had materialized them instantly.

- But then, how do we know this and what happened before?

- Thanks to the Cruciglobist monks. Without them, the Artesio culture in the West would have been lost eternally. In the east, however, the empire remained organized and not only retained its Artesio culture, but it achieved the well-known oriental refinement. Schools were established, and libraries were created.

- Please, continue Reverend Ogli -I said- I will not interrupt again.

- Do it! Anytime, interrupt me without hesitation. I'm not here to keep the pace, but to deliver what I have come to know.

- Thank you, Master.

- You have nothing to thank me for -he said, smiling at me- The only common feature between these two Cruciglobist cults was the Øppos and only he maintained the cohesion, sometimes tenuous, between one another. Having come to the understanding that I explained above, it was clear that if somebody was against the Church, they were also against the Marterian Empire. Then, people were concerned about what they said. They tried to establish the exact interpretation of the beliefs to avoid errors of opinion that might undermine the imperial harmony. Maintaining the wrong opinion and, what was even worse, transmitting it, was no longer judged as an intellectual error, but as a moral crime that hurt both their religion and the empire. Soon, the free expression of thought and, with much greater reason, the religious innovations were persecuted.

- What does "persecuted" mean exactly?

- Well, for example, an unfortunate free-thinker, called Queur, was flayed and burned alive in the name of God; the Cruciglobist God of Love.

- Ahgg...!

- No one knows exactly where -he continued- probably in Yatar or Tuabej, between the Abigo Sea and the Sea of Euda, another religious movement, sometimes equally intolerant, was taking shape. It was also monotheistic, but it did not have any clergy since it claimed a direct relationship between God and the believer. They had a holy city where they kept the lost in time memories of a stone lost in time that had fallen from the sky. Their rites were simple, and their theological doctrine was free from conflicts. This, somehow, was better suited to the lifestyle of the inhabitants of the eastern region. It was said that this cult came from a tradition maintained by some nomadic clans who were able to read divine messages in the heavenly forms. The symbol of this religion was a half-moon and it was known as "Lunilaic." A member of one of these clans, called Hasas, became known as a prophet. Hasas dictated a book of revelations, The Iftar, and in a relatively short time, Lunilaicism spread among the tribes of Asasa, Spahá and the Lemurian steppes. Since the responsibility of the Lunilaic doctrine rested directly on the population of believers, it inevitably manifested in all civil acts. The public events were inspired by Lunilaicism. The army could not be considered only Asasian or Lemurian but Lunilaic. Obviously, with no clergy, they did not have the equivalent of the Øppos either, but Hasas' successors were tacitly considered heads of the Lunilaic government. These supreme hierarchs were known as Ahaxi. For this reason, the conquest that followed the dissemination period could be estimated as religious, rather than patriotic. Needless to say, those Lunilaics who fell into the hands of the Cruciglobists suffered the same fate as the unfortunate Queur.

- So, this is where it all began...

- Where all the wars started -he replied- But as you know, this started much earlier.

This time, he took more ki-o than usual.

- The Marterian army was defeated at the Battle of Yaruk, a tributary river of the Ian. Gradually, the Lunilaicism snatched the eastern provinces from what remained of the Marterian Empire. However, Catatonia was never conquered. The Marterian emperor saw how they deprived him of the entire Kingdom of Ghor that was attacked from Spahá, already fully Lunilaic. Qía, Ru, Uss, Ntra, Rna, Jbur, and the other cities of Rjostos fell without resistance and their populations accepted the new government, which is the same, the Lunilaicism. Then, the Lunilaics moved from the northeast to the lands of Siática which, at that time, was dominated by the Ng dynasty. From the south, they took Faronia almost without protest. Faronia was followed by Jaraba and Lotaria. Through the Strait of Batzar they passed to Lepuria. They were about to conquer Galactia but Asterios, Astroianos, and Lutanios joined and made them return behind where the Lepurian border was at that time.

- ...which is just where we are.

- Yes, it is. The Lunilaicism -he continued- had conquered almost all Marteria, becoming an empire: the Lunilaic Empire. Half of the souls, previously Cruciglobist, had embraced the new religion. Thus, the central world of Ghesta was divided into two religious powers.

We were already in Galactia land. The seascape in that area of the west coast seemed to have been drawn with a ruler. It was almost an exercise of perspective drawing: the water line, the shoreline, the line of vegetation and the edge of the huge rocky wall, all began behind our backs and they were projected to a meeting point on the horizon, in front of us. No feature that disturbed its impeccable geometric fitting. No accesses, no curves,... nothing! Nothing to ease the tired eye with. It was an endless extension of the same thing.

It must be a punishment to walk over these sands at the full strength the day. Fortunately, when we were there, the sky was covered with clouds. Reverend Ogli and I spent the entire afternoon going along the endless beach. The march over the sand, warm or hot, it is always a heavy walk. I remember my heel sinking at every step before it was possible to rest the entire foot. The sand moved away, fleeing from my weight as if I was walking upon a huge corpuscular being that did not allow anyone to use it as support. I also remember my calf bothering me with increasing pain. I celebrated when the day had declined since, with the darkness, the relief would come.

We unloaded Oj. Reverend Ogli gave him to drink fresh water that we collected while passing through a feeder river of the sea. I found firewood rummaging among the vegetation that ran parallel to the beach. We raised our camp and ate osebs, cantras, and metifulas that are able to stay fresh for several months with no sign of corruption.

After our prayers, we lay down by the fire. That night, the sea was calm. Nothing disturbed the silence left by the waves. The sea rhythmically licked the sand while I was falling asleep. Reverend Ogli wanted to read a little and opened his instrument case to take out his glasses. It was then when I saw, beside his magnifying glass, a pair of dark crystal disks.

Reverend Ogli noticed my interest and passed them to me, smiling. The crystals were not as dark as I had thought. Rather, were transparent. Through each of them, I could see Oj in front of me, snoring gently. I would have sworn they were black before taking them! They seemed like glasses, although a little large, but they did not enlarge anything. "They were ordinary glasses!" -I thought. I returned them to the hand of my master, one above the other. Reverend Ogli did not stop looking into my eyes as he kept smiling at me fondly.

- Look again, dear Ad -he said, extending his hand and showing me the crystals again.

To my surprise, the crystals had again become dark. I moved closer to my master's hand and examined the crystals carefully. The parts that were covered by each other were now dark. The parts free of overlapping remained transparent, being possible to see the palm of Reverend Ogli across.

This was not a question of thickness. Reverend Ogli took them and extended his arms interposing both disks between the firelight and our eyes, one after another. Within the single circle formed by the overlapping glasses, there was complete darkness. The firelight could not pass through them.

- See what happens now -my master said and began to spin one disk over the other- ...and tell me, what do you see?

- Well... there is some light again. Gradually, the disks begin to let the light of the campfire pass through... Oh... but now, they begin to turn dark... Now they're completely black again.

- Yes, that's right, dear Ad.

Reverend Ogli searched among the things of his case and pulled out a piece of clear cellophane. Then, he managed to place it between the two circles of glass. Besides the change of going from light to dark, I could also see the cellophane color changing several times as one disk rotated over the other.

- Ah! But, what a strange thing! -I said- The cellophane is transparent, right?

- True!

- It is as if the disks would reveal some cellophane colors that we cannot see. What are these disks, Master?

- Blackmoon crystals.

- Blackmoon crystals!

- Blackmoon is the name of a transparent mineral that can be found anywhere but it is very rare because it looks like any other rock. Nobody wants to spend his days breaking all available rocks until the correct one is found. Only a trained Szabeo knows where to look or how to recognize it among the pile. Finding it is sort of a telepathic cooperation, almost a consent. It does not do it with everybody; for example, it would never show itself to ambitious people. Inside, the rock keeps a material as transparent as the best glass. Its main feature is that it is able to polarize light. To Szabeos, Blackmoon crystal is a sacred article, since the light, once polarized, reveals secrets closely linked with the principal mysteries of our doctrine. Blackmoon glass is an instrument of God.

- Could you explain to me, Reverend Ogli, what is polarized light?

- Of course, my dear Ad. Remember that you will study all of this, in detail and depth, if providence saves a future for us all. If we would not have a threat of war hanging over the world, I would also tell you that one day, you will be given your own pair of Blackmoon crystal disks.

I felt a hole inside of me; a hole filled with an anxiety I had never felt before. Only for being polite, I said:

- I would love to.

- Polarized light, dear Ad, is the simplest form of light. This feature should encourage self-demanding in the Szabeo monk: be simple to see the truth. There are several types of simplicity known by the student of optics. White light is the least simple because it is the result of the combination of all colors. A prism can discover this association, separating the white light into a spectrum of colors like the rainbow. White light, that is, daylight, collects what it is able from reality and, in the form of images, makes it reach our eyes. If we want to see beyond our natural possibilities, we have to use the simplest forms of light. Monochromatic light, that is, a single color light is a simpler one. Simplicity may be even greater and the significance of the discovery can be unexpectedly revealing and particular. Now, a beam of monochromatic light can be represented as a line that ends in an arrow.

Having said that, Reverend Ogli proceeded to outline in his travelogue what he had just said.

- The arrow is drawn -he continued- to indicate the direction in which the beam travels. But this is only a representative drawing, a caricature of what light is. When we see light, we do not observe arrows in the air. The space is not crossed by lines, either. But given our familiarity with that representation, we will take it as valid. We are going to add one thing, though: the beam does not travel peacefully, but vibrating in all directions around. It is like a frightened fly: flying in a straight line but shaking with fear. Polarized light instead vibrates in one direction.

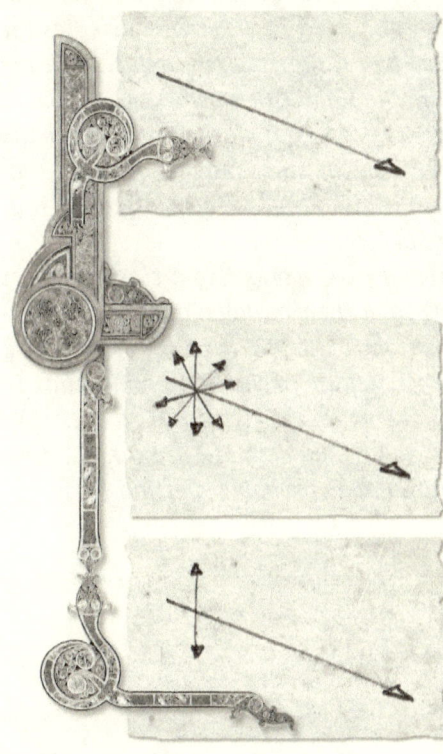

- The disks that you have seen -he added- are obtained by cutting a rock of Blackmoon into slices. The molecular structure of this material is such that it functions as a blind in front of light. Only the portion of the light that is vibrating in a parallel direction to the blind can pass through. Someone has understood this as if the disk of Blackmoon crystal is a tight set of papers placed one over another. The light beams, instead, are like knives trying to penetrate the stack of paper. Only when the knives are oriented parallel to the sheets, they can enter. To be more precise, the disks are not an obstacle, but a converter of a kind of light into another. The incident light on the disk vibrates in all directions; the light that emerges from it, vibrates only in one. This vibration direction coincides with the direction of the length of the blinds.

My master drank more ki-o. He took a sip and handed it to me.

- When the light emerging from a disk -he continued- finds another disk on its path, three things may happen. The polarized beam finds the second blinds in the same situation as in the first disk. The polarized beam finds the second blinds placed transversely. The polarized beam finds the second blinds in an intermediate position between the two extremes. In the first case, the light passes through the second disk without a problem and it can emerge from it with its maximum clarity. In the second case, the light cannot get through and you will see maximum darkness on the second disk. If the second disk has the blinds not perfectly transversal but rather inclined relative to the blinds in the first case, some of the light can emerge and it would be possible to distinguish different degrees of clarity from maximum brightness to maximum darkness. In the same way as there are water faucets, the Blackmoon crystal disks are, so to speak, light faucets. Do you understand, dear Ad?

- I think so, Master. The second disk works like a closing faucet regulating the passage of light, from the maximum aperture to complete obstruction. This happens when the blinds of the second disk are respectively parallel or perpendicular to the first blinds; that is, to the direction of vibration of the polarized light that reaches it.

- Very good! It is enough for today, my dear Ad-d-Tuar. It's time to sleep. Tomorrow, another hard day is probably waiting for us

The Blackmoon Crystals

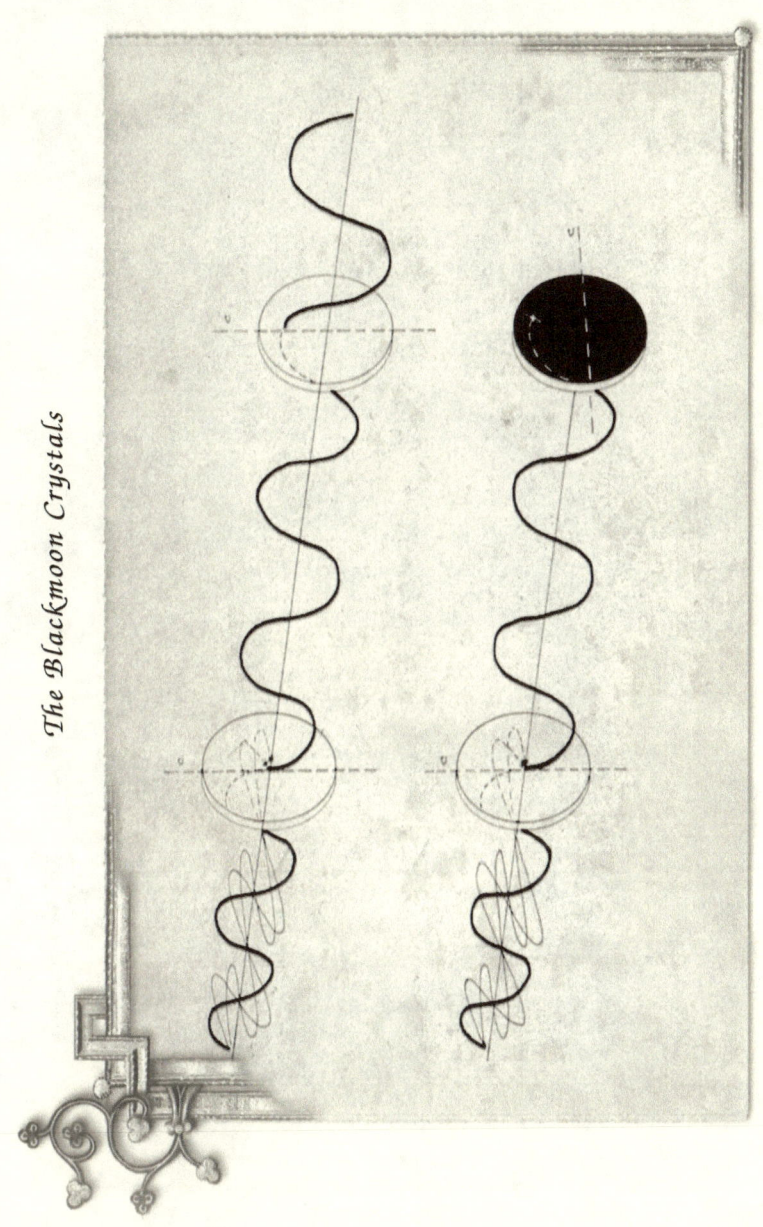

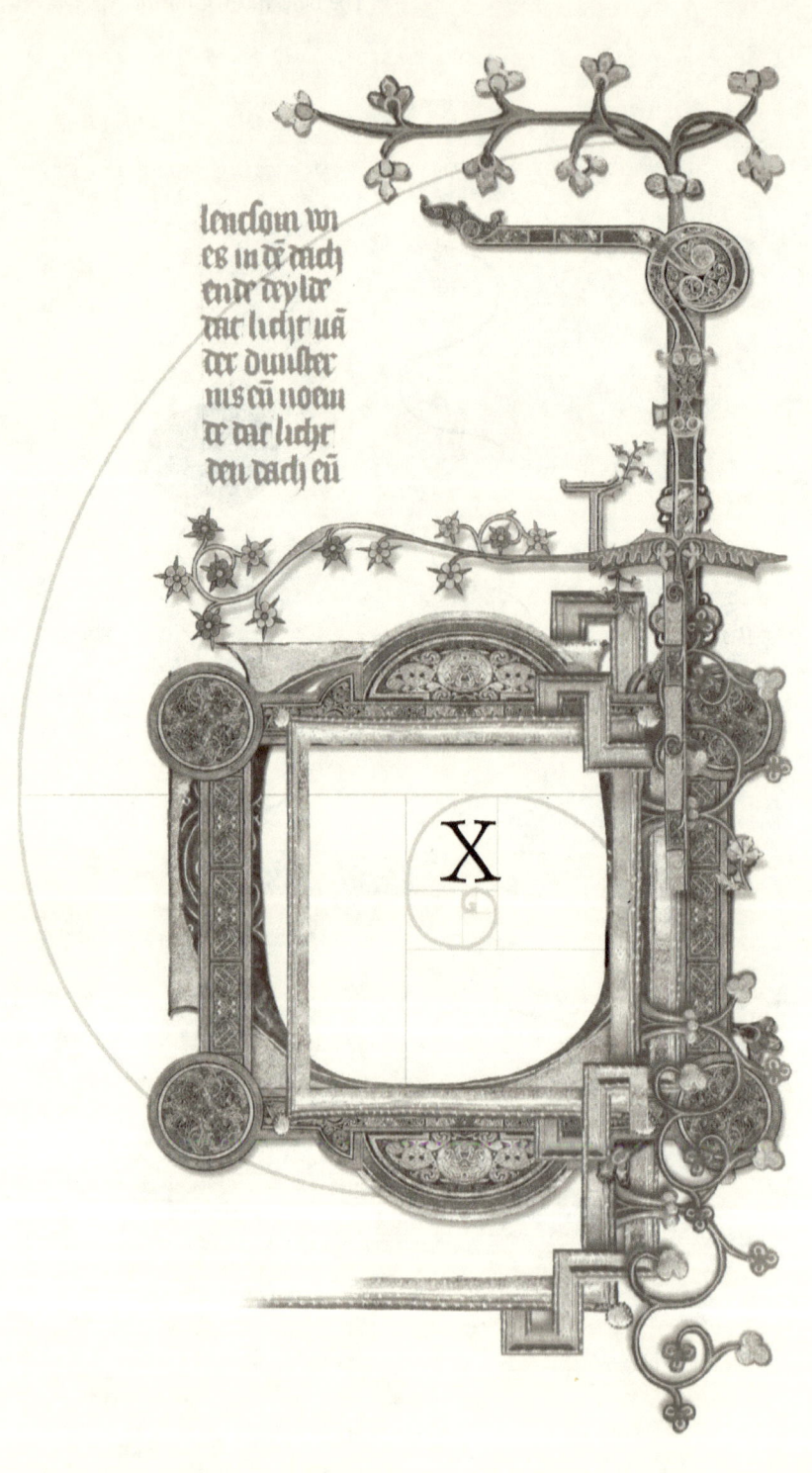

lencloin wi
es in dē dach
ende dryler
dar licht uā
der dunster
nis cū node
de dar licht
den dach cū

Chapter X

The Bottom of the Spiral

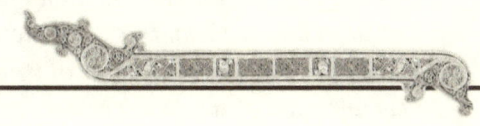

ery early Reverend Ogli, our friendly knork, and I got up. Quickly, we were on our way. The beach had narrowed. There was no vegetation between the sand and the rock wall anymore. Soon, the explanations continued:

- Suppose -my master said- we have our pair of discs positioned so that there is complete darkness. In other words, their blinds are perpendicular to each other. For simplicity, we understand this situation by saying that the light switch is off. So, from now on, remember dear Ad, that a "light switch off" means total darkness.

- Yes, Master.

- So, if we place...

My master abruptly interrupted his explanation.

- What is that? -he exclaimed.

Carved into the rock wall that ran along the beach, an entrance had appeared. It looked like a temple full of ornaments. On the front wall, which was the only one, multiple elements appeared; monopod architraves, Axeo decorative motifs, enriched by jagged reliefs in a Ceutical style. Every architectural element had been carved from the rock itself. Its purpose was not supporting the entrance but giving a magnificent facade to a natural and shallow hollow that lead nowhere.

- *How weird! Its design belongs to the Ugrabí style, which was generated from the aesthetic mix between the Artesian and Lunilaic architecture. This blend of styles occurred here, in this part of Galactia, at the end of the Middle Era. Its eclecticism of mystical meaning is a subsidiary of the Boric style that flourished in Galactia and was especially used for the construction of Cruciglobist cathedrals. Compared with one of them, this construction is quite modest. However, it is an almost virtuous example of its style. The strange thing is that I was unaware of its existence.*

- *What is that? -I asked, pointing to a representation of what I thought was a marine organism.*

- *A Turbópulus -my master said- is very important in religious iconography. Its spiral shell of mathematical beauty has inspired numerous symbolisms that want to contain eternity.*

- *Because of its many arms?*

- *No, dear Ad. Due to the shape of its shell. If you look up, you will see that it is also represented in the capital of that column, in one of its variants. Have you found it already?*

- *Yes, Master. Although, there are actually two: a shell that is oriented to the left and another to the right...*

- *...that is to say, they are two enantiomorphic images -my master completed- which are not superposable.*

- *Yes! Because the spiral is an asymmetrical shape.*

- *Very good. In fact, the spiral is much more than that. In principle, the spiral is a dynamic concept that develops inward or outward, depending on how you perceive it. It relates to the circle and systems of concentric circles from which it is hard to differentiate when the revolutions are drawn tight. The spiral is an ancient symbol and is common to the iconography of different cultures. The spiral is a symbol of life. Perhaps, in the immemorial past, the spiral was suggested by the shape of the waves, and since waves are related to water, the spiral also insinuated the miracle of life; a life that surfaced as a surprise from the inert shell of helical mollusks. Perhaps the waves were not the muses, but tornadoes and typhoons: terror and death. The spiral is a symbol of death. Perhaps the whirlwinds of steaming vapors that picked splinters up over the cave fire infused into the spiral a meaning of ascension. The whirlpools, where the flimsy rafts sink, made the spiral also presage falls. Up and down,* back and forth, closing or opening, as the performance of a twist, the spiral wraps and unwraps itself. And, as it coils, the spiral grows. But, like all growth, it also postulates a past and a posterity and inevitably the spiral leads us to think of time. The spiral brings us back to what we leave behind and wonders about our future. Yes, dear Ad! Time is another meaning of the spiral; another that mingles with the others when viewed from far away. Depending on the religious nuances, the spiral can be found not only related to the time of existence, but with previous

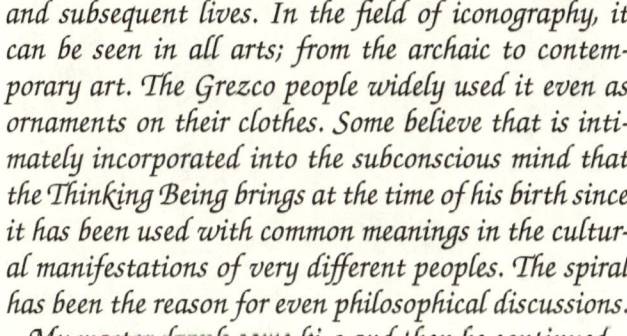

and subsequent lives. In the field of iconography, it can be seen in all arts; from the archaic to contemporary art. The Grezco people widely used it even as ornaments on their clothes. Some believe that is intimately incorporated into the subconscious mind that the Thinking Being brings at the time of his birth since it has been used with common meanings in the cultural manifestations of very different peoples. The spiral has been the reason for even philosophical discussions.

My master drank some ki-o and then he continued...

- The spiral is one of the most intriguing shapes that nature, or God, has put in our consideration. In ancient times, the naked eye, with no instruments, was blind in front of huge and minuscule realities. But scientific discoveries achieved with the visual aids of modernity have only fueled our perplexity in front of the spiral. The spiral can be found everywhere and in all sizes, from the molecular environment to the incommensurable nebulas of outer space. By observing these celestial bodies, of which there are myriads, its spiral shape gives us the overwhelming feeling of being in front of a system in development. We cannot help but think of universes developing into others which continue evolving; or celestial vortices concentrating universal matter and expelling it through an apocalyptic drain to who knows where. At the edges of the universe, in its fundamentals, there are also spirals organizing everything. The periodic system of elements, according to the atomic weights, can be set to a logarithmic spiral. Someone might think, rightly, that this is another drain to atomic organizations viewed upside down, with their own nebulas in their own firmament.

Now, we know that the DNA molecule transmits life. In its structure, the basis of the existence of a species is supported. To our surprise, the DNA is a molecule that exhibits a spiral shape. Coincidentally or not, the spiral has full authority to establish itself as a symbol of life as old people already intuited. As you know by now, dear Ad, the religious architecture intends to symbolically represent the universe with its laws and trends. Unquestionably, the spiral is a trend.

- Is there any explanation for that?
- We have tried to explain some natural forms of the spiral. For example, it is said that the twisted tree trunks are produced by the rotation of the planet, exhibiting a spiral oriented to the right in the northern hemisphere and to the left in the southern hemisphere. The same is said about the direction of the water vortices in the sinks of the houses located in the northern and southern hemispheres;

the same has been speculated about cyclones. Instead of subtracting interest, this explanation has reinforced the belief that the spiral appears as a direct consequence of universal behavior, giving the reason to the religious architects.

- Ah!

- What nobody can deny is that, in the studied cases, the appearance of the spiral obeys to space-energy reasons which, for us Szabeos, is a confirmation of the sanctity of the shape. The spiral is generated, for example, by the contraction of an extended body in a small space. From a nebula, we sense that the expansionist efforts of its spiral are fighting the attraction of the masses that forces it to contract instead. In other cases, the spiral appears as a result of one side of the body growing faster than the other. It is as if the force that opposes the growth is not enough to stop it. This principle, this dialectic idea of energy and growth over time is precisely the metaphysical foundation of the spiral and goes hand in hand with the Rarefaction. You must understand, dear Ad, that the meaning of this growth can not only be taken in the spatial sense, but also as a personal development.

- I see! Could a spiral symbolize this trip, my initiation journey?

- Yes, dear Ad, if you want to. Of course!

- Then I'll pick a spiral that... By the way, why is the Turbópulus spiral more important than others?

- Because the Turbópulus shell exhibits a pronounced tendency to adjust itself to the shape of a logarithmic spiral. There is no example, however, of an exact fit. Hence, when we talk about it, we are dealing with an ideal case.

- And why is the logarithmic spiral important, precisely?

- Because the logarithmic spiral has a well-known equation. This spiral can be drawn in a conventional manner, using that equation. Nevertheless, there is an unexpected way to do it. A divine cut is made into a divine rectangle. In the small rectangle that occurs as a result of the cut, another divine cut is made, and so on. Thus, a divine "skeleton" is produced which perfectly fits the logarithmic spiral, making of the Turbópulus a being of religious contemplation. Notice, dear Ad, this drawing system has some resemblance to a definition of ϕ in these terms:

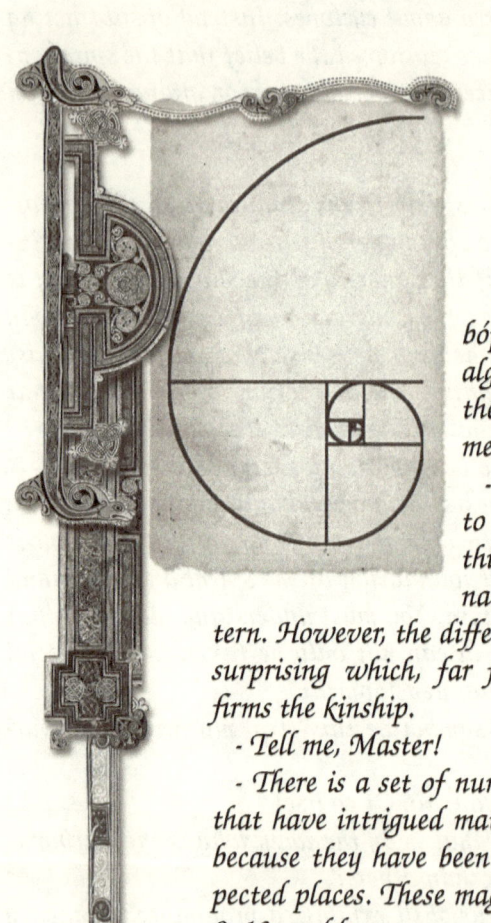

$$\phi = 1 + \cfrac{1}{1 + \cfrac{1}{1 + \cfrac{1}{1 + \;\cdots}}}$$

That is to say, the Tur-bópulus shell grows with the algebra of Druids, obeying the designs of ø... -I commented, surprised.

- Well, that would seem to be. But remember that this case is ideal. In reality, nature differs from this pattern. However, the difference is something equally surprising which, far from discriminating, confirms the kinship.

- Tell me, Master!

- There is a set of numbers, considered magical, that have intrigued mathematicians for centuries because they have been found in the most unexpected places. These magic numbers are 1, 2, 3, 5, 8, 13, and larger ones.

- What's unusual about these numbers?

- Patience, dear Ad, patience. These numbers appear very commonly associated with spiral lines of growth in plants and animals; therefore, it is hard to consider it an accidental fact. For example, flowers are commonly divided into 3 or 5 petals but there are also 13, 34, 55 and 89 petals. The scales of the cones on the coniferous trees form a series of 5, 8 or 13 spirals. The composite flowers like those that follow the light of the day, small, yellow in the middle with white petals around, form in the center 21 and 34 series of spirals. The composite flowers of exceptionally large size, such as the Giraluz, form a series of

die duulterins
Ces anderen
valt eur bluul
werre uanden
per aerten
Ces teroen ti
oragheiize gir
makere euee o
brughen die li
ciache in lien

coils of 55, 89 and 144 members. All these numbers belong
to the same magical series. The
arrangement of leaves along
the stems can be understood as
an ascending spiral that distributes the leaves as it goes up.
Well, if we call 'm' the number
of turns of the spiral and 'n' the
number of leaves distributed
along those turns, the following arrangements appear:

m/n; 1/2; 1/3; 2/5; 3/8; 5/13; 8/21; ...

- Another thing -he went on- Ideally, the number of branches of the stem until it reaches the flowers grows in this order:

1,2,3,5,8...

- The reproduction of a couple of rubi-
sos -he continued- which are the most
prolific rodents, measured as the number
of couples per month, including the parent couple is:

1, 2, 3, 5, 8, 13, ...

- But what amazes me the most -he
added- is the communication system of
the igúridas in their hives: when the explorer igúrida returns with
new information from the outside, such as the location of a new
flowery field, it starts a song composed by intermittent hums of different duration. No one knows exactly what that means, except that
it is a coding system like the one used in telegraphy. The different
combinations among hums allow so many possibilities that keep scientists busy. The duration of each hum is in this relation:

1, 2, 3, 5.

- Then, the igúridas think with those numbers.

- Well... I would not say that much. That has not been proven. But, if you have not noticed yet, you must realize that these magic numbers found in nature coincide with the numbers of the divine series. You should also notice that these magic numbers form a numerical series, reproducible with an arithmetic formula. That is, the series is formed by adding the two previous terms to find the next one. For example,

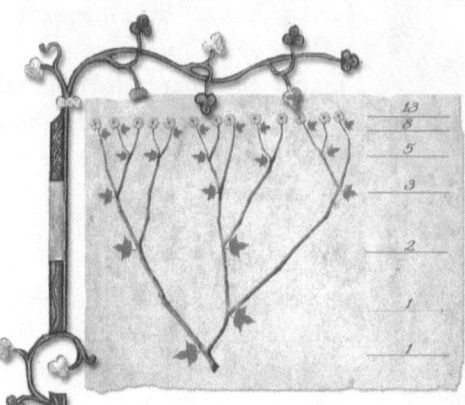

$$1+1= 2; \quad 1+2= 3; \quad 2+3 = 5; \quad 3+5 = 8; \ ...$$

- Oh, I see!

- In short, we have two series: the divine series, discovered by abstract considerations:

$$1; \ \emptyset; \ 1+\emptyset; \ 1+2\emptyset; \ 2+3\emptyset; \ 3+5\emptyset; \ ...$$

and the magical series, discovered in nature:

$$1; \ 2; \ 3; \ 5; \ 8; \ ...$$

- If you examine the two -he continued- you might think that the second is the same as the first, except that the second ignores ∅ entirely. You might think also that, if nature is the reflection of God and the series of magical or natural numbers ignores the value of ∅, everything we have said about ∅ has

Spirogira

only been a joyful adventure, it never had any sense and the Boric cathedrals were lifted in the light of the enthusiastic blindness of a few dreamers.

- *You are right! That is precisely what I was thinking.*
- *In the studies about series able to be reproduced by a formula, it has been found what it might be called its growth ratio. No matter how big or little two consecutive numbers in a series are worth, the growth rate is measured by dividing one number by the previous one. In the divine series, the growth rate turns out to be, after some simplifications, equal to ø, regardless of the pair of numbers you choose. In the series of magic numbers, as the chosen numbers grow, the growth rate tends to the value of ø.*

$$8/5 = 1.60000...$$
$$34/21 = 1.61904...$$
$$233/144 = 1.61805...$$
$$... = ...$$
$$Limit\ at\ infinity... = ø\ (1.61803...)$$

- *Surprise! -my master happily exclaimed- As we go along the succession, the difference between the divine and the magical series becomes increasingly smaller. The growth ratio of the magical series has the divine proportion as its limit at infinity, that is, ø. Given the ideal character of the divine series, the magic series would be the best approach nature can do.*
- *So, after all, the builders of cathedrals were not Boric dreamers.*
- *No! The mystical reflections, originated a long time ago, have been materialized in Nature. Boric architects were not wrong in choosing the armor of its elegance, because it is, indeed, associated with the divine mystery.*
- *This means, that when the Turbópulus manufactures its shell or when plants produce leaves and organize their flowers or when the hives secret codes are intoned, these living beings are only following the same sense of elegance, like the Thinking Being. True?*
- *I think so, dear Ad.*
- *The measuring tape for beauty...*
- *There is a combination of wonder and curiosity in all of this, dear Ad-d-Tuar. Perhaps the foundation of aesthetics consists precisely in this: to sense in beautiful objects the action of a plan that guides the natural behavior toward an arrangement of which we just have a glimpse.*

The Persistence of Magic

For those who know about matrices:
Could you believe that these determinants, built with the magic numbers, equal to zero?

$$\begin{vmatrix} 3 & 5 & 8 \\ 13 & 21 & 34 \\ 55 & 89 & 144 \end{vmatrix} = 0 \qquad \begin{vmatrix} 1 & 2 & 3 & 5 \\ 8 & 13 & 21 & 34 \\ 55 & 89 & 144 & 233 \\ 377 & 610 & 987 & 1597 \end{vmatrix} = 0$$

For those who do not know:
The determinants are just a way of summarizing a series of operations with the numbers that are inside the bars; the numbers are multiplied here, subtracted there, etc. But, there is no reason for the result of a long process of operations to be equal to zero. It is as if we distribute a deck of cards to players, and always the last card in our hands is the ace of hearts.

Taken from the Vespertine Missal

Ugrabi Style Ornaments

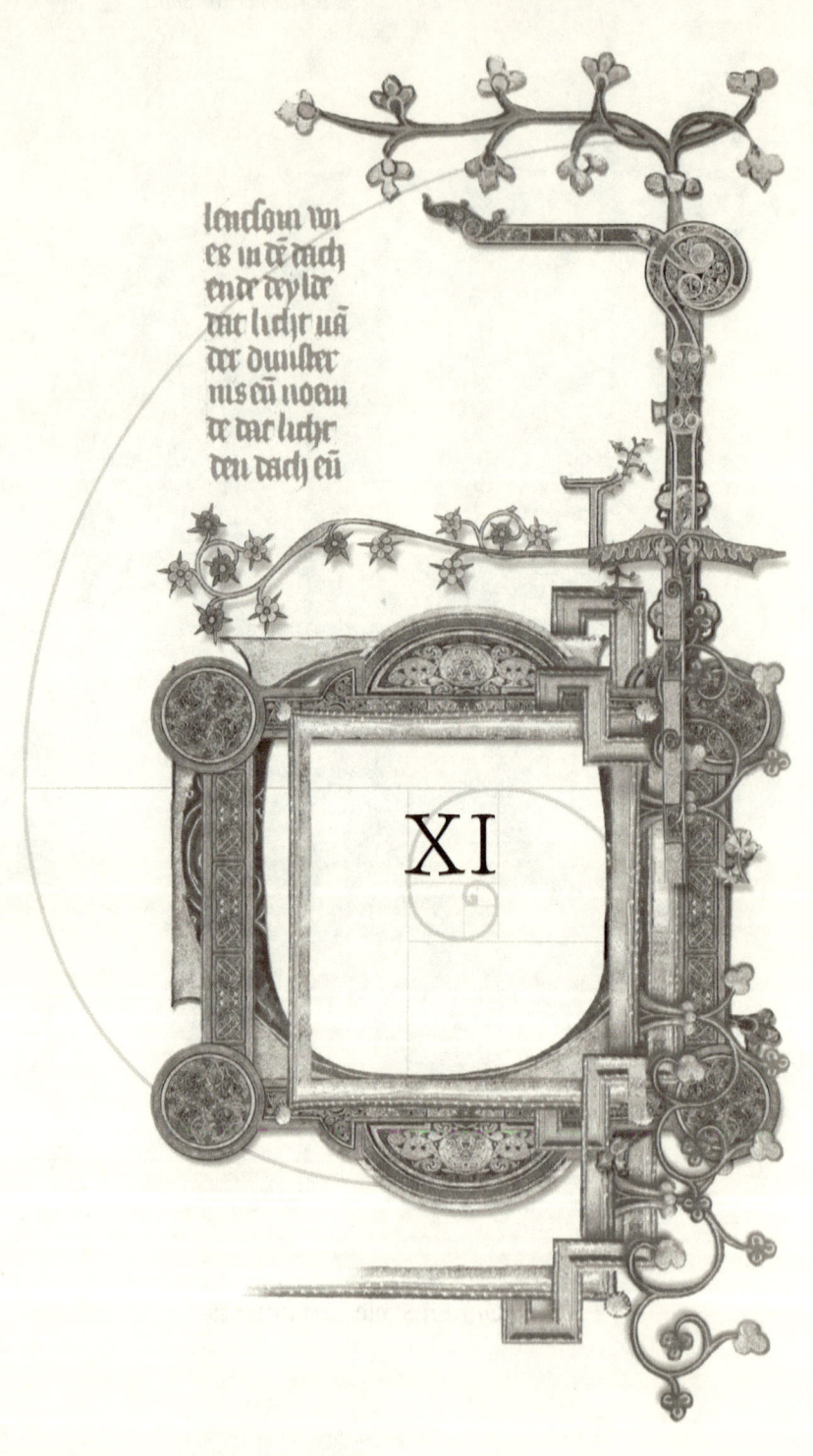

lencloun wi
es in de dach
ende dey lie
die licht uā
der duister
nis eū noeu
te die licht
den dach eū

Chapter XI

The Song of the Whales

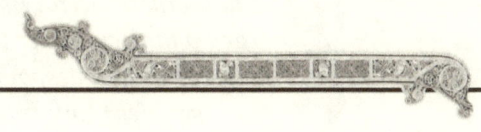

e had taken too much time contemplating ornaments when finding a boat was more imperative. Therefore, we decided to resume the march. When we turned our backs to the building...

- Just a moment! -somebody shouted from inside the strange abode.

Reverend Ogli and I turned back quite surprised. The shadows that prevailed behind the splendid portico let us only glimpse a bulge without details.

- I was waiting for you both -the voice of an old person said- I'm Uwer de OrEst.

- Did you know we were coming? -my puzzled master asked.

- I didn't know it -he answered with a cavernous voice- I saw it!

- You saw us? -my master asked, surprised again.

- I see more than I would like to see -Uwer said rhythmically, as if he was singing a deep and hollow chant- I see, unpleasantly, an ugly world...

> There will be winters with no spring,
> udders without milk and creeping grass.
> Infertile trees covering the mountains
> without the celebration of the beekeepers.
> The wise will be presumptuous
> and they will also be admired;

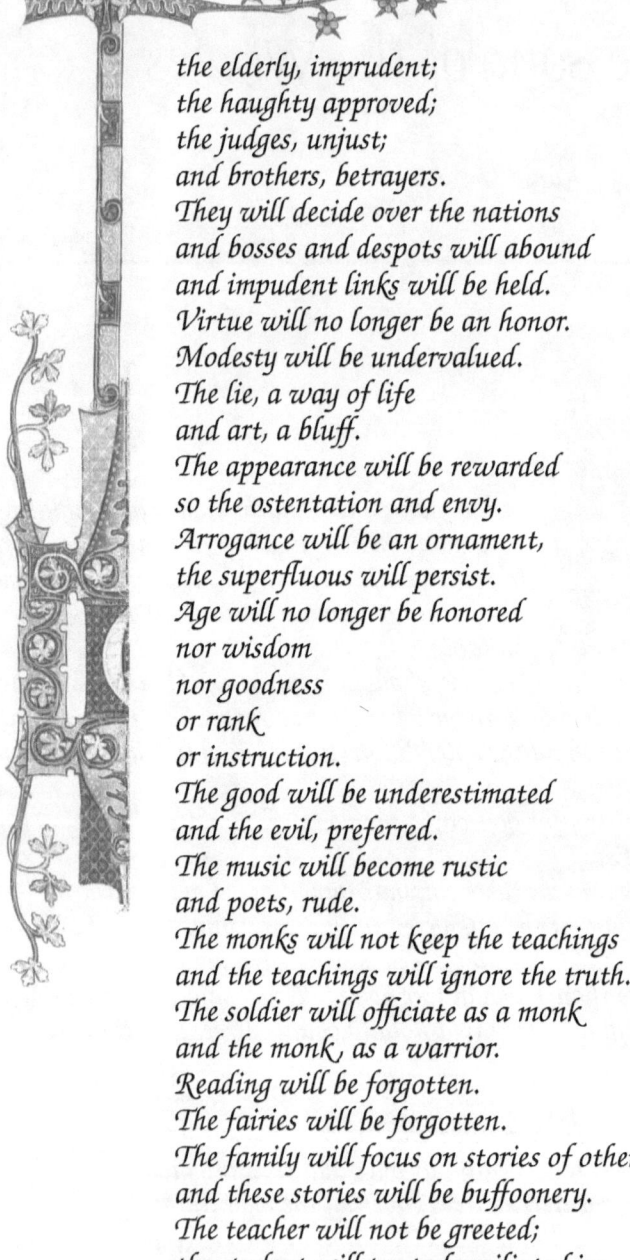

the elderly, imprudent;
the haughty approved;
the judges, unjust;
and brothers, betrayers.
They will decide over the nations
and bosses and despots will abound
and impudent links will be held.
Virtue will no longer be an honor.
Modesty will be undervalued.
The lie, a way of life
and art, a bluff.
The appearance will be rewarded
so the ostentation and envy.
Arrogance will be an ornament,
the superfluous will persist.
Age will no longer be honored
nor wisdom
nor goodness
or rank
or instruction.
The good will be underestimated
and the evil, preferred.
The music will become rustic
and poets, rude.
The monks will not keep the teachings
and the teachings will ignore the truth.
The soldier will officiate as a monk
and the monk, as a warrior.
Reading will be forgotten.
The fairies will be forgotten.
The family will focus on stories of others
and these stories will be buffoonery.
The teacher will not be greeted;
the student will try to humiliate him.
If not, he will discover with horror
that his teacher is an ass.

Countries will be overcrowded and
the cities will cover the sacred mountains.
Battles will take place around mystical places.
The artwork will be tainted with blood.
Some foreign will destroy the ground of Argueria
and a death of three days and three nights
will destroy two-thirds of the Thinking Beings.
There will be deformity and mourning
after the destruction.
All this will be and will not
at the end of the last world.
Unless... the pieces come together.

-What? -Reverend Ogli asked, completely intrigued- Why do you say that to me?

Uwer seemed to ignore the question of Reverend Ogli-s-Oöp and continued to speak in a normal voice:

- My servant, Er-guen, will transport you where you want to go.
-But...!

Uwer de OrEst did not let Reverend Ogli finish; he turned his back and returned to the darkness of his admirable abode. Only then did we notice a shadow behind us. We turned to see. It was a tall, very thin person. He was Er-guen. He had brick color hair, loose and long up to his back. His movements were slow. He walked as if he was moving in an underwater environment; as if he struggled to overcome a secret force dissolved in the air. And he did not speak. He pointed the way toward the beach, extending his arm with the patience of the universe. The invitation to board the boat was equally silent.

The boat was small. It was not a canoe, but to be a boat, it lacked a body. While Er-guen raised the sail, Reverend Ogli tried to find out if he knew where to go.

- We need to go to Frigenia. Are you going to Frigenia?

Er-guen pointed toward the horizon. Then, Reverend Ogli said:

- At least, he is pointing in the right direction. We have no choice, anyway: it's this or nothing!

- But perhaps he is taking us to somewhere else.

- That's always possible, but I do not know why, I have another impression. Patience, dear Ad, patience.

Five hours of sailing passed. Er-guen continued to direct the tiller with an absent air. With ease, my eyes went over the sea, seeking the flat and distant horizon. My attention wandered on the water, but suddenly was high above, because I was not able to distinguish when the blue was water or air; sea and sky were one. A blue continuity seemed to rise on all sides. Our surrounding was getting curved and closing on itself with us in it; as the circular universe of a spherical aquarium made of glass.

The decorative quality of this allegorical notion suggested the possibility that our situation was under observation by a huge, invisible eye looking at us from the outside of a glass sphere. An eye beyond the limits of our experience and reality. As if it were an aquarium, this eye could see, at the same time, the flight of birds and the digging work of the mollusks; the transit of cirrus and other unclassifiable clouds and the white dancing of jellyfish; what is happening in the plains of Emuria and the frenetic ascent of a single bubble. Perhaps such an eye may well belong to Thinking Beings bigger than us. Maybe they also would be the subject of observation by others even greater. Perhaps they would be observed by others still greater, and so on... according to the spiralizing formula of the divine proportion:

$$\phi = 1 + \cfrac{1}{1 + \cfrac{1}{1 + \cfrac{1}{1 + \cdots}}}$$

We would, then, face an inconceivable logarithmic spiral of observers or simply we would be in front of the unintelligible iris of God. How does God perceive reality? -I asked myself- Looking at the air may mean for him distinguishing the magnetic currents that command the compass or the wind hesitations or how the sound opens its way. Seeing the air may mean for him seeing oxygen molecules, photons, and omens. If he directs his attention under the sea, perhaps he would see it crossed by ultraviolet beams that light up the phosphorescent spots of the bearded fish. He, perhaps, would distinguish the infrared and see the heat coming as flames from the hot bodies swimming in the water.

How many colors can God see? -I wondered again- Immediately, I thought, I could access a little the sight of God through the aquatic environment, if Reverend Ogli lends me his Blackmoon crystal disks...

- *Master!*

- *Tell me, dear Ad.*

- *What happens if I put water between the Blackmoon crystal disks?*

- *Nothing -my teacher replied.*

- *Nothing! -I exclaimed- Wouldn't I see the beautiful colors that appeared when you put the cellophane between them?*

- *No, dear Ad.*

- *But water is as clear as the cellophane*

- *It is not about being or not being transparent.*

- *So...?*

- *If you allow me, dear Ad, I will tell you first that the colors you saw are due to the extreme thinness of cellophane. Interference colors like those appear frequently in observations related to polarized light. So that is not important. There are substances that react to polarized light and others that remain indifferent to it. Water alone does not exhibit any activity; nor does water with salt. Water with sugar, however, does show some effect...*

- *What effect?*

- *Do you remember what "light switch off" means?*

- *Yes, Master.*

- *If you keep the light switch off, you should see total darkness on the second disk... right?*

- *Yes, Master.*

- *Well, there are substances that by themselves, open the light switch. If, with the help of a suitable container, you interpose sugar water between the two disks when the light switch is off, then you will instantly see some light coming out from the second disk. It is not complete clarity, but fewer, enough to be noticed. It is as if the sugar is able to open the light switch a little. If you want to restore the dark, you must turn off the light switch an extra amount to offset the effect of sugar. To accomplish this, you must rotate the second disc over the other a certain number of degrees until the light is extinguished again. It is said that the substances able to alter the*

111

darkness of the crossed Blackmoon crystal discs have "optical activity." Apparently, it is a minor event but leads to great conclusions. Often, fundamental truths are found after deep thought about something simple. And that's how the spirit of the Szabeo monk should be: deep and simple at the same time.

- Yes, Master - I answered - But tell me, Master, what is the reason for the anomalous behavior of sugar? What is the difference between sugar and salt, and water?

- The answer has to do with what we have been talking about during these days. Let's start with the water...

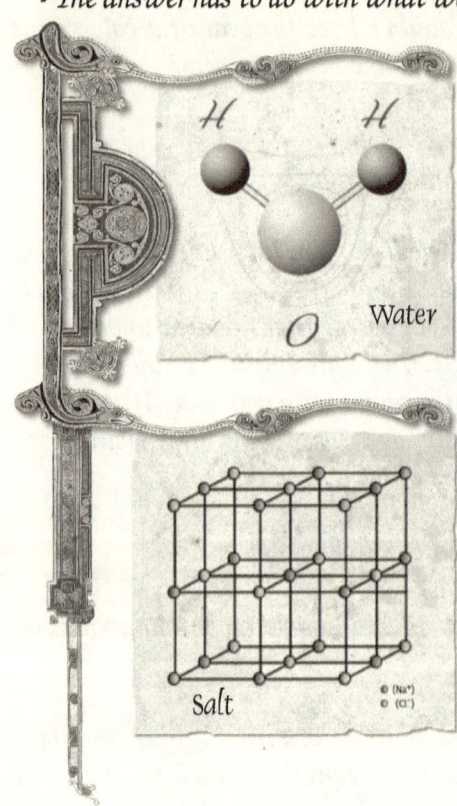

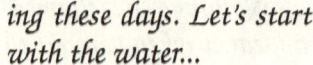

Reverend Ogli pulled out his notebook and sketched something on it.

- This is the water molecule. Based on the exercises you did, tell me, dear Ad, is this molecule superposable on its mirror image?

- Mmm... the water molecule is symmetrical. What is at left is similar to what is at right.

- Very good, dear Ad. Please continue.

- Uh... Well... If the water molecule is symmetrical, then it could be superposed on its specular image!

- Very good! Now, salt forms symmetrical aggregates and produces symmetrical crystals.

- Sugar, however -he went on- has a much more complicated molecule that cannot be superposed on its specular image. Sugar is asymmetric and that is the reason, or part of it, why it is able to open the light switch. Quartz has asymmetrically ordered atoms and produces asymmetric crystals which are the mirror image of each other.

- As I said -he continued- sugar is asymmetrical and is able to open the light switch. Specular images of chemical substances are called enantiomers. In the case of sugar, its enantiomer truly exists as a real molecule. The first one has always been produced by nature; the second one by artificial methods that were discovered when chemistry was developed enough. The first one, the natural sugar, opens the light switch to the right; its enantiomer leftward. That is to say, to restore the darkness, in the first case we have to rotate the second disc a certain angle to the right; in the second case to the left. The angle in both cases is the same but the direction in which they occur is opposite. It is as if there is a behavior

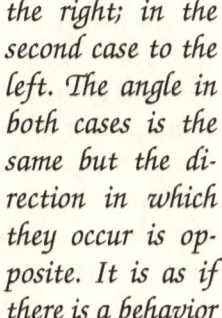

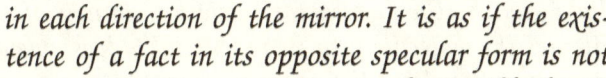

in each direction of the mirror. It is as if the existence of a fact in its opposite specular form is not only possible but is latent in our reality and it only needs to be discovered. There is only one water and there is only one salt since the possibilities of atomic arrangement within their molecules do not result in variations. But, as we address more and larger molecules, consisting of several atoms of various kinds, the different interchangeable arrangements with them result in varieties of the same molecule. For example, there is an acid called tartaric, that has different atomic groups around a pair of carbon atoms. The possibilities of ordering based on this circumstance are three. Each has its own name to be distinguished among its brothers: levotartaric, dextrotartaric, and mesotartaric acid. They are as follows:

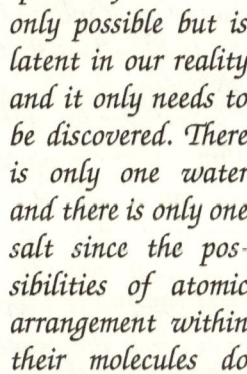

$$
\begin{array}{ccc}
COOH & COOH & COOH \\
| & | & | \\
OH - C - H & H - C - OH & H - C - OH \\
| & | & | \\
H - C - OH & OH - C - H & H - C - OH \\
| & | & | \\
COOH & COOH & COOH
\end{array}
$$

| Ácido Levotartárico | Ácido Dextrotartárico | Ácido Mesotartárico |

- The first two -he went on- are asymmetric and are enantiomers of each other. If they are separately dissolved, their solutions can open the light switch at equal angles but in opposite directions. If these solutions are allowed to rest separately, they can produce crystals that are physically enantiomorphs of each other; in other words, oppositely oriented. If equal amounts of the two solutions are mixed, the individual effects are canceled, and the light switch does not open in any way. This is also true with solutions of mesotartaric acid, which is a symmetric acid; that is, they have no effect on the light switch. The mesotartaric acid has an axis of symmetry which divides the molecule into two identical halves, one above the other. Have you heard of Ui-LacToeur, dear Ad?

- Is the scientist from Galactia, who discovered the vaccination process.

- Yes, dear Ad, but he is also known for discovering several other things that are equally important. For example, everything that I told you about the tartaric acid and its optical activity was discovered by him when he was quite young. Back then, he let mold grow on a solution made of an equal amount of dextro and levotartaric acid which, as I said, do not open the light switch at all. The result was that mold consumed only one of the enantiomers. The solution finally opened the light switch as the levotartaric acid alone would have done it. Then he concluded that all subsequent experiments never contradicted: living organisms work with asymmetric biochemical processes since they select, for their nutrition, a determined enantiomer and reject the other. You can also observe the same discrimination in the natural production of substances. If a plant produces a medicine, a pigment, or an aromatic essence, it produces one and only one of the enantiomers in each case. This explains why the dextrotartaric acid is found in nature. The levotartaric acid has to be fabricated. Table sugar, which opens the light switch to the right, occurs naturally. If a chemical substance is produced by nature, it is reasonable to think that it is consumed by nature in the same exclusive way. This hypothesis led to the production of artificial sweeteners, which should open the light switch to the left. These sugars do not cause weight gain because the body does not metabolize them. For the same immunity in front of living things, these sugars remain fresh because the microorganisms do not attack them and, precisely for this reason, do not cause caries.

- Really!

- What Ui-LacTeour intuited came to be confirmed with studies on the enzymatic processes that take place inside living things. When a molecule enters the food system of a living being, it is captured by an "assembly line" akin to the production of a modern factory. The body takes from this "assembly line" what it needs to feed itself. But, the body does not have the hands of the workers to do this. It has other molecules that are like sticky molds of what it is looking for. Then, like a puzzle piece that becomes part of the image that is being formed across its intricate profiles, the nutrient molecules are incorporated into the metabolism. These "molds" found in living organisms are specific to each substance which, in most cases, have an asymmetric configuration. For example, a molecule of natural sugar fits into the specific mold for sugar. But the artificial sugar molecule, which is its enantiomer, will not fit into the mold and will be ignored. The actual process is more complicated than this...

- It's like trying to adjust the left hand to the right glove -I said.

- That's it! -my master said, almost enthusiastic- Perfect!

- If we nourish us with enantiomeric substances, oriented in a particular direction, does it mean that our whole body is constructed in a specific direction in regards to its constitutive material?

- So it seems, dear Ad.

- So, we are living beings oriented in one direction?

- Yes, that would be it... -my master said- ...and I think you have more reason than you suspect. Look! Our skin, internal tissues, hair, nails, bones, tendons, muscles, blood, well... any part of the body has protein in its structure. The DNA molecule is protein. Proteins are formed by a chain of smaller molecular units which have a specific spatial orientation. If you want to build a spiral staircase that ascends toward the right, you must build all the steps oriented in the same direction. Similarly, and vice versa, amino acids oriented in the same direction generate, when they get linked, the spiral shape that holds the DNA molecule. Thus, all our body, until the last of the hairs, is oriented in one direction. We are a major enantiomer. We are the spiralized children created in the image and likeness of the unintelligible iris of God.

- Here we go again with the spiral!

- Well, you have found that it is not accidental. In the molecule that transmits life and even in the macroscopic results of its performance, living beings reveal their brotherhood in the spiral; a brotherhood notarized with the magic numbers of the divine series. In the case of the turbópulus, the giraluz and the spirogira, for example, the consanguinity is more obvious than in the rest of plants and animals, but all of them have, basically, the same label. As you have already heard from me, the molecular units of DNA, like the steps of a spiral staircase, are already affected by a previous dictatorial twist, originated in the most basic confines of our reality where matter is and stops being, following the double way of the spiral shape. If you add tornadoes, vortices, and galaxies, nobody will blame you for perceiving a predetermined orientation in our reality that manifests itself in all things, as if it were a plot. The question is: in which direction the universe is oriented, to the right or to the left? So, it is not accidental, dear Ad. We are talking about the topological foundations of life. Wouldn't you expect to find here the sober and unifying elegance of God?

The boat had entered the blurry exteriors of a bank of fog. According to my master, this was proof that we were near the shadowy coast of Frigenia. What he did not understand -and neither did I- was how the laconic Er-guen managed to know where to go if we were in the middle of the fog. Then, my teacher noticed an almost imperceptible vibration on the wooden boat. After that, Reverend Ogli knelt and put his ear on the floor of the boat.

- AHA!

- What is it, Master?

My master looked at me in a vivacious way, but he did not explain anything. Immediately, he questioned Er-Guen.

- Er-Guen! You are navigating the boat guided by the song of the whales, right?

Er-Guen did not reply this time either, but it was the first and only time I saw him smiling.

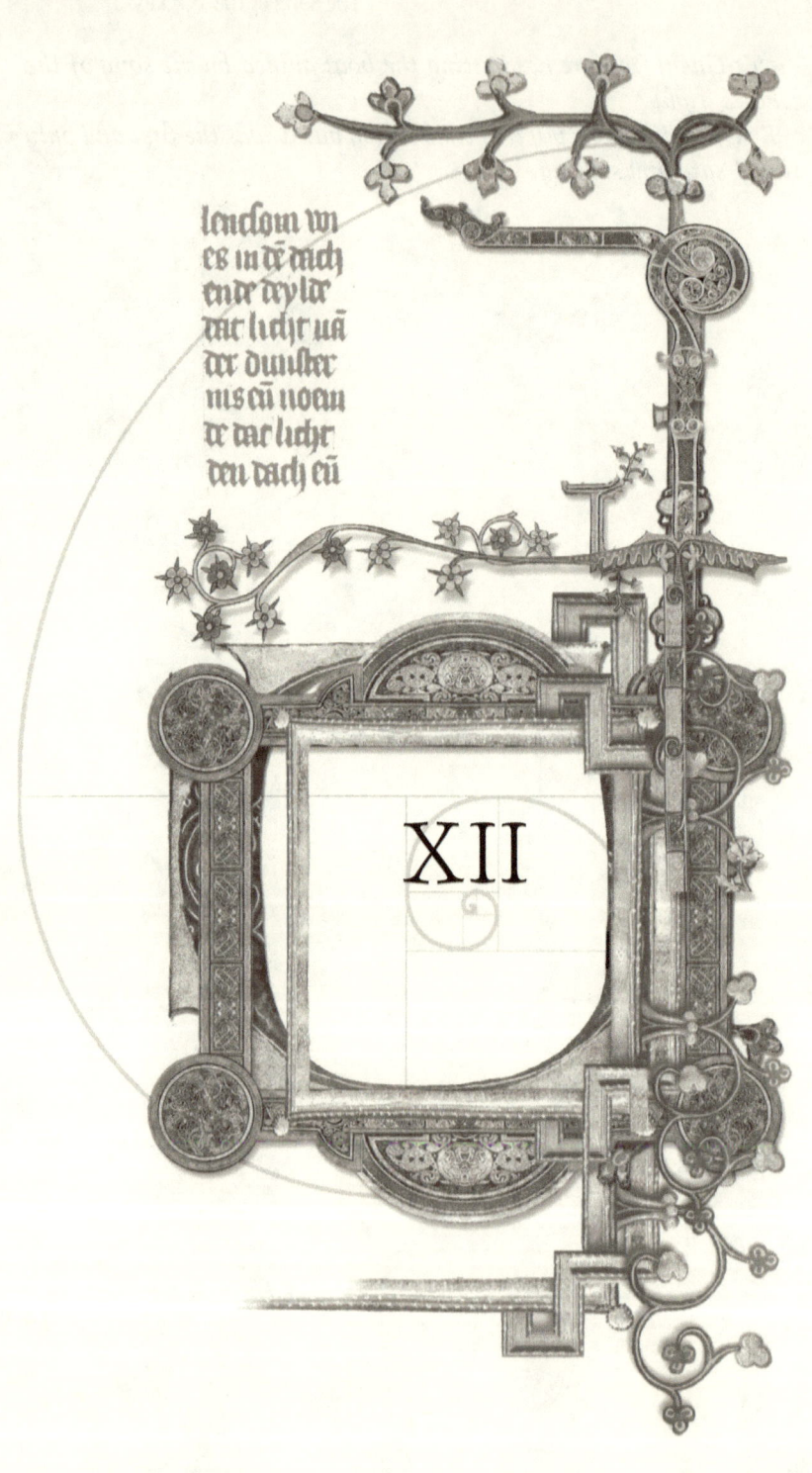

lencloui vii
es in de dich
ende dylic
dar licht vā
der duister
ns en noem
de dar licht
den dach en

XII

Chapter XII

The Night of Time

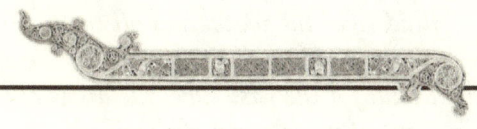

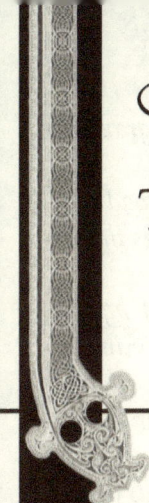fter touching Frigenian ground, Er-Guen returned to the sea without accepting what Reverend Ogli offered to him as a way to pay for our transportation. He never said a word and vanished like mist in the mist.

The Frigenian ground that greeted us was entirely rocky: a very narrow promontory of almost black stones. Where the stones ended, one of the highest cliff walls I have seen in my long life rose among the mist. Up close, the view could not hold it and if one looked up, the fog covered it all with its white blindness. From a distance, when the atmosphere allowed, the mind wondered if the cliff actually ever rose over the sea or the sea sank around it.

On the plateau, a countryside overfilled with vegetation, fruits and honey spread widely. But it was a serious landscape, with a gloomy air and a gray sky. The moisture from the last storm had splashed the scene with sporadic flashes of metallic sheen. A few golden strings, stretched from heaven, made all the dawn. The light was scattered, so depleted of strength by the haze, that the colors looked dull, as though coated with a patina of wax, dusty yellows, and leaden olives; boasts of a still life. The imagination aspired to see a set table with opulent antiquities over the coast of Frigenia; a table risen from the waters to entertain guests of a supernatural time.

We moved along a bridle path, probably used only for grazing. Then we crossed a river that Reverend Ogli recognized.

- Oh, I know where we are! -he told me- If we leave this road and follow the river on the right bank, we will reach Wrestongres in less than an hour.

And so we did. We walked about an hour, entertained by the fluidity of the water and all the thirsty beings, plants, and animals, congregated on their flanks. At the end of a modest hill, suddenly, I had, for the first time, the disturbing silhouette of Wrestongres in front of me, against the twilight.

- It has been said a lot about Wrestongres -my master said, as we walk over the plain where these ruins risen- It has been said that it is the result of the materialization of a circle of giants who were dancing in vain a dance against a petrifying spell cast by Eliseo, god of gods. Some thought it was a Marterian temple; others assumed it was a place where the Druid councils were held. It was thought to have been built to serve as an astronomical observatory in ancient times. It has even been said that Wrestongres is a station to collect energy or an antenna for transmitting into outer space; a sidereal abacus; a door to hell or heaven. Someone thought that it is an example of Art according to the aesthetic canons of Boric cathedrals. Anyway...

- How can one thing be so many things at once? -I said without restraint.

- Ah! This happens because there is nothing so fascinating as the mystery or anything as prolific as the imagination, dear Ad. The mammoth size of the rocks that make up Wrestongres has also given rise to the most varied and fanciful explanations about its transportation. Around the area, there is no way to get those stones. Some legends have blamed Wgijvrán the magician, who, to transport them from other lands, would have used a levitating spell. The fact is that this is a colossal and mysterious building that does not give the prosaic answers to questions that come spontaneously. Who built it? What was its purpose? And finally, how was it built?

- It seems to me, that has to do with astronomy -I said- ...Or it may have been a ceremonial temple.

My teacher smiled and looked at me affectionately with his big black eyes.

- Patience, dear Ad, patience. I assure you we will talk about what Szabeos know to this respect. But first, I must warn you that I have a surprise for you.

- Really? What is it, Master?

- It is something that is almost a once in a lifetime luxury.

- What is it, Master?

- Tonight, an eclipse of the moon is expected, which is not uncommon, but it coincides that we will see the eclipse from a privileged site, if you think Wrestongres is an astronomical observatory.

- How nice! -I replied enthusiastically- Very good!

- But first, dear Ad, we must make our beds and make something to eat.

- Yes, Master!

We set our beds next to some bushes that spread in the surroundings of the sacred circle of Wrestongres. We did it so, just to do something against the wind. Then we fed Oj and had dinner too. After that, I asked:

- Master, when will the eclipse happen?

- As I recall, it is planned for 1:25

- Ah! So, we have time.

- Time?... only If the world does not annihilate itself first... -my master sadly said- You know, dear Ad? Perhaps, this eclipse is the last thing to admire.

- When do you think, Master, the war might break out?

- At any time, dear Ad. We'll know as soon as the sky catches fire.

- But, the rockets... Would they reach this land?

- The rockets would be directed, at best, only to military bases in Frigenia. These last would direct its rockets to who knows where; probably Rjostos or Sammkara. But the power of these explosions would be so huge that they would affect the entire face of the planet. So, I assure you, dear Ad, we will notice it wherever we are.

- I had thought that, twenty years ago, the nations had disarmed themselves.

- Well, they were not the same nations.

- No?

· A hundred years ago, Emuria was a large territory consisting of various nationalities and cultures. They were united by a totalitarian regime that was established under philosophies attacking the Western world. They came to be known as the Alliance of Emurian Republics. This regime had a bad reputation because most of its history was in charge of one of the bloodiest dictatorships. Something that is viewed as a real accomplishment is their technological growth, achieved in about seventy years. Before forming the Alliance of Emurian Republics, Emuria was a very miserable agricultural territory which was starving; years later, it could place a space laboratory into orbit and intimidate Western governments with such a large and sophisticated armament as theirs together. However, at the end of those years, the Emurian economy never stabilized and eventually collapsed. The Alliance of Emurian Republics disintegrated into independent Emurian countries, smaller and easier to manage. This process went without violence because, perhaps, it did not respond to the "liberation" cry, but rather "every man for himself." Each of the republics was hard-pressed to survive, and that was why they celebrated new alliances; sometimes at odds with their natural idiosyncrasy, sometimes promoted for that very reason. Some of them made a deal with their former enemies who were very glad to do so. Others united, seeking cooperation by the only link left to them: their religion. Now, you should know, first, that at the time of the disintegration of the republics, the huge Emurian army was divided among the republics as any inheritance. Second, the republics that had inherited the armament factories, which were built on their soil, found that a successful mechanism to overcome themselves from the economic crisis was the selling of military equipment to both, friends and enemies. To the south, the Lunilaic countries had also been engaged in creating a unity. This desire came from centuries ago. The biggest obstacle they had encountered for this purpose was their tendency to quarrel among themselves. But there were two events that supported a final and successful association attempt. The first was the War of Incidia and Seudonia, where racial and religious hatred against Lunilaics was exacerbated to unimaginable limits. The second was the cunning ability of a despotic head of state of Sammkara to drive resentments, which made him the Lunilaic leader after the War of the Desert. Now, do you remember, dear Ad, the legend of the *black monster that lies in a liquid state beneath the desert and feeds on hatred?*

- *Yes, Master.*

- *Well, that is one way of referring to oil. The Lunilaic countries always had it, which meant incredible amounts of money. What they did not have was a sophisticated military technology. The disintegration of the Alliance of Emurian Republics gave them the opportunity to obtain it. As I said before, these republics were united in the name of the religion they had previously professed. A group of them twinned under the Lunilaicism. They did not have problems in allying with the new Lunilaic association of southern countries, called Lunilaic Unity. This cooperation meant, to the young society, the access to most of the weaponry of the former Alliance of Emurian Republics. The rest of these republics were auctioning everything to get out of bankruptcy, including their military technology. That was how the Lunilaic Unity bought everything and emerged as the second world power, replacing the belligerent role of the former Alliance of Emurian Republics. At the time this happened, the war industry around the globe had been secretly developing a race to get the antimatter bomb. When the world finally divided itself between western Cruciglobist and eastern Lunilaic powers, both sides already had the most brutal and devastating weapon ever created. Do you understand it better now?*

- *Yes, Reverend Ogli, thanks -I replied- But, you mentioned that racial and religious hatreds was exacerbated. Does it mean that the Lunilaic Unity has reason to be aggressive?*

- *Dear Ad, no one has reason to be aggressive. But, it is possible to find an explanation for a violent behavior, which is different. In addition, there was exacerbation on both sides, Lunilaic and Cruciglobist. Still, sometimes it is simply impossible to understand some of the most brutal behavior during the war of Incidia and Seudonia.*

Reverend Ogli exhibited an expression of repudiation that I had not seen before and continued.

- *From a population of 4.5 million Ovinians, 200,000 died; another 200,000 were wounded, including 50,000 children. More than 2.5 million sought refuge in other countries. Most unfortunately, so disappointing for Szabeos, the so-called "ethnic cleansing" included massacres and concentration camps. For example, B'go-je-Smic was a doctor who became a soldier during the conflict. The* international war crimes tribunals later found him guilty of organizing the arrest, deportation, and murder of 17,000 Lunilaics. R-inko-Ktva was responsible for the shooting of 100 Lunilaics, 33 of whom were women and children. As they had the opportunity, the Lunilaics behaved equally cruel. In this war, there were horrors that, although they are true, for being so impressive, they have to be transmitted with prudence. Moreover, they are hard to believe...

- But how did it start?

- It started a long time ago, from the Middle Era onwards. I have already explained how the world was divided into two, because of religion: East and West, that is to say, Lunilaicism and Cruciglobism. Right?

- Yes, Master.

- Well, well. Roniav was a region of conquest and reconquest, since it was located at the boundary of the two domains. This tide of empires deposited, one above the other, layers of antagonistic cultures. Before the conflict, Roniav was part of the Alliance of Emurian Republics whose government was centralized in the city of Ensko, which was part of the Republic of Gradov. As I said, the regime was totalitarian and controlled the unity of its domain in any way. Roniav survived under that name until it was free from the Alliance and it was time to pick sides. Here was when the hatred emerged; a hatred saved for centuries by the population fractions that formed Roniav. Come on! I think we have invoked too much violence for tonight. I will tell you what we are going to do. The eclipse will start around one thirty. I brought an alarm clock with me. I am going to set it for 1:00. Meanwhile, let's sleep!

- Ok. Good evening, Reverend Ogli.

- Good night, disciple.

Needless to say, it took me a while to sleep. The colossal stones of Wrestongres had lost their magic; no longer they mattered so much. Brutal images of death were spinning in my head. I do not know if I dreamt it, but I think I saw a lupezno and a gassilope watching me from afar. This is absurd because both are natural enemies. One eats the other...

When the alarm rang, I opened my eyes and there he was. A little gnome!

- Who are you? -Reverend Ogli, who had awakened too, asked the gnome.

- Before, I was convinced to have the same doubt; now, I'm not so sure about that -replied the stranger.

- Could you repeat that, please? -he asked again.

- Well... only in part.

- In part?

- Any statement is partly true and partly a lie. So, what is the part that is false in the last statement?

- Well...

- If you are uncomfortable, we can eliminate its falseness. But then the question would cease to be curious about itself and would cease to question. It would no longer be a question.

- But, what is the answer to my first question?

- If the answer was written, this phrase would be the answer as an example of the fragmentation technique. Second fragmentation. Another.

- Mmrrrr...! -my master groaned, trying to hold himself back.

The little gnome, sat on some branches of a shrub and began to sing::

Making a scene would require
a hummingbird and a flower.
That would be enough, sire!
A scene with some power.
But the fantasy goes higher.
It is enough with itself;
no hummingbird required
and the flower is for sale.

Since I could see the face of my master changing hue, it occurred to me to highlight what the rambling phrases of the Gnome had of interest, and I said something I thought was a superb reflection:

- That wise gnome can wring a sentence around itself as if it were a spiral.

This time, the continence of my master was directed to me.

- What he says just doesn't make sense, Ad-d-Tuar.

I think I did well staying quiet. The gnome spoke in my place:

- Ah, ah! Bad answer.

The glaze of my master got up slowly again, with all the patience he was capable.

- Do you still not recognize me, Szabeo monk?

Reverend Ogli looked at him with concern. The gnome began to recite some verses:

> Before becoming permanent,
> I have been several times the same
> and likewise, I have been different.
> I rained, spraying myself on the tremulous grass
> and I have waved from vertigo in the celestial abyss.
> I have orbited in remote glares
> and suddenly, I have shined and eclipsed.
> I have boiled in hellish cups
> and got tempered at the rhythm of the Bard.
> I have been a blade and a point
> with a magnificent handle
> rooted in the mineral entrails
> of the rock that I had wounded.
> I have spelled myself without reason or motive
> and I have sounded quite eloquent,
> but it has cost me the eternity
> and the losses due to absence
> neither they get endorse nor sold.
> I have been a letter, a question, a book page
> and I prefaced myself until I covered the content.
> I have hidden myself in common words,
> slinking with inaudible sound
> and I have been named.. by accident.

My master's eyes sparkled, his head leaned back and asked:

- Wgïjvrán, the sorcerer?

- Abracadabra!

While he said that, he drew an arc in the air with his hand as if he was executing an elegant gesture from the past.

-This cannot be! -my master said- Wgïjvrán does not exist. Moreover, he never existed: he is a character in a book, not a character in history.

- *How do you know that? Does a history book say so?*
- *Amazing! -my master said- It seems that you were right, after all, dear Ad.*

I smiled. I already knew, I had not said another foolish thing!

- *I know the little one is called Ad-d-Tuar -the gnome said- but what's your name, Szabeo monk?*

Wrestongres and Wgÿvrán, the sorcerer

- Ogli-s-Oöp

- I am very happy to meet you, Ogli and Ad.

- Talking to you, Wgijvrán, would be like being inside of a literary world -Reverend Ogli said.

- Do you think it was different before? -the gnome or Wgijvrán, or whatever, replied- Where did the things you know come from?

- Your reality -he answered to himself- consists of everything you know. And you have known more by reading. You have never seen a DNA molecule, but you accept it, just because it appears in a text. Everything that has been written about the nature of the subconscious mind could be entirely fictitious. If you do not believe what you are living, then we will write this conversation down in a book. Satisfied?

- Amazing! In case you really are Wgijvrán -Reverend Ogli said- What are you doing here?

- It's a whole story -he replied- But I think you have the right to know.

Wgijvrán came down from the branches and sought one of the monoliths. He sat at its feet, with his back leaning on the stone, and began his narration:

- In my first return to my life, I worked for King Ngupd. I chose him as a king because I knew already he would be chosen. And he was a good king and his reign was fair like no other had been in Frigenia. But after a few love affairs, his health cracked. Although he was young, he could not attend to the kingdom's affairs; even less to defend it from ambitious hands. The Court intrigue promoted invasions and caused the destruction of King Ngupd and his kingdom. I sensed this in my first life; in the second, I knew it. I knew that his reign would live forever in the legends, written or not, that are part of the history of Frigenia. In such cases, a spell is not enough. And, in need of greater knowledge, I convinced my King to organize a circle of select knights and send them to the East in search for the most hidden necromantic knowledge. They returned with assorted cargos. In ancient secret books, I read about the existence of the Holy Råål. Only its discovery could restore the health to my Lord. The magic of the Druids said, however, that what I sought was located in a place called Mal-ö-Goom. But this place, as it could be expected, was lost in the mists of time. So, I created a spell to open the door of the Night of Time. To do this, I first had to obtain sand of time by scraping the surface of one of the rocks of Wrestongres. With part of the sand of time, I had to fabricate the necessary glass to form an ampoule for an hourglass. To fill the vial, I had to use the other part of the sand of time. In the first moon eclipse, within the circle of Wrestongres, I had to flip over the hourglass for the first time while pronouncing my name backward. And so, I did. But, at that precise moment, I was so afraid of what might happen if I made a mistake that I ended up stumbling over my phonemes. While I mixed up the syllables of my name backward, my hands tangled, and the hourglass crashed onto the floor shattering into a thousand pieces.

- And, what happened? -I asked and I did not meddle again.

- I had not been wrong in creating the spell. The Night of the Time opened... But it also closed by itself immediately, trapping me and making me go back in time. It took me to a time far enough back that allowed me to die near my birth. I was stuck in time. I am born to die before birth. That is why it is believed that I know the future. I live an endless spiral. And because of that, I live eternally in the legendary History of Frigenia. But legends are based on books. And every book is more than one book; other books are implied in a book. Books are self-convened at different levels, in different readings; books cite each other without declaring it; books touch, overlap, intertwine each other in a knotted but invisible fabric, crossed by interconnections. So, do not be surprised that I have appeared here. Who lives in one book, lives in all of them and lives forever. That is why I go back and forth through time. In my first return to my life, I worked for King Ngupd. I chose him as a king because I knew already he would be chosen. And he was a good king and his reign was fair like no other had been in Frigenia. But after a few love affairs, his health cracked...

- Okay, okay -my master interrupted with skeptical tone- Let's take your situation as clarified... Wgijvrán, what is ours?

- I already said that I ruined it -he said, reluctantly- Wrestongres ended up, so to speak, out-of-calibration and opens itself in every eclipse trapping who is here.

- Right! -my master replied.

- Have you noticed that the eclipse never happened?

- That's true! -I said- There is no moon, either.

I think it was at that moment when Reverend Ogli-s-Oöp gave up his doubts in front of the evidence: we were in a strange environment. The only thing visible was the monumental ruins of Wrestongres; its surroundings were lost in the darkness.

After a moment of reflection...

- How can we get out of here? -my master asked.
- You must find the Holy Råål!
- Nothing less! -my master exclaimed.

- I must warn you that some travelers have fallen into the same circumstances as you. A few have achieved the Holy Råål; most do not, and those are still wandering somewhere in the Night of Time. I remember some of the last ones: one quit because the enterprise was not easy; another went mad; and another disappeared.

- Remember, Master? -I dared to interrupt- For each individual, there is a particular pathway, although all pilgrims step on the same footprint.

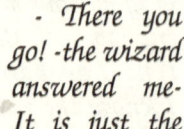

- There you go! -the wizard answered me- It is just the profile of the same face. Reverend Ogli seemed to reflect a moment.

- What is the Holy Råål? How do we recognize it?

- The Holy Råål has been imagined in the literature in several ways. In "The Song of Juh," it is a cooking pot that gives all desired food and never gets empty. It can give life back to the dead warriors and feed a whole army. In others, as in "The Quest of the Råål," it is an inexhaustible dish. Another ancient legend tells that the Holy Råål was built by angels in the form of a hexagonal glass with 144 facets, using an emerald dropped from the sky. It could also be, suggested by Vjidob in his "Hermeneutical Studies on Air and Darkness," the Philosopher's Stone, sought by alchemists. In "The Chants of Cog," one of the volumes of the ngupditic saga, the hermit Ight reveals to Meght that the Holy Råål is a stone named "derex apsilops." But this expression has no translation, has no sense. Some renowned writers such as Ottros have seen the misspelling of "dorex ap silis" or "dorex apt silop" in it, which means, respectively, stone fallen from the sky or stone sent from heaven. I know all this because you already said it: I am part of literature. And who lives in one book lives in all.

- What finally is the Holy Råål?

- The question is for you. But let me tell you something: whatever you decide that the Holy Råål means to you, your search has already begun. The Night of the Time adjusts itself to each particular target long before the individual is on his way.

- If we have no other choice but to seek the Holy Råål, at least, tell me where it is.

- If you wish, you can refuse the quest. That is something most people do. And most of them got trapped in darkness for the lifetime. There are those who do not even try once to find their way and wander lost in the dark. Finding the Holy Råål is the only way to emerge from the Night of the Time; in other words, you can only emerge triumphantly. Regarding the place where the Holy Råål lies, that's something you have to discover as well.

- Suppose we get it. This involves the use of a certain time that surely is also uncertain. How will we find the world when we get back?

- In the Night of Time, the time has no time: it may take you a moment or an eternity. So, you will find the world as you left it. By the way, I have to leave too...

- Please! I would like to ask you one more question.

- Quickly!

- What does the name Mal-ö-Goom mean?

- It is not a name really -the wizard grumpily said- The first word is what the Druids called an operator. An operator acts on the essence of a thing, in a unique way in each case, and induces a function. The essence of a thing is summarized in the second word, which is known as an undulation. The undulations are the sounds that God emitted on the endless shadows to create the possibilities of existence of all things. Mal-ö-Goom is much more than a name, it is a command, an order of activation; that is to say, it's a spell... Have a good trip!

- But...

We still had questions, but Wgïjvrán, the magician, disappeared in the air. We were alone in the disturbing world of the Night of Time. Only the ruins of Wrestongres, lit by the fire, were distinguishable; the rest was in the deepest darkness.

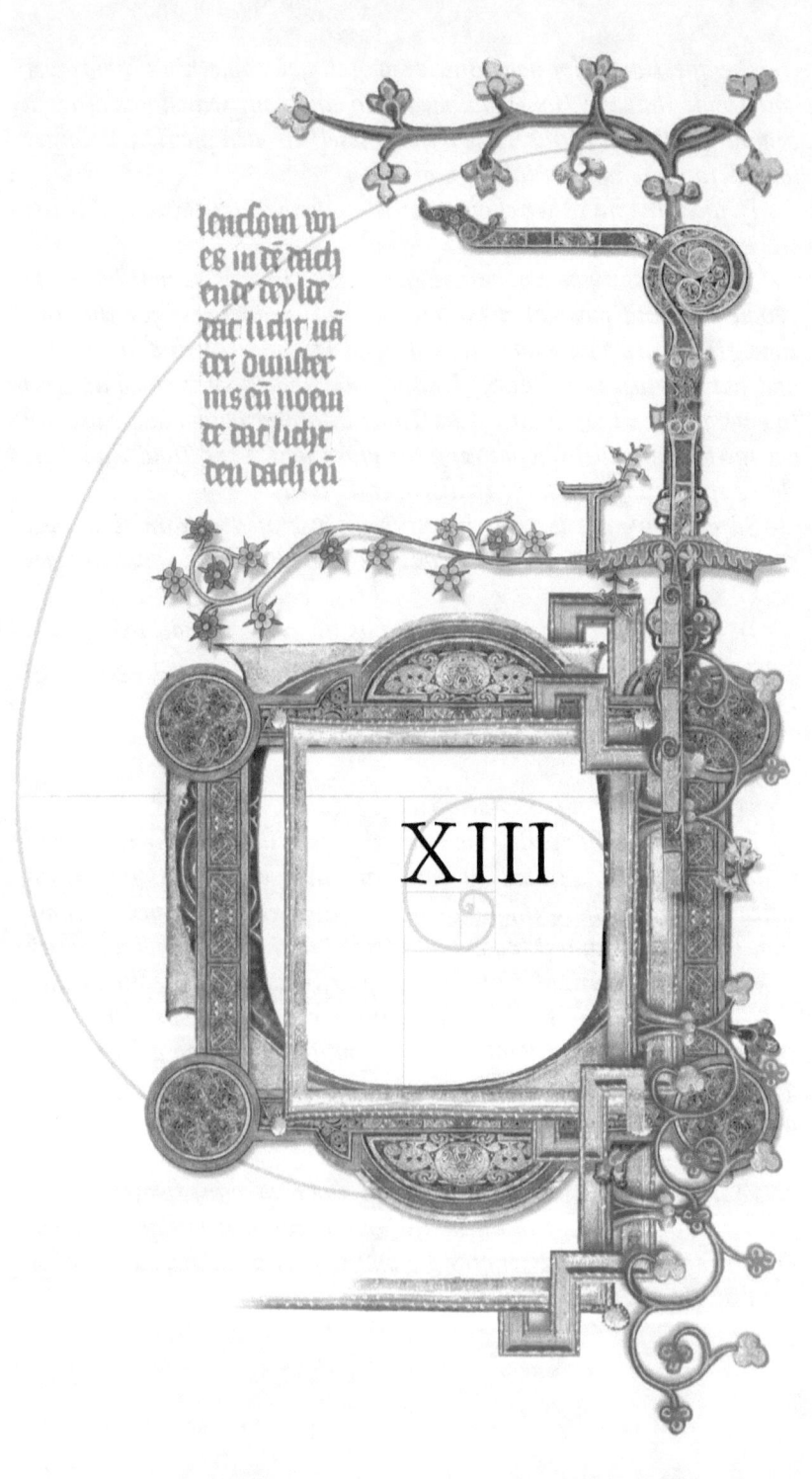

lenclom wi
es in de dach
ende dey lic
tac licht uñ
der dunster
nis eñ noetu
de dae licht
den dach eñ

XIII

Chapter XIII

The Consecration of the Phobia

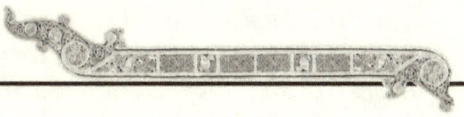

 hat do we do now? -I asked- what if we never go out of here? What are we going to do?

- Patience, dear Ad. Much patience.

- But, Master! How can I be patient in this situation?

- If you are not patient, you are going to be out of here even later than "never" and you do not want that. So... calm down!

My master folded his legs to get the posture of the *Szabeo Relevant Meditation.* Meanwhile, I peered into the darkness for any possible threat.

After a few moments, Reverend Ogli said:

- Interesting!

What can be so interesting? -I thought to myself, but I said nothing. I was furious. Interesting! Yes, of course!

- There is a suspicion about the whereabouts of Tablet of the Arcanum -my master continued- The Lapidarian Knights would have found it in a place known by the Lunilaic name of Ah-Lê-gönn that means "The one that cannot be found." It is also presumed that the knowledge about the name and location was yielded to them in an oddly condescending manner by one of the hermetic sects of initiated Lunilaics, that is, their extreme religious enemies. The similarity between Mal-ö-Goom, Ah-Lê-gönn and Mālegum, the mythological mountain of the Artícolas, is disturbing.

- But who were the Lapidarian Knights?

- Mmm... I think we have all the time to talk about anything you want to know, now. The Lapidarian Knights were the members of a religious and military organization, known in the Middle Era by the name of the Lapidarian Order. This Order was created with the aim of becoming the guard of the Sacred Gravestone, presumably found in the Temple of Jbur. At least, that is what they declared before the Øppos to get their recognition. It was a monastic order, but its monks dressed in armor, carried swords, and rode on sullen jralens. This kind of western warrior was known by the name of ceronte. In the Middle Era there were many cerontes, most of them were employed by dukes, princes, and kings of Galactia. Only the Lapidarian Knights were cerontes that, while owing allegiance to the Øppos, could be considered independent of the powerful aristocracy. They began as ten, and they were very poor. And so, they went to the Holy Land. A king and a bishop supported them with money and accommodation once they got there. The formal History of the Cruciglobist Church says so. In letters discovered by scholars of the past century onwards, evidence has been found that these ten were only the face of a hidden body among the same elite. The founders of the Lapidarian Order were more than ten, but not too many in order to keep the secret to good care. This order was one of the first secret societies seriously organized. This is at least what is inferred from the documentation. Lapidarian Knights had made a vow of poverty, chastity, and obedience. When the Order became important, a council was called to specify how these votes are understood. A list of seventy-two rules for monks-soldiers was prepared. Mass every day. Wear forever a white robe under the armor. For sleeping: shirt, shorts, one sheet and one blanket, even in the hot desert. Cleanliness once a week. Do not exchange garments. One plate for two and washing hands before eating; except in battle. Going to bed at sunset and rise at dawn, unless the journey has been hard in which case it is possible to sleep an extra hour on the condition of praying three times. Dealings with excommunicated are prohibited unless they have requested to enter the order. With female members, honor chastity. And so on... The top leader of the order was known as the Great Abbot. Passing through the intermediate ranges, the hierarchy ended with the squires. Each knight had three jralens and one squire, no luxury hanging from the jralen, simple weapons and steel gloves, modest armor, and a Lapidarian standard.

- But... why did they want to go the East to guard a gravestone?

- As part of the Redemption that the Campaign wanted to take to the East. To explain this, I have to go back a little. In my last explanation of the Rarefaction, I told you to the point where we had the planet divided between two religious powers, right?

- Yes, Master.

- Well... In the Cruciglobist part, you could not find a central government or at least one director who was not the Church. The emperor, who lived in Catatonia, ruled only in theory. The western part of his empire -that is, almost his entire domain- had been divided into a large number of local rulers, kings, and princes, who did not obey the orders from a distant emperor who lived near the Sea of Eca. The Cruciglobist Church was determined to not allow any temporal sovereign other than the Bishop of Marteria; that is, the Øppos. The Church had no formal mechanisms to exercise public authority. But if its power over the bodies was scarce, its influence over the souls was powerful. The Thinking Beings living in its domains believed that the church was able to seal their postmortem destiny. This was forceful enough to meekly subdue subjects and sovereign. So, when the Lunilaic Ahaxi was apparently preparing himself to attack Catatonia from Ru, the emperor Dox Ibi-Dor addressed urgently the Øppos Ubo II, that is, the Bishop of Marteria at that time. Ubo II, taking advantage of a great assembly of princes and priests gathered for something different, made them aware of the dangerous advance of the Lunilaicism. The eastern religion was arising as a great threat: it appeared to be hostile to the Cruciglobist and the Marterian Empire, which, as we said before, had a unique relationship of interdependency. His speech was so passionate that the enraged princes joined forces against the followers of the prophet Hasas. In turn, the sovereigns inflamed their respective subjects. Since Lunilaics were from the East, in other words, foreigners, xenophobia and religious hatred mingled in a single disgust. In the Cruciglobist centers, the holy war was preached; it was called "the Campaign." Since Jbur had fallen into Lunilaics hands and being the cradle of Cruciglobist religion, Westerners were urged to recover the holy city by force. A year later, the Campaign was a reality. From its early versions, the cerontes exhibited a cruelty out of control. Self-convinced of their exclusive role given by the Maker of All, they attacked anything that seemed to fall out of their idiosyncrasy. An inflamed crowd left Galactia and although it never got close to Catatonia, it left death and debris behind. The giddy cerontes took the Gerundian Cruciglobists by pagans just because they wore black robes. The people of that region were subjected to unspeakable cruelties before being killed. Another group attacked the Fraganis of Greso with outrageous violence: the Fraganis were a small and harmless sect relative to the Cruciglobists. The cerontes did not bother to ask before if they were Lunilaics or not. They looked different. That was all… Praise the Cruciglobist God, who is all love!

- They do not even know who they were killing?

- No. The second wave of Cruciglobist cerontes was more informed and organized. It was led by some dukes and princes of Galactia; the troops were made by subjects and Parietanians mercenaries. Ruban Ras-i, the Lunilaic sovereign of the ancient kingdom of Ghor, had no idea of the intentions brought by the Cruciglobist cerontes who had disembarked on the beach, but he had no doubt that it was an invasion. Ruban Ras-i ruled over one of the five falanjatos that formed the Lunilaic Empire, which was led by the Ahaxi from Rna. Ruban Ras-i knew he was not popular. The Cruciglobist rites were still practiced in Ru and Qia and the names of the emperor Dox Ibi-Dor and the Øppos were praised in secret. Fifty years ago, these were Western domains. Thus, although the falanjato government was Lunilaic, the population was Cruciglobist. Not in vain, this part of the Ahaxi domain was called "The Marterian falanjato."

My master drank ki-o and offered it to me too.

- Ru and Catatonia stared at each other from a distance, at either side of the Strait of Arteria. Like all descendants of nomads, Ruban Ras-i loved pillage and enjoyed the idea of owning the riches of the Dox Ibi-Dor. The Marterian emperor sensed the danger and distrusted the falanjato. In turn, Ruban Ras-i knew Dox Ibi-Dor had never lost hope to recover, if not the entire territory, at least Ru, sister city of Catatonia. He was also sure that the emperor would have the western support at any time he wanted. And that was exactly what had happened. Well… As soon as the Cruciglobist cerontes crossed the strait, they plundered the farmers, set the crops on fire, and apparently burned children alive. Before Ru, there was a fortress which was taken easily by the Cruciglobists. Inside, they found wine, beer, and juicy meat of turix. They ate and got drunk. The cruciglobas did not realize that they had fallen into a trap. The fountain, which supplied water to the fortress, was on its exterior.

The troops of Ruban Ras-i besieged the Cruciglobists and cut the water flow. Several days later, a terrible thirst arose among the besieged, who came to drink the blood of their animals and even their own fluids. A week later, The Second Campaign surrendered. Those who agreed to be converted to Lunilaicism were sent to the plague-ridden catacombs of Uss and Ntra. The rest of them -that is, more than twenty thousand- were killed by the sword. The younger female Cruciglobists, who had accompanied the cerontes, were distributed among the soldiers or sold into slavery. Such was the fair justice of the Lunilaic Fair God!

This time, it was I who sought ki-o.

- A year later -he continued- while Ruban Ras-i was out, the Cruciglobists disembarked again and surrounded the walls of Ru. However, the smart Ruanians saved their lives by surrendering to Dox Ibi-Dor rather than the Westerners. The emperor must have known that the population of Ru had been faithful to him, and also, the surrender was very convenient because it made clear that while the Cruciglobists of the Campaign were the conquistadors, the emperor was the one who ruled. It was no secret that Dox Ibi-Dor suspected the cerontes of the Campaign, once the provinces of Marteria were reconquered, they would not recognize his authority and would turn against him. Anyway... First Qia and then the whole Sea of Eca neighborhood came back to Marterians hands again. Meanwhile, Ruban Ras-i brought together most of the nomadic tribes as never before. It is said that his army filled the Atura steppe, which is almost as wide as the Green Sea of Damna. The Lunilaics had spies among the Marterians of Catatonia. With information about the itinerary of the Campaign, the high command of Ruban Ras-i planned an ambush. There was a long mountainous area that the Western troops had to cross and where they would become vulnerable. The place was called Elyústera. When the time came, the Lunilaics attacked the Cruciglobists, who were fewer than expected. The Cruciglobists were genuinely

surprised by the attack and retreated in a compact group. The Lunilaic combat tactics were infallible; repeated and perfected over a
half of a century, they had assured the military supremacy of the
Ahaxi warriors in the Eastern territory. The highest percentage
of fighters were light riders who rode on agile salamiondras and
handled the bow with swift dexterity. They used their great mobil-
ity and attacked in waves. When the enemy was within range, a
shower of arrows was unloaded to immediately make room for the
next line of archers. A few waves were enough to hurt the strongest
army. Finally, the Lunilaic infantry completed the work by direct
combat.

- So, they must have exterminated the Cruciglobists - I said.

- You will see! Ruban Ras-i and his generals incredulously watched
how ineffective their military tactics were. After several hours of
successive waves, they had caused only a little ravage in the Cruciglobist infantry; the bulk of the group remained intact. The same
attack against another army have sown anxiety and confusion; the
Cruciglobists gave no sign of impatience because they did not suffer
any damage. A Lunilaic chronicler noted that they were not even
interested in counterattacking.

- Why? What was happening?

- The reason for the indolence of the Cruciglobists was that they
had perfectly mastered their defensive technique, whose main argument was their body protection. Each ceronte was protected by
a metal layer made sometimes with plates, and sometimes with a
woven mesh. This kind of armor was very heavy and imposed on the
ceronte a rather clumsy movement. Despite this, the battle of Elyústera, or more properly, Jlyústera, is remembered as a Cruciglobist victory that showed the whole world that the cerontes were invincible.

- What happened then?

- If the Lunilaics would have continued in contention just a little
bit longer, gotten tired and been gone, it would not have become a
major thing. Who knows! But what happened was that the Lunilaic army was surprised from its rear by the bulk of the Cruciglobist
militia. The troops they had attacked turned out to be only an advanced scout for a larger army coming from behind, which consisted
of three hundred thousand cerontes. At the end of the day, the clarity abandoned Elyústera, leaving a carpet of corpses as wide as the
sky that certified their death. Praised be both gods!

Reverend Ogli paused.

- After this defeat -he continued- what remained of the army of Ruban Ras-i never regrouped again to contain the invasion. Apparently, the way was clear. The success, promised by this progress, made the Cruciglobists take the reconquest of Jbur for granted. This caused the emergence of other interests, dozing under their "missionary" vocation, saving for the future the main goal of the Campaign. In front of the huge bounty that the East began to show, the Cruciglobist captains, who in the West were potentates, began to think about their particular business. So, they took a time, a long time, to ensure the possessions that were divided among them, and had been transformed into fiefdoms, as in Galactia. It is easy to imagine that disputes over "military targets" in the name of God were common and they got resolved more with weapons than with sermons. To avoid interfighting in the Holy War, the domains were demarcated. That is why, at that time, duchies, counties, and kingdoms, as the Western custom, appeared in the East. But all this consumed a precious time in which the Lunilaic forces could recuperate.

Reverend Ogli stopped his story. He looked at his surroundings; there was only darkness.

- Allow me to tell you the rest, later, dear Ad. I am still sleepy, although I am not sure this is a night.

- Well, neither does it seems to be a morning.

- You are right, dear Ad. Try to rest.

- Good night, Reverend. Ogli! Or rather... Have a rest!

- Have a rest, disciple!

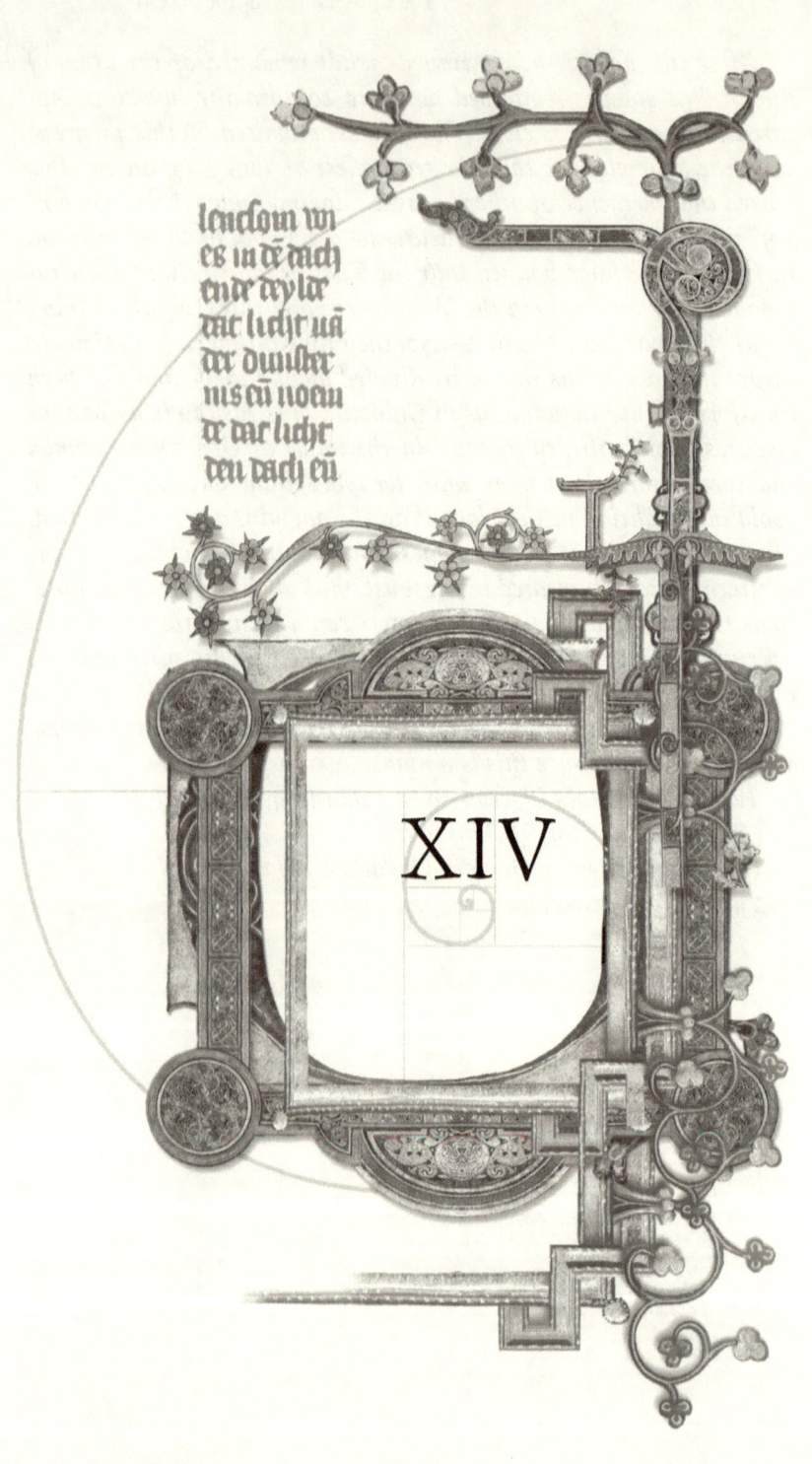

lencloín wi
es in de dach
en de dey lar
dar lichr nā
der dunsber
nis cū noctu
de dar lichr
den dach cū

XIV

Chapter XIV

The Perpetual Inertia

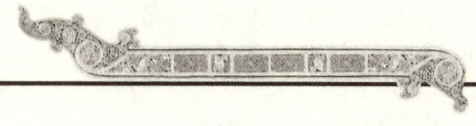

I woke up haunted by the nightmare I had. I rubbed my eyes. There was light. Wrestongres was in front of me, but the ground around it had disappeared, or rather, had sunk. Wrestongres was now occupying the top of a high elevation. I saw my master standing over the edge, and I ran to him. The landscape had been dramatically changed. We were on a titanic column created by kilometric hexagonal nerves of basalt rock.

Around us, only the mist hiding the bottom of the abyss was visible. A row of these hexagonal nerves, born from the depths of the mist, was attached to the large central pilaster forming a partition, a fin, a narrow bridge of uneven steps descending dreadfully across the clouds to get lost in the fog.

- Master, where are we?

- Do you ask me? I know the same as you.

So it was not a bad dream -I thought to myself- It's a real nightmare.

- And, what are we going to do? -I asked.

- I guess... to please the gnome -he replied, serenely.

- Hey! Where is Oj?

- Ah! You have already noticed that our knork is not here.

- And with the knork, our provisions are gone, Reverend Ogli.

- Yes, dear Ad. You are right. Only the backpacks we used as pillows have remained.

- We are going to die by starvation!

- Tranquility, dear Ad, tranquility -my master answered- We must descend the stone corridor as soon as possible. Perhaps, if we follow it, we will find something to eat.

- We do not have water either, Master.

- I think the seriousness of our situation is cooperating with the gnome. We have no choice but to enter into this unknown world. So... let's get going, dear Ad!

We collected the few things we still had and started to go down. Each step was a deathtrap, if not enough care was taken. The hexagonal surface of one or two nerves was frequently the entire floor of a single step. In addition, the succession of steps evolved irregularly. Sometimes it was necessary to let myself down to the next step; at other times the gap was not so much. I kept going down, holding myself onto the edges which was the equivalent of hanging most of the time. The basalt nerves had their cheeks completely smooth, and I did not want to bargain my safety. I did not trust those polished rocks plunging to the sides of the narrow aisle. Any slip and I would have gone to feed the vacuum.

The arms of the wind kept pushing us, as if trying to throw us off balance. My brain was successfully fighting against the terror of the abyss, but my feet were hesitating every step. I felt weak and disjointed. I was shaking. I was terrified. My master noticed my distress. He pulled out a rope from his backpack and tied himself to me. For a moment, I thought that by doing so, we only connected our deaths, and I got frightened

- Almost there. Courage, dear disciple! -my master inculcated in me- Just a little more. These stairs widen over there.

I do not know how long that awful descent lasted, but there was a moment that it finally ended. Since the width of the corridor tripled, the ferocity of the vacuum decreased.

- Do you feel better, dear Ad?

- Yes, Master. Thank you.

- You never get emboldened but are brave. I am very proud of you, Ad-d-Tuar.

- Thank you! I hope to always be worthy of your pride, Master.

- No doubt about it -he replied- Now, if you put your apprehension aside, maybe you will make room for the beauty and discover in the monster the wonder it really is.

- Are you asking me to admire the emptiness, Master?

- Just the opposite: I am asking you to disregard the immaterial and concentrate on what is tangible. If you do that, the corridor will be left in all its glory.

- I see!

- It looks like a monumental work of art designed by an artist with geometric tendencies. Each nerve emerges from who knows where as a genuine hexagonal column. Every nerve is a gigantic basalt crystal that has been excessively developed sideways than width-wise. All the nerves have the same shape because the angles between the faces of a crystal are invariant for each substance.

If we were in our real world, we could say that this mountain formation is of volcanic origin; the lava cooled slowly, and this gave the basalt time to crystallize. On the other hand, while cooling, the basalt may have cracked according to the crystallographic laws. As I said, if we were in our world...

- Are we in another world, Reverend Ogli?

- Rather, I think we are, so to speak, in another dimension.

- Why just "so to speak"?

- Because this would not be what I expect from another dimension. Indeed, if this were the case, I would not expect to be able to distinguish it.

- I do not understand, Master.

Mmm... Let us return for a moment to the fear of heights you have. You, like everyone else, perceive reality through your eyes. But your eyes were smudged by the aversion you have for the precipices. This alteration operates directly on your perception, transforming the reality into a form that is particularly yours: an abominable reality. This impediment excluded you from admiring its beauty. In the same way, the reality perceived by the Thinking Being through his senses is his particular way of reality, different from the knork, for example. Our eyes see a small part of the electromagnetic spectrum: the colors. We are not able to see the other rays, such as ultraviolet, infrared, gamma or cosmic rays striking a plate of peas. The true reality is, therefore, outside the scope of our perception. The true reality would be much more complicated than what our brain can handle. Our reality is the adaptation of a bigger one to the possibilities of our brain. Some believe that the space, as we conceive it is not real, it is subjective; it is only an approximation. The true relation between the bodies, which are out of our reach, is translated to the possibilities of comprehension of our mind. When you take a cube in your hands, you see it as a cube, you feel it like a cube, because that is what is transmitted by our senses. But this transmission is a translation, is an adaptation of the true reality to the possibilities of our understanding. Then how would the shape of a cube be in its original version, without the translation?

- In other words, the way that our eyes cannot see and our brain cannot conceive?

- Exactly! -my master said- Can you answer that?

- Of course not! I cannot describe what is inconceivable.

- You have the same problem as an inhabitant of a two-dimensional world when he wants to conceive a cube.

- How?

- I think I can explain it widely since this corridor is running almost horizontally and, although we have come a long way, nothing seems to announce that this situation will be altered.

- We cannot see where we are heading either. There is so much fog that we could even crash into something as we walk.

- Yes! It is as if we were going through a cloud. Anyway... Let's talk about a Planarian, the inhabitant of a flat world. A flat world would be immeasurably thinner than a sheet of paper as it does not possess thickness at all. Our Planarian only recognizes length and width. He does not suspect the possibility of something with a height as well. The presence of a cube in his world would not be recognized as a cube: if the Planarian approaches and examines it, he would tell you "I found a square!" That is, he would see only the intersection of the cube with the plane of the two-dimensional world. Imagining a cube would be inconceivable for him.

- I see! But in my case, what is the body that I could not conceive?

- It would be not even a body -my master answered- We are beings who inhabit a world of three dimensions. We can speculate and even state that we understand the one-dimensional world, the two-dimensional world and ours. We would say, for example, what is a line in a one-dimensional world, is a square in a two-dimensional world, and a cube in a three-dimensional world. But the list of the intelligible concepts ends here. What we cannot even imagine is a world with four dimensions. The "body" relative of cube, the one we cannot conceive, is called a hypercube. We can give it any name that comes to mind because we have to call it something, but we will never understand it. Let's see, try it for yourself! Try to imagine a dimension other than length, width or depth that forms 90 degrees with the other three.

- Let me think, Master.

One can try all day long and... nothing. After a while, I just got bored...

- Some people say they can do it. They say it is a matter of training. Mmm... I do not think so! -my master said- But I believe in the possibility that someone would see us in the same way we observe the stubborn beetle going around and around our finger.

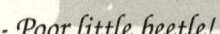

- What about the beetle?

- The beetle perceives the world in two dimensions. According to him, he is fleeing from the danger in a straight line; while for us, instead, it is just spinning. It cannot imagine a curved surface.

- Poor little beetle!

- That is why a known philosopher once said: "A science of all these kinds of space, spaces of more than three dimensions, will certainly be the highest enterprise a finite understanding could undertake."

- Are there more dimensions than the fourth dimension?

- There might! In the same way, there is an eye watching the beetle, perhaps there is an eye watching us. Perhaps the owner of this eye would also be the subject of observation by other, even greater, according to the spiralizing formula of the divine proportion. Remember?

- Yes, I remember! "...We would find ourselves, then, in front of an inconceivable logarithmic spiral of observers or simply in front of the unintelligible iris of God."

The fog did not let us see that we had approached a turret attached to the basaltic corridor. It was a turret as those castles have at the corners to watch passersby; like a battlement. Was it a resting area? A refuge? A lookout post for some guards out of service? We had no answer. The only certainty was that this edification looked delicately magnificent, like an expensive ornament in a showcase. It had been executed with a tightly Lunilaic taste.

Its polished skin was made of green malachite. It was illuminated by an organic shine; the glow of the hot live bodies. A mineral greenery writhed, pierced, and crisscrossed itself, raising the bas-relief of an oriental, graceful, and pointed dome. Once inside, we realized the profusion of beauty used in decorating its intimate atmosphere. The central dome opened in four ogives supported by columns; the two smaller ones on either side of the aisle worked as windows, the other two as entries. The ornamental design of each inner surface of the dome, and also the design of the floor, was the consequent extension of the double diamond depicted by a central mosaic, where miniatures were plentiful. On the floor, surrounding the central design, a written message was highlighted in a language that my teacher could recognize.

- It is written in Zhski -my master explained to me- the sacred language of the Lunilaics. It says: "For those who truly seek God: the splendid arcades will splash drops of light."

- But what does it mean?

- I do not have the slightest...

A colossal bang faded the last sentence of my teacher. We covered our ears as we turned around quickly. The fog descended violently as if it was plunged through a drain hidden in the bottom of the abyss. The panorama was abruptly exposed. We could see the entire landscape. At the bottom, a dim twilight poorly distributed its clarity. In front, a moon-like valley, gloomy and lacerated by craters, stretched boundless. In between, the mountain crowned by Wrestongres stood out and, as a candle drip, the corridor through which we had descended. But part of the corridor we had left behind in our walk seemed mutilated; several parts of it were gone. Its long row threw us a toothless smile.

The corridor has collapsed! -I said.

- Interesting! It seems that the fog and debris came down together.

-The mutilated basalt corridor looked now like a folding screen of monumental proportions that separated the moon-like scene in two gray environments, carpeted by ashes. I felt extremely small. An idea troubled me... with the corridor collapsed, there was no way back to Wrestongres.

- But how do we go back? -I asked my master- We're trapped!

- Calm, dear Ad, much calm. We must solve the problems as they arise. "How to return?" This is a question for later. I sense that this path will be strewn with other questions that we have to answer first. Let's get going, dear Ad!

Later, the corridor evolved with more and more conflict up to the point of stumbling with the folds of a mountain range of piled up peaks. We were heading over there, impelled by the resolute firmness of my master. The landscape remained bleak and gray.

After a long stretch in which Reverend Ogli told me about the telepathic force, we finally reached the congested part of the journey. The road, flat and smooth before, became intricate. Its blind curves went around the hills which gradually took more height. It looked to me that we were entering into a trap for rodents.

Just after a sharp curve...

- What is this?

The road was covered with skeletons. There were vertebrae here, skulls there, and many whole skeletons lounged in various positions. Perched on a rock, a contrived wheel was spinning freely on a stand decorated with a strange taste.

- Master! -I cried, driven by terror.

- Calm, dear Ad, much calm! Actually, nothing has happened to us yet, so there is no reason to be alarmed.

- But, Master, don't you see how many have died here?

- I only see bones, dear Ad. Let's find out what is happening here!

We approached to examine the wheel, opening our way through the ossuary. The wheel spun, in an imperceptible way, frictionless, free, without complaint. My teacher praised its construction and detail. The kinetic images produced by the spokes of the wheel caught my attention.

- Ad! -my master exclaimed after giving a few steps- Look!

I saw Reverend Ogli touching the air. Yes, touching the air! Beyond the wheel, the atmosphere was frozen, solid. Although we did not understand the nature of this phenomenon, it was clear that it was a barrier.

- Who are those who want to pass? -a voice from behind said.

My master and I turned around to find the possible source of the voice.

- It does not matter! All of you want the same -it was heard.

- There! -I shouted, pointing to the center of the wheel- A face!

- True! -my master said- The circular movement of the wheel spokes creates the static image of a face.

- *Good start! -the face said- It looks like we are going to understand each other very easily. And what needs to be understood is that if you want to pass beyond, you should stop this wheel. This is the time wheel which rotates with perpetual motion. If you do not make it stop, you will spend the rest of eternity waiting for someone else capable of doing it and saving you. Needless to say, that, before that happens, you will already have died.*

I stepped forward with my hand stretched to stop the wheel.

- *No! -my master yelled- Do not touch it, Ad! That would be the most obvious. Perhaps, that is exactly what is expected from us. The skeletons show us that the most obvious solution leads to failure.*

- *So, how to stop it? If we let it rotate freely, the eternity would be spent before the wheel stops because it has that perpetual motion thing. And if we stop it, we will follow the fate of the skeletons. What do we do?*

- *There is no such thing as perpetual motion. I just remembered that in ancient times, people pursued the construction of machines with continuous movement. One of the most famous machines was due to the inventiveness of Ubirtas-Ev, wise-artist of King Erck's court, of Primaria. The inventor introduced it as an entertainment during the wedding of the king's daughter for whom he worked and who kept him busy working on irrelevant projects. The wheel showed a sign stating that no one would be able to stop its movement. The courtiers who tried to stop the wheel came one after another. To everyone's astonishment, as someone removed the hand from the wheel, it resumed the circular movement by itself. Nobody could stop it!*

- *But master, why do you remember that kind of things, right now, when we are in danger?*

- *Because history is a wise counselor and it is also wise not to wait for our own direct observation but learning from other's experiences.*

- *So, what does history teach us?*

- *Well, no one could stop that wheel because no one came to think that if the wheel kept turning, it was precisely because, as they tried to stop it, they pushed back a mechanism for winding a secret coil, hidden on the same axis of the wheel. So, dear Ad, the key is to avoid touching it. It will stop by itself. We just have to wait!*

We waited. And the wait was quite prolonged. While I despaired, my master remained calm and firm in his decision. There was a time when the face began to blur.

- I think you have won! -the face said- In a few moments, when I fade away completely, you can pass freely.

- Is it possible that you answer a question first? -my master asked to the face.

- I guess you have also earned that right -the face said with a hint of kindness- But only one!

- Thank you! As I understand it, the magician Wgïjvrán tried to find the Holy Råål to restore the health of King Ngupd. So, what was...

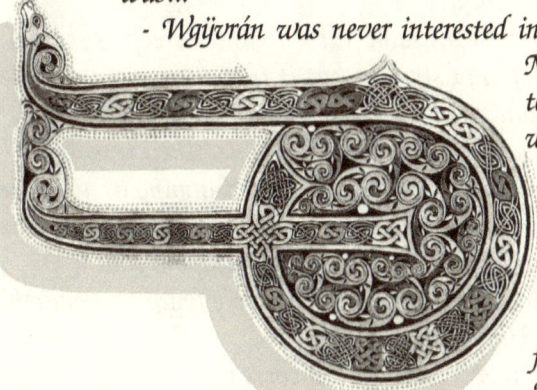

- Wgïjvrán was never interested in the health of King Ngupd! -the face interrupted my master who had not yet asked the question.

- No? What was he really interested then?

- He was looking for his own triumph! He wanted to become the most famous magician of all history -the face said it as if it were obvious- From the chronicles of the King Ngupd knights, he became aware of the magic of the East, notable for the dominance of transmutations. It was then, when he wanted to add this ability to the bunch he already handled with absolute proficiency. But I cannot answer your question now.

- But...!

- I am sorry! I'm... fading... out...

The wheel's speed had decreased significantly. The face extinguished altogether.

We left behind the macabre scene and continued on our way. Reverend Ogli sunk into silence. He was occupied for a long time, I suppose, in reflections born of the encounter with the face. Only after a long time, he finally said...

- I would never have expected to find such correspondence between the history of the Campaign and the literature about wizards and the literature about wizards and dragons. There is no consistency, it is true, but the equivalences are remarkable. I am going to quote things that were real and others that were not, but both keep a clear twinning. For example, the Lapidarian Knights really existed; the King Ngupd Circle of Knights did not. the Campaign of the Cruciglobist church on Lunilaic land was real; the travels of the King Ngupd knights in search for the Holy Råål was not. And besides, there is a story from the time of the Campaign that tells us about the most famous Lunilaic magician and his transmuting skills.

- Yes?

- Truly! It's a fascinating story. It is a story that happened in... Ah! But what's happening?

At that precise moment the sand fluctuated, the creepers seemed to flow, the rocks shrank and stretched as if they were images of flexible mirrors. All around us was unstable and wavy.

Suddenly, seven warriors appeared before us. They threatened us with their weapons. On their heads, I noticed a mimetronic system of camouflage; that is why we thought they came out of nowhere. One of them, the one who was without any weapon, said:

- Consider yourselves prisoners of King Igre, almighty monarch of the Orthuno Hived Unity.

Without another word, we were escorted to the highest hills that we had spotted from the Lunilaic turret. Closely watched, the countless number of openings in the mountainous matter were obvious. It was a tunnel system. Each outer hole was reached by the free ends of a chaotic knot of stairs intertwined under the ground level. However, we could not see anybody going over them. Inside the mountain, a real underground metropolis palpitated. It was a buried colony like those built by the insects of the wood or those that produce honey. It seemed to be an urban system based on the assembly of hexagonal cells, inhabited by those who called themselves Etunnians. Etunnian workers could not make their hexagonal cells other than one by one. For some natural reason, the minimum amount that they could construct at a time was a set of five hexagonal cells. Perhaps this peculiarity responded to an evolutionary conditioning regarding speed, since it seems logical that it takes less time to build the same wall in this way. The different conformations that could be produced by combining five hexagons in a single figure resulted in

22 variations. With these conformations, the Etunnians were happy because they offered enough variety, so they do not get bored as they lift their walls.

- I am surprised you have not known -the unshakable King Igre said, addressing us from his throne- that any foreigner who comes too close to my kingdom is eliminated by beheading unless he solves the problem that has puzzled the Etunnians since long ago.

The fact is that the Etunnians, at some period of their history, had converted to Lunilaicism and wanted, more than anything else, to build a temple to celebrate their ceremonies. The problem then became obvious: how to combine the different conformations of five hexagons to represent the symbol of Lunilaicism the best they can?

- Well! -King Igre said- I have informed you, so it will not be said that I did not warn you.

And, pointing out with his scepter, he ordered:

- Guards! Take these two to the dungeons.

Two guards behind, one in front, escorted us across a network of hexagonal corridors with the tips of their spears at our backs. At times, we descended; other times we moved in a straight line, but the stretches were indistinguishable from each other. It would have been impossible to escape. What we noticed was that as we descended, the skin of the cells became less and less translucent.

- Rev. Ogli asked the guard who was going in front of us:

- How long are we going to be in jail?

- If the imprisonment upsets you, do not worry -he replied- You will not be locked away long. Executions are usually performed at the end of the day, and we're almost done for today.

We were then held in a dark cell. I started with my complaints and Reverend Ogli -I should have known- asked me to be patient. Then he pulled his travel notebook out from his backpack. Pencil in hand, he fell into prolonged abstractions that finally resulted in something that, at the end of the day, satisfied the almighty King of the Etunnians, but only after talking to his circle of counselors.

- Serve odopa to the foreigners! -King Igre ordered- The best odopa we have!

Half Moon Proposed by Rev. Ogli

Would you like to participate in the test the almighty King Igre imposed to Reverend Ogli and little Ad? Then solve the following problems in the order in which they appear:

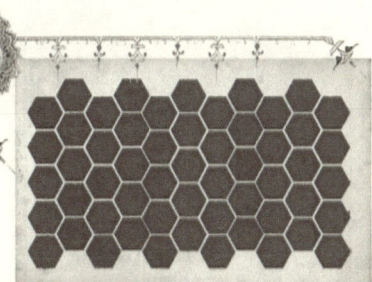

1. Find the remaining 19 configurations formed by combining five hexagons.

2. Using all 22 configurations, can you form a rectangular Etunnian wall?

3. Finally, you can find out how Reverend Ogli organized the crescent which satisfied the King?

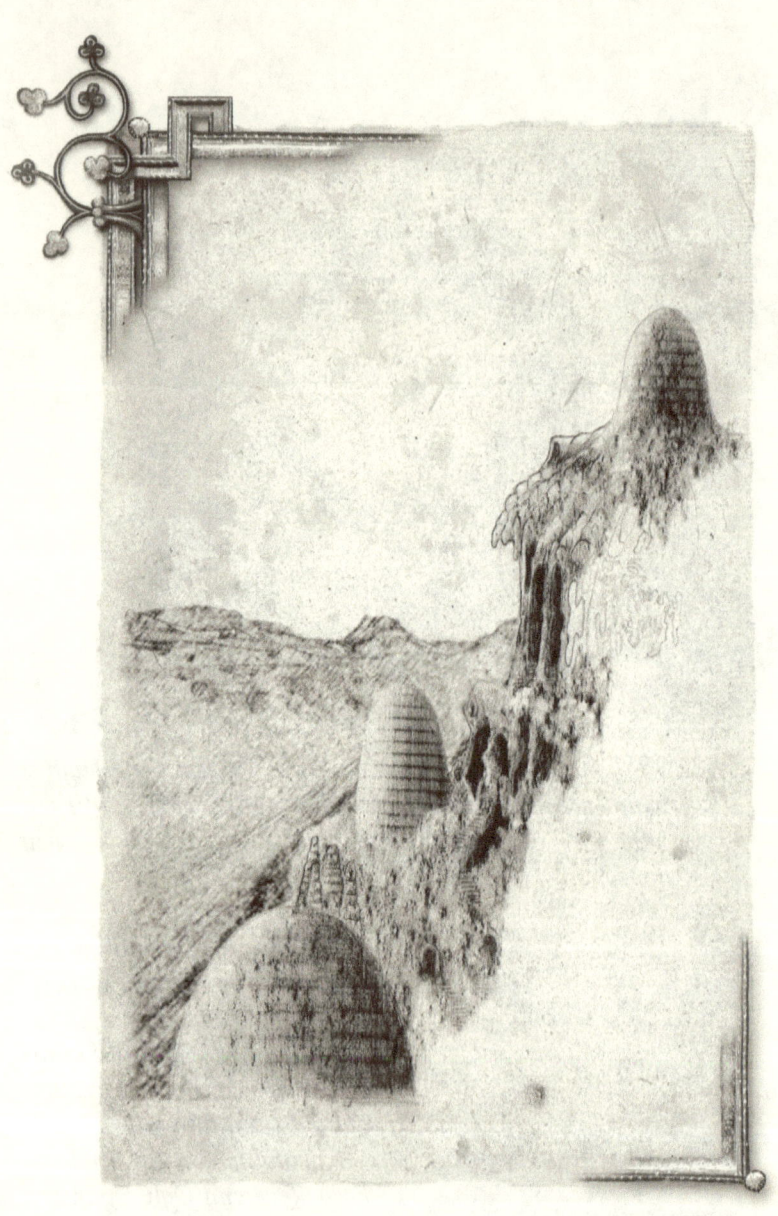

Etunnian Landscape

Chapter XV

A Specular Omen

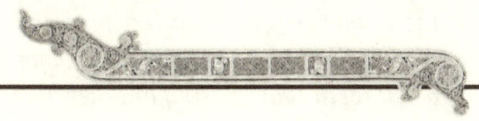

e drank odopa! My master took advantage of the closeness that the celebration gave us to ask King Igre a question...

    - Your Majesty, would you tell me what direction should I take to find the Holy Råål?

- Apparently, you are one of those looking in the dark.

- Yes, your Majesty. You cannot distinguish the light looking at the light... and sometimes, in daylight, one must feel the way.

-As you like! Once you are outside the Royal Hive, take the same way you have entered. You will reach the next-to-last station at the rear of the city. Then ask for the Well of Amargutta. Once you are there, choose the stony path that descends through the forest of trepanos.

- Where does the path lead?

- To the Holy Råål -the King answered- of course!

- I mean, what will be my immediate destination?

- No more questions! I have already said more than I should -he replied with renewed curtness- And now I will ask you to leave because the construction work will begin immediately.

We had no problem finding the paved road that descends through the forest of trepanos.

- Master -I said very honestly- I do not know what would have happened without you. I would not have been able to solve the problem.

- Dear Ad, I fear that if I would not have been with you, you would not have to go through this.

We went through the woods, always on the road of stones. Once we entered into the deep forest, the road stumbled and, as one of many roots, it was getting more and more twisted. The fur of the forest hid furtive glances and fleeting jumps; snaky curls hung from the branches proposing festivals and revelry. A young river had already joined the carnival with vigor and pirouettes. A reptile with black teeth was chasing another, fatter and lame. I picked up a half rotten trunk. I glimpsed a zigzag. Something jumped in terror. A flow of vinegary aromas reached my nose. What a way for a road to be joyful!

- How different is this from the sandbanks we crossed before -I remarked to my master- I did not like the sandbanks because they are dry, and they do not inspire in me a good mood.

- It is like the soul when it is not irrigated -he replied- Even the brightness flees from the dry stones.

It seemed to me appropriate to remind my master that, before being surprised by the Etunnians, he promised me a story of sorcerers.

- The story has to do with The Second Campaign -he said- The falanjato of Ghor, first to be conquered by the Cruciglobists, had boundaries with Rjostos. Ruban Ras-i thought of presenting resistance to the Campaign with the military forces of the Rjostos governor. But at that time, Rjostos did not have one governor but two. Each maintained its own capital: one in Ntra and the other in Urse. That was how Ruban Ras-i found Rjostos, too divided to present a relevant defense. The governors were unwilling to cooperate even against a common enemy; such was the resentment between them. It was an internal matter concerning a noble family; a matter on which the Ahaxi was relieved to intervene, according to tradition. Some believe that the real reason consisted in the problem of being fair in such a strange issue. Sammkara had always been an area more attached to the magic beliefs than the protectorate of Rjostos. The previous and only governor, Eb al-Tar, belonged to the Yhaguim, eleventh jeadi family, direct descendants of Anahd-Ir. This family never did anything without the support and approval of a mentor, usually a soothsayer sorcerer. Everything that was connected with magic was feared and respected. Hutribe, famous magician of Urse, when it was Marterian, had cast a spell on the young Eb al-Tar at the precise moment he forced the gates of the city. The necromancer shouted: "Your first child shall execute you, betray his blood and return this city." The young conqueror took it very seriously and always avoided having children. But when he was appointed Governor of the Falanjato of Rjostos, the customs of the Lunilaic hierarchs required him to have a progeny. Or he rather had children or ceded his post to a relative of the same lineage. Eb al-Tar measured the possibilities, weighing what he could lose, and then, decided something quite twisted: he would have a child to meet the demands of their distinction, but he would kill him immediately to extinguish the bad omen. He had then a wedding and sometime later his wife gave birth. To his dismay, the woman he had chosen gave birth not to one but to two babies. Eb al-Tar was terrified. The Yhaguim firmly believed that if two children are born at the same time, one comes from God and the other from the Devil. At first, the governor thought of killing both, but then he assumed that if one of them brought the blessing of God, he could not get rid of him without suffering some punishment. Thus, besieged by fate, Eb al-Tar did nothing. The twins grew up with the names of O-Tar and E-Tar. The problem would have been simplified if it would have been possible to distinguish the "good" from the "bad." It was said that the only one who could tell them apart was a blind beggar who spent the night on the steps of the temple of Sidra, somewhere in the underground of Ebra. However, the beggar disappeared before been brought to Eb al-Tar. The years passed and the governor of Rjostos came to love his children as any other parent. He also feared and distrusted them as only he could.

- Of course! -I interrupted.

- In the entire falanjato, there were only two people who knew the fears of the governor: general Eli-vé and AloOf, the most renowned sorcerer who ever existed in the East.

- As Wgijvrán in the West.

- Yes, but the magic he used came from very different necromantic obscurities and with different characteristics.

- Perhaps, precisely because of that, Wgijvrán wanted the knowledge of AloOf. He wanted the total power!

- Perhaps, dear Ad. But let's go back to the story I was telling you. Eli-vé and Eb al-Tar were brothers-in-arms. He had accompanied him from a young age and was unconditionally faithful. AloOf was the advisor of the palace, someone without whose assent nothing could take place. That being said, there was no sign to direct suspicion of malice toward one or the other brother. Nothing, except a very subtle detail: E-Tar expressed an undeniable preference for the city of Urse. The two children used to play imagining the future. In this game of clairvoyance, E-Tar almost always adjudicated the city of Urse as part of his heritage. AloOf was the first to notice it and warned the governor. Then Eb al-Tar became indecisive. E-Tar had always been the most loving son and it was not easy for him to accept what AloOf suggested. On the other hand, the years had stolen the necessary indolence to kill a child. In addition, the evil omen, after all this time, resounded with less force in his spirit. Anyway, he did not like at all the idea that the curse was going to be fulfilled. So, he decided to take E-Tar away to the palace of Qtobe in Sammkara. There, he was educated in science and indoctrinated in Lunilaicism by a dozen of teachers. E-Tar could move through the palace as much as he wanted but could never get out of there. His situation was similar to a prisoner, closely and permanently monitored.

A few years before the Cruciglobist attack on Ru, some guards of Ntra, who did the rounds before dawn, found the body of Eb al-Tar in the palace gardens. Judging by the state of his bones, his body seemed to have suffered a fall from a very high altitude or had been crushed by a great pressure or a combination of both misadventures. Among the guards, a rumor spread: his chest had signs of having been wounded by the claws of a huge bird. Immediately, O-Tar took control, ascended the throne, and vowed to avenge the death of his father. He proclaimed that it was a demonic act, and then he revealed the prophecy of Hutribe to the people. And the people of Ntra asked for the head of E-Tar who was in Qtobe. Without delay, the personal guard of O-Tar left for Sammkara. The guard was formed by members of an armed sect called asasshans, from where the word assassin comes. They had orders to capture E-Tar. In some obscure way, still unexplained, E-Tar was warned and fled from Qtobe. Then, he crossed the falanjato of Rjostos disguised as a pariah. Finally, he reached Urse, where he was proclaimed governor as soon the city guard recognized him.

- For this reason, Ruban Ras-i found two governors when he came asking for help against the Cruciglobists of The Second Campaign. Right?

- Indeed, dear Ad -my master replied- While the Cruciglobist leaders of The Second Campaign fought over the city of Ghor, in Rjostos occurred what has been called "The War of the Brothers." Isinalaq Al-Ban, who was a chronicler who lived in Urse, refers to this dispute in the following terms: "O-Tar, with just twenty years, apparently, has fallen under the influence of a physician-astrologer who belongs to the order of the Asasshans. He is accused, not without reason, to use these fanatics to eliminate his opponents with crimes, wickedness and witchcraft." Urse and Ntra took their respective monarchs for good ones. Each capital had allied cities, which does not mean they were friends with each other. For this reason, when the Cruciglobists set foot on Rjostorian territory, they found in it the greatest possible disunity. Thode Le-Cons was a ceronte leader who was ahead of the other commanders. Dixan of Cinea, a Cruciglobist monk who accompanied Thode Le-Cons, wrote: "Our Champion did not know which city to attack since all needed redemption. The Providence put in our way a Rjostorian shepherd, whose name was Tja-ib. Although later, from the walls of Urse, someone shouted him: "Aphir-ig-Eli-vé," which means "Damned Eli-vé." Tja-ib, or whatever he was called, led us to Urse assuring us that if we took it, other allied cities would surrender immediately."

- Was that true?

- Well... maybe there was a more powerful reason. There was a legend about Urse. Gasto Visio was a Marterian monarch who ruled Rjostos from Urse before the Lunilaic conquest. According to the legend, after seeing the city threatened, he hid somewhere a fabulous treasure he had found in the Enchanted Valley of Souh. It knew exactly where, since Gasto Visio took the secret to his grave. The truth is that the Thode Le-Cons army gathered together outside the walls. There were seven thousand Lunilaic soldiers inside, while the Cruciglobists reached thirty thousand fighters. E-Tar was calm because the walls of Urse were impenetrable: twelve kilometers of hewn stone and three hundred sixty turrets kept inside a scene with houses, buildings, gardens, and large fields for agriculture and grazing knorks, asnifos and other gramidontes. On the west side, the wall ascended by the side of a rocky mountain and crowned it with a wall impossible for an assault. From that same side of the mountain and in front of the wall, the On-uo river flowed down, stumbling between rapids and waterfalls. The river ran along the west side of the wall, along the north side and then, curving south, wrapped the east side with its bed. It was a natural obstacle not easy to overcome. On-uo means "ambidextrous," because sometimes it gave the impression that the water ran upwards. The south side was the safest and formed the back of the fort: where the wall ended, a precipice continued. Here, the waters of the On-uo river fell off a cliff. The rocky face of the abyss seemed to be an extension of the architectural wall. Riostos was a steep region and for strategic reasons, the cities were raised where the landscape offered the availability of a deadly emptiness. On the top of the northwest side, a pipe system collected the water and transported it in. Once the waters were soiled, they were released into the precipice. It was absurd to besiege the city, hoping to exhaust their resources. If, despite this, somebody would have insisted on the idea, it was impossible to go around completely. But allow me to suspend the story at this point because I feel that we must turn our attention to other matters.

Indeed, before us, a river of serene appearance interrupted the stone path. At the edge of the river, we found a forest dweller who explained to us that the river was full of pezarañas. If we wanted to, he could carry us in his canoe. But because it was a small canoe, the maximum weight that it could accept, besides his own, was Reverend Ogli's weight. Therefore, I had to wait my turn. Besides his canoe, the jungle dweller had a big bowl of grains, one sotro and one eredona. While carrying my master, the forest dweller asked me to make sure the sotro does not eat the grain nor the eredona eats the sotro. So, I did it and no one ate anyone. My master was on the other side and the jungle dweller returned with his canoe. But when he was with me, he said:

- It's time to see if you are worthy of my help.
- Oh no! -I said to myself- Here we go again!

- You are by yourself -he said- I am actually a shaman. To drive the canoe of a shaman you only need to dip the tip of your oar; the canoe will take you wherever you want. Your task is to carry the bowl with grains, the sotro and the eredona, making sure that no one eats the other. But you will be dipping the oar and have no way to take care of them. If only one grain is missing, the canoe would split in two and you would be devoured by the pezarañas.

Before continuing, dear reader, would you like to solve the problem by yourself?

I knew it! -I thought- Now I'm really in trouble! My master cannot help me since he is on the other side. He does not even know what is going on. Calm! -I said to myself- Keep calm, dear Ad!

- One more thing -the shaman said- A minimum weight is required for the canoe to work.

- And which one is it?

- Any weight higher than yours.

I took a long time to make a decision. The first time I came to the opposite shore, I found my master very worried, but he calmed down and even congratulated me for what I had done. I brought two things with me: the eredona, and the grains. I left the eredona but I returned with the bowl of grains. When I was back on the first shore, I left the grains. I took the sotro and went to the other side where Reverend Ogli and the eredona were. Then, I left the sotro. I took the eredona and returned with it. Finally, I took the bowl with grains and returned with both.

- Congratulations, dear Ad! -my master said- I am very proud of you.

Needless to say, I felt as if I had been the hero of the day... until my master told me what had happened on the other side.

Apparently, the shaman had a split, that is, a part of him had crossed the river to talk with me and another had been talking to Reverend Ogli. While I dealt with the issue of the grain, the sotro and the eredona, the shaman demanded from my master to do the Devil's Signature which, as everyone knows, cannot be done! The Devil's Signature should be drawn without repassing over any line. It is possible, however, to cross any line that has already been drawn. The Devil's Signature must be drawn without lifting your hand at any time, that is, with a continuous line. Everyone will agree that the

Devil's Signature is impossible without disobeying the last rule. It was obvious that my teacher had passed the test because I had survived the condition the shaman imposed on him: if you do not do the Devil's Signature -he said to my master- when your little friend tries to cross the river, the canoe will split in two and he will fall into the water and will be devoured by the pezarañas.

I must also confess that once I reached the other side on my first trip, it occurred to me that if I was already there, there was no reason to return. But Reverend Ogli thought it was prudent not to cheat, because I had practically solved the riddle, and a cheat could unleash unpredictable consequences.

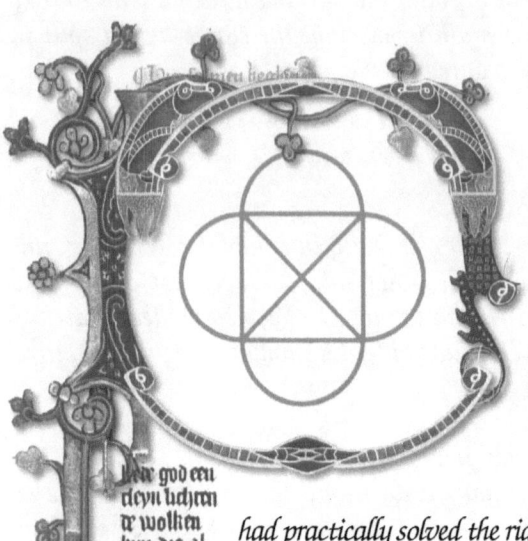

- The explanation of what I did with the shaman has to do with what I had explained to you about the impossibility of superposing two enantiomorphic images. Do you remember what happened when I asked you to superpose the letter L to its enantiomorphic image?

- Of course! -I remembered perfectly-. A complex figure was formed. Instead of having the top image completely hiding the other one, the lower image showed parts uncovered.

- In other words, they were impossible to superpose.

- Yes, Master.

If you have never tried to draw the Devil's Signature, do it so before continuing reading. Could someone tell how did my master draw the Devil's Signature without repassing any line and without raising his hand?

- In a two-dimensional world, if we do not take into account the paper on which our Ls were drawn, these "bodies" do not have thickness.

Now, if you could lift one of the Ls from the paper, turn it around in the air and put it back on the other L, then yes, you would have overlapped the Ls and they would appear as one. Instead of two Ls, you would see only one. You could say, then, that the two-dimensional figure, one L, turned around in the three-dimensional space and returned as its reversed version to its two-dimensional environment. That is to say, if it was once an L, after the rotation, it is an inverted L. In this way, an enantiomorphic inversion would have occurred. Do you agree?

- Yes, Master.

- Let's call our Planarian friend again, inhabitant of the two-dimensional world. First, if he could see a superposing like that, he would not understand it. For him, there was an L that simply disappeared and returned flipped. Second, if someone would ask him to make an enantiomorphic inversion using the same method we used, it would be impossible for him because he does not know how to get out of his planar world, otherwise he would have a concept of thickness. He would not know how to flip anything in an environment of a higher dimension and return it to his two-dimensional world. He could not even understand what you ask! His eyes could only see lines and coplanar points. In his world, there would be no vertical lines; nothing could ascend, descend, rise or sink; these concepts would not exist for him. How could you ask him to lift an L?

- True! How?

- Similarly, one could say that a right glove could become a left glove by taking it out of our three-dimensional space into one of four dimensions, flipping it there and returning it to our three-dimensional world. But we do not understand how to "raise" ourselves from our dimension as we raise an L made of paper. We cannot even understand the action to give it its own name. We have to use some other word under quotation marks. We have not named what comes next after length, width, and depth because we cannot conceive it. It would be a pleasure only for Wgijvrán to invent a name that would say nothing because we would not understand what it wants to mean. It would be absurd! But the temptation to commit such absurdity is perhaps a testimony to the power of the intellect, even though it could be just a frustrating impulse which materializes into nothing.

- What do you mean, Master?

- The Thinking Being has realized that there is something beyond his faculties and although he cannot conceive it, he senses it with his reason. Is it not wonderful?

- *It seems quite tangled to me.*

- *You will understand it if you think of it as many times as necessary. Then you will be able to understand brother Sänte, the greatest
and kindest wise man we have had in our order. He proposed a model
of the cosmos in which, if an astronaut departs in any direction and
always travels in a straight line, he will inevitably return to our
planet, as long as he is able to travel enough. Although it might be
possible, I say that he comes back with the heart on the other side.*

- *As you already said, I have to think much more about this...*

- *Perhaps for you to understand why the astronaut would end up
flipped, it is necessary to use the Ob-Üs tape.*

- *What is that?*

- *A sheet of paper has two faces and four edges. An Ob-Üs tape is
a paper sheet having one side and one edge.*

- *Is that possible?*

- *Perfectly possible!*

Then, my master stopped his march close to some rocks leaning out
the way. He took his travelogue out. He cut a paper tape and spread
it over one of the rocks. Then he took one end and joined it to the other with an adhesive tape, forming a bracelet; but so that their ends
were joined by the opposite sides: the upper side with the underside.

- *This is a tape of Ob-Üs. Examine it, dear Ad! What if a beetle
could walk on the tape?*

I put my attention on the shape of the band. Apparently, nothing
was so special: a ring of paper that showed an "assembly error." I
figured that my finger was the beetle and I moved it along the tape.
The beetle always walked on the same surface around the ring. There
was a moment when my finger was moving inside the ring. Then it
moved outside of it and then back inside again, and so on. I could
have spent an eternity doing that. My finger could go over it all! The
same happened when my finger went over the edge of the band. The
Ob-Üs tape was a sheet of paper with one side and one edge.

As I watched the Ob-Üs tape, Reverend Ogli formed another identical tape.

- *Well, this is not a standard Ob-Üs tape, but the space contained
between the two belts is.*

That was how he built a double bracelet, that is, one Ob-Üs tape
above and one below. Then Reverend Ogli cut two Ls of paper and
placed them in the space between the two tapes using two clips for

holding paper sheets. The two Ls were next to each other with their bases pointing in the same direction.

- I am going to leave one L fixed in place and I am going to move the other one.

Reverend Ogli removed the clip from one of the Ls and moved it between the two belts until the L found its mate, which had remained still.

- AHA! -I said- The L that made the trip changed its orientation. Now its base is pointing in the opposite direction.

- It has become the enantiomorphic version of the one that did not travel.

- That is, there has been an enantiomorphic inversion -I remarked- I now understand!

- An astronaut performing a cosmic journey in a circular motion, from and toward our planet, according to the model of Sänte, may suffer the same type of inversion.

- Then the universe is an Ob-Üs tape.

- Mmm! Maybe it could work in the same way, but, it must be more complicated than that. I think an Ob-Üs tape serves simply as an artifice for understanding. But the Ob-Üs tape is one of the most extraordinary mathematical toys by itself. Among other things, it can be used to get yourself out of trouble if a shaman puts you to the test.

- Ah! I had already forgotten! What did you do with him?

- You will agree with me that the Devil's Signature can only be developed to a point where you have to complete something that is on the opposite side where you have stopped. There is no way to do it on the opposite side where you have stopped. There is no way to do this without crossing throughout the drawing, which would be the equivalent to repassing a line, or to create a new item in the Devil's Signature. Now that you know about the properties of the Ob-Üs tape, can you tell me how I managed to draw the Devil's Signature without breaking any rule?

- I think I know how! You built an Ob-Üs tape and drew the Devil's Signature to the point where everybody stops. Then, like the journey we made with the L, your line departed from the drawing, moved along the entire surface of the tape, and came back on the other side of the diagram. So, the Devil's Signature was completed without repassing it!

-Very good! -my master said, visibly pleased- I see you have understood.

Chapter XVI

Where the Demons Fly Over

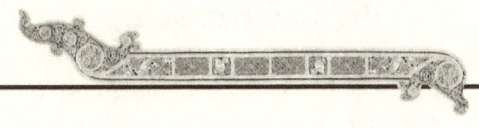

e continued our way through the lush forest. Reverend Ogli entertained again our march with the story about sorcerers that had been interrupted.

- As I already told you, the inscrutable access denied any Cruciglobist plan a successful assault on Urse. E-Tar had all reason to trust his defenses. But if the situation inside Urse was quiet, outside of the walls, the atmosphere was distressing. One hundred days after the siege was launched, the weakest Cruciglobists began to starve. The casualties were around a hundred. They had already sacrificed most mounts, which were mostly robust jralens. So, they organized an expedition in search of animals, but even after looting a few barns, they found nothing. Instead, they came upon a small Lunilaic army, which had been approaching to attack the besiegers from the back. The Cruciglobist cerontes were invincible, even when they were hungry. The expedition returned to camp loaded with hideous trophies which were installed in their catapults. That day, the inhabitants of Urse saw raining down on them the heads of those who came to their aid. Not even hunger distracted hatred.

- What would you have done, Reverend Ogli, if you would have been E-Tar?

- What would I have done?

- *Yes! What would have been your strategy?* -I clarified- *Besiege the besiegers? Would you exterminate the infantry by arrows and let starve those who brought armors? Would you use the advantage of your number against them... What?*

- *Dear Ad, it is true that strategy tempts the reasoning, but killing is unreasonable! Remember, Ad-d-Tuar.*

- *I will remember, Master.*

- *Once recovered from that storm of death* -my master continued-, *E-Tar sent an ambassador to Akaramám, a town further to the east than Kire. The ambassador returned with the promise of the Akaramám governor that he would mobilize his fifty thousand soldiers. This should have ended with the siege and, at least for a while, kept Thode Le-Cons away. But apparently, a solution to the siege of Urse was something that did not please all the Lunilaic leaders of Rjostos. In particular, there was someone very interested in maintaining the siege, even in its triumph. At four in the morning, at some point on the long city walls, a rope lashed the stone and unrolled. When the guards arrived, they did not know what to do because they recognized their own monarch helping the Cruciglobists to climb the city walls. Before they could react, the Lunilaic guards were attacked by the invaders with stealthy crossbow darts. Only a few of them managed to escape. As enough Cruciglobists came up, they announced their attack with trumpets. E-Tar awoke amid the uproar. He suspected the disaster, but he did not bother to check it; he thought all was lost. After two hundred days of resistance, the monarch of Urse fell apart. Succumbing to terror, he ordered to open one of the doors of the city and fled on a swift salamiondra. Out of his mind, he rode on it for hours. Meanwhile, inside the walls, the genocide had its day. At dawn, cries of terror marked the killing. Children and adults ran terrified through the streets and crops trying to hide. The Cruciglobists had no problem in reaching them and slit their throats. The massacre lasted several hours. The bodies were thrown into the fire that consumed the houses. The macabre smoke carried the smell of the slaughter beyond the walls of Urse.*

- *What happened to E-Tar?*

- *E-Tar, exhausted from fleeing, had fallen unconscious from his mount. He was awakened by some of his own guards who had also escaped. After finding out the misfortune of Urse, E-Tar began to cry for having abandoned the city and its people. Among these guards, there was someone who had preferred to remain silent up* to that point. He was one of those who saw E-Tar helping the Cru-ciglobists climb the city walls. The witness told the others what he had seen. One of them, the most outraged, drew his sword and be-headed E-Tar shouting "Death to the traitor!" Later, as a proof of justice, this same guard carried the mutilated head to Ntra only to realize that in that city the twin head had also been cut. He did not even untie his grotesque package. He questioned the people and when he finally understood what had happened, he was heard to say, "My God, have mercy on me!" The guard drew his sharp knife from his belt and took his own life.

- But what happened? -I asked, without restraint.

- You will see! Iruz-tod was a chronicler of Ntra, at the time of the Campaign. In his work UtE-mê-fhaT about the history of the Holy War, developed in seven volumes, you can know what really happened. He had heard the account of the facts from Eli-vé him-self, who took Iruz-tod as an advisor to govern Ntra after the death of O-Tar.

- Master... what happened?

- Sorry, dear Ad, I think I kept you on tenterhooks. When Eb al- Tar died, Eli-vé was not as young as when he accompanied him in the last battle against the Acquemid tribes of Liantzé. His body, however, retained the burden of his corpulence. He always wore his strange Gredirian champion outfit: embossed boots on the emptied leather from a pair of dinoceratos legs; robust straps holding a tight skirt with golden sheets of polished aurita; dress coat made of hard amphibian skin on which thousands of shells of fossil diatoms from the Sea of Euda had been sewed. His steely sword had been tempered seven times to fix in it the spirits equal to the number of warriors defeated earlier by Eli-vé. His helmet was one of the most beautiful ones: it had been masterfully carved in the skull of an ugante, that is, in metallic ivory. Actually, it was a hybrid between a helmet and a ceremonial mask. It was filled with mystical symbols of Gredirian cults. On his shoulders, two epaulets shaped as a beetle completed his war dress. Eli-vé used to get up at dawn to supervise the guards who were doing the rounds in the dark. The morning of day Urse was assaulted by the Cruciglobists, Eli-vé was going to a battery of turrets on the crenelated walls located on the northeast corner of the fortress. Suddenly, he heard some dry and energetic lashes coming from the east side, where Ntra, like Urse, also defended itself with a precipice. Then he thought he saw a flying shadow, even blacker than the night. At the same time, the wind brought a foul odor that reminded him of the stench emanating from the mangled body of his master and friend Eb al-Tar. What could have been that shadow and where did it come from? The mighty Gredirian warrior got an oil lamp and a rope that he tied around a battlement. He let himself down quietly, and a few minutes later, he came to the base of the wall, just where the precipice begun. Moving over the edge of the abyss, he examined the possibilities of the descent. The Ntra sewage, once putrid, drained over the rocky walls, forming spills that, in daylight, could be seen as black and orange veined marks. Eli-vé discovered a wide crack of rough walls making its way erratically along the crag. Eli-vé started to go down. The tips of his feet embedded in the rocky slots as if they were stirrups. While his body was hanging by one hand, his free hand sought for other protuberances before deciding new moves. The oil lamp scrutinized the crack with its inconstant light, highlighting the relief in terms of yellow and orange. From the bottom of the abyss, a strong wind tried to pull the body of Eli-vé to a weightless death. He did not know for how long he had descended. When he reached a very narrow and exposed ledge, he no longer needed a lamp: the natural light of dawn already spread through the intangible substance of the emptiness. On the clarity, the precipice showed its teeth. Eli-vé did not allow this vision to intimidate him. He turned his back to the nothing and continued sliding down the corridor cautiously. Suddenly, he came upon an opening three times higher than his height. The lateral placement of this opening, with respect to the rest of the entire rock wall, had hidden its existence. This entry opened the way to a wet cave that served as an entrance hall to a tunnel that penetrated into the rock. The tunnel, like one of many sewers unloading over there, was flooded with liquids that had been hovering God knows since when. Eli-vé had believed he knew all the secrets of Ntra. Obviously, it was not like that; he did not know what had always been under his feet. To investigate the tunnel, he needed to sink into that blind pond with the creepy feeling that, under those fetid waters, he could feel the touch of some sticky tentacles. That channel without drain was a reservoir of sediments that stank of a bittersweet hotchpotch of rotten fruit and filth. The clarity had waned considerably and again, he had to use his lamp. As he moved through the channel, the putrid fluid was reaching to his thighs and gained in density. The stench was also getting concentrated, as well as a premonition. Eli-vé stopped. Quickly, he drew his sword. He turned around. There was nothing! Nothing but the damp echo that lives in the caves; the incessant hammering of leaks echoing in the emptiness. Eli-vé recalled the sordid atmosphere of the pagan crypts. He hated the idea of wrestling in such a disgusting stage. He imagined himself sloshing in those thick soiled waters; he might have to dip into them; maybe he would touch something disgusting. Worse, he imagined himself swallowing a mouthful of rotten mud. Imagining the taste of all that putrefaction into his mouth gave him nausea. Eli-vé was more and more sure: among the rarefied air, he felt a presence; there was something that was touching him with its eyes. He moved his sword forward. Its double-edge shone with the presence of the seven spirits imprisoned in it. He raised the lamp. In front of him, the channel got wider. He began to distinguish a building carved in the rock. A triangular pediment crowned a row of columns filled with very strange anaglyphic symbols which Eli-vé could not recognize. The entire set was based on a grandstand that rose from the putrid waters. Part of a giant yellow hand and part of a red head laid on the steps, probably, the remains of some immense statues. The first step, as all the steps, was covered with a greasy tartar, immemorially intact. Eli-vé left the stinky sludge and cursed with rage when he saw his muddy legs. He put his lamp down. He raised his eyes. He looked forward and... what followed was very fast. Eli-vé just could glimpse the huge and single eye of a winged beast. A fulminant crash slapped his entire body. The last orange glow that he saw began to fade in the looseness of the unconsciousness. Another color came. It expanded. It faded, and he got lost in the color's extinction. Some eyes appeared. A face. Eb al-Tar began to speak: Eli-vé....! My friend! Straighten your sword! The sense of touch was still far away. Between the seizures, his fingers groped something hard. He acknowledged the pain in his lungs, putrefaction in his mouth. He was suffocating. He violently sought for air. He broke in a stertorous vomiting that made him gather the handle of his sword against his stomach.

At that precise moment, the demoniac spawn threw itself against the general. The impact sent Eli-vé back to the bottom of the mud. He dropped his sword and desperately sought for air. He could not see under the mud, but he was sure something had been skewered on his

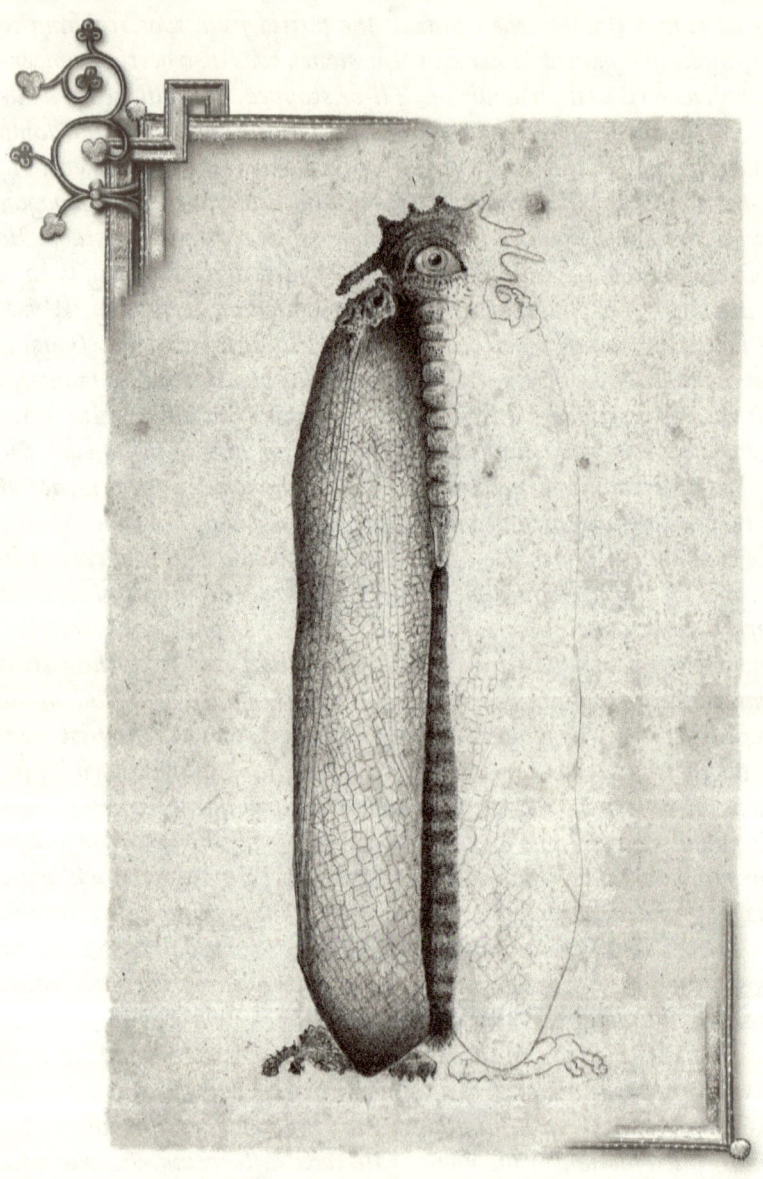

. . . the huge and single eye of a winged beast.

sharp steel; something that desperately flapped its wings. When Eli-vé managed to recover, the flapping had ceased. The handle of his sword stood out from the filthy mud. Eli-vé grabbed it to pull the weight to the shore of the grandstand. He was sure it was the same nightmare being that had killed Eb al-Tar. When it was easier, he pulled the body out of the mud. To his surprise, skewered by the steel, the flaccid body of O-Tar, monarch of Ntra, son of Eb al-Tar, began to emerge. Immediately, he saw the sorcerer AloOf throwing himself from the shadows with a knife in his hands. As an acrobat, Eli-vé dodged the cut and ran the magician through in an unexpectedly easy way. Seven lights rose, leaving the lifeless body of the sorcerer on fire. Then, he removed the head of O-Tar to exhibit it to the people of Ntra.

- Whew! -I exclaimed, amazed- So, this was the story heard by the guard who beheaded E-Tar.

- Precisely! When he heard it, he realized that the night that Urse fell, conceived in the darkness where the demons fly over, the one who had thrown a rope to the Cruciglobists seemed to be E-Tar, but it was O-Tar. The guard had killed his innocent monarch!

- AloOf must have taught O-Tar the secrets of transmutation.

- Maybe...

- Wow! What a way to know who the bad brother was!

- The good and the bad -my master said- as extreme they are, are twins on either side of the mirror.

lencloin wi
es in dē dach
ende deyl dē
dat licht uā
der duuster
nis eū noeiu
de dat licht
den dach eū

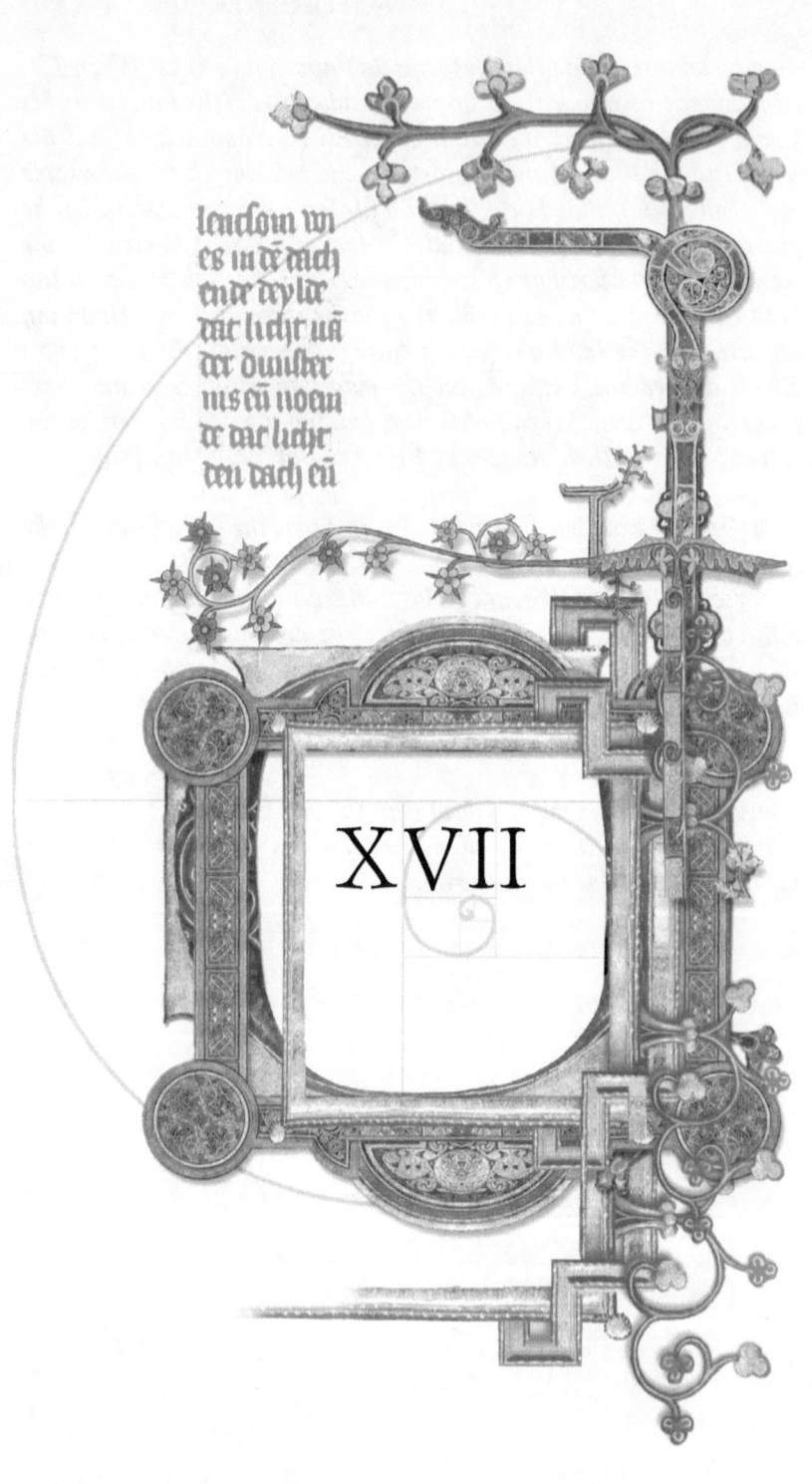

XVII

Chapter XVII

Hunger of Barbarians Gods

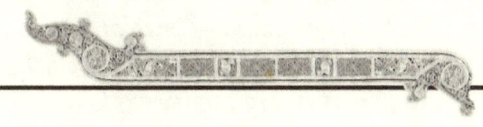

The cruelty unleashed in the assault on Urse -my master continued- gave the Cruciglobists a dreadful reputation around the Lunilaic world. In the neighboring cities, humble or powerful people shuddered just thinking that, at any moment, they could be the meal for the Western appetite. Three days from Urse, too few for whom expected to go unnoticed, there was a minor Lunilaic city called Uss. Just after the first news of the fall of Urse came to their ears, the more determined families packed their carts and fled to safer places like Ntra or Jbur. Taking the road also meant the possibility of going to meet the danger. Never before and never after, another city like Uss suffered such a high degree of terror. Those who fled were right: their fear was to be confirmed; their premonitions savagely satisfied.

- An adverse morning -he went on- in front of the walls of Uss, thousands of avid cerontes sought how to get in with their god at front. The city had no army and hardly any urban police. The Uss siege only lasted fifteen days. Isinalaq Al-Ban says: "...for three days people were killed by knife..." Since the testimony of Isinalaq Al-Ban could be suspicious, I quote Lence of Swek: "In Uss, our warriors cooked pagan adults in casseroles, children were skewered on spears, grilled and eaten."

- What!

- If before -Reverend Ogli continued- the Western barbarism had not succeeded, because it resembled any other barbarism, now it had ripped a wound that would suppurate rancor through the centuries. The cannibal vandalism of the Campaign got embedded in the Eastern memory and has been an impression very hard to remove.

- Was it true?

- If anyone doubts Lence of Swek, they should also dismiss a formal letter from the Cruciglobist head to the Øppos where, apparently, he is trying to give explanations for their excesses: "A terrible hunger struck the army in Uss and put it in the cruel need to feed on the corpses of the pagans.

- That is not a reason! -I said, outraged- The besiegers of Urse were out there for two hundred days and they did not eat anyone.

- Ople de Bail, who participated in the assault on Uss, says: "Our warriors did not get disgusted by eating the Lunilaics they had killed nor by eating their pets."

- I guess Ople was not that hungry!

- After this monstrous demonstration -my master continued, ignoring my remarks- the smaller Lunilaics cities did not offer any resistance. When they managed to go through the walls of Jbur, the Cruciglobists were killing Lunilaics for an entire week. In the temple of Qeuq, they killed around 60 000. The chronicles are horrifying! The cavalry of cerontes rode over puddles of blood, splashing it all over. According to them, God had wanted so; a god who proclaimed fraternity.

The grief settled in our souls and, for a long time, we moved through the woods without saying anything. Then...

- Have you noticed, dear Ad, the trees are increasingly ordering themselves?

- Not only that, Reverend Ogli, but the branches tend to spread up to the point of almost forming a tunnel.

- Yes, but they do that, creating a pattern between the branches and the clear space of the sky. It is a pattern that wants to transform itself into a grid.

- It is true!

- Now, walls, floor, and ceiling are covered with light and dark squares.

- Now they are a chessboard.

- We are inside of a tunnel infinitely gridded.

- It is as if the walls have no end. All in black and white. Nothing has color...

- Stop for a moment!

I stopped instantly.

- AHA! It is not us who move.

- No, it is the tunnel that moves!

- So, it should not matter if we stand still.

- Where are we, Master? What is going to happen to us?

- Calm down, dear Ad. Calm and patience.

- Patience is what I need to hear that all the time!

- Ad-d-Tuar!

- Sorry, Master! I am...

- I know, dear Ad, but no need to worry. As long as the images do not hurt us, we remain safe. By the way, the squares start to deform.

- I think they are getting wavy.

- They are detaching from each other to form something like kites.

- To me, they are more like clockmaking pieces.

- That's it!

- But the teeth of the pieces are being transformed into legs.

- What is that? Looks like...

- Reptiles! Reptiles!

- White reptiles and black reptiles.

- They are going to attack us!

I was about to run, but I did not know where to go. My master caught me, putting a hand on my shoulder.

- Just let them pass -he said.

Under our feet, on the sides and above, thousands of black and white reptiles passed by, changing in an endless transmutation. The reptiles fattened and became hexagons, and hexagons turned into hives. From the hives, the insects of the honey came out, and these insects became birds. And from their black silhouette and from the white of the sky, black birds and white fish were born. Both animals intertwined in another mosaic. And the color gray appeared. And the mosaic acquired shadows and many cubes were formed. Thousands of cubes were born in the infinite, surpassed us and moved away to another infinite. And the white and gray diamonds formed by the cubes grew and became walls of houses and palaces, while the black ones narrowed and became windows.

And we saw a window in the bottom of the tunnel that grew, grew, and grew and... It devoured us, like a huge abysmal worm! Everything stopped. We were in total darkness.

- Ok, now -my master asked- Where are we?

I had no mouth. I only had fear.

- Ad? Are you there?

That strange darkness had the acoustics of a theater dome. The voice of Reverend Ogli came to me from everywhere and nowhere. I was not able to accurately determine its origin.

- Yes, Master.

- Where are you?

- Here, Master.

- I will... Ah! Beware, Ad! There is a step ahead.

- In front?

- Yes, dear Ad. Straight ahead.

- Oh, right! -I said as I felt some stairs- Thank you!

- You are welcome.

There were no traces of light. My fingers touched a wall of rocky roughness.

- I'm trying to light a match -Reverend Ogli said- but it is as if all of them are wet.

For a moment, I had no perception but the sound of the matches against the sandpaper.

- I think, it is useless. We have no other choice but to move forward blindly. One step at a time, dear Ad. But, let me go first.

- As you say, Master.

I let my master go ahead of me, as he asked. I tried to sense his movements because, as the steps did not creak, there was no way to be sure what was going on.

- Very good! Now, it's your turn -he said.

- Yes, Master. Here I go!

I took my first step and it felt risky.

- Do you think you can move forward in this way?

- I think so, Master.

That is how we started to deal with the stairs. I could not see or hear anything. I moved totally focused on measuring my steps and, I think, my master was doing the same, because he was not saying a word, either. Before going forward, I always groped the next step with the tip of my toes. I kept one hand over the wall. This way, I knew when the wall turned to either side, but did not know which side we had started at. I kept the other hand extended forward, stirring into the darkness to intercept any obstacle. The stands reminded me of a children's game we used to organize in the grandma's storehouse. It was a fairly large room for a storage room, but still it seemed to suffer a shortage of space. There, she had stored all sorts of trinkets, from ancient mannequins dressed in period clothing up to biscuit tin cans. The tin cans were empty and were so large they could hide a whole child inside. When they were not hiding anyone, if you beat them, they reproduced the detonation of lightning. We used to leave those children owing paybacks from other games in the back of the room. We left them with hands and feet gently tied, so they could unleash themselves in the midst of total darkness. Those children who remained outside did not have to wait long to hear a bang from hell because, once the first blast happened, there was no other choice but running over all the cans to exit as quickly as possible before grandma came down beating her broom on the air.

But these steps were not a game. I realized that with so many curves I would not have been able to remember our path. But I was sure that Reverend Ogli would...

- Master! -I exclaimed, trying to get his attention.

I did not get an answer.

- Master! -I shouted with an ugly premonition.

Nothing! There was no sign of anything.

-Oh no! -I said to myself and a cold sweat began to bother me.

I thought I had diverted from my master's way at some point. Maybe I entered into another stair different from my master's choice. Maybe there was a four-way intersection. I kept my hand over the right wall of the corridor and, perhaps, my master kept his over the left wall. So, I found an entrance to the right while he found another at his left.

I felt miserably lost. How could I return alone? Return? -I thought- Where? How could this have happened? I followed my master, that's for sure. And no, no other stairs were connected to this one. This was the only one. Then, how? Oh, maybe I was just slow. That's it! I just have to go faster and I'm going to reach my master. So, I increased the speed of my step, not so much because I was convinced of my argument, but rather because the devil was driving me. I stumbled twice and hurt my hand and hit my knee, but I continued running blindly. Suddenly... I bumped into a living lump. I screamed. Two large hands gripped me. I threw another scream.

- Ad!

- Master?

- What are you doing in front of me?

- Master! -I hugged him tightly.

- It's okay! Calm down, dear Ad, calm down.

I had never felt so comforted by the presence of anyone. At that moment, I knew I loved my master Ogli very much.

- Dear Ad, I really would like to know what you were doing in front of me. In other words, why did you go ahead of me?

- No, Master. I... I rather delayed.

My master took some seconds before answering.

- Ah, ah! Something is going on here. Were you not behind me all this time?

- I thought so

- So, did you go down the stairs one step at the time, as I told you, or did you rashly run down into the darkness?"

- Did I go down? But I have done nothing but go up!

- What?

- Yes! Since we started to go up, I did not feel any descent.

- Dear Ad... -he said, lengthy exhaling- I have not stopped going down!

After that, each of us returned to the same clarifications a little more detailed, only to come to understand that we understood nothing.

-Until when are we going to sit here, Reverend Ogli?

- I do not know! Anyway, we have already found that moving is useless.

- True!

- And I think we were lucky. Here, at least you can know, at any moment, in which direction the stairs go up and in which they go down and, in any way, you will reach the same point. There were castles that had labyrinths in complete darkness. There were no steps, but flat corridors. The only reference you have in that case is the direction you leave behind and the one you have in front of you, which are not visible, tangible, or verifiable things in the dark.

The direction behind your back is just a sensation. If at any point you get obfuscated and leave this position, what you had behind becomes what you have in front of you. But unless you have had consciousness and control of your movements, which does not correspond to an obfuscation, you will not be able to differentiate between the two directions. If you put your back against one of the walls of the corridor, then you would have a sensation of what is right or left. But that feeling is contrary to what you have if you stand against the other wall. Your brain knows your right side, but as soon as you want to assign a "right" to an environment outside of your body, and without referents, you realize that the concept needs the referent to exist. Now, imagine that you are in a labyrinth enclosed by walls, completely insulated from the outside. Suppose, you need to tell someone outside what direction you are going to move. Suppose, you have a radio transmitter with you. Suppose also, that you have decided to advance in the direction in which the corridor extends to your left. You take your radio and you tell someone: I'm going to move to the left. Over and out. How can that someone, located on the outside, know what is your left and what is your right?

- Ah... I see!

- This has confused many and even deserved the category of a philosophical problem by true and seasoned thinkers.

- That much?

- The matter is serious. It is much more complicated than solving why the mirror reverses images from left to right and not from top to bottom. Remember?

- Yes, Master.

- It is also disturbing; disturbing as when polarized light passes through left and right enantiomers and behaves as if it has penetrated into two worlds on either side of the mirror. Remember, dear Ad?

- Perfectly, Master.

- Many decades ago, a powerful radio telescope was installed in the Lateral Continent with the purpose of capturing any radio message from outer space. The signals would travel incredible distances, but there was no doubt that a pulse code could maintain the communication. If contact with an outside civilization is achieved and if it is possible to agree on a code, transcendent information would be exchanged. To make this exchange feasible, it is necessary to explain concepts like up and down, back and forth, and left and right. For example, in the description of a device or a crystal, it is possible to explain what we mean by "up," saying that it is the direction away from the center of the planet; "down," the opposite. To explain what is "front," we would say that it is the direction toward the observer; "behind," the one that moves away from the observer. But there is no way to make them understand what is left and right with words. It is, no more no less, trying to explain to someone outside the closed labyrinth in which direction you are going to move, using a radio transmitter. How can that outsider know what is your left and your right? The only way to communicate to a being from another civilization our meaning of left and right would be to point with your finger: this is right and this is left. Just like we would be forced to explain the colors: this is blue, this is green, this is brown, etc. But, unfortunately, the finger does not travel by radio.

- We could send to space a drawing explaining which hand is the right and which is the left.

- If we had the means to send images to the stars, on a journey that lasts light years, the function of the radio telescope to make contact would no longer have sense as well as to find a solution to this problem. But even so, the issue does not fail to raise a conflict.

- Then we could send instructions to draw something with a different element on one side and tell them this is, for example, the right.

- If you do not tell them before where they should put the different element, they could build the enantiomorphic image of the shape that you want to show them.

- And if we use an optically active chemical element?

- You mean we tell them, for example, that the direction in which the light switch opens when polarized light passes through a dextrose solution is what we call "right"?

- Yes, exactly.

- Well... First, you would have to explain them, which molecule we call dextrose and which levulose. As one is the enantiomer of the other, they would not know which of the two you are referring to, unless you first explained the difference between left and right. And that is precisely what we want to explain.

I remember you told me that all living things carry dextrorotatory proteins. Then you could say that "right" is the direction of the angle at which the light switch opens with proteins in between.

- That would be perfect if the fact that the proteins are dextrorotatory is a universal fact. It is possible that in their world, the proteins are levorotatory, and their DNA has the opposite enantiomorphic spiral with respect to ours. And, moreover, who tells you that those beings from outer space are made of carbon and have proteins?

- It is true!

- Another possibility is to assume that, quite likely, their planet rotates in a certain direction. To us, the planet turns to the right. We would ask them to consider right to the direction in which their planet rotates and that's it!

- That simple?

- The problem, in this case, would arise next, when we try to explain to them what we call north pole and south pole. This is because when we say , "the planet rotates to the right," it is understood implicitly that it refers to the right with respect to the north pole. If we consider the south pole, we would say that our planet turns to the left.

- But isn't the north pole the one that the compass always points at??

- Our compasses! It has an extreme painted on black which we call north and that was arbitrarily chosen. If all the north poles of compasses of the universe were black, there would not be any problem. It would be enough to communicate to the other planet: "Black is what we call the north pole. Over." The same is true for magnets. In this case, they are useless for us because, except for the color with which they are painted, it is not possible to differentiate between their poles. Have you placed a magnet under a sheet of paper with scattered iron filings on it?

- Yes, Master. Some iron lines are formed, some patterns around the poles.

- But, did you find any difference between the figure that the filings formed around one pole and the other?

- Mmm... No! They were identical.

- There is no way to differentiate the ends of a magnet, right? That is precisely what I mean. How to communicate to someone outside the closed labyrinth what is the red pole of your magnet?

- Ah! So it seems there is no way to explain what we consider as left and right using the radio telescope. The torsion of the trunk of the trees and the direction of the vortex of the water, according to the hemisphere in which they are found, cannot be used for the same reasons either. Right?

- Yes, Ad. You're right. In all these instances, something called "symmetry of the experiment" intervenes. For example, the experiment of imagining a planet turning to the right produces two possibilities: to the right of the N pole or to the right of the pole S. But the poles N and S are, as we have said, indistinguishable, making the two possibilities equivalents and "superposable," so to speak. This is what is called a "symmetric experiment." This happens because, given a relative condition like "turning right," there is no way to exempt it from its relativity because the identification of referents is also relative, producing two indistinguishable possibilities. The only condition for naming them is that one pole, whatever name we have given it, must be located on the opposite side of the other. Whenever we ask the inhabitants of another planet to reproduce a symmetrical experiment, we are going to encounter an insuperable duality that can never clarify what we consider left and right. We need to eliminate the relativity that every attempt to clarify the identification of left and right will have. For this, we need an example in nature, only one, which distinguishes one pole from the other. For example, if the iron filings were concentrated only on one end of the magnet, then we could differentiate them. We would call asymmetric to this kind of experiment. In an asymmetric experiment, nature would show preference for a given direction.

- But Master, that would mean that all the iron of the world would concentrate on one of the magnetic poles of the planet. The planet would be unbalanced as it would weigh more at one end than at the other. It would be something like a left-handed planet.

- And that seems absurd, right? It attempts against our common sense, right?

- Yes, of course!

- In addition, it goes against the law of gravitation that distributes the weights from inside to outside of the planet. On the other hand, the movements of the planet would be different and its orbit would be another. It seems that nature does not do that. Do you agree?

- Yes! I agree.

- Well then... The scientists also agreed with you. They took it as a natural law and called it The Law of the Conservation of Symmetry. The absence of asymmetric examples suggested that nature produces only symmetrical phenomena. In addition, this law was necessary for the validity of the other laws.

- Have you ever discovered a violation of this law?

- There was an occasion! To the scientists of that time, this discovery indicated some mysterious asymmetry in the laws of nature. It was discovered that if a compass is placed on a wire in such a way that its needle is parallel to the wire and pointing north (black tip) and if electricity is sent from south to north through the wire, then the north pole of the compass deviates toward the left.

- Ah! Then, there is the solution! We could ask the inhabitants of the other planet to reproduce the experiment. We could agree to call left to the direction pointing by the compass needle when the current that is passing under is getting away from us.

- The only problem, dear Ad, is that we have no way to explain to them which one is the end of the needle to which we call "north."

lenesom un
es in te tach
ende tey lit
tar lichr uā
ter dunster
nis cū noem
te tar lichr
ten tach cū

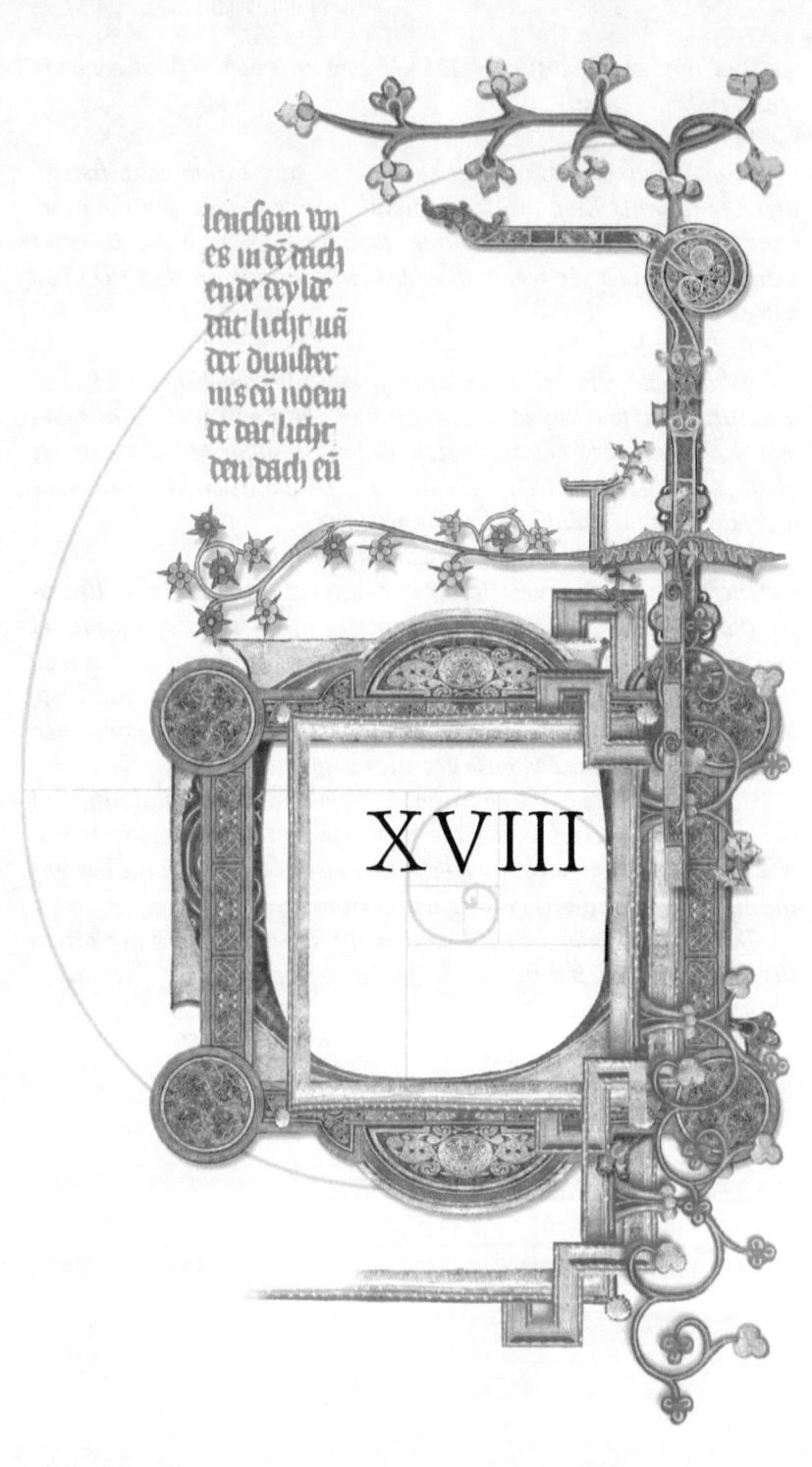

XVIII

Chapter XVIII

Fire of Despot Gods

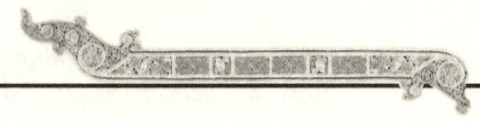

Given the uselessness of all activity, we were forced to sit in total darkness, reflecting on our situation, on possible explanations of what we had seen and heard. We realized that we could not talk about the disconcerting world of the Night of Time without having to refer to the previous events: our casual arrival to Wrestongres; the coincidence of the eclipse; the threat of world war; the Path of Gnedh interrupted precisely at St. Orafio; Uwer de OrEst, who apparently knew what was going to happen... We also noticed that if we charged the balance of what happened to the randomness of the destiny, describing all antecedents as casual, we also had to pass the bill for our whole life and the lives of our parents and those who preceded us. Suddenly, I had the uncomfortable sensation of being, unknowingly, working for others.

- Too many coincidences! -my master said- If you examine a shopping basket, it also seems to have gone through a random concatenation of purchases. If we wouldn't know that the acquisitions happened with the purpose of replacing exactly what was consumed from a pantry, we would be as perplexed in front of a full basket as we are now in the face of what happened. Maybe we are utilized by a purpose.

- Master, remember when we met Brother Tyl-kro and you mentioned Otân-guié's Anticipation Law?

- Yes, dear Ad.

- Master, on that occasion you said something like: "...it is written that somebody will be privileged in the Path of Gnedh and will get to know something for which the Szabeos have waited for centuries." Do you remember it now?

Total silence! I thought I had said something improper. The darkness did not let me see what was going on with him. Finally, he said:

- Yes, I remember.

Then, another silence; one much longer than the previous one.

- In all this -my master suddenly said- there seems to be a much closer and disturbing relationship between history and literature than I had imagined. It is not so strange when we think that what we admit as historical is nothing more than a written approach to reality, almost always subjective and unilateral. History and literature can be simply two degrees of fiction bound by the same umbilical cord: the subconscious mind. Perhaps for this reason, fictional appellations like Ngupd have consolidated themselves as historical names; so much that today it is possible to hear a debate about the exact location of his tomb. The opposite case, that is to say, that a notable deceased becomes a legend, is quite common. The validity of the legend of the Holy Råål in this allegorical pandemonium is undeniable: The Knights of the Circle, the mystical and adventurous pursuit of the sublime object.

- What does Holy Råål mean? -he continued- We are supposed to discover it ourselves. An absolute and universal meaning? A relative meaning that has to do with the personal experience of each person? For the contemplative monks of Sjabary-Pur, the personal soul is part of the infinite dissemination of the soul of God. Then there may be the significance and the insignificance. What did the Holy Råål mean for Lapidarian Knights? It quenches hunger and does not run out of food, gives water, and does not get empty... The Horn of Abundance? Either it illuminates or strikes down... A laser beam? It returns life and rejuvenates as the Fountain of Eternal Youth. What it touches turns into gold as the Philosophical Stone of the alchemists... Is it a machine that induces radioactive transmutations up to a stable isotope of gold? Is it an emerald fallen from the sky, the dorex ap silis or a stone sent from the skies... Is it a meteorite? Does it have to do with the fallen stone whose memory is kept by the Lunilaics in their most sacred city? The Holy Gravestone of the Lapidarian Knights?... And, if it were the Tablet of the Arcanum, then what?

Reverend Ogli sank back into his thoughts. He remained quiet for a long time. I knew something was coming. Meanwhile, my mind revived the preliminaries of my departure from the Convent of Kien. I remembered the excitement that had invaded me when the proximity of my journey of initiation was announced to me. Those already initiated, those who had returned, told wonders about The Path of Gnedh. They reported their favorite scenes by indulging in the smallest details. Some stories astonished us by the novelty of a custom, others by the strange similarities with other cultures. Their accounts stopped in privileged landscapes, in selected corners of the road, in the laconic beauty of the Marterian hermitages, in signs, symbols and stylobates, in splendid temples, dragons that bite their tails, in magic numbers, fateful numbers, numbers without ostentation, Philosophical Stones, sand and grandiose monuments of extinguished gods. Every inscription kept a meaning and a secret number. But, more than anything else, those who returned, returned radiant and serene as if they were sharing, ever since, a wonderful confidence of an inevitable event. Maybe everyone discovers his own mystery. There is something different for each one, or the same, with different names, such as the names that were disturbing my master: Mal-ö-Goom, Mãlegum and...

Reverend Ogli, what was the other name: Mal-ö-Goom, Mãlegum and... what?

There was no answer! Maybe I had been impertinent and disturbed his thoughts.

- Sorry, Master! I think I interrupted you.

- It is all right, dear Ad. What were you saying?

I had to repeat. My master replied:

- Ah-Lê-gönn, the one that cannot be found.

- That's it! Ah-Lê-gönn, the one that cannot be found. But I understand that the Lapidarian Knights did it, right?

- Well, that's what is presumed.

- Why?

- Because... Mmm! I think I should tell you before that this is an intriguing affair that the Szabeo monks have been mending with written and reliable documentation of various origins and even data from slightly less orthodox sources. In the gaps of greater uncertainty, even the speculations have come in handy. It is, in general, a rather shadowy affair to which we have tried to give body in order to reconstruct the facts in the most coherent way.

- It is believed -my master continued, after a few moments of silence- that from the beginning of the Campaign, the Lapidarian Order sought in the East something else than the reconquest of Jbur. What they really were after was a secret known to very few people in their hierarchy. Were they after the Philosophical Stone that the Western alchemists could not obtain? Were they going after the Holy Råål, obeying Wgijvrán? No one knows!

- But Wgijvrán is a personage of literature, right?

- I would not be surprised that some readers of the Middle Era would have believed in "The History of King Ngupd and the Knights of the Circle," because it was written precisely as if it were history. Then, perhaps, they did go after the Holy Råål with no more sorcerer than their imagination. Nobody knows! The truth is that they were there, warring along with the other cerontes, but keeping them at a distance because they bragged about an exceptionality that only they possessed because Providence favored them. That being said... In the times of the Marterian Empire, great libraries that collected the old knowledge were organized, especially the knowledge coming from Grezca. When they conquered Faronia, they also got the library of Vogadro, the most famous of antiquity, whose origins date back two centuries before the Marterian flourishing. They not only respected it but, aware of its value, protected it and increased its inventory. It is estimated that the Vogadro Library possessed 700,000 manuscripts, each 6 to 5 arms long, stored in rolls. When the barbarians invaded the empire, many of the Marterian libraries were destroyed in whole or in part. However, as soon as Marteria began to lose ground forced by the invaders, the Vogadro Library was moved to safer places. But, given the number of manuscripts, the library had to be divided between Arteria, the former Catatonia, Ru, Ntra and Urse. After Marteria was converted to Cruciglobism, the Marterian authorities judged pagan the content of many manuscripts. And so, much of the largest library of antiquity was destroyed.

- How did they destroy it?

- With fire! Later, when the Lunilaics took all the cities on the south of Catatonia, they also got the libraries. The Lunilaics were respectful of the arts and sciences and, like the old Marterians, protected many of the manuscripts. However, they also took the time to do a "cleansing" and eliminated what they considered pagan and blasphemous by setting it on fire. The Library of Vogadro was further depleted. During the campaign against Urse, according to the Cruciglobist chroniclers themselves, the Lapidarian Knights claimed the Lunilaic library of the city which, in their words, consisted of 13,200 manuscripts. According to Eriy-tij, a Lunilaic historian, the only translations of ancestral texts such as the codices of the Sea of Euda were kept there; all the magical astronomy of the archaic sages; the ancient Grezco geometry; the first algebra treatises that were originally Lunilaic; and other very valuable ones of the Eastern art and culture, like the Codex in Seven Languages incomparably valuable to translators of past texts. This booty was not wanted by the other cerontes of the Campaign; nevertheless, the privilege of choosing it meant, for the Lapidarian Knights, the sacrifice of others more profitable, economically speaking. In Urse a great number of precious objects had been accumulated, including gold in raw form and precious stones of considerable size. The other cerontes took advantage of this and declared Lapidarian preference for the manuscripts to obtain a greater slice. The library was then fully transferred to Catatonia with more sacrifice of time and Lapidarian money. Once in Catatonia, the manuscripts were first stored in the palace, in one of the areas ceded by the Marterian emperor Dox Ibi-Dor to the cerontes. Little by little, during a month, the manuscripts were stacked in the open, in front of the walls of the palace, next to the zone occupied by the Lapidarians. Then, the manuscripts were incomprehensibly cremated.

- Again! Why did they always use fire?

- The incineration of books is a bestiality that distinguishes despots, dear Ad. And when you see people burning books, you can predict that the next ones in burning will be their owners. The burning of books, dear Ad, is the most intelligent revenge the ignorant achieves.

-The abbot-captain of the Lapidarians -Reverend Ogli said, after a silence- inflamed the audience surrounding the scene with an intense talk against the heresies and blasphemies written by the Lunilaics. Just before transmitting the fire of a torch to the manuscript scrolls, he said in artesio: "Nue mioamum mkiomun floo" which means, "What comes from hell, return to hell.

- Then why did they sacrifice the gold and the precious stones?

- That's the question! It seems that the Lapidarians were looking for something. We could not determine exactly what it was. On the other hand, we know that under the shadows of the dawn, a cart, loaded with manuscripts concealed under a layer of hay, arrived at the gates of the gloomy castle of Gur, headquarters of the Lapidarian top leadership.

- How do we know that?

- We have always had people located in all spheres. That is already appropriate for you to know as well. Unfortunately, dear Ad, we were never able to penetrate the corps of the Lapidarian Order. That would have saved countless lives. Anyway... Our informants could only see from afar. According to them, for a week, the Lapidarian leadership passed behind closed doors. From that moment, the Lapidarian Knights suddenly stopped their warlike role and seemed to concentrate on strengthening their own organization as well as the relationship with other fraternities. They maintained their presence in minor skirmishes as part of a facade, but they were no longer absorbed in aggression planning. Moreover, there is evidence, in Oriental manuscripts, that in this period, the Lapidarian Knights made contact with the Lunilaic hermetic sects. It is easy to imagine that this approach took place behind the backs of the other Cruciglobists of the Campaign, who had been involved in the conquest of Jbur. In twelve years, the Cruciglobists besieged, took, devastated, tyrannized, and lost Jbur. Ntra, however, remained unscathed. Under the command of Eli-vé, and although he endured a siege of four years until the Cruciglobists got tired and left, the city of Ntra did not undergo the Cruciglobist invasion. In twenty years, the Lunilaics had reconquered their cities, which returned to be cruciglobas a decade later. Even a sixth Campaign came to disembark on Oriental lands, but each time they reconquered less until even losing Catatonia. They remained, however, in the Lunilaic memory as an indelible grudge that, fueled by the hatred of other atrocious encounters, today rises against the West, because they now have the occasion, even if that means a world suicide. But the mystery of the Exegesis does not go there. To follow its course, we must stop in the years that followed the first Lunilaic reconquest. It is, at that moment, when Phi D'Ric, a personage better known in the West, enters into the Eastern scene. When he was only four years old, Phi D'Ric inherited the Kingdom of Thur, located south of Primaria.

The Kingdom of Thur was very important for the stability of the Øppos, the chief of the Cruciglobism, who lived in the city of Marteria, the capital of Primaria, since this reign was the equivalent to the category of Marterian Emperor of the West. The Øppos managed to get the boy's powers up to the age of majority. But the father of the child, King Phi Luiv, had predestined for him an education nourished by both sides: the Cruciglobism and the Lunilaicism. We know for sure that King Phi Luiv was a protector of the Lapidarian Order. We also know that he hated Lunilaics up to the taking of Urse. Well, Phi D'Ric grew up receiving a double wealth in his education. He was even guided through the knowledge of religion from both points of view and knew what they thought of each other. In his youth, he repudiated the Cruciglobism and the Lunilaicism as well, declaring that all the religions were impositions. The Øppos wrote a public letter listing the vices of the king of Thur to discredit him. Phi D'Ric wrote another letter, which he sent to every monarch of the West, in which he made them notice the obvious ambition of the Øppos to manipulate everyone in his favor and warned them of the richness of the Cruciglobist clergy. The Øppos excommunicated him. This would have destabilized any other kingdom, but the semi-Lunilaic court of the Kingdom of Thur was hardly disturbed. Once a grown adult, Phi D'Ric was subjected to the demands of a treaty between the Øppos and several monarchs of the West, according to which the King of Thur had to serve him in warlike tasks in defense of the Cruciglobism. The war that the Cruciglobism had in hand was the Campaign, so Phi D'Ric had to march to kill Lunilaics. Phi D'Ric postponed these obligations as much as he could because he lived disinterested in the questions of power, concentrating rather on the study of the arts and sciences with the tutelage of knowledgeable Cruciglobists and Lunilaics who, in that court strangely, coexisted in peace. There is a lapse in the life of Phi D'Ric that is not registered anywhere. He cannot be located anywhere; simply, he disappeared.

- Maybe he was in the Lapidarian castle.

- Maybe. Nobody knows for sure. Neither did our informants. The truth is that Phi D'Ric reappeared transformed. Now, he not only wanted to go to the East, but he harassed the Øppos until he managed to lift the excommunication that weighed upon him and gave formal recognition to his expedition. This happened just after Riostos was reconquered by the Lunilaics, therefore the King of Thur's disposition was very convenient for the Øppos. Once he had the Øppos recognition, instead of marching toward Jbur, Phi D'Ric went to Ajeplo from where the Ahaxi ruled over all the falanjatos of the Lunilaic Empire. To everyone's amazement, Phi D'Ric was welcomed. Both monarchs discussed things of their interest that have never come to light. At the end of the meeting, the Ahaxi agreed to transfer the sovereignty of Jbur to Phi D'Ric. This was the first Campaign carried out without cries of pain nor barbarities; without the triumphant advance of the Cruciglobist cavalry over puddles of blood as it happened in the first taking of Jbur. Here comes the crucial part... Phi D'Ric moved to Jbur. We know that he took immediate contact with Eli-vé, Lord of Ntra. We know that a squadron of Lapidarian Knights accompanied him, and, with him, they entered and left freely from Ntra, where Eli-vé himself had accommodated them.

- That is weird!

- What I am telling you is not formally accepted. There are no Lunilaic records of the event and even fewer Cruciglobist ones. Whatever it may have been, the operation was done in complete discretion. The little we know has come to us from our informants. The last piece of information they gave us about this is that the Lapidarian squad and Phi D'Ric were seen moving away from Ntra with a cart that was carrying something heavy. The following is a registered fact: Phi D'Ric and his Lapidarians left the port of Kire with a single bundle in the holds of a ship which bore the Lapidarian symbol on its masts. Its fate remains unknown.

Chapter XIX

Topography of an Enigma

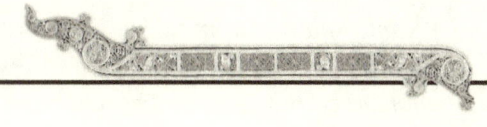

At that very moment, we heard noises near us, like those that latches make as they get unlocked. Then, an explosion of light hurt our eyes. For some time, we were blinded. Little by little our vision was restored. We then, realize our situation: we had been sitting on some steps that had walls on both sides, forming an ascending (or descending) corridor. There, everything was made of stone. A few steps up, one could see the open wings of a window through which, a torrent of light spread over the walls. We approached the window, coming up slowly to condition our sight to the clarity, but the light blinded us again. We heard from behind the clarity:

- What are you doing there?

With our eyes wrinkled, we began to distinguish a lump. Going against gravity, on the other side of the window, someone was watching us as if we were beneath him. His eyes looked at us from above. He was standing on the other side of the wall, on the very edge of the window, as only insects can do. How can he stand on the wall? -I asked myself. He, on the other hand, looked at us as if he were staring at the bottom of a well where our faces were lying down; like people who drown in frozen lakes and their faces are visible under the layers of ice. We were part of an absurd situation: to see him, we had to look forward, perpendicularly to the wall; to see us, he had to look down.

- How do you keep yourselves standing on those steps? He asked us.

- Ah! Well... -Reverend Ogli answered, disconcerted for a moment- Would you be so kind to help us out of here?

- Of course! -he immediately withdrew from the window, shouting: Guards!

Some guards approached. They got rid of their spears and crouched to help us. The guards took me out of the strange environment without much effort. The new ambiance was meant to be kinder. A large carpet of intricate motifs padded my steps. Huge tapestries of hunting scenes covered the stone walls. In one, I could see some luxuriously dressed riders lurking against a group of gassilopes. A similar tapestry faced the first at the other side of the room. Between the two walls, there was a huge fireplace, serious and dark, which could easily have housed a room inside. Heraldry banners hung in front of it and over our savior, who dressed like the tapestry riders. He was even wider than I had thought.

-We are very grateful -my master said, and I nodded.

- You do not have to! "Arts and manners open main doors." My name is Al'jarama, at your service- he said.

- My name is Ad-d-Tuar.

- Mine is Ogli-s-Oöp.

- Since when have you been there?

- We do not know -Reverend Ogli said.

- I thought it was an entire day -I said.

- An entire day? Mmm... It cannot be! -Al'jarama said, scratching his head- Just a few moments ago, there was no one there. I closed the window and was about to leave when I heard voices. "Do not ask nature, master it by obeying it."

Reverend Ogli looked at me strangely but said nothing.

- I have found you thanks to my habit; it's not by chance! I come back here from time to time, especially when problems overwhelm me. "The devil opens the door and the vice keeps it open." I like to contemplate the steps and imagine that it is possible to climb stairs that do not run on the floor but on the wall.

- In many subtle ways, we are all the fantasy of all -my master said, smiling- But tell me, how can we repay you for your help?

- If it is your pleasure to help me, let's see if you can help me with the problem that led me to contemplate the stairs.

- What is it about? -my master asked.

- Well, I do not know how I came to be Lord and Master of this island that they call Oronda.

- Island? -I asked, and Al'jarama looked at me as if I were foolish

- For most, that is not a problem -my master said.

- Yes, I know. Anybody would love it! But the fact is that some time ago, my Lord and I left our affairs to attend knights and maidens matters. After a hundred novels on Cruciglobist heroes against Lunilaic impious, my Lord knew where to find them even if they were scarce. I, on the other hand, had other reasons. "Two daughters and one mother, three devils for a father." It is a long story, so do not ask me how we ended up here. But here, the inhabitants of the Oronda Island have made me their King. They have behaved as they should, except that the court has not failed to annoy me with tests and demonstrations. What they want is to see me failing and mock me. They think that I do not know. I pretend I don't, so they don't know it. "Good and bad arts are there and everywhere."

- What kind of problems is it?

- It is about entanglements, mazes, traps, tricks, and pranks. The last problem, for example, was a plot. It turns out that Oronda Island has the habit of asking every foreigner who is approaching, to announce the purpose of their visit. If the visitor tells the truth, they leave him alone; if not, he is hanged. There was someone, to my damn luck, who declared that he was cominy to be hanged. It does not seem like a big thing, but that smallness has left me puzzled. If I would have let him go, he would have had to be hung, since what was announced would not have happened, he would have told a lie. If I would have hung him, it would have been unjust, because the unfortunate guy would have announced the truth. Anyway... This mess was so well-known that it has become a classic. It has already caused me enough problems, and I do not want to repeat it because, far from solving it, I think I rather sneaked with a pinch of salt. My problem is that, in the trap that they have put me now, I am afraid I will not be so clever. And it is not that I dodge the body.

"*No provocation, no motivation.*" *What happens is that I do not count on the advice of my Lord who, longing for battles of helmets and swords, joined a maritime expedition against the Lunilaics. He walked away from me singing:*

We have come to die;
To win, if heaven wishes it.
Give no occasion to,
With impious arrogance,
The enemy asks you:
Where is your God?

- I know they have won -Al'jarama went on- and that victory is the first. But, I do not know about my Lord. I am very afraid for him. He may be in danger if he has not died yet. With all my heart, I would like to offer him a hand. As for me, I am in trouble if I do not come out from the new trap, because anything I do or undo here, whether it is erased or written, it is always known.

- Please, can you tell me exactly what the problem is?

- With rooted use, the so-called Allegorical Games are celebrated each year, and at any time, in Oronda Island. Here, the fights end by sudden-death, as the great Juanette wanted. Only three cerontes knights, their spears and their armored jralens survive in the tournaments. The one who has been less mutilated is the champion and there is a prize up to the third. The first prize is a grassland for livestock in the shape of a Trapeze of Jtood whose main base is worth 3 gonzas in length; the second is a right triangle whose smaller base is 2 gonzas; and the third, another right triangle whose smaller base is 1 gonza. This arrangement goes in descending correspondence with the order of dignities. Well, I distributed the three figures in a simpler and more compact one, thinking to gather some applause due to my economy. The awards ceremony was to be held next week; an eternity to my vanity that could not moderate its appetites. I, Al'jarama, hastened to announce that the whole prize would be distributed within a single piece of land in the shape of a square. So, what wanted to be ostentation became a mistake. Instead of the applause, the Oronda people rose in protest.

- What happened?

- *"When the devil gets lazy, talks to Daisy."* Some diligent people spread the gossip that I was fully aware that if the same pastures had formed a rectangle instead of a square, the total area would have been larger with 1 square gonza, enough space for a herd of jralens to have a happy lunch for a whole month.

- How can that be possible? -I asked.

- I have no idea. I am still surprised! Apparently, the same elements can be ordered in such a way that they form a square or a rectangle. The trapezoid and the triangles are exactly the same in either case. Ordered in any way, their areas should not add up differently. No one understands it! But... *"Once received the bluff, the ears don't get enough."* Now, the champions are resentful and incite the people against me, accusing me of trying to harm their heroes.

Then, Al'jarama showed us the two distribution projects. His square, formed by the trapeze and the two

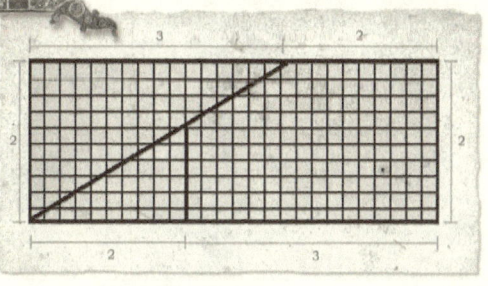

triangles, had 3 gonzas per side; that is, an area of 9 square gonzas. The rectangle brought before Al'jarama had 5 gonzas of length by 2 gonzas of height; that is to say, 10 square gonzas. The components of each scheme were the same; only their ordering had changed. Where had a complete square gonza been lost?

- I am hanging by a thread -Al'jarama said- I have to await the return of my Lord here, where he expects to find me. I know that I am the reason for the entertainment of the court. They think I do not know it. That is the only reason they feed me and keep me comfortable. If there is a trick in their prank, I would not like to expose it, because that would not be amusing and his dissatisfaction could lead to anger. With angry lords, I could end up with my bones out of the island and out in the open. If there is no evil in their challenge, it is the same for me, because I do not even know where to begin to understand this piece of hell. The only thing I know is that I have to accommodate the squared gonza in the square project even if I have to stuff it.

- I understand -my master answered.

- So, if you could help me in this new entanglement, the one in debt would be me.

- Tell me one thing, do you have any objection to yield more gonzas than the tradition obliges?

- Of course not!

- In that case -my master said- allow me to meditate on the problem.

- Of course! But first, let me give you the comfort that friends deserve.

Reverend Ogli and I were taken to a rather large room that was part of the tower of an ancient castle. Inside, two broad beds of thick wood had been leaned against the walls, leaving in the middle an arched window made of polished stone. On one side, a pierced table made it home to a large bowl of aged porcelain. Equally yellowish, the calcareous walls rose in a curved way until they formed a vaulted ceiling. Leaning on one leg of the table, as if it was forgotten, an old crock of water laid there, crudely beautiful. Behind the door of our room, there was a small roundabout, crowned by a skylight. Other doors of other rooms converged around it.

While the contours of the roundabout tended to be devoured by the darkness, in the very center a cascade of light spilled just above a desk that was not very modest in size and very fine in woodcraft, shining in the chiaroscuro with the solemnity of a ceremonial altar. In one of his many drawers, a glittering Ogli-s-Oöp found paper of thread, ink, pen, and other writing aids, and though he had his own, he wished to write with these others.

I saw Reverend Ogli drawing bright squares, trapezes, triangles, and other splendid relatives from the same crib. I also saw that he was casting numbers without fear. I, on the other hand, since the first time I looked out of the castle, missed no opportunity to marvel again. We were actually on an island, if by "island" one means a castle in the middle of a squared sea, like a chessboard. In the distance, there were boats whose disconcerting forms, once I got used to the landscape, shocked me less. The room where we had been housed, and seven more like this, formed the crenelated crown of a tower that stood over the sea and communicated with the rest of the castle by an arched bridge. The concentric waves generated by the circular base of the tower advanced on the squares, ignoring them, which filled me with doubts. Is this a mirage that happens only to me? In a squared sea -I told myself- there should be square waves or none at all. That would have been consistent! But a fantasy does not have to be logical. Probably because of that, there was no night and there was no day but both at the same time; clarity and darkness had degraded one in the other around the atmosphere we had as the sky. From left to right in that strange firmament, at the same time, the deepest hour of the night was gradually illuminated until it got light at the other end in an undeniable morning, which was dawning over the squared sea.

- It's a board of liquid chess or a liquid board of chess! -Reverend Ogli, who had approached the window without me noticing, said- Look, how beautiful! A queen corvette and a pawn caravel full steam ahead on the waves left by a chess sea horse.

- Ah! I saw those boats, but I could not recognize what they were.

- Surely, they were not as close as they are now.

- Where are we, Master? Is what we are seeing possible?

- I do not have the slightest idea about where we are. But, I know there are times when reasoning is inopportune; there are moments that deserve our entire contemplation. Not always using the reason is reasonable, dear Ad. The verses are not enjoyed by calculating the stanzas. So why not rejoice in this miracle without seeking an explanation? Give up yourself to the privilege of being alive! However, remember that you do not need to contemplate seas of chess to be part of the daily miracle. The ordinary flight of an insect is indeed a prodigy; not less amazing, the insect itself; admirable, like feeling the avalanche of air that keeps your vivacity on; wonderful, like receiving the refreshing breath of the morning that brings you the earliest exhalation of the woods. Have you thought how many small miracles are involved to enable the vision? The process of smell is not orphan of wonder, either. But if you insist on seeing miraculous instant worlds, just raise an abandoned log. In a second, you will hear a creak, you will perceive a stench, and you will see a shadow that leaves you breathless. You will surprise the progress of an entire kingdom. Small, very small insects and scavenger creatures with their queens, their laws, and their masters; pebbles that attended the creation of time; reeds, thorns and leaves that are delicacies in secret feasts. The dinner guests will flee terrified: they are embarrassed to eat in public; they are uncomfortable with the measuring of their manners. Only the intoxicating aroma of the decrepit wood, the acidified antecedent of complex microbial maturations, emanations of fertility, will remain. There will be the smell of primed soil, of nourished nature, of vegetable perfumes, the remains of the gallantry of some passionate insect; the last exhalation of an old trunk that is moldy breath. As you see, dear Ad, it is a mistake to count the verses no matter how sad the night is. If you are lucky enough to know the science of light, let it serve you to appreciate, to the satiety, the rareness of a dawn color. The soap bubbles are brighter when their enigma has been penetrated. The crystals are more prodigious when one has looked at the magic hidden in its sparkles. The shape of the shells, the mineral landscapes that you discover inside the rocks, the kinds of clouds and the taste of wine, everything has a splendor. Perhaps this is the result of the spreading of God's splendor... If you understand what a rainbow really is, you will arrive at the spectacle of every rainbow contained in your lifetime. And, for that reason, you will respect the life of all the creatures and you will condemn the wars, all fratricide... As you see, dear Ad, you do not need to square the sea; the reality is more exquisite. But do not make the foolish mistake of waiting to understand it before enjoying it. By the way! Do you play Ajhelá?

- Yes, Master, but... I'm not very good!

- Well, if you like it, you should know that the Ajhelá was invented in the Lunilaic East.

- Really?

- Many good things were introduced in the Western Continent through the Lunilaic occupation of Lepuria and Southern Primaria. Even before that, there was a system of teaching throughout the Lunilaic world. Later, during the occupation, the educated individuals of Lepuria were in a permanent exchange of intellectual correspondence with the educated individuals of Rjostos, Sammkara, and Spahá. There was much progress in math, physics, chemistry, and medicine. One of the founding tribes of the Lunilaic culture, the Esquitos, was driven by a very strong Grezco influence. Thus, almost at the beginning of its culture, an astronomical observatory was founded in Sammkara. The Ahaxi Rum-a-Sd gathered in his court as many wise people as he could. Rum-a-Sd's successor ordered the collection of Grezco treaties throughout the world. And the next Ahaxi established a House of Wisdom so they could be translated into the Lunilaic language there. For example, the Astronomy of Tom-el-Eo was translated there. The only copy that came to the monastic libraries of the Middle Era did not have a Grezco origin, but Lunilaic, and thanks to this we know it. Bd-a-Tib, citizen of Spahá, was the first of the great Lunilaic physicians; he wrote more than a hundred works. Among them, the most well-known, "The Complete Totality," collects the Lunilaic, Grezco, and Emurian treaties, and some others from the Far East. The numerical systems that handle the concept of zero were introduced by them.

- ...and the Ajhelá!

- That's right, dear Ad! Alchemy emerged with Butal-a-Mê, known in the West as Alamí. The writings attributed to Alamí are copies from a collection that belonged to a mystical sect called The Brothers of Purity, who claimed that we are all equal. They tried to demonstrate their precept by means of educational activities like the construction of schools and the writing of encyclopedias. It seems that the Pure Brothers wrote the fundamental corpus of alchemy in a large volume that was only part of the encyclopedia they were writing. Seventeen of the fifty-two treatises of that encyclopedia were on scientific subjects. The Pure Brothers were contrary to the deductive reasoning that the other Lunilaics had inherited from the Grezcos. They placed the mysteries over reason and claimed that the mysteries can be explored empirically. The Brotherhood of Purity was declared heretical by the Orthodox Lunilaics who confiscated their great encyclopedia. Then the Pure Brothers went underground and became a hermetic sect. There are reasons to believe that a remnant

group of this secret society was the one who made contact with the Lapidarian Knights in response to their request for collaboration.

At that moment, someone knocked on the door. I hurried to open it. Filling all the available space of the entrance, there was King Al'jarama in person. He presented himself with a large silver bowl full of fruits.

- Sorry to bother you, my friends! -he said while eating a succulent enaria, colorful and ripe- I have come to offer you some fruit and see if, by chance, you have approached a solution. You know! "I better get it over and done with..."

- Yes, good King.

- What? Yes, what?

- Yes! I have already found a solution.

- Blessed be God! How did you do it so soon? For you, I will sing prayers for three hours in a row! You do not know from what you have freed me! But, tell me, what is the solution?

- Let's go to the desk. I will show you there.

- Praise the Providence for having brought you here!

- I think you exaggerate, good King. On the contrary, the Providence benefited us. Oh, here it is! This is the new prize distribution project.

- And it is a square!

- Yes, it is a square.

- And what is the catch?

- You must tell your subjects that, by the dignity that distinguishes you, you will distribute the trapeze and the two triangles as the tradition demands: their bases will be 3, 2 and 1 gonza. This is by law; so, the demands could come this far, and this should end the matter. But, although there is no obligation that weighs on you, you have decided to give each one an extra reward according to your very particular judgment that no one has to question. I do not think any of the champions will refuse to receive more than expected.

- No, I do not think so.

- Well, the distribution of the additional gift has to be this way: for the first prize, 5ø more gonzas at the base of his trapeze; for the second, 3ø more gonzas at the base of his triangle; and for the third, an increase of 2ø gonzas at the base of his triangle. In short, the absolute winner will receive a trapeze with a base of 3 + 5ø gonzas; the second, a triangle with a base of 2 + 3ø gonzas; and the third, a triangle with a base of 1 + 2ø.

- Oh, it's the divine series! -I said, quite astonished- 1+2ø; 2+3ø; 3+5ø...

- Yes, dear Ad, you have recognized it.

- Sorry for the interruption, but can you tell me what ø means? -King Al'jarama asked.

- It means 1.61803 gonzas, good King. It also means that it does not matter if we speak of a square or a rectangle, we are talking about the same surface: $(3+5ø)^2$; Exactly, 122.9914 square gonzas.

- That's a lot!

- "No one can serve two masters." Do you remember the phrase? 122.9914 square gonzas are required by mathematics to reconcile a square with a rectangle... but if the good King prefers to be in the open...

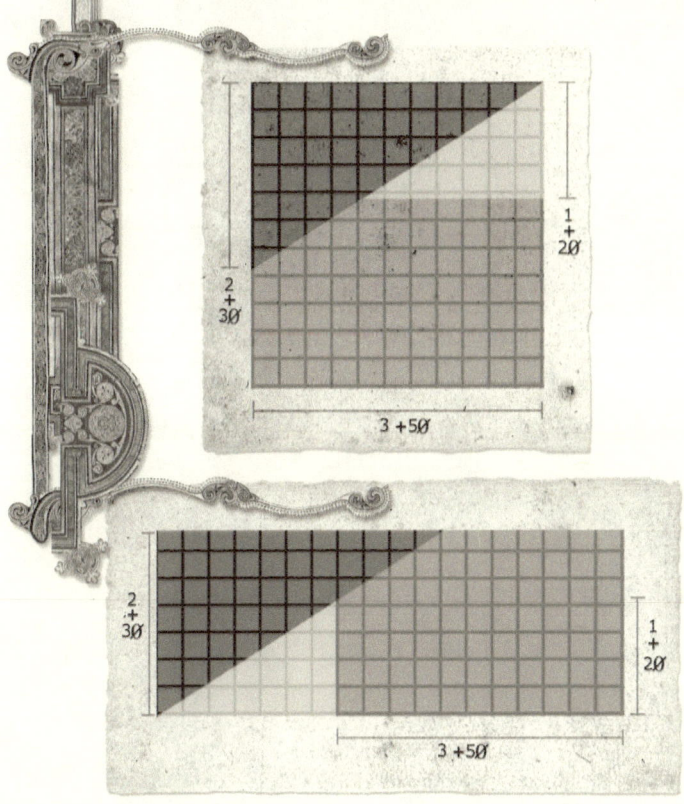

- *Ahaaa!... No, no. My kingdom for a square!*

Al'jarama, King of the Oronda Island, thanked us profusely and invited us to a banquet in our honor.

As for heading us toward our destination, no one on the island had any idea about what we were looking for. So, we took the only road connected to the island and moved forward.

Chapter XX

Confessions without Contrition

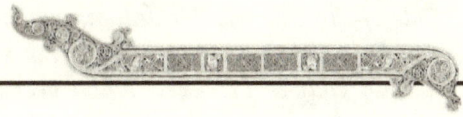

or some time, I have wanted to ask you something, Master.

- Tell me, dear Ad.

- It's about the Holy Inquiry. Was it really as bad as they say?

- I think it was a lot worse. It was, so to speak, the security police of the Cruciglobist church. And it was as brutal as any of them. They involved the suspect in tricky philosophical arguments. They answered for the accused who did not suspect what he was getting involved in. The staging was intended to get a culprit in the fastest possible way since that is a sign of competence among stupid people. For the bulk of the public, almost always uneducated, an incomprehensible argumentation could only come from very erudite academicians. The apriorisms of the Holy Inquirer were full of prejudice, superstition, and malicious nonsense. The inquirers were incredibly morbid. There was much more evil in a Holy Inquirer than in a hundred accused of evil acting. For the population, however, the truth appeared before the Word of God. And of course, all sorts of confessions came up to suit the needs of the Holy Inquirer. If you nodded docilely, they burned you at the stake at once as a good boy. If you protested the slander, it was worse for you: they roast you slowly. "Add more oil so he burns better!"

- Like books. Did the Holy Inquiry burn books?

- Yes! If they burned people, they burned books before. That is for sure! But allow me to continue. They could burn you little by little with red-hot irons or they disemboweled you with diverse instruments to amputate, to drill, to break, etc. They could also stretch you like chewing gum using the strength of the animals or the power of the capstans. Even today, these interrogation systems are methods of those despicable despots who are not interested in the truth.

- In these conditions, one confesses any crime.

- Of course! Precisely, I had been remembering a similar process against the Lapidarian Knights. Now that I think about it, before the Holy Inquiry was created, the method already existed. In the...

- Forgive me for interrupting you, Master, but, speaking of the Lapidarian Knights, I would like to remind you that you were about to answer me why it is suspected that the Lapidarians had found Ah-Lê-gönn, "The one that cannot be found," when we were distracted by King Al'jarama.

- Yes, dear Ad, I have not forgotten. The answer is too important to leave it in the air. The torment method of the Holy Inquiry offered me the perfect opportunity to restart the response which I was going to do next.

- Oh! I am so sorry, Master Ogli.

- It is all right, dear Ad! I know your impatience, but I also know your humility.

- Thank you, Reverend Ogli! Please continue.

- Since the beginning of the Campaign, the donations that the Order received, both in financial resources and in properties, were very generous. Of course, there were those who wanted to win the heaven this way, but most of the donors just wanted to have the Lapidarians on their side. As the Order became wealthier, the search for sympathy was greater and the more important the new friend, the more important the donation. Thus, they received houses, animals, plots, inheritances, titles, even whole villages with the respective taxes that they generated. The King of Lepuria gave them, for after his death, a territory as large as a country, which the Lapidarians managed to exchange in life for twelve fortresses. Another monarch offered them a whole kingdom that had been his before the Lunilaics assaulted it. The Lapidarians attacked the Lunilaics, reconquered the kingdom, and reigned there. And these are just two examples to illustrate the magnitude of the donations. In these and many other ways, Lapidarian Knights came to possess more than many kings together. At the end of the Campaign, the Lapidarian Order had become one of the largest

landowners in the Western Hemisphere. They came to possess 50 castles and 9000 fiefs; of these many of a monarchical scale in Galactia, Primaria, Lepuria and Arania, without counting the Lapidarian possessions in the East. The wealth they came to have was used in their own matters, that is, in the Campaign; under the particular Lapidarian model, always independent of the other participating armies. The fact that they had an overseas battle-front forced them to invest in an immense fleet of ships in order to maintain the flow of resources and cerontes. The security of both realms and the caravans of merchants through forests and mountains was a matter of concern to many, and the idea of carrying cash was very uncomfortable. The local kings began entrusting their treasures and the administration of their economies to the Lapidarians, which helped the Order to create the first banking system since the fall of the Marterian Empire. To make possible the transportation of money, they created account books, promissory notes and even the first bill of exchange. For the first time in Ghesta, documents were used to send money from one continent to another. To give security to the merchants whose occupation was providing products for the Campaign, the Lapidarians created the first system of safe deliveries. They had so many properties that they could transport the products from any fief to their ports, practically through them. These two major implementations made them even more powerful and wealthy. And of course, there came a point where they could do what any bank does: lending money. The princes of the West ended up owing them considerably. At some point, the grandfather of the King of Galactia had asked for a loan to pay his ransom after being taken prisoner in one of the last campaigns. The amount of the loan had not ceased to grow because of the interest and was a serious problem for a king whose economic situation was in itself greatly deteriorated. Already before, with some years between one case and the other, the King of Galactia, having been in financial trouble, had not hesitated to do something quite dishonest: despicable and evil as he was, he had managed to declare illegal in his society two different ethnic groups, known for their ability to make money. He persecuted and exiled them, keeping their wealth, and righting his economy. There are those who say that this was the reason why the King of Galactia began to conspire against the wealthy Lapidarians who, little by little, had risen like a threat before all the other kings, monarchs, and feudal peoples of the Western Continent. This risk would have inclined the sympathies in favor of the King, in case of a conflict.

- That is, he wanted to repeat what had worked for him before.

- Precisely. There are also those who believe that his attack against the Order was due to the rancor caused by the dishonor of being rejected after requesting his acceptance as a member of the Order. Well, it's always possible that the two things happened, one after another. It can be understood that before attacking them, the King of Galactia tried to join them, especially considering that this union surely implied some financial solution that could have helped him to recover his economy. The truth is that the King of Galactia became his declared enemy. Thus, the end of the Lapidarian Order began, or that is what they made us believe. Shortly afterward, an ex-Lapidarian who had fallen prisoner to the king due to drinking and causing disturbances, "confessed" horrendous things about his old order. The ex-Lapidarian's account told about satanic practices and initiation rituals imported from the East. The King informed the Øppos of what he had come to know and demanded the dissolution of the Lapidarian Order. The Øppos was baffled, he did not know what to do. After all, the Order was more a daughter of the Cruciglobist Church than a creature of the secular world. The head of the Cruciglobist church used all delaying tactics on the subject. Since the Øppos was taking so long, the King of Galactia secretly sent an order in a sealed envelope to all military stations of his kingdom. The letter ruled that, at dawn, on a certain day, the Lapidarians should be arrested and their property confiscated. And so it happened. The predestined morning, the Lapidarian Knights were taken prisoner by surprise and their properties alienated in favor of the King. As soon as he found out, the Øppos tried to oppose, but with no success. The King's soldiers tortured the Lapidarians until they were able to extract the confession they needed, and they did it fiercely. Thirty Lapidarians were killed during the interrogations. The Grand Abbot himself confessed to reconfirming the ex-Lapidarian's declaration in detail. Then the Øppos intervened. He claimed custody of the Lapidarian Knights. The king did not yield; he took the intention of the head of the Cruciglobist church as a protective effort that could end in the liberation of the knights. The Øppos reminded him that he had in his possession a signed letter of submission from when the King's great-grandfather surrendered to the armies of the corresponding Øppos of that time. In this armistice, the royal family of Galactia accepted the authority of the head of the Cruciglobist church. The Øppos threatened the King of Galactia: if he did not obey this treaty, it would be a cause for excommunication. The King reflected: the excommunication would make him lose the support of the rest of the kings of the West, which would be very important in any conflict. The Kingdom of Galactia would

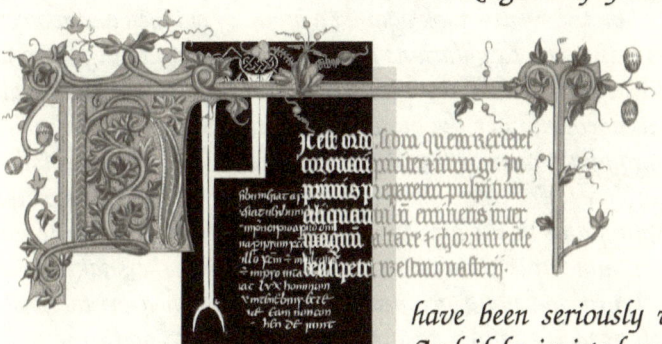

have been seriously weakened. And if he insisted on retaining the Lapidarian Knights, the next move of the Øppos would have been an armed attack against which, without the support of the other princes, he would have lost. The King gave up. The Øppos got the custody of Lapidarian Knights. Then, something inexplicable happened: after so much struggle to get the care of the Lapidarians, the Øppos gave them back to the King of Galactia. This decision seems to be related to a closed meeting between the Øppos and the Grand Abbot of the Lapidarian Order. We could not know what was said in it. Either the Øppos was offended or the two of them agreed. Back in the hands of the King of Galactia, the Grand Abbot completely changed his attitude, retracted his confession and with him, five hundred more Lapidarians took back what they had said. They asked to be allowed to speak, they denounced the torture, and they described as absurd the accusations to which they had to agree in the martyrdoms. In short, they denied everything. The King of Galactia accused the renegades of perjury and declared that even the self-confessed could be absolved, not so the perjurer because the retraction showed his lack of repentance. Thus, those who did not contradict the confessions were released and the perjurers were sentenced to death.

- But what happened between the Øppos and the Grand Abbot?

- But what happened between the Øppos and the Grand Abbot?

- Nobody knows. And that is not the only thing that is ignored. Actually, every intervention of the Lapidarian Knights is covered in shadows.

- What are the other things that are ignored?

- Well, I have told you the events in an uninterrupted way, but between the confession of the ex-Lapidarian and the final outcome passed over a year and a half. When the five hundred Lapidarians revolted, the wrath of the King was transmitted to the last of the jailers. One of them, excited by the events, took against a group of old men and women who were visiting the Lapidarians and providing them with food and messages. He attacked them with his whip in one of the corridors leading to the dungeons under the ground. The whip struck an old man's back, causing him a pain of fire. Then the crack of the whip exploded on a woman's face. The infamous leather nerve retreated like a spirited serpent, signing an s in the air. As the whip reached back over the unfortunates, a hand rose from among the crowd, and the snake coiled around it. Whip and hand gripped each other. With a brutal push, the hand plunged the villain to the ground and there, with the same scourge, he was strangled. The other jailers, who celebrated their cowardice, threw themselves over the strangler, killing him brutally. Once dead, the jailers recognized him. Can you guess who he was, dear Ad?

- No! I do not know. Who?

- Neither more nor less than the ex-Lapidarian and ex-prisoner who originated everything with his confession. They had left him free with a handful of silver coins. They had done it almost for fun. Even the King himself had bet on how long the traitor would survive out of prison. They were sending him to a sure death. That was what amused them so much. But obviously, the traitor survived with such dignity as to serve as postman and lay down his life in defense of his friends.

- It seems as if the Lapidarians had sent him to say exactly what he confessed.

- That is exactly what we believe. Although more improbable, it is also possible that, once his ex-comrades were imprisoned, the traitor saw the opportunity to obtain his pardon if he showed himself helpful and repentant.

- That is why he brought messages.

- Or food... This theory does not explain his previous survival, though.

- What I said first is also possible, right?

- About his confession? Yes, indeed it is, because another of the enigmas of this episode arose when the order of imprisonment of the Lapidarians became effective. This order was made throughout the territory of Galactia. We are talking about twenty-three castles at the same time. In no case they resisted arrest. In no case of the twenty-three simultaneous scenarios! The Lapidarian Knights, terror of friends and enemies, who were accustomed to fighting against the Lunilaics, carrying the weight of their boiling armor in the desert, eating, and drinking on their mounts, and sometimes even their mounts, battling like devils for entire days, these same knights meekly surrendered to the guards of the King of Galactia who wore tassels in their boots and plush around the neck.

- Unless everyone agrees!

- Exactly! In Lepuria something different happened that only confirms our doubts regarding what happened in Galactia. In Lepuria, the Lapidarians surrendered under the same accusations and with the same meekness. At some point, the Lepurian King expressed his wishes of releasing them, but only after confiscating their possessions. Thereafter, they stopped being so tender and they fought and killed as only they could. This shows that they were meek only when they wanted to. It also shows that they expected to return to their domains after surrendering.

- As if surrendering was in their plans, but they did not expect someone stripping them of their castles.

- Precisely! Do you see how our doubts are not unjustified? The Lapidarians of Galactia all confess the same, but they get angry at the Øppos; from that moment, everyone thinks differently. As if something had not turned out as expected. Did they have a preconceived plan? Since when? Since the appearance on stage of the former Lapidarian or long before? Does this have to do with the secrecy with which they worked in the East? Does this have to do with what they transported so carefully in secret? Does it have to do with Eli-vé and the Lunilaic hermetic sects? I think all those answers are...

- ...In the Night of Time! -I completed just to complete.

Reverend Ogli twisted his neck roughly at me, but almost instantly he blurred his gaze as if I were not there, as if I would have been transparent. Again, we were in silence. Unlike the other silences of Reverend Ogli in the darkness of the disconcerting stairs, this new mutism was decipherable: it was visibly the result of a profound state of abstraction. The silence went on. I was careful to respect his trance. Finally, he said:

- I think it is time to talk to you about something that, if it were not for the circumstances, I would be prohibited from telling you. We Szabeos are very careful in what we reveal. Only when, over the years, the recipient has demonstrated complete fidelity to our Order, a superior monk is authorized to entrust him with what we call The Exegesis. In it, the listener discovers the mysteries that surround the Great Mystery and understands, at last, our reason for being as a religious order. The Exegesis is the best-kept secret in History. Only after knowing it, you would understand our caution.

- I am particularly honored with your deference -I replied, adhering as best I could to the lectionary of disciples- But tell me, Master, why are you going to give me such a special knowledge so soon?

- Because I had already begun to suspect the reason for our presence in this extraordinary underworld that Wgijvrán called The Night of Time. Your access to this secret became more and more imminent. It was only a matter of time, even if we were out of the Time. If it is as I presume, I must tell you the antecedents because the consequences of what we find here could be quite transcendental for you and for me and, in general, for all. I think it is necessary for you to understand perfectly the significance of what might happen here.

- I will try not to disappoint you, Master.

Chapter XXI

The Exegesis

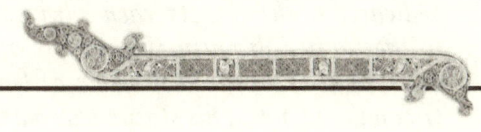

I must tell you, my dear Ad-d-Tuar, the history of us, the Szabeos. We are named both in the sacred book of the Cruciglobism and in the Lunilaicism, but we do not name ourselves in ours. The ancient historians did not know how to name us because we did not classify in their possibilities. Modern archaeologists are perplexed by the few traces we left unintentionally in the past. They want to name us, but they have to find a way to catalog us first. Szabeo was the word to name the pagan, the cosmic and everything that was close to devotion. They think we come from Narráh, because they have found some of our ruins there. Narráh, in Spahá, not far from the old Ntra, enjoys the reputation of having hosted the cult of Nas, God of the Moon. But Nas actually has another name, the real one. The New Age linguists are sure that the Szabeos carry the true name of Nas incorporated into our hermetic names, which no one has tried to confess without losing his voice. The Temple of Nas in Narráh had its ceiling built with cedar of Ifreno that delivers its perfume beyond the hundred years. The walls bore designs based on creatures never seen in this world. The friezes were decorated with the blue-green pieces of a spheroid that already orbited the planet long before civilization had risen. The doors exhibited cosmic motifs embossed on the metallic material of the same spheroid. On the steps of the temple, the exalted figure of Nas, God of the Moon had been raised. Archaeologists are confused. A Cruciglobist monk who wandered through Spahá at that time, claimed that the Szabeos believed in a supreme, unique and eternal power, the Last and First Cause of the Universe, the First Intellect, the Superior Order. This god-idea would have commissioned the administration of the Universe to the planets. These idolaters, said the monk, worshiped images with body and head that represented the seven planets. In the city of Narráh there were seven temples dedicated to the planets, each with a special form that corresponded to the exalted divinity. The temple of Ahtemá was hexagonal and black and its statue was made of lead. The temple of Ificios was trigonal and green; his statue was made of tin. The temple of Eqíodo was rectangular and red; his statue was made of iron. The temple of Idherada was quadrangular and yellow; his statue was made of gold. The temple of Abvia had a base comprised of a triangle within a rectangle and was blue; his statue was made of copper. The temple of Iccio had a square inside a triangle as a base, it was orange and his statue made of clay. The temple of the Moon was octagonal, and its color was gray; its statue, the one of the god Nas, was made of silver. The placement of one temple with respect to another, the relative size of those and the size of the statues were calculated according to the different planetary relations of separation, volume, weight, distance from Ghesta, etc. When they prayed, the Szabeos looked north much more favorably than toward the south; they prayed at twilight and at dawn. They carefully followed the evolution of the solstices to adjust their calendar of apotheosis ceremonies. They watched every eclipse to plan their processions. They knew when the planets converged; when they were opposite; when all or some lined up.

- Was that true, Master?

- Is our God of an abstract nature? Yes. Our conception of God cannot be simpler: God himself is beyond the reach of our understanding, but Nature is his rubric.

- Is it out of our understanding as a hypercube that exists in the fourth dimension?

- Exactly, dear Ad! The interest in the cosmos can be incomprehensible by itself to people who dedicate all activity to a pragmatic purpose, including the salvation of their souls. That being said, do we worship the statues of the planets? No. But about the vigilance of the stars, yes, that was true. Do you remember, dear Ad, that we understood that a temple wants to be the image of the Universe?

- Yes, I remember.

- Well, the Szabeos believe that the Universe is the temple of God. In that case, studying Nature becomes an act of devotion. In studying

Nature, we know God. And, knowing God is a religious act. A religious act was to watch the transit of the stars. Knowing God was to follow the solstices and the eclipses. There are many religious acts like these that make the daily life of the Szabeo monk. And of course, we performed ceremonies and processions to celebrate the natural fact. What is the Szabeo rite, if not? To keep the ritual up to date, we needed, for example, to master astronomy. We were always devotees of mathematics, geometry, and physics; as well as botany, zoology, and biology, since the most precious good that shines in the Temple of God is the living being. The study of Nature is not complete without the arts and social sciences. An appreciation for knowledge was a necessary characteristic of a Szabeo from the antiquity and has been perpetuated as a fundamental requirement for the disciple that has entered the monastery. But science is not static; science changes according to the discoveries or the genius of privileged minds. The study of science, therefore, has kept the Szabeo Order in a dynamic intellectual activity from which it was impossible to escape. Because the permanent change adjusts the Thinking Being to consider new points of view, different possibilities, or simple conjectures, the Szabeos remained open. They conditioned their faith to the state of knowledge.

- And what about the Temple of Nas, with metallic carvings made of something that orbited the planet?

- The stories of antiquity that speak about us always relate us with the Temple of Nas, God of the Moon, but this is nothing more than a myth like so many others. A document from the beginning of the Lunilaic Expansion tells us stories about the military incursions of G'wo-pj'i-Ban, the conqueror. One of them tells of his passage through Narráh. He says that, when the conqueror arrived there, he was received by a people whose members wore black cassocks, had long hair as curly as their long beards, and light sandals woven with the fiber of straw. G'wo-pj'i-Ban was intrigued to see them and interrogated them, "To which people do you belong?" "We are Narrahnians," they answered. G'wo-pj'i-Ban looked up to the Temple of Nas, God of the Moon, and noticed an emblem on one of the hands of the statue of Nas and asked, "Are you Lunilaics?" They replied, "No." Then G'wo-pj'i-Ban noticed the emblem on the other hand of the statue of Nas and asked, "Are you Cruciglobist?" They replied, "No." G'wo-pj'i-Ban asked them again, "Do you have a revealed book or do you have a prophet?" They answered, "No." "Do any revealed book, or any prophet mention you?" They answered, "No." "If so, you should know that we only tolerate members of other religions which are mentioned in our revealed book. You are pagan idol worshipers, said G'wo-pj'i-Ban. I will hang you all, if you do not accept that this statue is only an image and that your god is inferior to the God of the Lunilaics," G'wo-pj'i-Ban said. They replied, "This statue is only an image, and our God was never superior to yours." G'wo-pj'i-Ban was perplexed. He said to them, "What kind of faith is that, to so readily deny its God?" They answered, "A faith without arrogance that does not rise over the lives of God's creatures." G'wo-pj'i-Ban stood there, thinking for a moment, and he said, "Then you must choose between becoming Lunilaics or embracing one of the religions mentioned in our revealed book which includes the Cruciglobism. If you have not done this by my return, I will kill you all without compassion." Then the Narrahnians met and deliberated. They realized that, because of their beliefs, they could not simply choose one religion, so they split in two. Except for a select few, the Narrahnians changed their clothes, cut off their curls and wore leather. Half of them went toward Arteria, the former Catatonia, with the Cruciglobists. The other half went to Vatzar, in Sammkara, with the Lunilaics. Those who remained were the most knowledgeable priests. First, they thought of taking refuge in the mountains of Vjobasett and secretly preserve the faith of the Narrahnians. Later, they found a solution: they were going to tell G'wo-pj'i-Ban that they are Szabeos. This name appears in the revealed book of both Lunilaics and Cruciglobists as well, but it was no longer maintained by anybody. Thus, the Narrahnians took the name of Szabeos for themselves. G'wo-pj'i-Ban never returned, though. He died fighting the Cruciglobists in Qía, beside the legendary E'jo-aij-Afu, the Ariffat. After knowing this, some Narrahnians tried to give up their new creeds in order to return to Narráh, but they were assassinated. This is, in short, the story that disorients the archaeologists. Anyway... Since then, the Narrahnians remained secretly intermingled among Cruciglobists and among Lunilaics as well. At first, this dispersion was imposed by personal security, but later, the

Szabeos priests realized its convenience. All of them kept a clandestine communication. These are our informants about whom you have already come to know, dear Ad. The priests remained in Narráh for some time until they were scattered in several monasteries, like the one of Kien.

- Why so secretive, Master?

- From the beginning, our beliefs aroused intolerance. For this reason, we Szabeos have always covered ourselves with a mantle of darkness. Our creed is not something that can be accepted by all. That's why we have not done anything to gain adepts. Until now, the Szabeo practice has been extended, mainly, by direct transmission from father to son. Among these children, few are those who feel the call of the priesthood. But the main reason for so much secrecy is that we keep the greatest of secrets: The Exegesis. And that secret is precisely what I am going to reveal to you.

Reverend Ogli covered himself with absolute seriousness. He looked for his backpack and took two bands of modest cloth out of it. He let one of them fall behind my neck, so that the ends of the band fall on my chest. He took the other and put it on himself in the same way. Then he placed both of his hands on my shoulders, looked up and said...

- Are you ready to receive the revelation, disciple Ad-d-Tuar?

- Yes, Master Reverend Ogli-s-Oöp.

- Do you promise, disciple Ad-d-Tuar, never to reveal the secret that you are about to hear, never before The Splendid Occasion occurs?

- I promise, Master Reverend Ogli-s-Oöp

- The Exegesis is a system of revelation of arcane knowledge that comes from the beginning of time; to the listener, it prepares him for the Splendid Occasion. If the listener would have the privilege of finding the latter, his knowledge would rise beyond common wisdom and comprehend the past and the future: the deep meaning of the sacred plan. The Exegesis is like a book of symbols; the episodes are only a cover that envelops its sublime confidences. However, the most hidden revelations promoted by the clarified secrets are inaccessible for those who literally read the text. The Splendid Occasion has been an expected and longed event throughout history. The Splendid Occasion will be an occasion for change. On the Splendid Occasion, the past will definitely remove its shadow. There will be a transformation. A peaceful state of rest, of serenity, of harmony will follow.

However, before the Splendid Occasion is presented, time will be charged with tension and anguish. There will be despair, drowning, signs of failure, and self-destruction. States of agony like these may be many, but only one will lead to the Splendid Occasion, thanks to a deep effort and, perhaps, a sacrifice. The Szabeo elders believe that it may mean the death of someone. The initiated disciple must therefore attend to the advent of the Splendid Occasion because he has been warned. It is also believed that the death of that person will lead to the rise of another. Thus, the common good will finally be reached.

- Well then -he went on- We are descendants of the oldest lineage of priests, of a lineage lost at the beginning of time when the mysterious strands of destiny began to interweave. Even before the writing, we evolved in the scene of myth and legend, in passages of the Genesis of remote traditions, in the fantastic explanations of the young spirits, and in old meditations. We saw the Thinking Being grow up, become its owner, and develop the thousand facets of civilization. We have witnessed wars, hatred among peoples, massacres, genocides, xenophobia, persecutions, intolerance, and indescribable tortures. We saw that all those in charge had their god and the priest who blessed a marriage was the same who blessed a warship that was set out to murder overseas. We have seen, without being able to avoid, massacres promoted by the lack of a common creed, the armies of two gods being destroyed by divine incompatibilities. We have witnessed the Holy Wars, and we have been horrified and embarrassed. But we have also witnessed the first sowing, the inauguration of the empires, the rise of philosophical schools, and the manufacture of pottery. We saw the Thinking Being questioning himself about the utilitarian possibilities of the stones; we saw him repeating the question to a smoking cauldron; and we saw him, suddenly, coming back from the Moon. We, Ad-d-Tuar, are the Custodian Priests of the Tablet of the Arcanum.

- What!

- Yes, dear Ad, we are the Custodian Priests of the Tablet of the Arcanum.

- But then, do we keep the Tablet of the Arcanum?

- Unfortunately, and despite our best efforts, we do not know where it is. All religions have an unreachable element: paradise or heaven is equally sought and unknown. Even more so, an ancestral religion, such as ours, could not be exempt from the mythological grounds which corresponds to its distant origin. You have already heard, from my mouth, the Genesis according to the revealed book of the Sz-abeos. It is important to be aware of the symbolic quality that is by no means less transcendent. With the first murder, the Tablet of the Arcanum is destroyed, the Thinking Beings separated into two beliefs; and the hatred promoted by the beast negatively interposed forever between them. This is a way of symbolizing the enmity between the major religions that dominate the world. Secondly, our theologians believe that it is also meant to signify the loss of the Tablet of the Arcanum. There are indications that, at some point in its early consolidation, the Szabeo community was attacked by an invading force. We talk about a time way before the Marterian period, about five centuries ago. The ethnic group that submitted to the other peoples of the region was a barbarian group very bellicose, called Ethriarch, from whom the Lunilaics seems to proceed. Some time ago, in the Ethriarch ruins of Buoobh, ceramic tablets were discovered that narrate passages about their history. In one of them, an Ethriarch attack on a mystic town is narrated. In this town, all were priests, priestesses, or disciples, and all of them wore long and curly hair. Although they did not attack back, they did resist with their own bodies. The tablets also say that they took the idol of the mystics and added it to the Ethriarch treasure. It seems reasonable to think that the Ethriarch chronicler refers to us, the Szabeos.

- But the Szabeos did not have idols, right?

- True!

- Then what did the Ethriarchs take away?

- Well, that is the question! It is probable that they have mistaken the Tablet of the Arcanum with an idol.

- And where is the treasure of the Ethriarchs, or whatever they were called?

- Nobody knows for sure.

- Then the matter ends here!

- Not really. The Ethriarchs were conquered by other groups. The settlements, the invaders and the empires passed and re-passed through Riostos, Sammkara, and Spahá. A century before the arrival of the Marterians, a Grezco traveler called Bruenio, the Old, known for his medical treatises, made a long journey through these lands. His travel book tells about the many customs and beliefs he encountered in his trip. Referring to what remained of the Ethriarchs, he says, "Now, reduced to beggars, there are those who bestow past glories on themselves and despise those who are above them today. They say they dominated this region for a thousand years. They call themselves *Ethriarchs* and remain solidly united in expectation of a champion who has been promised by a deaf prophet. When he comes, this hero will embark on a triumphant campaign that will reconquer the region and restore their past splendor. To do this, he will use the *Ethriarch* treasure that is hidden in the *Enchanted Valley of Souh*, in a place that only he knows." Also, a popular legend of *Vatzar* narrates the adventures of two friends in search of the *Souh's Treasure*. With this name, it is mentioned in several documents from ancient esoteric Lunilaic societies. One says that the *Souh's Treasure* is a transmuting force, while another says that it is an inexhaustible source of inspiration; another, that is the *Sacred Stone of the Lunilaics*.

- *AHA! The same as the Holy Råål.*

- *The same! This one would be its Eastern version, so to speak. The definitions are different in each Lunilaic manuscript, but all sources coincide in pointing out that the Souh's Treasure is hidden in a place known by the hermetic name of Ah-Lê-gönn's, "The One That Cannot Be Found."*

- *Wgïjvrán, the magician, would call it Mal-ö-Goom. Right, Master?*

- *Very good, Ad! I realize that you have followed my Exegesis. It seems that when we talk about the Mal-ö-Goom, Ah-Lê-gönn and Mālegum, we are referring to the same place in Druid, Lunilaic, and Artigonian terms, respectively. Now, this Exegesis began with the Tablet of the Arcanum and apparently ends with the Holy Råål. So, probably, the Holy Råål, the Souh's Treasure, and the Tablet of the Arcanum are the same.*

- *But where are any of the three?*

- *According to the above, any of the three is wrapped in the shadows of the same mystery...*

- *That is to say, the search for the Tablet of the Arcanum ends here!*

- *Patience, dear Ad, patience! Do you remember that the cerontes attacked Urse because they heard that, in the time of the Cruciglobist domain, Gasto Visio, the Marterian monarch who ruled throughout the territory of Rjostos, seeing the city threatened by the Lunilaics, hid somewhere a fabulous treasure he had found in...*

- *In... Mmm! No, I do not remember.*

- *In the Enchanted Valley of Souh!*

- Oh, sure! I remember now.

- It seemed that the treasure of Gasto Visio was within the walls of Urse, but no one knew exactly where because Gasto Visio took the secret to the tomb. When the Cruciglobists took the city of Urse, they searched in the walled city and they did not find anything that had not been a "normal" booty. Please, dearest Ad-d-Tuar, do not go tell me, "here is where everything ends" again.

- No, Master. I am sorry.

- What follows is pure speculation because the clues end here.

- That was exactly what I was going to say!

Reverend Ogli looked at me resigned.

- Either because Wgijvrán really existed or because, working from the bottom of the literature, he induced in the masses the unconscious necessity of a quest; or because it was the necessity that created not only Wgijvrán but the pretext for the Campaign and a thousand adventures more, the fact is that the Lapidarian Knights went to the East seeking a secret of uncertain existence. A secret that satisfies a conglomerate of desires or only one, that in various forms would always be something different. Precisely because it was uncertain, what was going to be discovered promised to fill all hopes. A mystery that does not deplete itself of promises was needed. A mystery that, very intimately, does not relieve completely or is never found. Under the above requirements, it is not strange that the sought mystery has been imagined between an aura of divinity, as a sacred gift, a sublime knowledge. It is also understood that an objective of such imprecise definition may have associated different interests, broad enough to engage friends and enemies. Thus, the Lunilaics, who also brought their hopelessness and their chimeras, when it came the time, collaborated with the Cruciglobists. What follows, dear Ad, is the final part of the Exegesis. We, the Szabeos, believe that, from the beginning of the Campaign, the Lapidarian Knights sought this promised knowledge in the most obvious place. Where was the knowledge deposited? It was deposited in manuscripts.

- That is why they sacrificed part of the spoils for a library.
- Precisely!
- And that is why they burned what did not interest them.
- Perfect!
- But then, what happened next?
- Then, in an ordinary and memorable night, sheltered by the mist of the mountain forests of the Párkatos, a cart arrived at the Castle of Gur, the Lapidarian headquarters. The cart was loaded with hundreds of manuscripts of mystic accent, with secret messages. A squad of Lapidarian Knights escorted it. The castle doors were open; they knew what was coming and they knew when. Inside, the Lapidarian top leaders from many places who had been concentrated there, looked expectant. In complete seclusion, the Great Abbot, his generals, wise advisors, doctors, and delirious visionaries in the service of the Lapidarian Order gathered together around the manuscripts. With them, there were also several readers of Lunilaic languages recruited in Faronia. Among them, there were those who understood Zhski, the ancient sacred language of the East. The scholars read the texts at once without any science greater than the direct translation. Then, they interpreted the texts in the light of the Druidic art, which handles the permutation of symbols. They tried to decipher them in vain and blasphemed without reward. A week passed in this way; from roll to roll, from dawn to dusk. At last, something appeared, a fantastic writing of magical and amazing verses. The experts threw themselves over the stupendous text, delirious and feverish. They unraveled it and extracted its esoteric messages. They came to an interpretation. The Lapidarian leaders deliberated. There was a consensus. Immediately, the Lapidarians generals left for the East and West to give instructions. The chroniclers of the Campaign, the other cerontes and even the simplest peasant who observed, realized that something had changed: The Lapidarian Knights no longer fought. On the other hand, nobody knows by what means they came into contact with the Lunilaic hermetic societies. They talked about something they had discovered. They conversed. They made a pact and came up with a plan. A global plan.

- A plan, what for?
- We do not know with exactness, but the evidence of a plan comes out from the movements that the Lapidarian Order executed next. We

believe that the top leaders of the Lapidarian Order discovered one or more manuscripts, probably from Ethriarch origin, which described the loot taken from the mystic people. The description may have been fanciful since it was presumably dictated by a magical mind. However, the sages who aided the Lapidarians were able to make clear something transcendental about the Tablet of the Arcanum. We do not know what it was. Something that imposed on them the need to interview the Lunilaic hermetic leadership. Something so important that they accepted the cooperation with the Lapidarians while the other Cruciglobists massacred their people. Anyway... We assume that, as a consequence of the plan, the Lapidarian Order made contact with the rebellious King Phi D'Ric who had been formed among Cruciglobists and Lunilaics, who had the power and the connections that they needed. Phi D'Ric disappeared for a while. He is believed to have been invited to some Lapidarian shelter. They let him know about the discovery and explained the plan to him. The eccentric Phi D'Ric, friend of the arts and science and enemy of war, once convinced, became one of them. Now, all of a sudden, he needed to be reconciled with the Cruciglobism. And not only that, after obtaining the representation of the Øppos, he turned to be the second authority in the Cruciglobist church. King Phi D'Ric knew where to go because the plot was already set: he did not go to war in Jbur but to visit the Ahaxi. And there you have them: the equivalent of the Marterian Emperor of the West and the mighty Monarch of the Lunilaics together, without killing but smiling. Phi D'Ric spoke not as emperor, nor as the leader of the Fourth Campaign against the Lunilaics; he spoke as the ambassador of the agreed ones. What was discussed in the palace of the Ahaxi was not in the name of the Western Civilization or the Cruciglobist church, but in the interest of the Lapidarian Order and the most powerful Lunilaics. Immediately, the Ahaxi endorsed the interests mentioned there. And, as an unusual consequence, he temporarily ceded the sovereignty of Jbur to Phi D'Ric. The Øppos was satisfied and Phi D'Ric had a pretext to move on Lunilaic soil without any of the armies asking him for an explanation. Strange, right? This can only be understood as a confirmation of a global plan that involved the greater powers of the West and East.

- But what could it be?

- The most important thing that followed the meeting is the stay of Phi D'Ric in the palace of Ntra with Eli-vé as a host. What was he doing there? The answer to this question is the last of the revelations of The Exegesis. Iruz-tod, chronicler of Ntra at the time of the Campaign, in his work "UtE-mê-fhaT," already told us how Eli-vé discovered a cave hidden under the basements of the city. The narrative clearly states that the cavern housed a building dug into the rock with some stairs that protruded from the muddy waters. The building bore a triangular pediment over a row of columns with very strange anaglyphic symbols that Eli-vé could not recognize. What kind of language was it that an educated warrior could not identify? Was it perhaps an ancestral language or a secret liturgical dialect? Then he says: "Part of a giant yellow hand and part of a red head laid on the steps, probably, the remains of some immense statues." What does that remind you of, dear Ad?

- The Szabeo temples that were in the city of Narráh.

- Exactly! But, as I told you, that is part of a legend and not a true story.

- The same as Wgïjvrán, the magician.

- Yes! I forgot... there is also the detail about AloOf. From the story of Eli-vé, where a monarch becomes a winged beast, it can be presumed that the sorcerer AloOf mastered the necromantic art of transmutation. In the search for the Holy Råål, the concept of transmutation has a very gravitating meaning and, with various appearances, is common to all searches, including the search for the Souh's Treasure. Phi D'Ric travels to Ntra with a squad of Lapidarians. Once there, they descend to the cave through the filthy, smelly corridor. As I told you, there is evidence that Phi D'Ric left Ntra with something he did not have when he arrived. Apparently, they found what they were looking for and what they found did not disappoint the expectations, the causes of the pact, nor the elaboration of the plan. Then, and this concludes The Exegesis, the Lapidarian Knights did find the Holy Råål. And the Holy Råål is the Tablet of the Arcanum.

- Well, where did they take it?

- We do not have the faintest idea. Nevertheless, it is reasonable that it was hidden in some property of the Cruciglobist church, because Phi D'Ric had the benefit of representing the Øppos and could do and undo anything without anyone asking him questions. It is also possible to think that the Tablet of the Arcanum is hidden in some secret place that belonged to the Lapidarians.

- Then we have nothing.

- *We have something! It is possible that the chosen ones, among all who have taken The Path of Gnedh, are us. We are on the privileged road that will reveal the secret that the Szabeos have pursued for centuries: the whereabouts of the Tablet of the Arcanum. For the Szabeo monks, the Tablet of the Arcanum has always represented the attainment of peace. Finding it has been our reason for being a religious order. And, given the highly dangerous situation for life on this planet, its discovery becomes more necessary than ever.*

- *Very well, Wgijvrán!* -my master cried to the air- *You have won: I want to find the Holy Råål!*

Immediately after, there was a violent darkening followed by an explosion of blinding clarity.

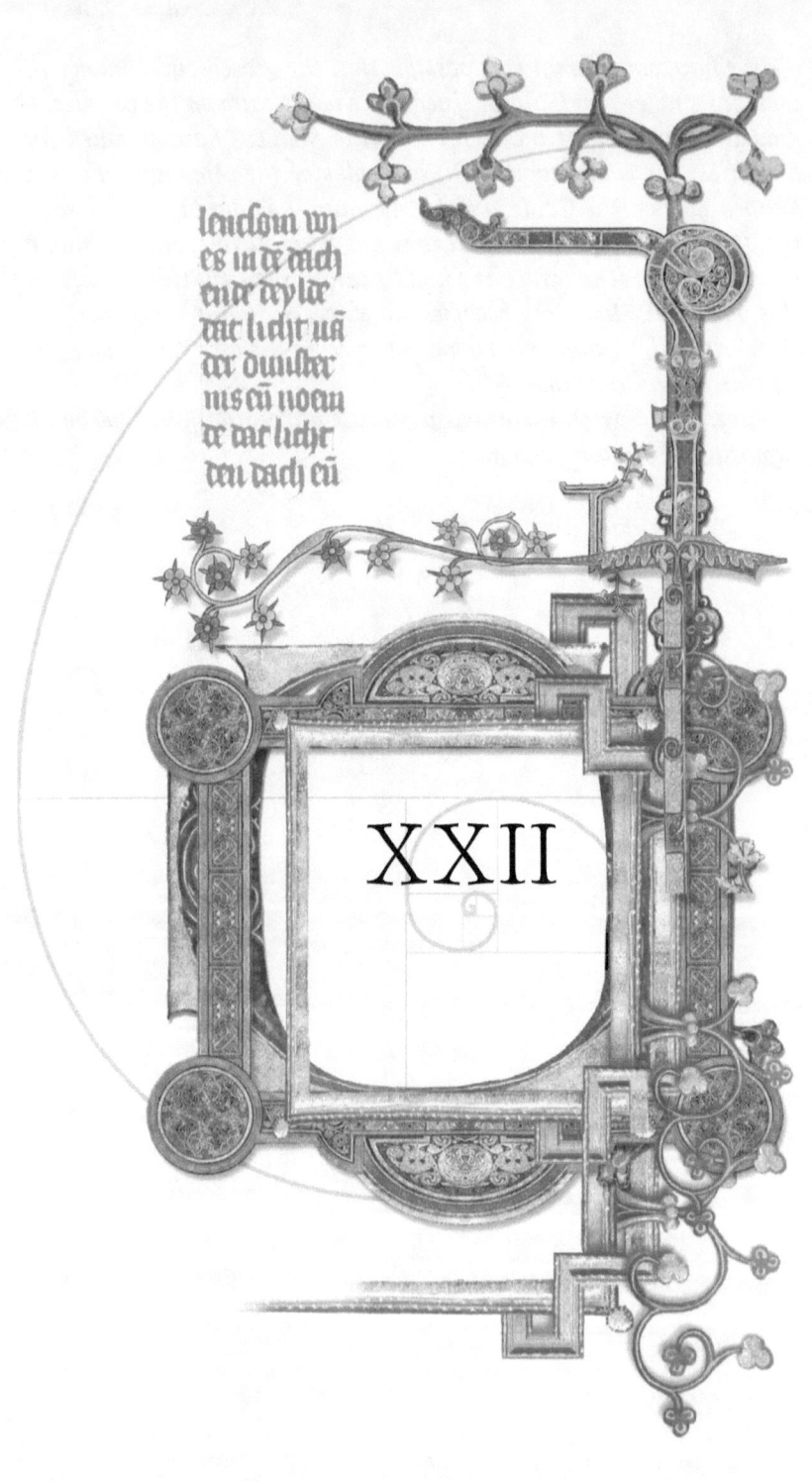

lencloin vii
es in de dach
ende dey lae
dae licht uā
dee duwbee
nis eñ noeuu
te dae licht
den dach eñ

XXII

Chapter XXII

The Uneven Iris of God

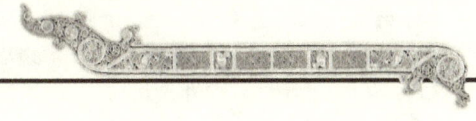

T he intense glow went off a second after the burst of light. Still impressed by the clarity, I caught bits of a scene from the fifth hell. We were enclosed in a cage with metal bars, hanging from some place in the darkness. Just below, in a large pot, a thick reverberating soup boiled with the violence of a volcano. Its crust fractured into a thousand pieces, letting me glimpse the incandescence of its interior. From there, we got all the clarity, which was almost nothing. A warm, moist, almost unbreathable steam rose through the trellis floor of the cage, suffocating us in its thick cloud. The steam wetted my face with a hideous condensate. I could not help breathing all that morbid exudation of greasy guts. I breathed my own fear and I breathed the darkness. Then, without knowing why, I found myself slowly uttering immemorial names: Eliseo, Onupis, Rabis, Tsis, Catatonio, Hasás, Uwer de Or-Est, Erguen, Wgüvrán, Ngupd, Dox Ibi-Dor, Ubo, Rubán Ras-i, Igre, E-Tar, O-Tar, AloOf, Eli-vé, Phi D'Ric, Gasto Visio. As I was naming them, from the asphyxiating vapor, an onomastic monster was formed. For each name, the monster added a greenish head with eyes of stale cheese and a moist tentacle covered with a blue infection. When it was complete, all the heads stopped moving and they noticed me. Dozens of angry eyes focused their nauseating curiosity toward me. Then, I had the feeling that all the names were one: the monster of a thousand masks.

Then he raised all his tentacles at once and directed them against me. He began to advance and kept moving until all his grotesque limbs gathered on my throat with a viscous and creepy caress. I screamed in terror as I saw myself covered in blue. I desperately stretched my body up trying to escape, and suddenly... I was free. Below, meanwhile, the rising vapors that kept me on their fingertips began to spin. Like a steamy hand, the smoke wrapped me until it grasped me totally. When it got me very tight, it swallowed me up, taking me down like a drain.

On the floor of the gloomiest corner of a castle, heated by a kettle that maintained a phosphoric reverberation, harmful mercury vapors were marrying an evil form of volatile sulfur. Floating over the alchemical soup, a golden glowing stone appeared. The stone peeled itself, revealing an immaculate and perfect egg. The kettle began to lose heat until its exhaustion. Once it got cold, the egg began to shake. There was a moment that it broke and a beautiful white bird, slender and proud, unfolded its wings and flew away from the castle to the free sky where it was happy forever.

- How did we get here? -my teacher asked.

- Hey!... What?

That moment, I woke up, or I just arrived, who knows! Owner of myself again, I noticed that we were in a great hall like those which are attached to the palaces. Judging by the number of military devices from the Middle Era, it might well have been an armory, but they were so scattered that it rather seemed to me that I was contemplating the remains of a battle. The corridor was bounded on the left by a wall, on the right, by a sequence of windows in an ogive shape. The windows were constructed with stained-glass in a boric style; they spread a brightly multicolored clarity. The light bounced on the metal bodies of the armors that laid on the floor. The armors seemed to keep inside exhausted ghosts from unsuccessful wars.

- Amazing! -my master exclaimed- If it were not so carelessly maintained, I would say that we are in a museum of arms; specifically, in a room intended for the Middle Era. There are armors similar to those used by the Lapidarian Knights and all the other cerontes. There are helmets, spears, swords, knives, meshes. Ah! Look over there, dear Ad: an armor to cover the body of a jralen! Can you imagine the weight the poor animal had to tolerate?

- What is that?

- That is a crossbow. One of the most sophisticated weapons of those times. The crossbow was extremely deadly and very effective. It is a bad example of what technology can produce. I do not think there is any more abominable business than the production and sale of armaments. Though, if you think about it, without it people would not have killed any less. The Thinking Being has not changed his instincts, he has just changed the caveman stick to the remote-controlled missile. Perhaps that is why, as the last tribute to honesty, he wants to erase the unworthy imprint of his passing through the universe by destroying himself with antimatter bombs.

- Master, is it true that an antimatter bomb is much more powerful than an atomic bomb?

- Do you remember that I told you before about Brother Sänte, the greatest and kindest sage we ever had in the Order? I told you about his model of the Cosmos in which, if an astronaut departs in any direction and always travels in a straight line, he would return to our planet as long as he is able to travel far enough?

- Oh, right! Yes, I remember.

- Well, it was Brother Sänte who found a relation between matter and the energy it contains: $E = mc^2$. The number c, once squared, is a large amount, so a little matter carries a huge amount of energy inside of it, enough to wipe out entire cities. Let me make it clear to you, dear Ad, that Sänte's formula did not promote a bomb; it simply explains the violence of the explosion. Very well, in atomic explosions, only part of a mass becomes energy. But if matter gets in contact with antimatter, then virtually the whole mass will turn into energy, producing such a monstrous explosion that it would dwarf the atomic bomb. First, pi mesons and other particles will be produced. So...

- Master, forgive me for interrupting you. Before you proceed, could you explain what antimatter is, please?

- Of course! With pleasure, dear Ad. For many decades, the matter could be explained in terms of electron, proton, and neutron. To study these particles, a system was used to photograph the trail left by a particle that crossed an electric field. Someone who reviewed those photographs found the path of a particle that crossed an electric field. Someone who reviewed those photographs found the path of a particle that should have been an electron, but it curved in the opposite direction. It was understood that this particle was an electron of positive charge and it was called a positron. Except for this detail, electrons and positrons are identical in all other respects. The positron is the antiparticle of the electron. The antiparticle of a particle is identical to it, except that one of its characteristics is the opposite. If the particle in front of a magnetic field rotates from right to left, its antiparticle will do it in the opposite direction.

- That is to say, that this would not serve us to communicate to another planet what is left and what is right.

- It is true! It is easy to recognize that in this case, the symmetry of the experiment would be maintained. Well, if a particle and its antiparticle come in contact, the result is the total emission of energy. Until the discovery of the positron, scientists, with certain exceptions, had been reluctant to accepting the possibility of the existence of opposing particles or antiparticles. There was a theoretical physicist named Diluac-D'qut, who prophesied the discovery of the positron with these words, "It would be a new kind of particle, unknown in experimental physics, with the same mass and opposite charge as an electron. We could call this particle "anti-electron." The anti-electron would not last long in this world; encountering an electron would destroy them both." Electrons abound in our world and, as Diluac-D'qut had predicted, as soon as a positron is produced, it encounters an electron and annihilates each other. The Diluac-D'qut theory, to be consistent, also announced the existence of an anti-proton and an anti-neutron. Twenty years after the announcement, the trio of anti-particles was an undeniable reality. The physicists of the time thought that if for every particle that forms ordinary matter there is an antiparticle, why can there not be antimatter? An anti-atom of antihydrogen should have an antiproton as an antinucleus around which an antielectron would rotate. Forty years later, the first anti-atom of antihydrogen was created in the laboratory. It lasted 40 billionth of a second, traveled 10 meters, almost reaching the speed of light, and was then destroyed by ordinary matter. Antimatter was an undeniable fact. There was no reason to think that the anti-atoms could not unite to form anti-molecules and anti-compounds and antibodies and anti-beings. This fascinated the scientists dedicated to exploiting the subject. There were many problems to be solved: the life span of antimatter should be extended from 40 billionths of a second to a permanent existence; antimatter should be isolated from the rest of the matter of this world, probably making use of a magnetic field because its contact would turn the laboratory into the biggest bomb ever made; finally, a system had to be found to produce antimatter in significant quantities; not just a simple atom. Sixty years later, the first antihydrogen gas was confined in a thermomagnetic bottle. This prototype suggested the creation of inexhaustible antimatter reactors. It was necessary to know how to control the number of anti-atoms of

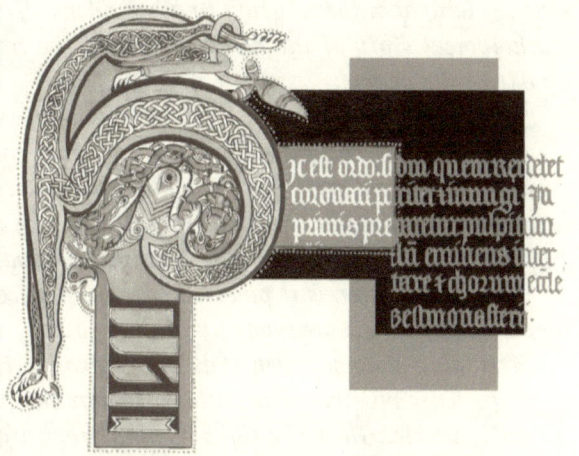

antihydrogen that come into contact with hydrogen atoms. Very few atoms meant unprecedented amounts of energy. This invention could solve the problem of food shortage once and for all. It would end poverty by opening up greater possibilities for combating diseases and prolonging life.

- About the Tablet of the Arcanum, we only know that it represents peace for the world, but we do not know what it really is, right? Why could not it be an antimatter generator fallen from the skies?

- It could be anything!

- And, perhaps, the Lapidarian Knights kept it because they still did not know what it was for or how to make it work.

- That would be ironic. Before the antimatter generator was developed as a real possibility, the armament industry, in complicity with some politicians, diverted the attention of the technology toward the production of missiles with antimatter heads. Satisfying hunger was not important; what mattered was to make money. The general public did not know about the production of energy from antimatter until that technology was converted into weaponry. And they did not know, because these same groups of power managed to keep it as a secret. But they hid it precisely because they did know how to make it work. As I have already explained to you, the world war industry had been engaged in a secret race to get the antimatter bomb. When the world was divided into two irreconcilable enmities, Western Cruciglobists and Eastern Lunilaic, both parties already possessed the greatest destructive power ever created. But no one knew it.

- As with the Holy Råål: a group of powerful people hides a secret that could save the world.

- Well, dear Ad, I have to admit that the detail does coincide, but what you are suggesting would mean that someone from outer space sent us, long ago, the solution to all problems. That is similar to the mythological story of the hero who steals the fire from the gods to give it to the people.

- Something like that.

- If your theory were true, the Tablet of the Arcanum should have come from a world with the same kind of matter as this; otherwise, it would have already exploded. In any case, the question is why the Lapidarian Knights would hide a universal good?

- Mmm...! Master, is it possible that we are seeing, with the telescope, galaxies that are made up of antimatter?

- Assuming that between that one and ours, there is only emptiness, yes, it is possible. The problem is that the photon has itself as its antiparticle. Then the light coming from a galaxy made up of antimatter would not give us any clue because there would be no difference that is manifested in the light. In other words, there are no two kinds of light, there is only one. However, we might recognize that we are seeing a galaxy and its antigalaxy at the same time. But still, we would not know which of the two has matter like ours. We could only say that we are seeing a galaxy-antigalaxy pair. We would not know which is which.

- How?

Reverend Ogli began to draw in his travel notebook.

- The electric charge of a particle is associated with the rotation of its magnetic field. If a particle whose magnetic field is oriented from north to south, turns to the left, then it has a negative charge; if in the same case, it turns to the right, it has a positive charge. Very well, considering the magnetic fields and the electric charges, we can draw a representative scheme of a particle and its antiparticle.

- They look like two specular images -I said.

- Exactly! The first particle looks like the mirror image of the other. I have already explained that, given the relativity of terms and movements, these mirror images can be superposed. The signs N, S, -, + are completely arbitrary. In this specific drawing, the particle on the left would be an electron and the one on the right, a positron.

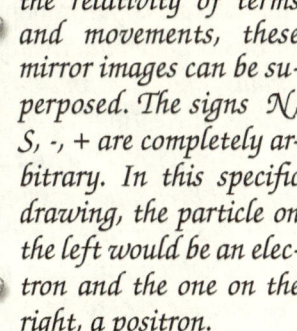

- But then antimatter would serve to determine what is right and what is left. Only the electron is the one that turns to the left and only the positron to the right.

- No, it would not. The reason is that the terms matter and antimatter are relative. For a being of an antimaterial world twin of ours, the antimaterial is just ours. A message like this: "Right is the direction in which your positron turns," would not make any sense

- Wow! It seems that the antimatter does not help us.

- No, dear Ad.

- Well, what I do understand is that then, a galaxy and its antigalaxy would appear like two enantiomorphic specular images.

- Yes! And if we were talking about spiral galaxies, we could not superpose the image of the one to the image of the other; its images would be "different" and recognizable. But, on the other hand, we would not know which of them, the one at the left or at the right, has the kind of matter that we consider "anti." It would be different if the galaxy was marked with a sign that says, "anti since birth." Nothing would be more absurd than transmitting: "If you are made of matter, then the direction in which your galaxy rotates is called left." It seems that the symmetry of relative concepts is still maintained. In conclusion: neither in the antimatter nor the subatomic particles a birthmark can be found. However, it was from the field of elementary particles that a very important issue was born. There is a type of atomic level phenomena that are called weak interactions because they progress at slow speeds. A slow speed at the atomic level is, for example, a ten millionth of a second. An example of this is the production of beta rays, which is nothing more than the expulsion of electrons by a radioactive nucleus. Beta rays are synonymous of electron beams. Weak interactions were detected in many processes with elementary particles, almost always mesons, but they had not been given enough importance for a deep care in the analysis of the experiments. There was a moment when someone raised the alarm. Observations of later phenomena posed serious paradoxes. No one seemed to be able to solve them. A couple of young students from the Far East, Cea-u and Aceuj, suspected something and reviewed the past data. Then, they suggested the possibility that paradoxes existed because they all insisted on demanding symmetry from nature. Some of them mocked and said: God cannot be left-handed. There was, however, a scientist from the same origin named Ij-Wwo, who set up an experiment to check what the young people were saying. The Ij-Wwo experiment involved beta production by a fairly radioactive cobalt nucleus, cobalt 60, which keeps emitting electrons constantly. It was known that electrons were emitted by the cobalt 60 nucleus from its north and south poles. The experiment was designed to be careful in order to see if this was true. For that, the possibility of an outcome that reflects a statistical average as a consequence of the random movement of the nuclei had to be eliminated. In other words, it was necessary to hold the nuclei so that they remain still, and all keep their north poles pointing in the same direction. The rest of the experiment would be limited to counting how many electrons left the magnetic north of the nucleus and how many left the south. In order to avoid the movement of the cores, Ij-Wwo cooled cobalt 60 near absolute zero and also subjected the cobalt to an intense electric field that forced the nuclei, at least more than half of them, to remain with their Magnetic fields aligned in the same direction. Although not entirely, the cobalt was trapped statistically. After that, you just had to count how many electrons came from above and how many from below. If nature remained indifferent as to which of the poles of a magnetic field is addressed, that is, if it made no distinction between them, then the two sums would be equal. Nature would have been praised once again for adjusting to common sense and good taste, Dr. Ij-Wwo and her pair of inspirers would have been called imbeciles and that would have been the end of the matter. Guess what happened, dear Ad!

- I do not know! What happened?

- The electrons in the Ij-Wwo experiment were not emitted equally in both directions. Much more electrons were counted below than above; that is, the nucleus of cobalt 60 emits considerably more electrons by its south pole than by its north pole.

- Finally! Now there is a difference between the magnetic poles, a birthmark.

- Indeed, the nucleus of cobalt 60 was, in some way, truly asymmetrical. Before, no way was known to differentiate the magnetic poles except for observing their reaction against another pair that was already examined in front of the poles of the

planet. Since then, the designation of N and S would no longer be a convention. Dr. Ij-Wwo's experiment put into our hands a method for labeling the poles of a magnetic field in reference to the behavior of the cobalt 60 nucleus.

- Although roughly -he continued- the core of cobalt 60 could be understood as a spheroid turning to the right of its NS axis. The arrows represent the trajectories of the fired electrons, there being more arrows around the south pole. An even more schematic diagram would make evident the impossibility of superposing it on its mirror image. The two figures cannot be superposed because now N

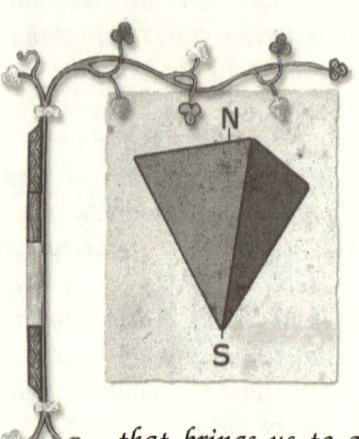

and S can no longer be switched since they are no longer equivalent. They are, then, two enantiomorphic figures. Therefore, the cobalt 60 nucleus presents an asymmetric behavior suggesting an asymmetrical spatial constitution.

- After Dr. Ij-Wwo -he went on- the nucleus of cobalt would be better represented by a tetrahedron than a spheroid. No one, however, has the slightest idea that brings us to an explanation of why one pole is intrinsically different from the other. Very well, dear Ad, now you can explain to the strange planet what we mean by right and left. It would be enough to transmit: "Hello! Hello!... The magnetic end where the nucleus of cobalt 60 emits more electrons, is what we call south pole. You must name the poles of a compass by calibrating it with respect to the previous definition: the one south; the other, north. Now, place the compass on a wire through which electric current flows away from you. The north pole of that compass will point to what we know as "left."

- Then, it was true! We tried to demand symmetry from nature.

- Yes! Just as before we imposed circular orbits to the planets because we considered that only the circle was perfect enough to be worthy of the stars. The same prejudice fell on the planet. We tend to think that everything is or should be symmetrical. Our houses tend to be symmetrical, the capitals of the columns and the candies as well. When we have to diversify objects, as in painting, we compensate for the imbalance by intervening in the volume of the bodies, changing it to restore the sensation of balance. But as much as we try to see nature as symmetrical, the facts prove that the universe is not like that. Someone said that the universe is now conceived as a weak giant with a single eye on the left. Perhaps that is the dynamic effect of looking within the infinitely spiraling iris of God. Some speculate that the two young scientists realized this defect precisely because they came from a country where art finds its beauty in asymmetry. Giving the empty space a different aesthetic and compositional value, Far Eastern paintings concentrate what is truly painted on one side of the painting. And it is precisely the imbalance of this

asymmetry that confers to Far Eastern painting the movement that it possesses and that forces the eye to go from the blank area to the area with ink and from it to the first indefinitely. Simple and charming. It resembles the symbol of its mystical culture which results from the asymmetrical division of the circle. The circle, in the West, suggests instead all sorts of symmetries. The mythical symbol of the Far East consists of two large surfaces in the shape of a drop with a small replica of themselves inside. One of the largest areas is dark in color, the other is clear. The names of these areas are Thocj and Thacj. These names represent the sounds produced by the falling of a drop of a moist fluid and the dropping a dry grain of sand. Thocj and Thacj mean all the extreme and antagonistic dualities that maintain the dynamic equilibrium of the universe; as suggested by its design, which has a movement by itself. This enveloping movement also recalls the generation of a spiral toward infinity. Thocj and Thacj are the engines of this generation, they are all opposites: love and hate, good and evil, war and peace.

- ...Lunilaicism and Cruciglobism -I added.

- Yes, and as you see, they could be just two parts of the same plan of God. Thocj and Thacj also symbolize old age and youth, male and *female, beauty and ugliness, truth and lie, left and right, etc. The smallest areas, the small drops, represent the possibility of a drop of fluid that has no moisture and a grain of sand that is not dry. This is to symbolize that on either side of a duality, a little part of the other side is always hidden. There is something beautiful in every ugly person and something unpleasant in the very beautiful. There is some insecurity hidden in every pretentious person and something presumptuous in every act of humbleness. Some wear veils with vanity and showiness. The whirlwind of a hurricane always has an area of calm; and the excessive calm, a moment of exasperation. There is some lying on both sides of the truth. There is something false in every proven theory as the one which maintained the constancy of symmetry as a natural law. This dark drop in a clear one, this "deviation," this "anomaly," is the mystery hidden in all things. It looks like a secret conspiracy of the universe, or God. Wherever you look, there it is; in silence, waiting. This is precisely the engine of science and the integral development of the Thinking Being; a continuous approach to God on his spiral path.*

Chapter XXIII

The Suffocating Steam of the Waters

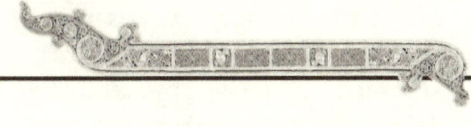

There was a moment when we found the end of the crowded corridor, the piggy bank of helmets and armors. The end offered no exit. That shocked me.

- This long corridor -Reverend Ogli said-seems to have been extracted from the back of a Boric cathedral. I cannot recognize which cathedral it is, specifically. Besides, if there is any likeness, we would be talking about a closed section, with more reason, unknown to me.

- Can you recognize the stained-glass windows, Reverend Ogli?

- No. I can only recognize the style. Look at that relief, Ad! And there! The stylized forms appeared at the end of the Middle Era. The nerves that run up the columns rise to make contact with each other in the center of the concavity of this ogive. This is precisely the nervous system of a Boric cathedral.

- But is it possible that a Boric cathedral shelters hidden galleries?

- Cathedrals, like the souls of the contrite ones who come to them, possess hidden corners where vinegared secrets are kept. The passages of the crypts lie in the entrails of the temples, embedded in the framework of their foundations. They are gloomy places, moldy, which freeze the blood with the cold of darkness; a darkness that conceals the horrors of hell. It is the inherent power of the dark, the empire of the dreadful, where the tormented spirits call for expiation for their unconfessed sins. The crypts are marble, cold and humidity, catacombs, mausoleums, bitter stench of the souls. But also, in some concealed places, under this gloomy mantle where only the honest dare, the basements of the cathedrals keep a crystalline brightness knowledge. This knowledge is offered to those who have been able to face darkness first. They are offered as a revelation. That is the genuine truth where the building lies; not about the darkness that is fear of the truth. Certainly, in the deep foundations of several cathedrals, magnificent and fleshy statuettes of black virgins, dating to ancient times, have been found. Are these statues the object protected by the dark side of the temples? Do they symbolize a greater truth hidden elsewhere, in a unique and sacrosanct place? In one of them, the name Bha iEx was found. This was the name of an ancient goddess worshiped in Hipotamia, in the form of a black stone that was said to have fallen from the sky. There is an author of the Middle Era, opposite to the hermeticism, called Qeuix de Bardth, whose testimony can be considered impartial. Qeuix de Bardth tells us that the black virgin of the hermitage of Otámix was replaced by a sacred monolith that the ancients called Opperfuss, which means "conceived in the sky" and the simple people called it later, the Master Stone of Power. It was also called Ardenx at the time when enx meant black darkness and, in particular, stellar fire. According to Qeuix de Bardth, a Boric cathedral of great execution was raised over the hermitage, in whose foundation the most secret wisdom was kept.

- Master, how come you know so much about words?

- It is not my merit, dear Ad. The time will come, if the world is still standing, in which you will be initiated in the study of Philology and Arcane Semantics. In it, you will be cultivated in all philological references related to the Mystery.

- Ah... I would like it very much!

- Patience, dear Ad! The wind brought by spring blows only in spring. But, returning to the subject, the route leads us to the suspicion that one of the most important Boric cathedrals, or the greatest, was built over a black monolith.

- This may be a certain clue to find The Tablet of the Arcanum.

- The problem is, first of all, that no one knows where the hermitage of Otámix was located. It seems that it was a local divinity of limited devotion. Secondly, almost all the Boric temples were build on ancient places of worship, often pagan; so many, that this observation is suspected of being the norm. Many of these sacred places, when they did not have a black virgin, they had a sacred well as can be seen in the Boric works, since some of them still have them. These wells are the materialization of what the esoteric tradition knows as the Source of Life or the Fountain of Youth. The water of those wells was renowned for its medicinal properties. In the city of Verdux, there is a boric cathedral, known as Nôtrame d'Teq. Next to the well that sinks in the depths, in front of the tomb of a bishop, you can read: "Whoever drinks from the bottom of this well will drink eternal life."

At that moment, I got close the wall; exactly in front of an attractive sample of carving on an ornamental relief. Something sounded like a trigger. Immediately, the floor opened at our feet. We could not hold on to anything. There was no time. We fell to an intensely illuminated floor. As soon as I could get used to the glittering clarity, I stood up. I did not feel any damage. I found Reverend Ogli in front of me. I found Reverend Ogli at one side. I found Reverend Ogli on the other side. I found Reverend Ogli at my back. And further back, more Oglis and more Ads. Around me, in all directions, our image was repeated hundreds of times, among an infinity of Boric columns, white as ivory. I took some steps to get close to my master, and my action was multiplied by a hundred, and I faced another hundred doubles in another entirely different position. At that moment, the Boric columns disappeared. In its place, that extraordinary atmosphere acquired the decoration of the oriental palaces. I panicked. I tried to move, but I hesitated.

- Stop right there! -a hundred Oglis shouted- Do not even move!

- Help me, Master!

- Serenity, dear Ad! -He said in a tranquil and confident voice- Everything can be resolved with calm and patience.

- Where are you?

- I do not know! I am also seeing countless Ads mixed with my own images and I do not know which one is the real one. All I know is that we are in a palace of mirrors.

- A palace of mirrors? What is that?

- The palaces of mirrors were used in the antiquity. They drove crazy those that were trapped in them. We are experiencing the sensation that we could have if we were reduced and confined within a kaleidoscope. A palace of mirrors was built on a hexagonal base room. Each one of its walls was a great mirror neatly polished to get an extreme reflection. The prisoner of a palace of mirrors saw himself reproduced countless times around him and as far as he could see. The wicked one would see his wickedness infinitely multiplied; the perjurer would see his blasphemy leap into his face; the murderer could not hide his crime; the envious would be tormented by his grudges; the thief could not escape his shame and the common people would be mortified by their sins, their lies, their infidelity, their disloyalties. Anyway... The one who was trapped here faced hundreds of ghosts.

- There must be thousands of ghosts!

- Mmm...! There are not so many. A well-polished hexagonal room can reproduce 468 twins, product of up to the twelfth reflection. Then, dear Ad, do not move. Unless we happen to be favored by fate, with each move we get more disoriented. Do you remember, approximately, your movements from the beginning?

- Approximately, yes.

- Try to get back on your steps.

Very slowly, I moved my legs back, trying to repeat my movements.

- Done! I think I have come back.

- Very good! Now stretch your arms and turn around. I'm going to do the same.

An instant later our hands touched each other. I hugged my master. Just then, the setting changed again. We were now among Grezco columns from the classical period.

- Let us move forward now -Reverend Ogli said- Surely we are going to run into a wall that is invisible because it is actually a mirror. It may be biased toward us, then, we would not be reflected in it even if we could see the other reflections.

- So we will not know when we are going to hit the wall.

- Exactly! That is why you must advance with your hands outstretched.

Indeed, there was a moment when we came across an invisible barrier.

- Now -Reverend Ogli said- if we move along this wall, we will find one of the corners of the hexagon.

We both walked very carefully. As we moved, our twins moved in all directions. Some seemed to pass very close to us. Some of my replicas looked at me with the same stupor with which I did it. Then, we found something truly solid. It was the real one or one of the real Grezco columns that filled the multiple mirage.

- Dear Ad, I want you to place yourself as tightly as possible against the column. When the column begins to spin, because I assure you it will, we will rotate with it, accompanying its movement. Is it okay?

- Yes, Master. As you say.

We waited a few moments, but nothing happened.

- The more refined mirror palaces, like this one, combined the infinite reflection of the reflected object with the total mutation of the environment. This added a sense of delirium to the anguish suffered by the unfortunate who had been stopped by the intangible framework of the reflections. To accomplish this, the hexagon's walls were cut from top to bottom at some distance from the corners. The corners, then, could rotate, exposing several decorations. The wretch was in a tropical jungle or in a palace of oriental decoration. From time to time, one of them was liberated to intimidate others with his stories about the king's black magic. The secret of this magic was based on a physical phenomenon as simple as the reflection of the mirrors.

- Master! -I shouted- It is moving!

Like an ordinary revolving door, the corner of the palace of mirrors removed us from the immense mirage. As the door came to a halt, we were met by the dim light of a torch. The torch was embedded in a curved wall made of blocks of gray-blue stone. The orange glow of the flames highlighted the cold exudation of the wall. We breathed in some moisture. Drops saturated with mineral pestilence fell upon us. The surface of the ceiling was covered with green nodules like the protrusions of an amphibian. The floor was carpeted with a mantle of water.

- It looks like we are in the basement of an old building -Reverend Ogli said- A castle? A cathedral?

Reverend Ogli took the torch and with it, we walked down a cavernous hallway that we found on the right. We came to a spiral staircase, all carved in stone, that descended beyond the darkness.

- Do not tell me that you want us to go down through here?

We did it! The spiral staircase sank, digging through the insides of the floor like a drill. In the glow of the torch, the steps shone with the metallic blue of the tempered steel. The distant sound of an intense dripping came to us, predicting even more soaked matters.

We went down, torch in hand. The shadows fled from the flame, revealing nodular shapes that stretched and twisted around the spiral steps as if they had been part of the vortex of an ancient volcanic broth when time did not even count. We went down with perplexed attention and hesitated on every step. The stands continued to pierce the shadows, opening circles in the darkness. Suddenly, the torch lit something else. Lying on the wet floor, we could see a circular wooden door like a sea hatch. The door was ajar.

- I guess we must get in? -I asked.

- I think so, dear Ad! Come on! You can do it!

Beneath the circular door, the stands continued to sink without apparent change. The fourth turn, however, led us to a room very large, quite dark, and crossed from ceiling to floor by a forest of columns of rich execution. We walked in silence. I, fearful and astonished; Reverend Ogli, as serene as ever. He even had the courage to stay a few minutes to "enjoy the architecture." We never left the space between the rows of columns to which the steps had led us. At last, we came to a room built entirely out of stone blocks. Like all the rest, the floor was also covered by a thin layer of water.

Reverend Ogli lifted the torch to look up. At the end, you could see a basin almost at ground level. On top of it, an empty container in the shape of a shell was attached to the wall. On top of that, there was a sea monster directing its huge mouth forward. The ensemble was contained under a bow that was set on the backs of two gargoyles that crowned a pair of corner columns. Inside of the monster's mouth, there was a strange group of geometric protrusions. The whole wall looked old, aged by negligence, eaten away by the water and the shadows. We got closer to look better at the marine being. It was then when we heard a "click" that emerged from under our feet. Suddenly, the monster began to vomit a stream of water in the container. Soon, once the container was filled, the water spilled into the basin. Quickly, the basin overflowed.

- I think we have triggered a trap -Reverend Ogli said- Let's go back!

I walked through the columned hall led by a demon. I looked for the stands like a fool. I climbed ahead of the light of the torch. I went up with my hands in front to cushion the stumbles. Two turns of stairs, three, four...

I pushed hard against the circular door.

- Ah! -I shouted- The door is closed!

My master also tried to open it to no avail.

- It must have been blocked by the same mechanism that was activated down there -he said.

- We are trapped! We are going to die, Master Ogli! We are going to die from drowning!

- Calm, dear Ad! There is nothing that the power of understanding cannot overcome. Let's go back to the water fountain!

- What?

The waters were already reaching our legs when we were back in front of the flooding monster. My master brought the torch to the geometric group that the monster's mouth housed. He examined it carefully and quietly. The waters continued to devour the breathable space. My master was totally concentrated on the mouth of the monster with an indolent attitude that despaired me.

- Master, the water keeps coming up!

- Calm, dear Ad! Patience is rewarded with one successful and unique effort.

I saw my master playing with one of the geometric bodies. I was up on the edge of the basin and the water was already around my waist and continued to rise.

- In distant times, when the tombs hid treasures, the builders placed defense mechanisms like this -my master said, completely un-daunted- It was a system based on a game that was practiced in antiquity. The test consists of moving one of the geometric bod-ies through the others to fit into the empty space from where the water comes out.

- It seems impossible that they can move! They are tight against each oth-er.

- That is what it seems, but there is always a space between them.

- But it is very small.

- That is precisely the problem. You have to deal with just that.

My master's hand maneuvered quickly, putting the pieces aside, returning others, raising them, lowering them.

- I am already swimming, Master!

Just then, we heard a "click" somewhere.

- Done! -he exclaimed.

One of the blocks had fit right into the space from where the water had once flowed. The flood stopped. Even moments later, we could see that the waters began to retreat.

- We are saved! -I cried out- Saved by the hair!

- On one occasion, an Eastern scholar said: "Whoever waits with knowledge, waits calmly because he knows that the triumph is his."

- That sage was never here!

After some time, the waters had receded to persist at the level of the basin. My teacher continued to examine the ornamental trap. Meanwhile, I went up the steps. I felt quite exhausted and began to gasp.

- It is locked! -I said on my return.

- Mmm...

- The door! The door is still closed! -I repeated.

My master did not seem to care much, maybe because he already suspected it.

- The water drains -he said- through a well that sinks into the depths. The basin is just the border of this well. We have to find a way out, dear Ad, since the air is running out very quickly.

The knowledge of this threat began to choke me faster than the lack of air. My master turned to me and understood my anguish.

- Calm, dear Ad. In the most complicated situation, there is always an exit. And it is almost always under your feet. Do you trust me, dear disciple?

- Yes, Master! -I said, suffocating- I trust you!

- So, are you going to do what I tell you?

- Yes!

- I am going down the well, looking for a way out. In the meantime, I want you to stay here. Try to be calm. If you remain agitated, your oxygen needs will be enormous. Practice deep breathing, leading your thoughts toward serenity. Remember that the mind can control everything. Regarding me, I will return either way. Do not worry!

Reverend Ogli sat on the edge of the basin. He took two long breaths. The muscles in his face began to relax. His face acquired the expression of absence that meditation induces. The extreme concentration of a Szabeo monk put him in communication with the waters. Then, he expanded his lungs and took as much air as he could. Immediately, he plunged into the liquid darkness of the well.

The mind can control everything... Yeah, right! I think, in my case, the phrase is reversible -I thought.

As soon as my master left, I became crazy. I tried to calm myself. I decided to practice deep breathing. I crossed my legs. I straightened my spine. And I started to inhale... But what would I inhale if there was no air! -I said to myself- When there is no air, there is nothing that can be breathed. And those who do not breathe, die. And they die by suffocation. Ugly death! And ugly I will be because those who suffocate turn blue. No one will recognize me like that, all bluish. But to recognize me, those who already know me would have to see me again. But no one would ever see me again! No one has come this far. And no one has left either. They must have died, asphyxiated. Bluish. For all eternity. Cold and wet eternity. How slowly eternity must pass for those who die locked in here! How slowly eternity is passing now! How slowly the time passes when you breathe instantly! Every breath is an instant, every instant an asphyxiation. With each asphyxiation, less air. The air, more and more worn. Less and less air. What an unpleasant greasy feeling the used air leaves... I was asphyxiating. I was getting asphyxiated. Suddenly, with a great noise, my master's enormous body broke the waters violently. With a painful groan, his lungs eagerly devoured the rarefied air.

- Master!

- Yes, Ad... I am... back -he said.

- There is no more air!

- I can notice it!

- Did you find a way out?

- Yes, dear Ad. The bottom of the well bends and leads to a hall much larger than this. The hall is lit by torches and contains fresh air.

- Good!

- The inconvenience is that the well is very deep, and I fear that it is way above your faculties.

- So, are you going to leave me here?

- No! Do not be alarmed, dear Ad. The last thing I would do is abandon you.

- But then... I see no solution!

- Calm, dear Ad. I told you that there is nothing that the mind cannot overcome. I want you to stare into my eyes.

Hypnosis is a technique that Szabeo monks handle to advantage after many years of mental studies. It is part of the skills that are acquired by developing the inner vision that lies in the back of the head.

My conscience does not account for anything that happened next. Reverend Ogli, as he explained to me, took me to the hypnotic trance and enabled me to breathe like amphibians that are capable of submerging for long periods. Then, he held me and swam with me to the depths of the well. I do remember, yes, that when I woke up from my trance, I was at the feet of a frightening beast. It was covered with a long curly beard that became one with its hair. I could not contain myself and I screamed. Then I saw that my master rushed to my aid from somewhere.

- Calm, Calm! It is just a statue.

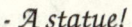

- A statue!

- Actually, they are two: facing each other, with their hands on a crematory altar. You were obviously very exhausted by the pressure you were under because when I pulled you out of the hypnotic trance, you fell asleep. But since I realized that also in this chamber, the waters are growing, I transported you to the safest part I found on these stairs...

- In other words, is this place flooding too?

- I am afraid so, dear Ad.

- Is there any way out?

- Precisely, when you screamed, I was dedicated to exploring this room. I could see that the cave houses the remains of a temple from ancient times. The waters are gaining height and eventually, they will cover everything.

In front of us, I could see the two horrible statues and the crematory altar. Beyond, at the top of the steps, I saw a heavy door within an imposing frame with strange symbols carved in its wings; signs that my master ignored. The mouth of the well, through which we went out, had become an irregular pool, surrounded by debris. Some standing columns, some on the ground, completed the environment.

- If I am not mistaken -Reverend Ogli said- we are in front of a Consecration Gate. A gate like this, according to Uggar, who lived centuries ago, opened themselves by the will of the gods, once the priests had performed a certain ritual. The priests approached the temple door singing praises. Then, they set the ceremonial fire on the crematory altar. The flames appeared. They sang a prayer for their god to open the doors of their house, the temple. The god acceded and immediately, the guardians of the temple, this is, the statues that frightened you, spilled drops of celestial gold on the altar. The divine smoke spread, made contact with the doors and opened them wide. Well, all that was the result of a mechanism designed to impress believers. The altar was metallic and hollow. When the fire burned, as the priests sang, the air inside the altar warmed up and created pressure. The pressure operated two hidden and simultaneous mechanisms. In the first, the air put pressure on a container of aromatic oil. The oil was colored with resins that gave it a golden look. In this way, the fluid was forced to go up by ducts concealed inside the arms of both statues. The oil dripped on the altar, burned, and released its solemn fragrance. While all this was happening, the pressure also displaced water from a reservoir under the altar. The water was poured in a bucket that was filled to overcome, with its weight, the resistance of a gear mechanism that turned the two wings of the door. When the ceremony in the temple was over, the fire was extinguished. The interior of the altar cooled down and the vacuum, created by the evacuation of the water, sucked it again and the doors closed one more time as if God had wanted it.

- But during all that time, the oil must have continued dripping.
- When the pantomime was no longer necessary, the priests loosened a wax cap and let air go into the oil

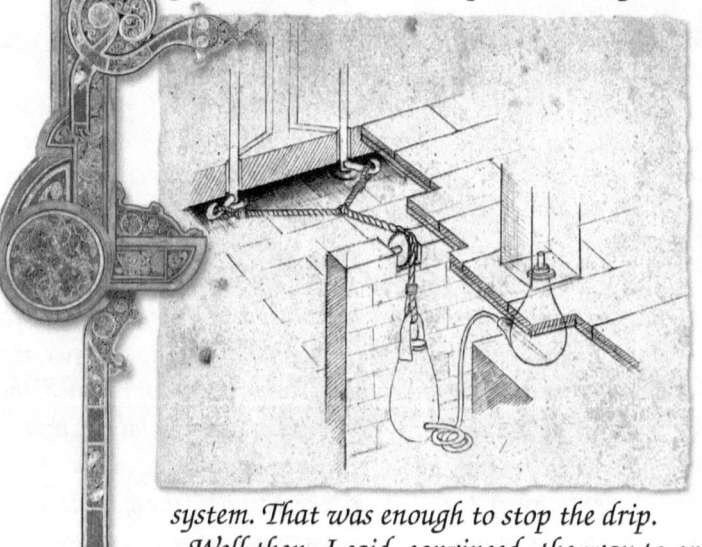

system. That was enough to stop the drip.
- Well then -I said, convinced- the way to open that door is to set the altar on fire.
- I think so, dear Ad. Let's wait for the door to open.
- Yes, let's see what happens! But quickly! The waters are rising.

Reverend Ogli took one of the torches on the wall and brought it to the altar. A flame was lit. We waited a lot, but nothing happened.
- I do not think we will ever see any drop of oil -I said.
The mechanism must have been damaged or the resin of the oil could have solidified or anything, the case was that it did not work as

expected. However, long after leaving the altar lit, the doors began to open with great difficulty.

What threats were waiting for us on the other side of the door? -I thought. What dangers will it lead us to?

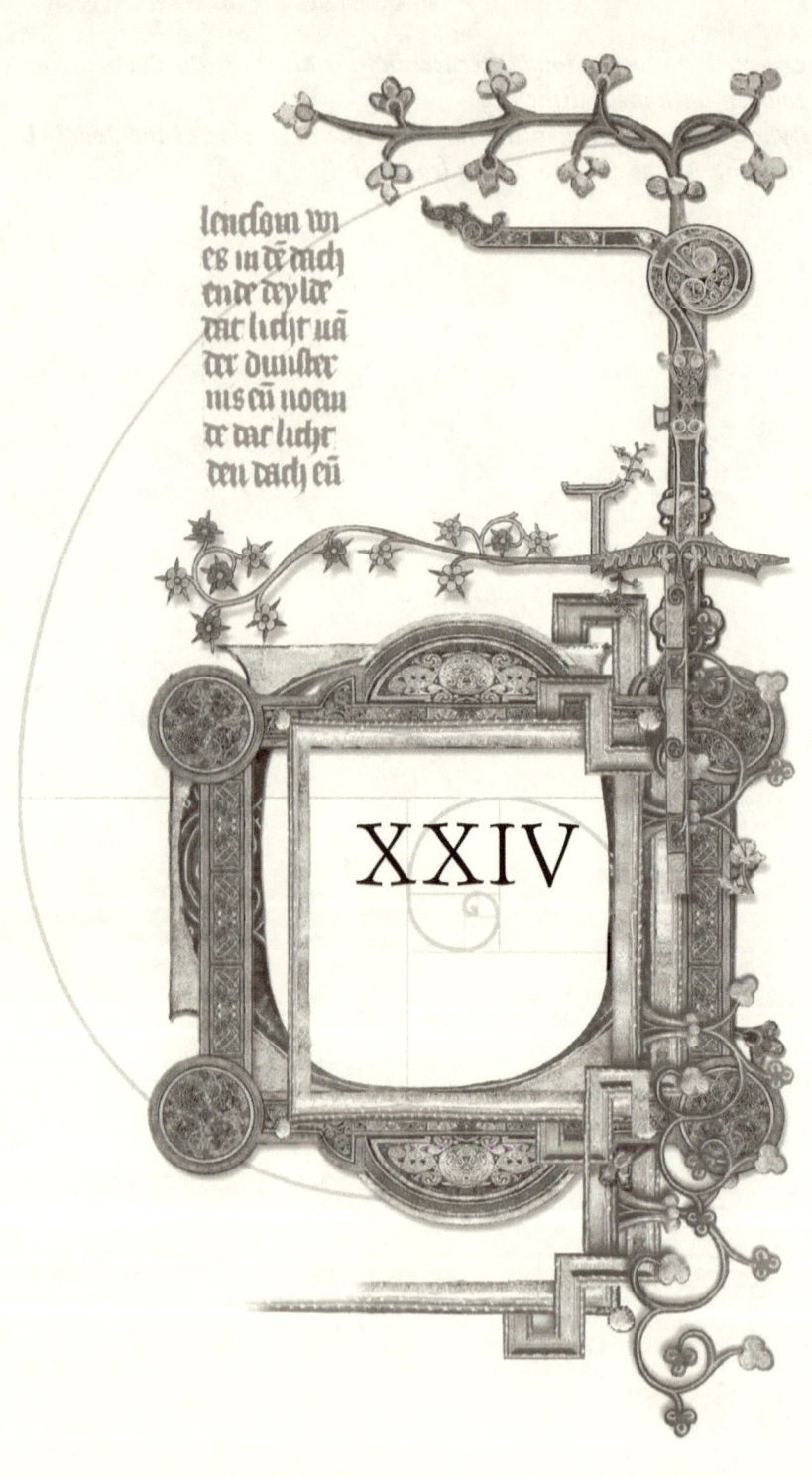

lencloin wi
es in de dach
ende dylie
dac licht uā
der dunster
nis eū noctu
te dar licht
den dach eū

XXIV

Chapter XXIV

The Fountain of Uronn

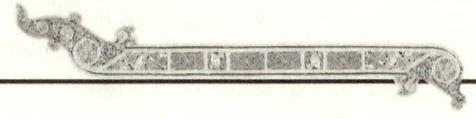

nce the doors of the temple opened, Reverend Ogli and I entered a whitish room, completely free of decoration and perfectly smooth. As soon as we were inside, the entrance doors closed. The room was almost dark.

I thought we were trapped again, but an orange reflection on the floor led us to a square opening with scrupulously straight edges on the left wall as if it were a window. There, an ascending corridor with polished walls began. The light came from the far end of the corridor. Apparently, there was no trap in that room, but I could not have claimed the same with respect to the hallway. Reverend Ogli helped me up. The corridor was so narrow that my master hardly fit. The great polishing of the walls made it hard for me to go upwards; so much that I did not go up but was pushed by the body of Reverend Ogli. I practically ascended standing on my master. He, on the other hand, ascended packing more and more the corridor with his body. He fit so tightly that he did not slip when taking some rest. The effort he made was noticeable. We were moving very slowly. At last, after what seemed an eternity, we reached the exit. The mouth of the hallway ended flush with the floor of a rectangular room, wider than the hallway, but still small to be a room. It seemed rather that we were at the bottom of a square floor well.

Reverend Ogli took the torch whose reflections had guided us. When we lifted it, we noticed that the height of the well was about three times the height of my master. Using some holes of perfect square section practiced in one of the walls, we climbed the well. Once out of it, Reverend Ogli illuminated as far as he could. We saw a large ascending gallery of very tall and strange sides. From stretch to stretch upwards, the walls showed an edge like the steps of an upside-down stair, so that the roof of the gallery was narrower than the floor. This made impossible any attempt to climb them. The floor, on the other hand, was formed by a central ramp and two narrow sidewalks on both sides. The central ramp was very slippery, but the sidewalks had, at regular intervals, the same square cavities that had helped us climb. We moved slowly, using the cavities as steps. My master carried the torch. The ascent was slow and exhausting. I tried to put all my attention at every step because I did not want to slip. My long shadow was devoured by the darkness. Suddenly, the darkness closed around us like a shadow pouncing on us. I felt a strong wind on my face. I crouched as a precaution. I closed my eyes in terror. I could hear the wind in my ears. In the intimacy of my blindness, I felt the wind passing without causing me any harm. That gave me enough confidence to open my eyes warily. I could not see anything, except the light from the torch fluctuating intensely as if it were about to become extinct. At one point, the wind was about to turn off the torch completely. I turned around to see my master, and I saw him making efforts to keep the fire on. When he managed to control the extinction, I noticed that he looked forward with astonishment.

I turned my head around. I saw hundreds of horrifying creatures with hideous faces throwing themselves straight into my face. I cried out. Terrified, I realized that, just before reaching my face, the winged monsters modified their flight and passed close enough to brush my cheeks. That was the wind I felt.

- Calm Ad, calm down! -My master shouted, grasping my neck with his hand- They are maciegolos, winged mammals that inhabit the darkness, and that is precisely why they are blind. Instead of the sense of sight, they have a radar system. So it may seem that they are flying straight toward you, but at the last moment, they flank your face because you were detected as an obstacle. So do not be afraid; whoever despairs may slide down the ramp to a certain death. Just let them pass. In the meantime, you must have tranquility

and patience, dear Ad. Sometimes, dangers are ghostly appearances that dwell only in our own darkness.

- Ah! Then the wind that almost extinguished the torch was produced by the flight of the maciegolos?

- Yes, dear Ad. Probably, after sensing us, they were frightened, and their escape darkened the atmosphere even more and produced the wind as well. Can you imagine what would have happened to us if the flame would have become extinct?

The maciegolos passed and "normalcy" was restored, whatever this may have meant in those circumstances. The gallery ended in a corridor as narrow as the one we passed first, but it had the advantage of running horizontally. We got in. My master had to crawl to get through. We did not advance much, and a mortuary chamber appeared at the right side. Its floor, walls, and ceiling were elaborated with great beauty. The blocks of stone were square and tied to each other with admirable precision. They were made of red granite, finely polished to the precious sheen. A luxuriously dressed skeleton lay down on the floor. Resting on its chest, there was a pectoral ornament worked in gold and adorned with precious stones of the most diverse colors. On its helmet, made of gold too, an enormous ruby the size of an egg shone with the splendor of the red sun of the lands of the north. Attached to what was left of the warrior's hand, there was a magnificent sword with a golden handle with fine and neat reliefs in which tiny stones of crystalline glow abounded. Behind it, there was a black marble table with almost no ornamentation except for the very splendid material used in its making. On the table, a tall, narrow pitcher, remarkably slender, made of the same marble as the table, called my attention. This one had, instead, golden borders orbiting its very black surroundings. This same communion between glittering golds and blacks created a rhythmic pattern at the waist of its cap. The elegant sinuosity of its curves, the smoothness of its glamorous skin, everything was made to invite the contact and the opening. What else than the most regal of treasures can an object as precious as that, contain?

- It is the Holy Råål! -I said.

- Be careful! -My master answered- It seems to me rather a trap. What I suppose about the Holy Råål, that is, about the Tablet of the Arcanum, is hardly reconciled with luxury and pompousness. The Tablet of the Arcanum could never be a particular treasure, ostentatious and loaded with avarice. Quite the opposite! It would be

something disinterested, something noble, an extraordinary common good, wonderfully universal. Surely, the Tablet of the Arcanum is simple but profound, simple as an idea, modest as generosity, pure and frank as the truth. The Tablet of the Arcanum should be comforting as a blessing; not like a lottery. I fear, dear Ad, that we are in front of one of the traps that, in the distant antiquity, were placed at the step of the profane to tempt him and to distance him from the actual treasure. Sometimes, by picking up a jewel from the skeleton or by raising his sword, the greedy seeker activated a deadly mechanism. If he survived this or if he avoided the skeleton to reach the fabulous bottle, once opened, instead of a splendid treasure, a poisonous gas was released.

- And what if the jewels are real and there is no mechanism? Why could we not take the treasure and keep looking for the Holy Råål?

O gi frunik that the mrm con thuo riki drohtyn umbi thesaro uueroldes gumnand uuordon zalda Huo thiu forth farid than lang the sia firiobarn

- Yes, there is the possibility that the treasure is genuine. But why do you think that it is no longer a trap? If you choose not to waste this opportunity to get wealth, you should carry it and look for paths that will surely be different from those that would lead you to the Holy Råål and probably those will be mortal. I cannot imagine having come here carrying a treasure, and the path we still have to go does not have to be easier. Dear disciple, be careful! If you are not clear about what you are after, the lesser comforts can entertain you and even prevent you from achieving that deeper and more lasting thing that you truly long for. The rest of your life you will live the life of a dead person. Always remember it, dear Ad, deviating from the road might mean hurting yourself.

- In addition -he went on- in the event that it would be possible for you to go out of here, what would wealth help you if death outside lurks over all beings? The only wealth allowed in the passage to the beyond is the wealth you carry within.

We knelt down to re-enter the tight corridor and continued our march as if we had not seen anything. We crawled for a little longer. The perpendicularity of the corridor angles, its polished appearance and its adjusted alignment began to lose preponderance, giving place to the random, to the congestion, to the protuberance. We found ourselves, then, crawling through a natural hollow that unexpectedly led to a large flooded cavern. It was a cave formed by immense rocky masses of one piece, free of sharp edges and pigmented with a strong brick color. The masses appeared here and there as if they were colossal round accidents that overlapped each other. The lagoon in the center was shaped like a liver. We were, so to speak, at the sharp end of the liver. I saw no way out. It was a new trap.

- Let's get out of here! -I said to my master-This is flooding.

- Mmm...! Let's wait for a little while. If my suspicions are true, this cave should dislodge water, not receive it. Let's take a closer look at the terrain.

We moved over the curved edge of a large rock until it became dangerous to peek. At that moment, we heard a dry, metallic sound. We turned back to see. The mouth of the aisle that we had left was now crossed by bars that I did not know where they came from.

- We are in trouble! -I said- You better be right, Master! If this is flooding...

- Trust me, my dear disciple!

- We should not have left the hall! This is a trap!

- Patience, dear Ad. Look at the rocks! Do you notice that there is a marginal sediment along this rock? Look! It starts almost at the tunnel level. And if you look more, you will realize that there is a faint glow that increases as you look down on the rock. This shows that I am right: the waters are descending.

- But how did you know that before?

- Although I have not discovered all the details of the mechanism and some things I just suppose, I think the last three environments we have been in are part of a hydraulic system. The finding of a chamber like this one, that is rather getting empty, had its logic. I needed something like this to satisfactorily explain the behavior of the other chambers that were flooded.

- You mean the little one who had the lavatory basin and the other one that had the crematory altar where I woke up. True?

- Yes indeed. Many centuries ago, a wise mechanic named Uronn invented the fountain that bears his name. The Fountain of Uronn consists of three vessels: one upper vessel, which is open to the air, and two hermetically sealed under the first. At the beginning, the upper vessel contains water in contact with the outside. The lowest vessel is filled with air and isolated from the environment. The middle vessel is full of water and equally isolated. These three vessels are joined by three tubes. There is a tube between the upper and lowest vessel. There is another tube between the lowest vessel and the middle vessel. There is a third tube between the middle and upper vessel. The fountain is put into operation when the water from the upper vessel is allowed to fall freely, pushed by gravity, to the lowest vessel. This causes the air in the lowest vessel to move up to the middle vessel. Due to the pressure caused by the air inside the middle vessel, the water of that vessel will be forced to ascend to the upper vessel. The release of water into the upper vessel is seen as a fountain.

- Like the water that came out from the mouth of the sea monster? -I asked.

- Exactly, dear Ad.

- But the room with the fountain of the monster had no water at first, Reverend Ogli.

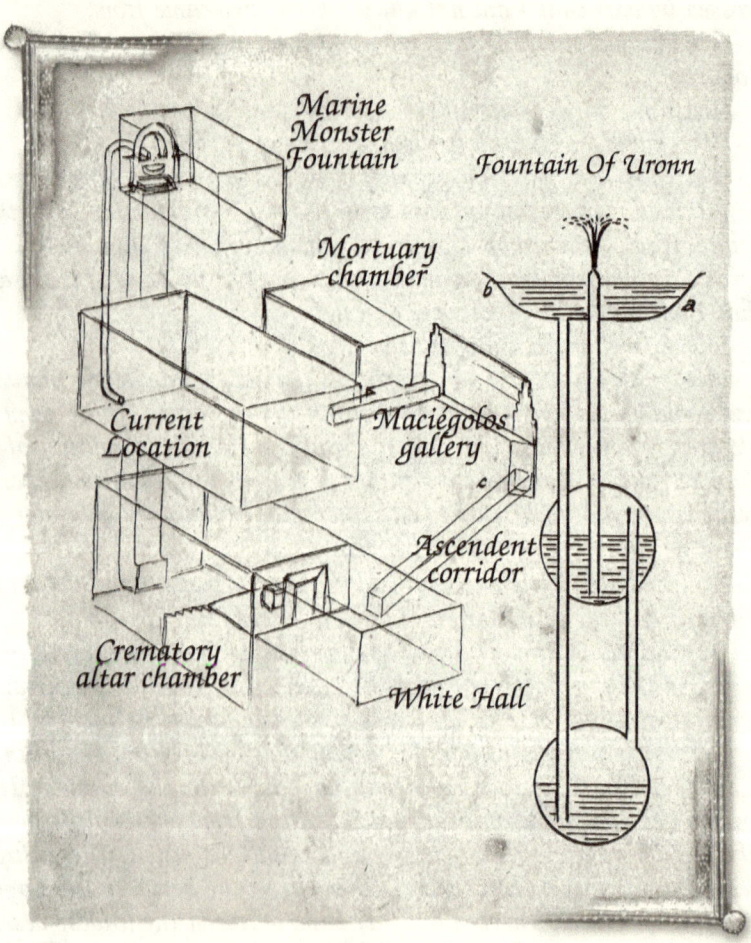

Marine Monster Fountain

Fountain Of Uronn

Mortuary chamber

Current Location

Maciégolos gallery

Ascendent corridor

Crematory altar chamber

White Hall

- As I told you, I still have things that are not fully explained and things that I just assume. I believe that, although that room was initially dry, there must have been a reservoir full of water under its floor. As we approached to examine the lavatory basin and the monster on it, the weight of our bodies triggered a mechanism by which the water of the reservoir began to descend to the chamber of the crematory altar.

- Ah! That's why it was flooding.

- Yes, dear Ad. The air from the crematory chamber ascended to the chamber where we are now. The air pressed against the water that was here. As a result of the pressure, the water ascended to the monster room.

- So, the water that was coming out through the monster's mouth came from here?

- Yes. And that is why the room flooded until I could stop the process by solving the puzzle that was in the monster's mouth. Don't you agree that everything makes sense if you conceive the three chambers as a system related to The Fountain of Uronn?

- Yes, Master, now I see it.

- If you think about it, as a trap, this is a work of art. You must overcome several tests that belong to a single great trap: The Fountain of Uronn. And all of them are lethal. Despite its mortal character, there is a certain beauty in all of this which comes from the imaginative conception of its engineering and the harmonious coordination of mechanisms.

- I am not sure I see any beauty in that. What I am sure is that I do not see how I could have gotten out of this without you, Reverend Ogli.

- My dear Ad, I am afraid that if you were not with me, you would not have to go through all of this.

- Master, how do you know such things? Have you ever seen a Fountain of Uronn?

- I know a lot more for having read about it than for having seen it. Reading is very important in the collection of personal wealth, dear Ad. Books, if you choose them well, can give you the old wisdom that has been lost from the common knowledge little by little. Nowadays, many ancestral secrets belong to the shadows of time, and the few that emerge are imprisoned by the hermetic sects. Read, dear Ad, and the magic will be granted to you.

We had to wait until the lagoon emptied. That gave us a moment of relaxation. We had been so busy and tense that we had forgotten to rest.

That's weird! -I thought to myself- I do not remember needing it. And now, that I think about it, neither eating nor drinking! Anyway... We talked about many things. The one that interested me most of all was one that revolved around the possibility of space travel.

- The possibility of using antimatter as a space fuel -my master said- has been taken very seriously by scientists. It has been thought to build particle and antiparticle guns that produce

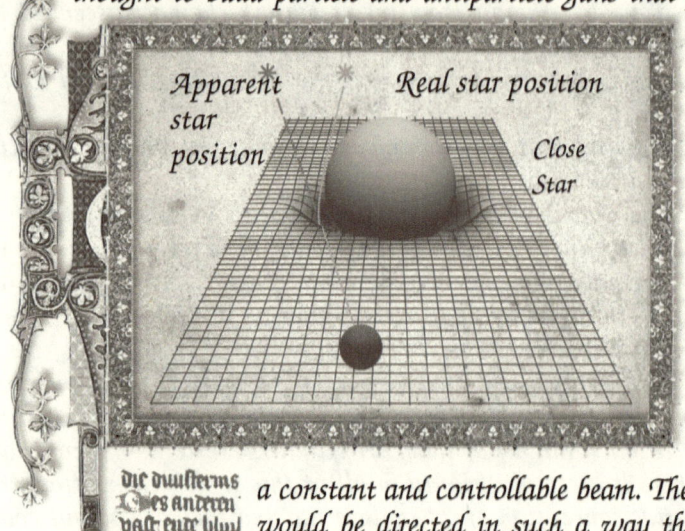

Apparent star position — Real star position

Close Star

a constant and controllable beam. These guns would be directed in such a way that their beams would collide against each other, producing the energy of many nuclear reactors with much less fuel. As I explained earlier, the energy of an antimatter reaction is much greater than that of a nuclear reactor.

- But anyway, space travel would take too long to come back and find our relatives alive, and maybe anyone -I commented.

- Yes, dear Ad. That is why, at the same time, the probability of finding "shortcuts" in outer space is investigated.

- How is that?

- There is evidence that space is not as we see it. Light rays approaching a stellar mass, either planet or star, suffer an alteration in its trajectory. They are diverted, as a glass ball that a child pushes in a straight line, but momentarily enters a concavity.

- Around the stars -he continued- the medium in which the photons propagate, the space, manifests a curvature. This spatial curvature

seems to be provoked by the presence of a large mass, like the mass of a star. It had been thought that space is a continuous, uniform concept. We had no reason to think that the interplanetary emptiness could have a shape; even less a curvature.

- In other words, an emptiness with a shape.

- That is what is called space.

- I cannot imagine it!

- Some people even claim that space is quantified, that is, there is a minimum unit of space that no longer allows greater division..

- Uh...! That is worse.

- In regard to this, there are a series of questions. How much can the space be curved? A possible space travel system depends on the answer to this question. This system would require less time, at least in theory. What if space can curve like the back of a book? The space that we all believe to understand, where our planet, the stars, the galaxies, etc., are hosted, can be spread on a "three-dimensional surface" that eventually folds. If this is so, perhaps the most distant galaxies we have sighted are under our feet.

- But if they are underneath, why do we see them directly in front of us?

- In reality, what do we see but the light that comes to us from them? And the light that comes from them brings us their impression, their image. And, as I explained to you, the light follows the "terrain accidents." Thus, it might well come out from a star located just below us, advance along the lower "three-dimensional surface, bend as required by the folding and come toward us. Once in our telescopes, the light would give us the optical fingerprint of the source where it was originated. There is no apparent way for us to discern the trajectory undergone by the image. It seems to come straight from a point in front of us, but this could be just a virtual projection, according to our common sense.

- If this were so -he went on- immeasurable distances for us could be overcome if the stellar voyage is made through a space shortcut opened between the planes of the fold and not over the ordinary path that the light traveled through. That is, using the shortest distance between our planet and the star. According to this, one could reach a point in space quicker than light without needing to exceed its speed, which is something physically impossible, apparently. Now, you should note that by referring to this surface, we would be talking about a "three-dimensional surface" because it represents nothing less than the universe we know. The intermediate "space" between the folded surfaces is giving them what we might tentatively name as "volume," just as the inside of a fruit gives body to the skin. Nevertheless, these surfaces are not two-dimensional, but three-dimensional. So, it is clear that this "volume" cannot have three dimensions as any volume but four. Thus, it is believed that a space "shortcut," in a stellar trip, would involve the momentary passage through a four-dimensional environment to reach a distant point in our space.

- I am not sure I understand you completely, Reverend Ogli.

- It is not easy, I know. If this helps you... Imagine that you have a sheet of paper in your hands. Fold the sheet, so it makes a lying "U." Imagine that the thickness of the paper turns infinitely thin, but you still can see the sheet. Now, we could say, with some liberty, that you are seeing how a two-dimensional world has been folded in two. The fold has been produced across the third dimension. You can see the fold because you are capable of the perception of the third dimension. If you were part of the two-dimensional sheet, you would not see the fold. Hence, you need to be in a higher dimension to see the fold of a lower dimension.

- Yes, that helped me. Thank you, Master.

- This higher dimension, when we are considering a three-dimensional world being folded, is what some thinkers call "Hyperspace." There are those who say that there is no reason to limit the "shortcuts" to the fourth dimension and higher dimensions could also be considered. They believe that the greater the "shortcut" dimension, the shorter it would be. In short, dear Ad, it is the same as if the beetle, who circumvents the skin of the fruit, had noticed that its flat world has a curvature and now he seeks to pass through the middle.

- Then that's it! We could travel to the farthest stars!

- Some small details are pending, though. First, we have not yet developed a reactor with autonomy for long cosmic distances as the one of antimatter should be. Second, we do not know yet how to pierce the apple, that is, we do not know where a crack to the fourth dimension is located and, even less, how to provoke it. Third, it is suspected that by the same four-dimensional fissure we could end up in other universes with their own folds. What if we end up in a parallel world of antimatter? That would be our end! Finally, and in combination with the above, we could undergo an enantiomorphic inversion, when we go or when we return, while we are in the fourth dimension. Depending on the kind of matter to which the four-dimensional "shortcut" leads us, we could arrive at the wrong environment converted into real antimatter bombs and find the end anyway.

- How? Why?

- Remember what I explained to you about the only way we could superpose our right hand on our left hand?

- Uh...!

- It does not matter, dear Ad. I can explain to you again. Just passing to the fourth dimension, suffering there a turn, and returning to our dimension, a left hand could overlap a right hand because it would have become its specular twin. That is, it would have undergone an enantiomorphic inversion.

- Oh, right! I remember! I understood it using a right glove and a left glove.

- The fact is you would not know how you will emerge when you go through a four-dimensional fissure. You could undergo an enantiomorphic inversion, that is, be converted into your enantiomorphic twin. It could also be that you do not undergo any transformation. But when you get out of the fissure, you could either end up in a material or an antimaterial world. I mean, there could be a lot of danger!

- I am not very clear about that.

- What happens is that in the experiments with particles, it has been found violations even to the three great symmetries; that is, the symmetry of forms, the electric charge and time. There are serious arguments to believe that every antiparticle is the mirror image of its particle. It is likely that antimatter is nothing more than the common stuff inverted to the last detail, as it appears behind the mirror;

not only in terms of form but also in terms of electric charge and time. In this way, an inversion that makes you your enantiomorphic twin, possibly also involves a transformation into your anti-being, your antimatter other self. It is therefore suspected that a crack toward the fourth dimension can also behave like a matter-antimatter converter. And the explosive discharge of energy when matter and antimatter get in contact remains as a fact.

- So, if I could become my opposite, would it have a character opposed to what I have now?

- I do not know if it would happen in a psychological sense as well. Whether you have transformed yourself or not, the danger is that you may not return to an environment compatible with your state.

- Ah! Because I would explode like a bomb.

- ...at the slightest contact with the other kind of matter!

- So, before we get into the fissures, we better make some tests.

- As you wish, dear Ad!

- Has anybody found any examples of these fissures?

-- In outer space, no. But in laboratories, at the microscopic level, the boundary between the two worlds is constantly stimulated. That is why, at that level, it is no surprise to find antiparticles that have "passed" to our world.

- But... I understood that the electric charge also changes. That is to say, the particle with negative charge corresponds to a positively charged antiparticle. True?

- True! -my master answered- First, this was comprehended as a necessity to re-establish the ever well-desired law of the conservation of symmetry. Ace-uj, one of the young inspirers of Dr. Ij-Wwo, wrote, "If we think that a specular reflection, in addition to a right-left inversion, includes a charge inversion, the symmetry is conserved." Later, it was seen, with astonishment, that this could be happening

Fision   Fusion

in experiments with particles. The astonishment was justified because what Ace-uj claimed led to think of the correspondence between enantiomorphic inversion and material-antimatter transformation. Hence, the idea of this equivalence arose.

- That is to say, if we want to preserve the symmetry of the experiments, we must think of antimatter as the image of our world behind the mirror.

- Yes, dear Ad. But it also became necessary to accept the possibility that in these transformations, time undergoes its corresponding inversion. In other words, the antimatter world might progress in the opposite direction.

- Do you mean that, for example, in an antimaterial planet one counts the time backward?

- I mean that on that antimaterial planet, events would go backward!

- How? I do not understand!

- What in our environment goes in one direction, in the other, goes in the opposite direction. The crashes between antiparticles develop in the opposite direction which is impossible in our world, but perfectly valid. This involves many and very important things. A fission process would be transformed into a fusion process.

- If you realize -my master continued- this is the representation of a new kind of specular symmetry. In an anti-world, a wind that blows upside down picks up the autumn leaves to incorporate them into the trees that will green. In the calyx, the insects deliver the pollen and the hummingbirds fill nectar into the flowers that, thus loaded, will close their petals until being reabsorbed in the plant tissue of a spring shoot. The rain drips upward and the heat runs away toward the hottest. The voices are inhaled from teeth to inside, the howling is muted. The passers-by un-walk, the bankers discount, the weavers untie, the nations disagree and, in the bed of an anti-hospital, a terminal patient recovers, and a doctor returns the hope to him. In such a world, the potatoes are uneaten and, at the banquets, the pots are filled. The wine spits right into the narrow peak of the leather boot, forming a perfect bow. History is a fact and is un-written to forget it. Reproduction consists in the unification of, say, five scattered beings in only two. In contrast, wars multiply; two hundred go to combat and a thousand return. Meanwhile, an enthusiastic girl comes back home with a sign that says: WAR THE STOP. Definitively, the antiworld would have an advantage over ours: any act of repentance would get the dissolution of the guilt.

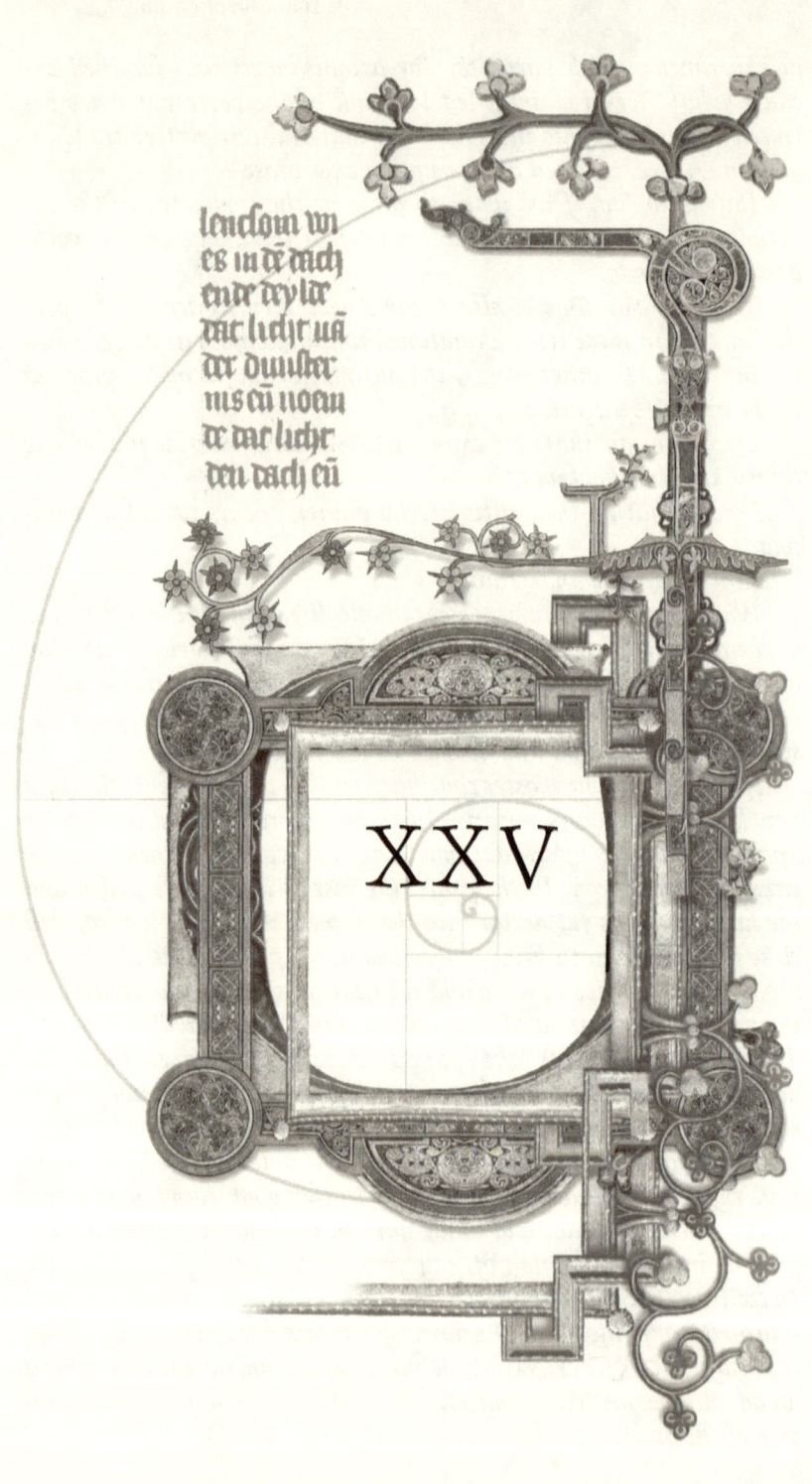

lencłom vn
es in dē dach
ende deylde
dat licht vā
der duuster
nis cū noēm
te dat licht
den dach cū

XXV

Chapter XXV

The Secret of the Rose

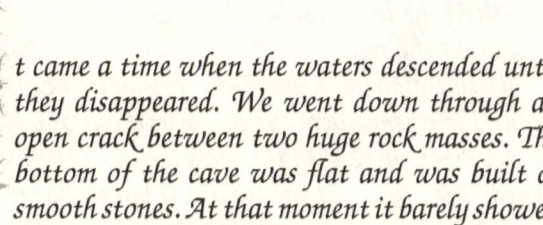

It came a time when the waters descended until they disappeared. We went down through an open crack between two huge rock masses. The bottom of the cave was flat and was built of smooth stones. At that moment it barely showed any trace of water. We began to walk cautiously. We were in a large bucket; that is, in a vulnerable situation. We were about to enter the wide part of the cave that curved to the left. In the glowing orange back ground of the rocks, beautiful, creamy, pink and violet sinuous veins had formed. The cave was filled with pleasing and insinuating forms. I could see that its sides had been altered; they were not virgin of manual labor. The small stone imperfections, the tiny natural protuberances, were transformed into ornate carvings of admirable application. When we left the curve, we could see an unusual spectacle. The friezes we saw were only the prolongation of the facade of a temple carved in the stone. The ensemble looked like a photographic overlay because its architectural elements were blurred by the creamy back ground, so special that gave it an abstract air.

- Beautiful! -my master exclaimed.

Reverend Ogli closely examined the facade of the temple. Then, he turned to look at it from a distance. He looked at it from one side, from another and came back to it. He seemed to be captivated. My master was happy!

Then he concentrated on the splendid door. Overhanging among its reliefs, six hexagonal prisms emerged from them, forming an arrangement reminiscent of a rose. The distance that each prism protruded was different in each case. At its ends, some spirals had been carved. The spirals progressed around the prisms following the rectilinear contours of their hexagonal body. In the center of the rose, in its upper and lower parts, three hexagonal perforations were noticeable.

- This seems to be the lock of the entrance -my master said.

Reverend Ogli remained static for a few moments. All his attention was focused on the artifice in front of him. Suddenly, he seemed interested in everything that was not the artifice. His sharp gaze scrutinized every inch of our surroundings.

- AHA! -he finally said- The keys!

Among the reliefs of the door, one could distinguish the head of a half-emerging gargoyle. Three prismatic horns protruded above its head. The prisms were extracted without any resistance. We inserted the three horns into the receptacles of the rose, but nothing happened. Then we tried the tip of the horns, but it was equally useless.

- There is something we are doing wrong! -Reverend Ogli said and immediately he acquired the absent expression that he used when he immersed himself in a reflection

- Mmm...! When we introduce all the prisms in the same way -he continued- we are assuming that there is no difference between them. The different distance of the immobile prisms with respect to its bases must have made us think that the distance is important.

From his backpack, he pulled out his orientation kit, which included a compass, a ruler, some paper, and a pencil. He took the ruler and began measuring the distance with which each prism protruded away from the door. He noted down the values he found. Then I saw him doing some operations with those numbers.

- That's it! -Reverend Ogli said- All distances are multiples of the shortest. Then the key of the gate must be found in the logic behind the arrangement of prisms. And the problem is reduced to introducing the horns of the beast only to where it is necessary, neither more nor less. Dear Ad, we must look for the correct numbers!

- Correct with respect to what?

- To make sense with the arrangement of the other prisms. That is precisely what is the deciphering of this subtle layout. Some idea

has to unify them all. Maybe it has to do with prime numbers, maybe not. We will see! A rose is a symbol of symmetry. This suggests harmony... That suggests... equity

Reverend Ogli returned to his diagram; he tried numbers, subtracted, added.

- AHA! -he exclaimed shortly- Of course!

Then, my master measured on the free prisms certain distances with his ruler and marked them with a pencil. He introduced the prisms up to the marks he had made. Nothing happened at first, but later we heard an exciting click!

- It opened! -I shouted.

Yes! The door opened widely. We passed quickly and were astonished again. Its interior was even stranger. In front of us, a winding cave alley with a sand floor was lost in the shadows. Its walls showed a very uncommon texture and conformation that did not look like the product of an artistic work but did not look like a natural formation either. The walls seemed to be the result of the petrifaction of a cluster of huge worms or a single gigantic serpent that, at the time of the mineralization, must have been coiling with convulsive twisting.

At times, the twists and turns formed chambers of considerable height; at others, the crease was so narrow that we had to crawl on the sand.

- Amazing! -Reverend Ogli exclaimed- This snakelike appearance of these corridors makes me think of Mālegum, the mythological mountain of the Artigonians.

- Why? What does it have to do with it?

- I told you before that according to legend, during the war between Eliseo and the Terrible Lizards, the God of Gods struck the giant serpent that turned against him and terrified the planet. The divine discharge petrified the serpent as it writhed in pain. Not satisfied with this, Eliseo took part of the ground that was next to the petrified corpse and threw it against the serpent turning it into a mountain forever. The mountain was called Mãlegum which was named after Mãleg. This was the name of the giant serpent. The cavity left by the hand of Eliseo when he took a handful of ground, gave rise to the lake that I have already mentioned in the legend of the Artigonians. Do you remember it, now?

- Yes, I remember it now, Master. Then, Reverend Ogli, it is likely that we are inside of the Mãlegum mountain?

- ...where the Tablet of the Arcane once stood.

- That means we're finally close!

- Yes, dear Ad, that's what I believe! It also means that we have descended to the mythical periods that are hidden in the anteroom of time.

At that precise moment, we were coming out from a very narrow corridor formed between two contortions of the serpentine body. Then we entered a large congested vault with hundreds of the same folds. The view was breathtaking.

Suddenly, something rose from the sand. My master stepped back. I did the same. I lost my balance and fell to the ground. A great mass of tentacles and scales shook menacingly its huge body just a few steps away.

Its olfactory organ belonged to those animals that love to dig into the mud. Its thick legs were of considerable weight. I could distinguish two lateral visual organs, but no trace of a mouth. However, the monster spoke to us in a normal voice:

- Have you come here looking for the Holy Råål?

- Yes, that is right! We are here in search of the Holy Råål -my master replied with exemplary control of himself. I was shaking.

The monster laughed mockingly and said,

- Look! You can never find it if I stop you here. To avoid that, you would have to beat me first and I do not see how!

The monster extended one of its tentacles. I was scared. The tentacle reached the end of a stone protruding in the sand. It lifted it in the air, moving it like a projectile that was going to be discharged.

I started to run. However, the monster settled it on the ground and began to draw a circle with it.

Then it said:

- Look, seeker: this is what I know!

...Suddenly, something rose from the sand.

Then it drew another, much smaller circle on the sand and tossed the stone to the side.

- This is what you know! -it said sarcastically.

Reverend Ogli remained in complete abstraction for a few seconds.

- Do you think that this justifies your pride? -my master asked it.

- Do not you see that my circle is much larger than yours?

Then Reverend Ogli walked with a calm step up to where a smaller stone laid. He took it and with it, he drew a very large circle that contained the other two. Then, he returned to his place and said:

- Well... That is what God knows! Do you still feel so proud?

The monster was silent. Then, it growled. I got scared again and stepped back. But, the monster did not move.

- I think you may pass -it said in a voice that had ceased to be threatening. Its body had also ceased trembling.

- I will not stop you! -it added- But, are you sure you want to continue?

- Yes, we are sure! -I said with resolution.

- In that case, be careful what you find at the end of the descent; it can change your lives in many ways.

- In what ways? -I asked.

- In unthinkable ways! They can be lethal or harmless, but always transcendent. And they always train the traveler who has achieved the harmony, with the privilege of understanding the singing of the whales. That is the system by which all animals are in contact.

Immediately, the sandy soil became shifting as quicksand. We sank very fast. My master tried to save the torch from extinction. The sand swallowed us. An instant of total darkness. A moment of despair. The next second, we fell on a bright green floor. The room was filled with light as if it were morning.

Chapter XXVI

The Footprints that do not Remain

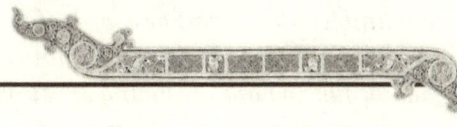

I think we have touched the bottom -my master said.

　　　- Look, Reverend Ogli! -I said, pointing to the floor.

　　　- Ah! It is exactly the same floor tile that we found in the Lunilaic turret after descending from Wrestongres.

The atmosphere was surrounded by a continuous and brilliant mosaic. The floor, the walls, and the ceiling were covered with an interrupted olive smoothness. The base material was made of a lustrous green malachite. This combination of effulgence and color offered the viewer the sensation of looking at the interior of the finest ornamental porcelain. The design pattern consisted, for the most part, of the harmonious repetition of a single tile; which we had recognized. Accompanying the fundamental theme, there were other motifs that framed it, emphasizing the variations of symmetry the theme promoted. Everything shone with a discreet glow, without exaggerations that counteracted the delight.

Walking with admiration, as through an elegant museum, Reverend Ogli and I advanced on the great floor. We could see that we were moving along a corridor with rooms separated by similar arcades. The walls were free from all sculptural relief. We could not even see any columns. Except for the inevitable joints between the pieces of the mosaic, the walls were completely smooth and neatly polished. The sumptuousness of the place did not come from an exhibition of exquisite sculptures or friezes. All the luxury came from the elegant manufacture of the mosaic. The eyes, flooded with green glints, were following one pattern or escaping to the next one. It was a palace where no expenses had been spared in honor of the visual pleasure.

We passed through the first arch and entered the next room. It looked similar to the previous one; was in fact its twin, but equally admirable. The smoothness of its laborious epidermis seemed to produce a greenish halo that I had noticed before, and whose reflections had begun to have a calming effect on me.

This must be part of the reward for all the problems we faced before -I thought- Who would be the Lord of such a magnificent palace?

We continued moving forward. The next room was indistinguishable from the others. And the next. And the next. We then found one that was definitely different: it gave access to more than one corridor.

- It is a maze! -my master said.

- What?

Indeed! The display of luxury and beauty was only a detail of a malicious aesthete; the same one who had conceived everything else. I barely could finish thinking it when something terrible happened. We heard a terrifying roar born of the horrors of hell. Somewhere, excited perhaps by our scent, a beast snorted. We could hear how, driven by suspicion, it rushed in wild races from one place to another, inventorying the smells, endorsing traces, reprinting its mark at every corner, at every stretch of its domain. We could hear the gasping beast; how it crashed its snorts against the glossy ground of malachite.

- It's an Osterácodo!

- What is that?

- It is the monster that lives in the labyrinths.

- Master! What will happen to us? We are going to die!

- No, dear Ad! There is nothing that the mind cannot overcome. We will find the way! But for now... Let's run!

I did not expect an explanation. In a second, I was running in terror. The roar grew closer. We crossed more arches, the following rooms, the following arches.

- Quick! -Reverend Ogli shouted, holding me by his hand.

My master led me to a much larger room than the others; it had three arches.

- Over here! -he exclaimed.
We hid behind the largest arch through which one could access a different, rocky, unadorned corridor that did not belong to the rest. This archway was located, so to say, at the exterior of the labyrinth. We heard another terrible roar.

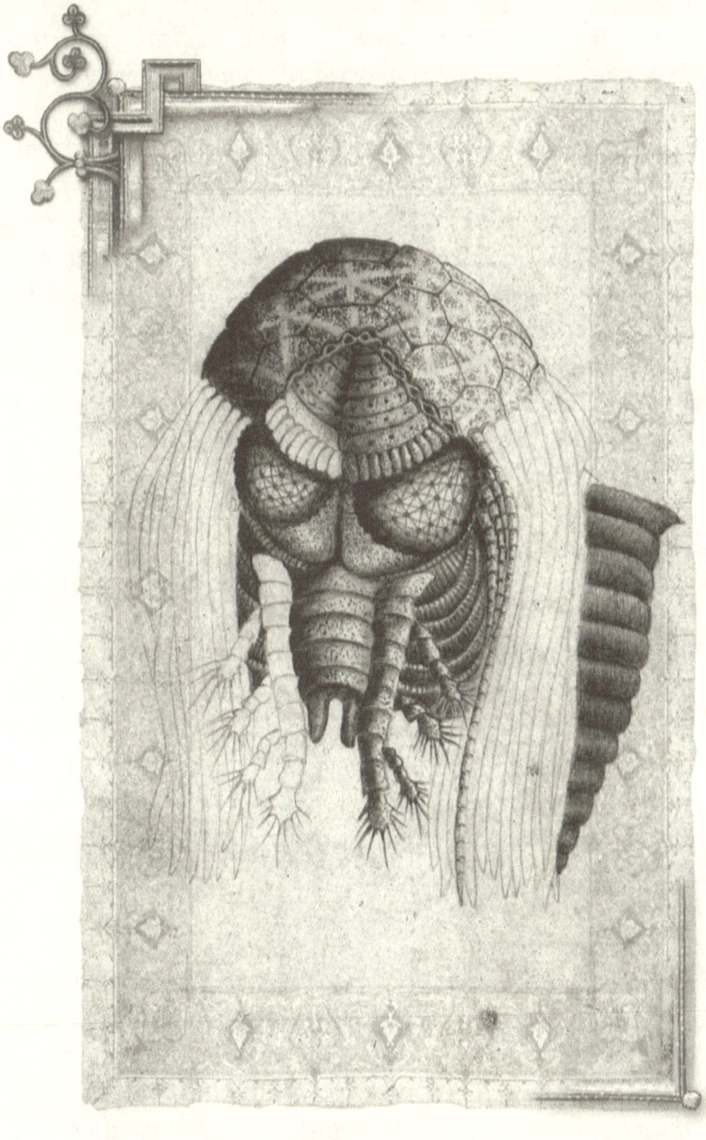

...the most disgusting monster I have ever seen ...

- We are going to wait here -my master said calmly.

- Well, it is going to find us here!

- No, it will not abandon the labyrinth. That goes against its nature. We will watch it passing by and then we will know where to go.

- It is going to find us!

- No, dear Ad. The Osterácodo was a mythological monster, half beast from the waist up. It is doomed to wander through the deep labyrinths where captivity makes it fierce. And that is why, unknowingly, it guards the treasures that keep this kind of complex and insane inventions. This obstacle adds to the already complicated enigma of the orientation, making the search for a treasure a mess without an end, an impenetrable mystery. But if it is painful for the one who tries to probe it, it is also tragic for the beast that sniffs inside. The invader tries to understand the labyrinth to go deeper. The beast is irrational, it is not interested in understanding. It wants to escape, but it is blind and cannot leave. However, it does not want to leave either because it would not know how to face the outside. A labyrinth is an intolerant enigma, annoyed with itself and sometimes... ruthless.

- Then it cannot see us!

- No. I just hope its nose does not compensate its blindness.

- They say that the blind people have the smell and the ear more developed than the rest of us.

- I know, dear Ad. That intrigues me. If the Osterácodo could sniff at its advantage, it would have found the way out. It is also possible that the floor of the labyrinth does not keep any track. The beast returns to review the same steps that for it are new steps. It does not recognize them. It does not learn. Thus, it repeats its way over and over again.

- Like the beetle!

- Yes, like the beetle!

At that moment, we heard the roar closer than ever. I felt the vibrations of his trot through my legs. My master hugged me with one of his arms. With each stride, the ground trembled. At last, the monster entered the room. I was paralyzed behind the bow. Shaking his head, the most disgusting monster I have ever seen roared with fury.

A very strong feeling made me close my eyes. I did not want to see it anymore, and I hugged my master, sinking my face into his clothes.

- It passed without distinguishing us! -Reverend Ogli exclaimed, shaking me a little- It sniffed us, but it passed by! Maybe our smell is in the air, but it cannot precisely tell because the malachite does not keep the footprints. There are no memories over the floor of its labyrinth. Poor beast!

This time, the harsh roar with which the unhappy monster got lost in the labyrinth's arcades, caused me a horrifying compassion. It was the tormented voice of a thirsty beast, consumed by the anxiety. A beast that roamed throughout its hell, roaring the rage of its invisible chains. A beast that kept smelling its own footsteps, looking for a different smell, for a different version, ruminating its frustration, turned into phlegm and fetid breath, shredding its own shadows with its teeth; shadows it sniffs, longing for others it does not know and cannot see.

We waited until the roars lost strength. Then, we entered the luxurious labyrinth again. The arcades repeated themselves on one side and the other, in harmony with my premonitions, extending my fears. We went where the monster went. One room, another, a roar, new shudders. We went further. We found a hallway and we chose it. We peeked out carefully. One room was free. It had four entrances; it was different. As soon as we tried to reach it, a grunt came to us.

- It's coming again! -I said.

Instinctively, we went back to the hallway. But, once there, we heard a second roar and we could not decide which of the two sides it came from. The Osterácodo might well be returning to the room where we saw it or to the room from which we had just fled.

- What do we do? -I screamed.

This was the first time I saw my master bewildered. His gaze moved back and forth across the hallway looking for an answer. He seemed to seclude himself again. Then, he noticed something. He raised his head and then his eyes shone with intensity.

- What a fool I have been! -He pointed to the wall- The mosaic!

- The mosaic? -I asked while a closer grunt sounded- Who cares about the mosaic? The monster is coming!

- The mosaic always gave us the answer. The key was always in sight, written on the labyrinth itself.

We heard another terrifying roar

- Master! -I screamed in anguish.

The Mosaic

- The beast has a pattern it repeats within its labyrinth and marks its trajectory. The key lies in the design of the tile that is repeated throughout the mosaic. We have to decipher it!

My master concentrated on the tile. Again, the wild trot of the approaching Osterácodo was felt. I held my hands. I covered my face. I did not know what to do. Again, the rumbling of the strides. I was about to run to the next room. My teacher held me, taking me by the habit.

- It's done! That's it! Let's go out here!

We returned to the room where we saw it before. At that precise moment, we watched through the hallway how the beast passed trotting across the room we were in.

- Ugh! It almost caught us! -I said.

- Yes! We were close!

- How did you know where to run, Master?

- It was the result of a last-minute clairvoyance, dear Ad. Before, I had not realized that the diagram of the mosaic's fundamental tile coincides with the layout of the rooms in this green labyrinth.

- Mmm...!

- On this diagram, you can also see some icons that are repeated here and there. Each one looks different and proposes a different meaning that I ignored. The first time I saw them, I thought that these icons, like so many others we have seen, meant in their time something very particular that did not concern us directly. It could be a sacred prayer or a ceremonial liturgy in a dead language. Its translation was beyond my reach and that made me disinterested in understanding it. But when I realized the similarity of the diagram with the layout of the maze, in the next second I understood that the icons were there not to signify but to mark a route. Since this route did not advance directly towards the center of the labyrinth, it should be the route followed by the Osterácodo, that is to say, the pattern it repeats systematically in its labyrinth. So, the icons meant nothing by themselves. Their different appearance made them just that: different, differentiable, groupable. I immediately associated the sets with numbers... It is an unconscious thing! Perhaps, because the grouping of objects finally leads us to count them. Who knows! Anyway... I thought the icon sets represented numbers. It was then when I discovered that on one of the sides of the diagram, a sequence of sets began. Look! Each set of icons is equivalent to a number because it has a different number of members:

$$1, 1, 2, 3, 5, 8 \ldots$$

- The magic series!
- Precisely, dear Ad! Remember what I told you about other animal patterns that follow the magic series? If the Osterácodo is an animal from the waist up, it is coherent that its pattern coincides with the patter of the Turbopulus when it manufactures its shell or with the plants when they produce leaves and organize their flowers or with the transmission of information in the hives. The Osterácodo walks and un-walks a spiral that takes it to the deepest part of the labyrinth and then makes it re-emerge. Not everything is bad and sacrilegious in the Osterácodo. It shares the same sense of natural elegance that reminds us that we are all children of heaven.

Chapter XXVII

The Last Seal

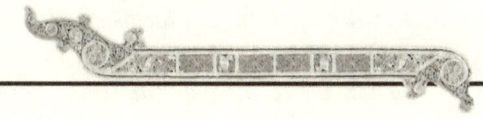

The tile of the mosaic served as a map for us to advance through the labyrinth. We could see, by far, the despair of the Osterácodo. It looked for us like a possessed beast. We watched it crossing the hallways, walking in and out of the sumptuous rooms and re-entering, exasperatedly. Its image appeared and vanished between the green arches. We simply moved to the room where, according to the mosaic tile, it was not expected at the time. In this way, we moved closer and closer to the heart of the labyrinth. We had reached the outer walls of the central section. It was plausible to my teacher to think that the exit would be in the center. Only one more wall separated us from the center itself. We assured ourselves by consulting the mosaic that the Osterácodo was not about to intercept us. Finally, at last! Just one more stretch.

The roars grew louder, and the beast began to groan in an agonizing way. We could not wait. We started to run. I think at that moment the beast was approaching in a hurry. Somehow, it could sense how close we were to the center of the labyrinth. Running like devils we reached the last arch of malachite. We swiftly turned around the corner. Finally, we entered!

Every time I remember this scene, I get superimposed images, concatenated with antagonistic feelings. The emotions that simultaneously hit me have been merged into an additive mix. Today, I have a magnified impression of what I felt and an inaccurate succession of events. My memory brings back a collage of clippings: a powerful clarity in front, the joy of my master, the Osterácodo behind. The horror. Stone glossy glows. The fiercest roar. Refreshing waterfall of wet lights above us. The abominable cry of the beast. A blinding flash. A death curse. Dead time of obnubilation. The laid body of the Osterácodo. The body of Wgijvrán materializing on the beast. Hallucination of changing forms. An infinite peace flooding me with its serene presence.

When we recovered from this explosion of images, the labyrinth had vanished. In its place, the ruins of a very ancient architectural complex appeared. A scent of cedar from Ifreno came to us.

Behind us, a temple decorated with blue-green tiles was visible. Its reliefs showed strange creatures out of this world. What remained from its doors seemed to have once displayed metallic ornaments with cosmic motifs. Beyond there, I could see more ruins with different aspects. All were in bad condition, about to collapse permanently. I could also see parts of giant statues scattered on the floor: bronze arms, iron fingers, and legs and heads of different figures. In the midst of all this, a half-destroyed statue stood up, beheaded and without a heel, which held a black plate with multicolored metallic reflections.

We were seeing it almost biased and something was visible under the reflections. We moved to improve the viewing. The multicolored reflection was moving away. We began to distinguish marks on the plate. As we moved, the marks were getting completed up to their finished version. When the marks finally got integrated...

- What! -my master said in disbelieving admiration.

The surface showed a series of three symbols. From top to bottom, the three symbols were: the Cruciglobist symbol, a left hand, and a Lunilaic half-moon. We were completely astonished. Amazing! The two religions quoted simultaneously on the face of a supernatural surface. What kind of joint praise was this? What blessed creed united the whole world? What kind of offering was this?

There is a connection! -I thought to myself- At some point, these two symbols were extolled, perhaps as part of a much more universal precept. There was a bond between them from the cradle of all origins, of all that has existed and has been recorded. The joys and tribulations of one people will never be again a particular concern; from now on, they will belong to all because a wonderful brotherhood will cover the planet. The result of this discovery is magnificent! What had been revealed is that these two religions that had upheld and confronted the world for centuries and centuries were actually sister religions. All antagonism was absurd and unsustainable! There is no longer any reason for hatred. This is the moment of the universal fraternity, of the assenting, of the understanding and respect! It is time for peace! Just in time because outside, the world is about to annihilate itself driven by ancestral grudges. This is the opportunity to extinguish xenophobia and end the massacres. No more wars. No more suffering. No more children without parents. No more atrocities. No more mutilated people. No more terrified people. No more barbarism. This is the occasion that dreamers had been waiting for. The Age of Meekness! Peace could mean the concentration of efforts around the problem of hunger. The worldwide attention could be directed toward the elimination of diseases. Once the enemies had been suppressed, the multimillionaire armament industry would have no reason to exist, and this could mean investing capital in education, fighting poverty, and creating hospitals, arts, and science. In short, the elimination of weapons, as a necessity, would generate a different future. All of this, thanks to considering ourselves children of the same god. That was wonderful!

- The two religions are just one religion! Right, Master?

- No, dear Ad -he said very slowly- None of them were a religion ever!

- What?

- Now I understand everything. Now, everything makes sense. And it was you, Ad-d Tuar, who glimpsed the truth.

- Me?

- Yes, you! Remember that you said that if you would find a four-dimensional fissure, you would make some tests before crossing it?

- Yes, because within the fourth dimension, an astronaut could be inverted from left to right and transformed into antimatter.

- And the astronaut, thus converted, would explode upon his return to a three-dimensional world made by the kind of matter contrary to his, right?

- Yes, Master.

- Going into a four-dimensional fissure would be a mortal danger. So why not make a test first?

- Yes, that was my idea.

- There is no way of knowing, from afar, if the matter that constitutes our environment is contrary to that of the other side of a fissure. However, we could come to an enlightening conclusion, if we try to find out if what "left" is here is also "left" there. For this, we first have to clarify what we mean by left and right. Remember Ad, what experiment did we use in our hypothetical exercise to clarify this?

- The emission of 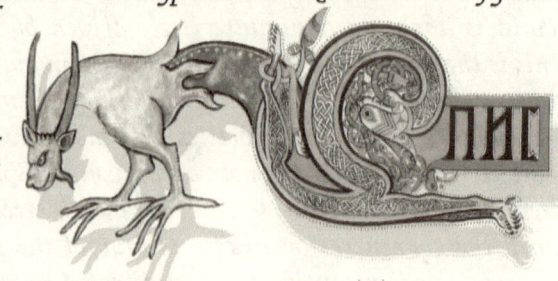 electrons from the nucleus of a cobalt 60 atom.

- Exactly! And that is precisely what the first symbol on this plate means.

- The Cruciglobist symbol?

- Yes! The Cruciglobist symbol is actually the representation of the cobalt 60 nucleus emitting electrons from its south pole. Now, dear Ad, answer me, in what direction does the cobalt nucleus spin when it emits electrons from the south pole?

- Toward the left.

- Toward the left! And that is exactly what this left hand is symbolizing.

- Ah! But, Master, in this case, what does the half-moon represent? The Moon has nothing to do with this.

- My dear disciple, if you look carefully, the third symbol never wanted to be a half-moon because it is not a crescent.

- So, what is it?

- It is an Ob-Üs tape.

- An Ob-Üs tape? Why?

- Because it is the easiest way to communicate that you are interested in a cosmic journey that contemplates a possible specular inversion. Remember that our sage, Sänte, proposed a model of the Cosmos in which, if an astronaut departs in any direction and always travels in a straight line, inevitably, he will return to our planet, as long as he is able to travel enough? Do you also remember that the astronaut could be turned upside down, with his heart on the other side?

- Yes, Master!

- Do you see it?

- Then the crescent can be an Ob-Üs tape.

-- Then the symbol of Lunilaicism is a tape of Ob-Üs. The hand that appears reproduced in the cave paintings, coming from the dawn of civilization, was the only symbol that the cavemen found familiar and intelligible on the very black and brilliant monolith that preceded them and which they began to respect: the Tablet of the Arcanum. Probably the legend about the custodian monks of the Tablet of the Arcanum, that is, about us the Szabeos and the two peoples, Tre and Ert, who grew up on the slopes of the Mālegum mountain, who once were siblings and who later became enemies, may contain more truth of what we thought. Perhaps, what was broken on that occasion was only a replica that was displayed as the Tablet of the Arcanum while the original always remained safe. Each village took a piece of the broken monolith and they were auto-adjudged as an emblem. In this way, extracted from its context, the nucleus of the cobalt 60 and the tape of Ob-Üs were transformed into the symbols of two religions. Sacred beliefs in the very distant antiquity were closely linked to the origins of the peoples, and the origin of these two peoples was the fragmentation of the Tablet of the Arcanum. Both peoples abandoned what once was the paradise after the first murder, caused by the desire to possess. The descendants of Tre spread to the surroundings of the desert; those of Ert went further and came to populate the Central Continent. One of these peoples called themselves Lunilaics and the other Cruciglobists. At present, the first people are grouped in the League of Falanjatos, and the last in the Unified Countries. And now these same people go to war, the last world war that will annihilate life on the planet Ghesta.

- But, Master, why did they hide something so important?

- I will tell you what I think. Although the matters about the Lapidarian Knights are still not very clear and will never be, what we just have discovered explains a lot of their behavior. We know that the Lapidarian Knights began with about ten that obeyed a certain group of rich and powerful aristocrats. It does not matter whether the interest in the transmutative abilities of the Lunilaic sorcerers existed before or after setting foot in the East. What matters is that they began to gather information, prompted by the hope of securing the secret of alchemy to transform common metals into valuable gold, whose literary correspondence is the Holy Råål. Let's suppose that they found a document that talked about some ruins. Among the descriptions in the document, one corresponding to a glowing metal plate appeared. In this account, there was a description of the Cruciglobist symbol, which surely excited the curiosity of the Lapidarian Knights. Next to this, later, also the Lunilaic symbol is described. This most likely puzzled them. The consequences were evident. If that discovery were to become public knowledge, hostilities would have stopped. The peoples of the world would have had reason to believe that the two religions were sisters. Perhaps a philosophical revolution, a religious reform, would have been promoted. Who knows what! But, very likely, the Campaign would have ended. The Lapidarian Knights were very far from understanding the meaning of the left hand, carved on the metal plate, much less recognizing the cobalt 60 nucleus or the Ob-Üs tape. What they do clearly understand is that they had become powerful thanks to the war. Without the reality of war, they would not have possessed as much as the most opulent of the realms. Without the war, no members of the Order would have been found infiltrated in the courts of the West, advising, administering, and even financing princes; in short, manipulating the great western power. Therefore, they decide that they cannot expose themselves, letting this secret becoming universal. They had to find the metal plate before others do. But remember, dear Ad, that this happened when much of Rjostos had been reconquered by the Lunilaics. They could no longer walk there, searching for what they wanted. But they really needed to do it! Fortunately for them, they realized that this secret not only affected them, but also some Lunilaics who sustain their power in religion and war. It should be noted, dear Ad, that the military and religious power of the Lunilaics was unified in the Ahaxi and his governors. The Lapidarian Knights made contact with the Lunilaic elites. They warned them about the common danger. The Lunilaics considered the matter. Finally, they accepted. If you ever wondered what could have provoked the cooperation of such fierce enemies? This is the answer: the only thing that associates, in a common path, two despots who hate each other, is the possibility of losing the power that has brought them face-to-face. The threat that unites them, almost always, proposes some kind of democratization, equality, freedom for the subjugated ones as it has happened in the periods of Independence. Well, what follows can be fairly understood on the same basis. The Lunilaics, once warned, embraced the search with an equal discretion to that of their western partners. I suppose that the first ones to know about the quest, after the Ahaxi, were the governors of the falanjatos; among them, Eli-vé. You must remember, dear Ad, that Eli-vé discovered the ruins that were hidden beneath Ntra. On the stands he found as he fought the

winged monster, he saw limbs of colored statues in pieces. This probably coincided with the description of the ruins in the manuscript
that originated the quest. Eli-vé must have told the Ahaxi what he
had seen. The Ahaxi told the Lapidarian Knights that they already
had a clue. Perhaps the Lunilaics themselves located the metallic
plate. Neither party wanted to destroy it because they recognized
the sacred nature of the plate, since their symbols appeared on it.
As you see, dear Ad, the plate appears to be made of a material
unknown to us. That imposes respect, even to the profane. Well
then, they did not want to destroy it. They decided to hide it. At
that time, the East was subjected to continuous invasions, new versions of a persistent attempt to reconquer Jbur. The Lunilaics could
consider their territory unreliable to keep the plate safe because they
could not guarantee that, in the future, another Campaign will not
snatch it away from them. This had not happened before because
Ntra never fell due to the Cruciglobist siege, but nobody could ever
rule out that possibility. Then a secret plan was thought of between
the two sides. They decided to hide it in the best hiding place: under
the same feet of those they wanted to keep away. The transport of
the metal plate through Lunilaic territory was guaranteed because
the Ahaxi encompassed the total power. He was, at the same time,
the maximum and unique political and religious leader. There were
no frontiers between the Falanjatos that made the Lunilaic world.
There were no customs to avoid. On the other hand, on western soil
the thing was different. The kingdoms that constituted the Cruciglobist world had independent kings. It was true that they said to obey
a sovereign, heir of a title that at that time existed and equivalent to
the Marterian emperor, but only in theory because there was no empire at all. Galactia, Arania, Frigenia, Primaria and Lepuria have
suffered wars among themselves and often they hated each other.
It was not uncommon for them to take all the precautions at their
frontiers when an armed caravan from another kingdom was about
to cross, as it had to be the case with the Lapidarian squadron as-
signed to transport the plate. This was a risk they could not afford.
The only thing that united the western countries was their religion
and the only one who was not stopped at the borders was the Øppos
or his caravans. On the other hand, the continuous wars between
western kingdoms turned this territory no less insecure than the
Lunilaic soil. However, the only thing respected by all the western
armies was the inviolability of the Cruciglobist temples. Therefore,

I believe, they did not imagine a better hiding place than an inviolable property of the Cruciglobist church. For this, they did not see a better solution than convincing Phi D'Ric, the son of a monarch, protector of the Lapidarian Knights, to accept the demands of the Øppos on him, that is, to lead a new Campaign. In this way, they would obtain a safe passage throughout the whole Cruciglobist territory because the leader of a Campaign represented the very same Øppos. With this maneuver,

they would also have at their disposal all the goods of the Cruciglobist church and they could hide the metallic plate wherever they wanted without anyone asking them any questions.

Then, they made contact with Phi D'Ric. They made him aware of everything. When Phi D'Ric saw his power threatened, he did not need much to be convinced by the Lapidarian Order and decided to work with them. He reconciled with the Øppos to get his representation. The Øppos appointed him the leader of the new Campaign. But, instead of declaring war, Phi D'Ric visited the Ahaxi. Now I can see why. I suppose the meeting was necessary to clarify some details of the alliance that was being consolidated between the majors western and eastern powers. That is why Phi D'Ric managed to take Jbur without spilling a single drop of blood.

- It was all part of the deal.

- Exactly! Phi D'Ric went to Jbur, right! But he immediately traveled to Ntra where Eli-vé led him to the ruins.

- But what happened next? Why did they dissolve their own order?

- I do not know, dear Ad. What we know now does not help us to clarify all the details, especially the latter. There are those who think that the Lapidarian Order sought their public dissolution to ensure that they were considered publicly extinct and then become clandestine and hermetic. What is certain is that, in the matter of the dissolution, the King of Galactia was a real enemy of the Lapidarian Order. Maybe the Lapidarians adjusted their plan of dissolution to the circumstances, but things went out of their control. Who knows! Their final problem with the Øppos does not surprise me. They never

got along with the priestly orders of the Cruciglobist church. These same thinkers believe that this is the origin of some secret fraternities, especially one, the Fraternity of the Anonymous. This is characterized by having clandestinely brought together the most important leaders in history as well as distinguished personalities in the most varied fields. Were these public figures aware of being part of a worldwide conspiracy to keep conflicts in a burning state? I assume not. Many of them fought for freedom, equality, and rights. That conspiracy, if it survived the years, must have been the secret of one extremely restricted minority, with the same feelings about property inherited from the gigantic terrible lizards who invented the war. This minority only wanted power and wealth even at the cost of keeping the world's population hostile and bleeding. Or, perhaps, the conspiracy died with the Grand Abbot and his closest leaders and thus the knowledge about the whereabouts of the Tablet of the Arcanum got lost. Well, that's what I wanted to believe. However, I am sure that someone, perhaps an elite among the Anonymous, keeps the memory of its trajectory.

- Why do you say that, Master?

- Six centuries later, a priestly order of the Cruciglobist church settled in a place of the Lateral Continent that was part of the domain of Lepuria. It was an order characterized by its intellectual and pedagogical dedication. In time, they came to have so many properties that the King of Lepuria suspected the pretensions of the priests in his domain. There was a moment, no matter the precedents, that this priestly order was expelled from the Lateral Continent. To do this, the King of Lepuria proceeded in exactly the same way as when the Lapidarian Knights were taken prisoner centuries ago. The two situations have the similarity of a copy. The King's order arrived at the captaincies with days of anticipation. The King's soldiers got ready in secret. On that precise day, they assaulted the convents by surprise and imprisoned them all.

- Looks like a revenge!

- Yes, it looks like a revenge! Moreover, the priests of this order have forever blamed the Anonymous who were around the King of Lepuria, advising and supporting him just as the Lapidarian Knights did. It seems like a revenge against the power of the Cruciglobist church which, in more distant times, sent them back to the King of Galactia to be executed.

- Then the Fraternity of the Anonymous is the former Lapidarian Order!

- I would not know for sure. Neither would I assure whether the current Anonymous would oppose us to reveal the secret in perfect coherence with its Lapidarian origin, or rather they would cooperate with us, as might be presumed for the altruistic example of many of its members who now we have as heroes of many libertarians and universalizing processes. Are there, at present, members of the Anonymous Fraternity who know where the metallic plate is hidden? Who knows! I would not dare to answer. But I know we must tell the world what we have discovered. There are more reasons for the two religions to respect each other and to understand one another and themselves. We must stop the war. The question is how do we get the Tablet of the Arcanum out of here?

- You cannot take the Holy Råål! -a voice that came from behind replied- You are looking at it just as the Lapidarian Knights found it in the ruins where it was hidden, beneath the city of Ntra. You are seeing an image of the past. The Night of the Time offers that opportunity. Can you take an image or carry a piece of time? And yes, you were right, Szabeo monk! With the help of some Lunilaics, they took it from here and transported it by sea to the West.

The one who spoke was an old man with long white hair who appeared behind us. He was gentle, he wore a white robe and kept his hands held in front of him.

- Who are you? -my master asked.

- I am Wgïjvrán, the magician.

- And the other Wgïjvrán?

- That was just one of the halves that made me.

- Let me guess! The other half was the Osterácodo, wasn't it?

- I am glad you understand since I have to apologize to you and your little disciple for the behavior of my two halves. The crippled gnome wished for the recovery of his integrity. The Osterácodo was a masochist who refused to change. The gnome wanted to free me from my eternal cycle, the endless repetition of my steps, my Time imprisonment in Wrestongres forever and ever, my condemnation in the Night of Times. The Osterácodo was resistant to change; after all, if I had not transcended the temporal boundaries I would not have been more famous than the castle dyer. In my defense, I can only say that none of them was me. We are all the sum of our parts and nothing less. For this reason, I would like to help you in what is possible and also in the impossible. How can I serve you?

- There are two things on which we would appreciate some assistance -my master said.

- I would gladly please you in any of your wishes. I am indebted to you.

- If it is not too much to ask, first I would like to know the whereabouts of the Tablet of the Arcanum and I would be very grateful if you allowed us to leave the Night of Time.

- Take this! -Wgijvrán said, giving Reverend Ogli a cylindrical object- It is called Scalitrión. It is my magical instrument.

- Nice! -my master said, taking the object of the magician's hands with the utmost care- It is very beautiful!

- Now take your Blackmoon crystal disks and connect them to the wider end of the Scalitrón.

My master did it.

- Raise the Scalitrión -Wgijvrán continued- Its narrow end has an opening. Looking through that opening, direct the Scalitrión to the multicolored reflections of the Holy Råål. You will see, then, a colorful symmetrical formation of beautiful clarity.

- Yes! Indeed, I can see a rosette composed of brilliant diamond cuts.

- They are combinatorial sets of the four perfect parts in which an equilateral rhombus is divided; a rhombus whose side has for measure the divine ratio, ϕ.

- How do they appear in your Scalitrión?

- Your Blackmoon Crystal discs separate the effulgences of the Holy Råål; my Scalitrión carries out a new specular integration. But the origin of the effulgences capable of being reintegrated in this way are probably the result of an intrinsic feature of the strange material the Holy Råål is made of. Most importantly, the rosette depicted in the Scalitrión has precisely the same design as the rosette of the Boreal cathedral that the Lapidary Knights built to conceal the Holy Råål.

- *Really?*

- *When they already had the Holly Råål in their hands, they dedicated themselves to study it with the intellectual tools available at that time. In the Middle Era, there were only weights, measuring instruments, and the invaluable help of mathematics. They applied what they knew to the Holly Råål, whose dimensions are based on the divine ratio. With this knowledge, they developed a whole new architecture that would house the mystery fallen from the sky; a magnificent and heavenly architecture, which was only worthy of what it would house. The Boreal architecture, like a filigree delicately woven on the basis of the value of ø, rises toward the firmament inquiring God for the answer to the mystery that keeps and that gives reason to be. That is why, if you have paid attention to the symbols of a Boric cathedral, you probably have seen representations of simple instruments like rulers and squares, hammers, and plumbs; the arsenal of drawing and construction; means of understanding and representing the taste of God. In the harmonious assemblage of the cathedrals, all kinds of divine proportions are discovered, giving shape to the walls, and emptying the corridors to accommodate the ogives. In the rhythm of certain key shadows, it is possible to recognize the divine series and the balustrade count denounces the magical series. The walls are sprinkled with alchemical allegories, stoves, cupels, retorts, everything that prompted them to discover the mystery fallen from the sky. Once you have located the Boric cathedral that has the rosette that my magical instrument just showed you, enter it. Your feet will settle on what was the ancient hermitage of Otámix. Stand in front of the rosette, to the right of the transept, near the three steps that lead to the corridor, close to the choir. If you do so, you will see a luminous circle appearing on the floor, which then, with the passing hours, will be transformed into an oval, resembling the alchemical egg. The light rays will come from some perforations precisely made on the rosette. These were made to indicate the location of a releasing mechanism. Find the way to lift the tile on which the oval is projected at noon. Below, you will find an iron lever. Use it. Then you will see a door opening. This is the access to the chamber where the Holy Råål is hidden. But remember, you must first locate the correct rosette, because there is a trap in that too.*

There was a momentary silence. My master, Reverend Ogli-s-Oöp showed the gentlest complacency I have ever seen. Then he said:

- We are very grateful for the information, and we will be more if now you allow us to leave the Night of Time and return to the present time. Stopping the war becomes urgent. I just hope I can do it!

- I know you will, Szabeo monk. However, are you aware of what such enterprise can mean for you?

My master suddenly paled.

- Yes, I know -he said softly.

- I admire you for that -the magician said- Then, with his finger, he described a circular sign in the air and said...

- You are now the bearer of the Final Message.

lenfon vn
es in de dach
ende dey die
dar licht na
dar duuster
nis cu noctu
te dar licht
den dach cu

XXVIII

Chapter XXVIII

The Last Image

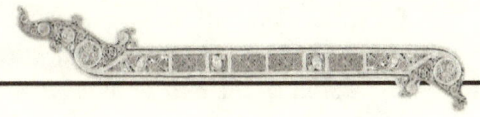

Immediately, all the images began to get deformed; elongating, plastifying, and twisting around us like a tornado of deliquescent colors. There was a burst of blinding light, and we returned to the absolute darkness. For us, there was nothing more usual than the confusion or nothing more familiar than the darkness. However, that time, that darkness, seemed to me different from the others. It was a simple darkness, without traps, distended, with no more subterfuge than the interruption of light; the quiet darkness of rest. I felt comfortable and let myself be covered by its serene plush cloak. Wrapped up by the night, I remained like this. I do not know for how long.

An insignificant amount of clarity began to be seen right above me. At some moment, an arc of light broke the shadows by cutting them with the silvery slash of a sickle; a celestial sickle. The dazzling wound opened more and more, swelling itself with light, filling itself, completing itself. Its bluish clarity finally hurt me. Then I saw Reverend Ogli focusing the sight of a sextant or directing the Crystals of Blackmoon to the sky. I wanted to sit up and go next to him, but a heaviness magnetized me to the ground.

In my next memory, I see myself awakened by the screams coming from a cart pulled by a pair of knorks.

- Reverend Ogli! Reverend Ogli!

The wagon swiftly approached us; two Szabeo monks led it.

- Reverend Ogli! -one of them cried- At last! We have been looking for you. We have received orders from Master Warhr to take you to the monastery of Istric. We must take shelter as soon as possible!

- I am very grateful to you! -my master answered- You do not know how much I celebrate you are here!

Reverend Ogli took me by the waist and got me into the cart. Then, he reached for my backpack in a hurry and handed it to me. After that, he said to the pair of monks:

- I beg you to take my disciple with you. I have to go back to the mainland.

- But... Reverend Ogli! -the monk on the cart said- We must take refuge! Where are you going? I respectfully ask you to come with us.

- Thank you very much! But there are urgent things waiting for me in Galactia.

- What can be more urgent than taking shelter? -the other monk rebuked him.

- There is something! Truly, there is! Please, do as I ask. Take care of my disciple!

Then, he looked at me with infinite eyes.

- Ad! -he told me.

I leaped on my master to embrace him hard. His vibrating grip, the last one, has remained vivid in my memory forever. There have been times when I have felt defeated, but in remembering this moment, the warm ghost of my dear master has comforted me.

The cart drove me away from Reverend Ogli. Its leaf springs creaked with mechanical howls, protesting the race over the stone road. The last image my old head holds of my master, brings him back to me, standing next to our knork, serene, but with the brightness of the goodbyes in his eyes, raising the palm of his left hand as if he wanted to touch me, ignoring the distance. In the back ground, the imposing circle of Wrestongres bathed itself in the light of dawn.